POISON

THE SPIRIT RUNES BOOK THREE

C J WALLINGSFORD

Poison
Book Three of The Spirit Runes

For more information, address: cjwallingsford@outlook.com

First edition 2021
ISBN: 978-1-954426-05-4
Cover design by Storywrappers.
Storywrappers.com
Editing by KillingItWrite.
Killingitwrite.com
Author website: Cjwallingsford.com

Sorry Bee, this one is for Eric. I need to apologize that his name is so similar to Erac.

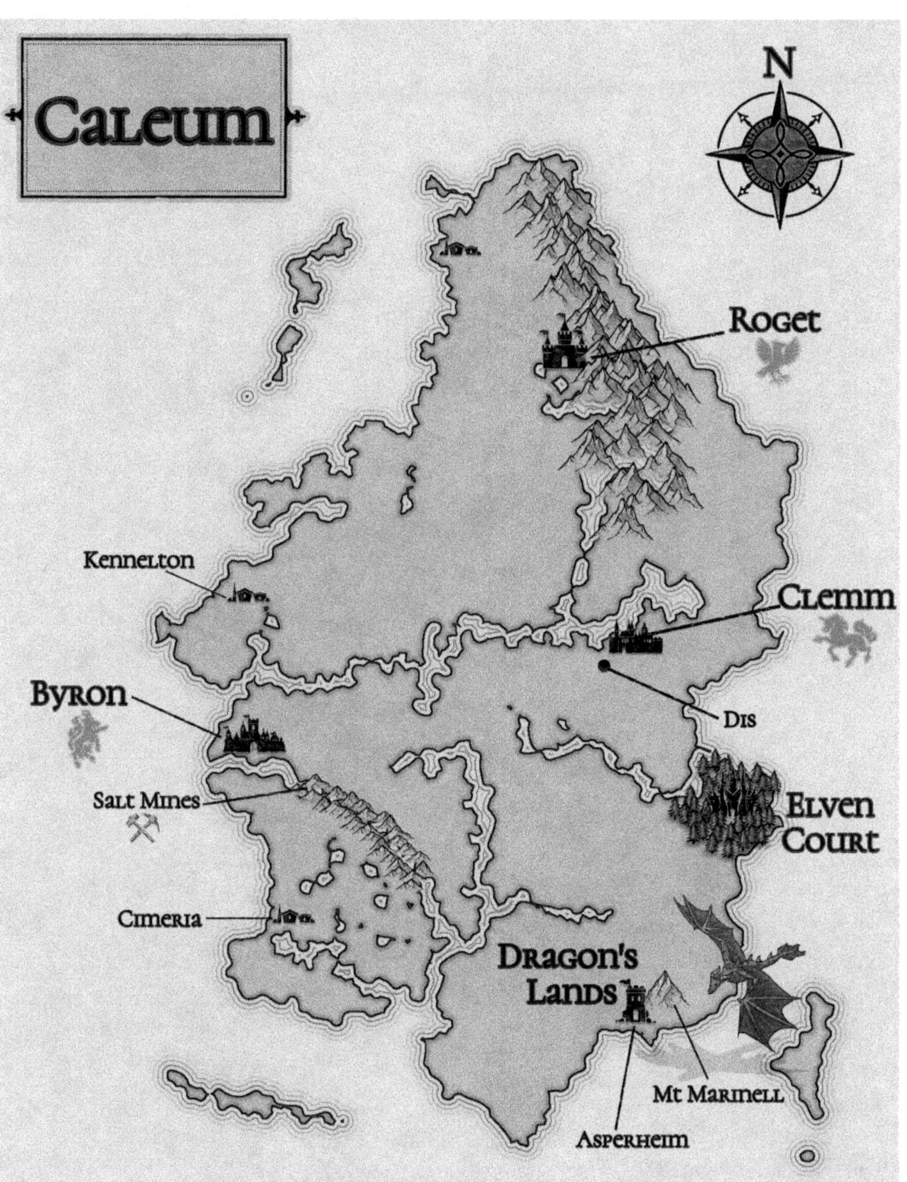

Caleum
N
Roget
Kennelton
Clemm
Byron
Dis
Salt Mines
Elven
Court
Cimeria
Dragon's
Lands
Mt Marinell
Asperheim

“There will be blood. I will taste it, the ichor of my enemy. They stole from me, took my life and tore my mind apart, and I will return the favor.”

Morella Rowena Annabelle Byron

CHAPTER 1

DECLAN

The scent of blood hangs thick in the air. The scent is floral, something strong and full of pollen, like jasmine and lavender petals, is rammed into my nasal cavities. I sniff, trying to dislodge the pressure and regret it. I sneeze, eyes watering, wondering how I ever managed to feed off her in the first place as I glare at Selene slumped on the floor.

She lost consciousness about half an hour ago. Her pink ball gown is splattered with dark splotches. The blood is dried, but the noxious scent is still overpowering. The gold diadem secured to her head by the pinned up blonde hair is askew on top of her head.

The crown doesn't belong to her. It should be on Ella's head, her sister, and the rightful queen as far as I am concerned; the rest of the court be damned for believing otherwise.

Ella. My wife.

I stare at Selene as I drop to sit on the bloodstained mattress, knees bent, arms resting on my knees, gripping a dagger in one hand. The stench of her blood is revolting, permeating the air from where it coats the metal blade.

Selene has a small nose, round at the tip. She usually stares at it with a vacancy in her crystal-clear eyes. Ella's jealous of her, though, for the life of me, I can't understand why. The two women seem to be ever envious of the other, but Selene has reason to be.

I need alcohol just thinking about Ella, her beautiful face, slim, toned body. She's always working on perfecting her punches. Haven only knows why given the powerful magic she possesses. My wife doesn't need to punch someone, just merely think, and she can cause pain, turn them to ash.

Curling my lip, I throw the blade away from me, and it clatters against the stone, the sound ringing harshly in the frigid air. I shove fingers into my hair at the top of my forehead to push away the brown strands in front of my eyes.

Ella was taken away by Erac on some arrangement with Viktor only hours after I married her. I had just enough time to consummate the marriage and reinstate the bond between us, a mental link we share through blood magic. Just enough time to fall in love with her all over again. I grip my fists, close my eyes, and breathe through my mouth.

The bond tears our souls in half so that we both have one-half of each of our souls within us. I have half of her soul in me, and I reach out for it, trying to find the glimmer of good she brings to my black soul. I need more than the emptiness of myself right now.

Selene doesn't know much about the plans that were made and enacted, which is stupid of her and smart of Erac and Viktor. Her only purpose in this mess was as a pawn. She knew her part, what to do, what to dose us with to interrupt our bond and leave us immobilized, helpless to fight back. In exchange, she was promised that Ella wouldn't ever come between us again. As if Selene and I could live happily ever after together as king and queen of Byron.

I scoff, rubbing a hand down my face and bare my teeth. I doubt Selene realized that promise was based on the foundation that I was supposed to die. My mother slit my throat, true to design. Selene didn't know that was part of the plan, according to her blabbered confession. It was stupid of her to believe that I would be allowed to live. Viktor knows damn good and well I'll come for Ella if there is even a single breath of life left in me.

This whole stupid mess–Ella gone, again. *Fuck this. Fuck Viktor, but most of all fuck you, Haven. I've had enough of this.*

I roll forward, arms dangling between my legs, glaring at the bitch. I hate that she gets the blissfulness of unconsciousness while I am left to suffer in awareness. In a swift motion, I stand, grabbing at the iron collar around her neck, not feeling it but hearing my skin sizzle at the sound of contact with the iron. I unclasp the band, tossing it aside. It clanks, and the chain rattles, but Selene remains asleep.

There's a red ring around her throat of chafed and burned skin. Iron disagrees with us, blisters the skin, sucks energy from the core of elementals, even shades like me. I check that she's breathing, and then I grimace, lifting her off the floor.

The woman is small and frail, like a doll, and she broke as easily as one. I cradle her in my arms, fuming about what I am about to do. I am a lot of things, an arrogant bastard and an ass, maybe even sadistic, but I am not heartless. My heart might be shrewd and shrunken, broken and cracked, but it's there, somewhere. I know it is because it belongs to Ella, the whole fucking reason I am doing this. I blame the half of Ella's soul in me for even caring to do this at all.

I close my eyes and concentrate on pulling apart the elements that create my body and Selene's, dissipating us as air back to Byron Palace. I blink against the bright light in the infirmary, looking around at the dozens of beds where injured and unconscious elementals rest.

Casualties of war, but these aren't wounded fighters. Those are in the gardens of Byron Palace. No, these poor bastards are nobility, probably hurt when demons swarmed the palace, and my bitch of a mother made a second attempt on my life. Ella was kidnapped, and Selene, the queen she most certainly is a failure of, helped to orchestrate and enact the ruin.

Fuming over cradling Selene in my arms, I glance around. I could put her in one of the empty beds if I could be bothered to search for one. Finding a bed for her is a waste of time, so I just let go, her body thumping to the floor.

She doesn't even stir, and with all her other injuries, she won't be able to tell that I couldn't be bothered to find her a bed or even bend over to lower her to the floor. I should have left her chained in that forsaken cell to rot.

Healers glance our way, exhaustion mingling with shock as they stare at me. I toe the body before my feet. "She's going to need your attention."

"What happened?" a young male dryad asks. "Was there another attack? Calest, quick, it's the queen!"

I curl my lip back and tear my elements apart, dissipating to the kitchen where my body reforms. I stalk to the cellars, nabbing a bottle of amber liquid. I lift it, pulling the cork, and sniff. With a smirk, I take a drink and drop the stopper to the floor.

I chug until the need to breathe outweighs the need for alcohol. Swiping at my mouth, I catch sight of movement, my eyes training on the fae entering the cellars. He stops short, blinking at me, then grins.

I snarl with silent ferocity, baring my teeth at him.

"Declan," he laughs. "Your Majesty." He gives a short bow and stands upright, watching me.

Medium height, blond, and scrawny. I jerk my chin at him, taking another drink with the bottle tipped to the side of my face to keep an eye on him. I know this man, but I cannot place from where.

The young man's face drops, and he sighs. "I heard about Ella again." He scowls. "Is there any news?"

I stop drinking, licking the remaining liquid from my lips, staring at him. My eyes flicker over his thin face, noting the noble nose and purple eyes. I grind my teeth. "Dean."

"I'm surprised you remember me."

"Ella nearly started a lynch mob trying to save your life and could have been hurt."

He nods, tucking his hands away in the front of his apron. "But, she saved my life."

One side of my mouth curls back. "She's like that." The words are a wistful whisper. *Fuck, I want my wife.*

He shifts, leaning against the entryway, angling his body to block the door. My skin crawls at being caged in here, even if I could rip this boy in half.

Dean bobs his head. "She is, and I keep fighting for her, telling anyone who will listen that she's not the murdering monster they are saying."

I take another drink, grunting at him. "No, that would be me, and they're all still so fucking quick to call me king and scream for her head." The neck of the bottle shatters in my hand as I clench too hard. I shake the wasted liquor from my hand, the cuts stinging and warm as they heal over.

"You're going to bring her back, right?"

My eyes jerk from searching for another bottle to his.

His eyebrows lift. "You're going to get her home and let her be queen?"

My stomach twists and slithers like something foul and slimy. I turn away from him, pulling another bottle off the wall, and dissipate somewhere no one can reach me to ask stupid questions.

I sit on the turret, drinking whiskey and staring south. The scent of blood makes me queasy. Selene's blood smells like I shoved my nose in a flower and sucked in seeds and pollen.

I take another drink, the alcohol hot and sharp on my tongue. The blood staining my hands is visible, and if I want the atrocious scent to go, I'll have to wash. I spent the last day getting any information I could out of Selene, and since I haven't been able to bring myself to shower, to change, to do anything. I probably smell terrible and look worse. I feel gross, but I just can't bring myself to face the truth.

I grip my whiskey tighter, feeling the glass cracking, wondering why bottles are not made of a stronger material. I set the whiskey aside before I shatter the glass completely. I clench my fists, feeling my skin pull tight, the caked blood cracking as my fingers stretch.

At least I know here no one will find me. Here I have a fleeting moment to close my eyes, lean my head back, and I picture her.

Ella. My wife.

I breathe out, holding tight to the visual behind my eyes, her smile, her dark hair, something purple and red strewn on the cave floor beneath her. My heart slows and rolls over. This close, I can almost reach out and touch her.

A rustle of feathers and cawing bursts me from the daydream. I crack an eye open to see a raven perched next to me. It caws, hopping and flapping its wings.

I snarl at it. The bird squawks, adjusting its wings against its body. I bend both knees up to my chest, resting my arms around them and flex my aching muscles. I have been tense for far too long.

"Caw."

I frown at the bird. "What do you want?"

"Caw. Caw."

I show my teeth. "Fuck off."

It hops a bit closer and flaps its wings. I wave a hand at it, trying to get the thing to leave. It hops back, and its head bobs forward, neck straining.

I lift an eyebrow and scowl. "What? What do you want? Go." I point south. "The one who would feed you or stroke your feathers or fucking be nice to you, she's that way." I realize I'm yelling at a bird and drop my arm to my knee once more.

"Caw. Caw. Caw."

I lunge for it, grabbing it by the body to pin its wings to its side. It's shrieking and trying to break free of my grasp, and I shake the damn thing. "What? Erac drugged her, took her south to fucking Asperheim, to the heart of Viktor's forces."

"Caw?"

I tilt my head to match the bird. "If she weren't dead, if she were able, she'd have come home, she'd come back to me."

"Caw." The bird is tilting its head back and forth. "Caw. Caw." The wings make a half-hearted attempt to break free.

"I don't know if she's fucking dead, I don't know what is going on. The bond—" my voice breaks on me. I grit my teeth and squeeze harder to get a hold of myself. The bird starts to struggle free. "I had five fucking hours. Five, six, who the fuck was counting? Not me. She wasn't supposed to—she fucking promised."

It keeps trying to break free, and I crush it between my hands. I want to hurt something, want to squeeze the life from Erac until he breaks under my hands into tiny pieces so that I'd never know he had bones. There's a pop beneath my grasp. My eyes focus from a red haze of the world around me to the thing in my hands. The scent of vermin mixes with floral, and I snarl, hurling the thing over the edge and watch it disappear.

If Ella were here, she would be heartbroken that I had killed the thing. I drop my head, grabbing at my hair, desperate to pull the thoughts of her out of my skull as if it would make this agony go away. I lift my face, my burning and blurry eyes pegging south.

I feel for the bond, getting a sharp, cold stab in my left temple. She is alive. The bond is interrupted, so she is alive. I know that. But that's all I know. I grab for the whiskey, chugging, and then hurl the bottle with all the force I can muster.

I frown. *I need to be stronger*.

Standing on the roof of the highest turret of Byron Palace, staring south, I see the soul star setting on the horizon. My wife is alive, and I am going to get her back. I catch a whiff of the breeze and my nose wrinkles with disgust. I should start with a shower.

I'm coming for you, lover, just hold on, fight back, don't give in, don't let him control you again. I'm coming to get you. I just need time.

I get no answer, nothing, not even a wayward feeling or bright swirls in my mind. There's no response from her. I'm not surprised, but it still feels like my teeth have been kicked down my throat.

CHAPTER 2

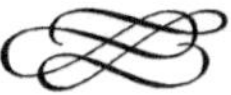

DECLAN

Showered, I stalk naked and cold through my rooms to a chest of drawers for clothes. I grab the necessities and pull them on. I tug a thin, black sweater that half zips up over my head and ram my arms through the sleeves. The zipper is cold against my chest, but I wrench it down, giving myself room to breathe. My mother would have a heart attack if she saw me dressed like this, jeans and a sweater, no dress shirt beneath, my bare chest exposed.

I stare into the mirror on top of the dresser and bare my teeth. My brown hair is too long, a reddish-brown beard growing in. The days when I cared about appearance are gone. My mother, the former Duchess of Kennelton, had always demanded perfection. I was to appear clean-shaven, my hair neat, always wearing a button-down shirt. She nearly lost her mind when she found so much as a wrinkle, and jeans garnered a disapproving *tsk* of her tongue.

My sight focuses on my black eyes sparkling in the light of the soul star filtering through the windows. They stare back at me, soulless and broken. My mother helped Viktor arrange the death of my father and me at the hand of mercenaries. I escaped with my life at the mercy of Marx, the King of Clemm court.

Mercy is an odd word. He used me to his own ends, keeping me locked up, sealing my memories and implanting false ones to create a monstrous tool to collect the spirit runes from around Caleum. He was not the only one vying for those runes of power, his ambitions bringing me back to Ella again.

Ella.

I splay my hands flat on the dresser, using it to support me as the thought of her and our bond tries to bring me to my knees. Marx was unaware he couldn't break the blood bond she and I shared, and in the end, I came home, returned to my former life with all the memories and skills he gave to me. I thought they'd be a curse, with what he'd made me a struggle to hold back. Haven has a sick sense of humor.

That should have been the end. Ella should have been safe, having found her own salvation in a blood rune from the monks of Mount Marnell in the south, but Viktor was not about to give up his tool as easily as Marx let me go, and I did what I had to in order to have Ella. I never cared about being king, just Ella. I was never going to watch her marry someone else, to let him touch her, have her.

Like Erac. I punch the mirror attached to the dresser, watching it shatter, blood left behind in the epicenter.

I traded the runes for a full reinstatement arranged by Viktor, handing over the runes I had collected. Ella had the Vitale rune. I never thought things would get this far. I never thought Viktor was capable of surviving, that he could bring forth demons from Damnatus. The idea of the Gammet brothers coming to court, Erac preying on Ella's naïve mind and bleeding heart, and letting them steal her away to Medius—the possibility never came to fruition in my mind.

I shove away from the dresser and the broken reflection of my narrow face, lips twisting with fury to stare out the window overlooking the orchards. I spent an entire revolution believing she was dead, staying king to honor what I thought she would want. I made mistakes, namely a sexual relationship with Selene, her sister, who is nothing more than a stupid version of Viktor, but Ella forgave me. That's who she is, forgiving and soft.

I grip my fists and inhale through my nose until my lungs are full. We made it through it all and found our way back to each other. The rest of this damned dimension did not matter. I married her.

Then Erac betrayed us, the spirits, and his own brother, all for the sake of having Ella, taking a set of spirit runes to Viktor. Those spirit runes are the ones I assume my mother wears now, the same ones she used to command me to my knees in front of Haven and everyone else. I kneeled at her feet, staring at my wife as she slit my throat from ear to ear.

I have no idea how Marx managed to keep me alive. The only thing I remember is gorging on blood and a whole hell of a lot of pain in my neck. I exhale and release my hands to hang at my side, leaving them to tremble.

Erac took Ella back to Viktor. I ram my fingers into my closed eyes and rub hard, growling in the back of my throat. She married me. She can destroy hordes of demons with magic, unlike anyone or anything else. After her time in Medius, she came back powerful, appearing self-assured and strong. We should have been able to get rid of the demons and Viktor once and for all. Things weren't supposed to go this way. She was supposed to stay by my side, safe with me, and we were supposed to rid Caleum of this scourge. We were supposed to win the war.

I drop my hands again and tip my head back, staring at the ceiling and thinking of Haven, our god and creator. "I used to think I was the monster, but I'm not. You're the fucking monster," I whisper, throat clogged and eyes burning. "What part of this is your plan? Haven't we paid enough? Suffered enough for you?" I clench my jaw and work my throat enough to swallow the lump. "We don't deserve this!" I yell. "We've done enough, paid enough. Where's our happy ending?"

There's no answer, just silence ringing in my ears.

I need to focus on getting the army to the fight right now, and then I'll figure out how to get my wife back. Another step closer. I reach for her through the link, getting a stab of cold in my temple.

I sit on the edge of my bed with a frown and take a moment. The interrupted bond hurts when I try to use it. My head hangs down as I take a few deep breaths through my nose, trying to hold together all the chaos in my mind. I need clear thoughts, and giving into my blood lust or the urge to try and smash through this problem with brute force isn't going to help me or her right now.

All I want is to bury my face in Ella's hair and breath her in, curl around her, keep her under an arm for safekeeping and ride out the after-burn of this curse of shades. But she's gone.

Asperheim. South. Where it's warm. I ache to feel the heat of her pressed against me. The ache starts to grow, blooming in my lower abdomen. I wince, sitting up and glancing down, expecting to see a knife protruding from above my dick. There's a sense of warm blood, but no wound.

Exhaling, I grunt, putting a hand over the spot as the pain starts to increase. I can barely breathe through the agony as my head starts to swim at the overwhelming sensation. I squeeze my eyes shut, dropping back onto the mattress and groaning, curling into a ball.

Daftly I start to realize this is Ella. I feel her affliction and reach out through our link. A wave of panic and torment slam through my mind. I can hear her begging for it to stop, but I can't tell what other than the feeling of my dick being shoved inside out and back into my gut. Opening the link increases the burning throb through my balls, and I pant, gripping at my lower stomach as if I could force the feeling away.

"Ella?"

It hurts.

"Ella—"

Haven, make it stop, please.

"Love—"

Please just let it be over.

Her begging breaks something loose inside of me, and I roll over and throw up. Vomit splatters back into my face as I fight to just breathe. Horror wells up and forces another retch as I realize what I am experiencing.

"He's raping you."

Erac's raping me.

The world turns gray as my vision slips out of focus. I try to fight it off, getting to my feet, but double over at the intense burning between navel and knees. "Fuck," I growl, and I blink as I lay on my side, staring at the wall.

Pressure recedes from my gut, and I can breathe again. I shake in pain and horror, unable to do anything but lay there. I need to clear my mind to dissipate, but I can't collect my thoughts enough to even begin to start. My eyes slip closed, and I reach out, trying to let her know I am here, and I feel this too.

How can this be love?

I groan loudly and grit my teeth. *"That's not love. This is love."*

I shove a random memory through our link, one where we sat naked under a blanket in her window seat as I massaged her neck and shoulders in a blissful state.

The pain starts to become bearable as I concentrate on wrapping her consciousness in mine, trying to protect her even in this useless state. *"You're going to be okay."*

Yes, I'm okay.

"Lover, that's not right."

No. He's not a lover.

I feel like I've been kicked in the balls when I realize she has no idea she's talking to me. She thinks I'm some kind of inner voice giving her strength. I roll over, trying to get off the floor.

"Ella, I'm here, I'm real. It's the bond."

What's a bond? I don't remember anything.

I can hear the thought but realize she's spoken aloud, not just responding to me. Panic brings bile to the back of my throat, then there's a lot of fear and a sharp pain in my temple before the world goes black.

CHAPTER 3

DECLAN

When I come to, I groan and squeeze my eyes shut, then roll face down and plant my palms flat on the cold stone floor to push up. I get my feet under me and stand, rubbing sleep from my eyes, then glance around. The room is flooding with light. I slept through the night. My heart tries to twist free of its connections, and I growl, rubbing a hand over my chest.

Ella is in Asperheim at the mercy of Erac. She doesn't remember me or the bond. My hands drop, and I clench both into fists.

I don't know where Viktor is or what he's doing, but right now, I don't care. The previous King of Byron is no longer my top priority. He has an army of demons from the lower dimension of Damnatus here in Caleum, fighting to take back what he thinks belongs to him. None of that matters.

Erac has moved himself to the top of my priorities. I am going to get to Asperheim. I am going to rip his head off, and I am going to get Ella back. I'll worry about Viktor and his demons after I make that prick eat his own dick.

The whispers start begging for me to split open skin and

watch blood well up in an open wound, to watch how easy skin can be sliced open, to hear something squeal in pain.

An echo of the pain I experienced through the bond leaves me clenching my jaw. Erac touched her, hurt her, forced himself deep inside of her even as she begged for it to stop.

I curl my lip and tear my elements apart, dissipating to the war camp in the southwest corner of Caleum, where the Byron army is facing off against the hoard of demons Viktor has let loose upon our dimension.

I come together in the middle of the war camp. This blasted war seems more hopeless than ever, but I cannot give up. Ella's waiting on me. I run a hand over my face, and when I see a servant trudging down the muddy, trampled path, I take my first step toward getting my wife back.

I grip the panel of the tent set up as our head of operations and step inside, blinking to let my eyes adjust to the dim light. No one stirs at my entrance. Four men are gathered around the table in the middle. Two are familiar, Seth and Samuel. The other two are a pair of dryads, one with the darkest skin I've ever seen, borderline obsidian. The other is a lighter brown, but both are built as strong and tough as their ancestral treefolk made of bark and wood, with scowls of desolated and exhausted fighters.

My brother, Seth, lifts his eyes to meet mine, the same pitch color that reflects no light. His eyebrows lift under shaggy brown hair, and he scratches at his jaw under dark facial hair with his free hand. His other is wrapped around the hilt of a sword splattered with yellow demon blood. "Dec?"

The other three turn to me. Samuel, a shorter man with wiry limbs, reflects a shocked expression. "You're back."

My gaze moves to the two other men, both dryads who look sturdy enough to pack a punch and take a hit. The darker man stands as tall as Seth, north of me and every other man I've met.

The other is burlier and shorter, maybe my height. They both incline their heads.

"Your Majesty," the taller says in a thick accent from the southern border.

"King Declan," the other acknowledges. His words are tinged with the same accent. "It is good to finally meet you."

I jerk my chin up at them. "Who are you?"

"I am Gamal, and this," he puts a hand on his companion's arm, "is my brother Lumor. We heard about Ella being taken. We came to help."

I bare my teeth, my pulse kicking up a couple speeds. "Why? Everyone here thinks she's a murderer."

He frowns, crossing his arms. "We care about Ella."

"Fuck you and your bullshit," I snap, blinded in rage and stalking to the table. I can see the king chess piece resting on top of the map tacked down to the surface. I pick it up and slam it down over the image of the palace of Asperheim. It cracks in half lengthwise but holds together.

"Gamal is not being kind," Lumor says. "We know, Ella. We care."

I scowl and eye them with a sneer. "I know everyone Ella knows, and I've never seen you two before."

Gamal shakes his head. "We were recruited to help Ella track Viktor when she was consigned to the palace."

"The orange-haired woman can vouch, she introduced us."

Legia. My heart slams against my ribcage, my temper fast deteriorating. "Legia fucking brought Ella to you? Took her out of the palace—"

Seth laughs. "If you think Legia forced Ella to do anything, you've lost your mind."

I squeeze my fingers into fists so tight they might break.

Gamal stares at me. "We believed that which is said about Ella, but we saw her determination to kill Viktor, the compassion she had each time we found ruins and wreckage left in his wake. She might be a murderer, but she has a pure heart." As he speaks, his eyes shift over my shoulder. "She is not what they say."

I swallow a lump in my throat and relax my hands. "Fine. I believe you don't think she's what they say, but that doesn't mean you fucking know her."

Lumor inclines his head. "We have heard she was taken, and we came to see what we can do to help."

I drop my gaze to the map, staring at the king piece over the image of a dragon curled around a mountain and a conical-shaped castle. I need fighters. "We fight back. We do what she tried to. We kill Viktor." I lift my head and glance around at the other men. "Now," I grunt. "Ella's in Asperheim with Erac and Viktor."

"Yeah, and it's a fortress," Seth says in a dark mutter.

"We need to talk to Sordello. Get the mages ready to move this—" I hold up a finger and make a circle, gesturing to the whole camp, "—to Asperheim."

"Where have you been," Seth asks.

I scowl. "Busy."

"For two days? What the hell were you doing?"

"Getting answers." I lift and drop one shoulder. "Facing facts." *Trying not to fucking lose my mind. Experiencing Erac raping my fucking wife.* I breathe out, long and slow through my nose, and pinch the bridge.

Seth jerks his chin upward and grunts. "Wyatt had some things to say."

"Ella's south, taken by Erac. She's at Asperheim, with Viktor, and Erac, and our mother." My voice is flat even to my own ears, the words coming out in a mechanical manner. "The plan was to kill me, capture her, weaken this court—"

"Yeah." Seth lets the tip of his sword dig in the ground. Sighing, he leans on the pommel, using the weapon as a prop while he runs a hand over his face. He stares down at his feet. "And it worked. We're a right old mess now. Chase is dead. A few others too, don't recall names right now. Gia's in fits and hysterical. Wyatt's locked up. Ella's gone. The Medici family's been wiped out by the fighting. Blackburn family's toast now. Noble families are dropping like flies, and us? We're just trying to keep our heads above water right now." His head turns left to right, then he faces me and shrugs.

I drop into a chair, and Seth hops on the table, the wood groaning under his weight. He has a rag and starts to clean his sword. Our eyes meet, and I stare into ones as dark as my own. It's a weird sight to see my brother with black eyes. Even in the worst of times, prior to this mess, his eyes were never darker than the color of storm clouds. I look away as others enter the tent.

Most are familiar faces of warrior leaders, their skin blistered and splattered with yellow and red blood alike. I run a hand over my face and lean back, the chair squawking its resistance.

"Report," I say, too tired to give a damn about etiquette.

Samuel steps forward, parchment and pages clutched against his chest. He lays them out on the table and starts rambling off demon horde locations and mapped out parcels by scouts about possible landscape advantages on battles. I don't pay much heed. The only advantage elementals will ever have over this war with demons are the spirits. My mind flickers to images of Ella, memories of times I enjoyed.

I sigh, kicking one foot up on the edge of the table, mud splattering Samuel's papers. "How many have we lost?" There is silence around me in the tent. I check behind me at the two warrior guild leaders. "How many?" I repeat through bared teeth.

Talwarth, a man that looks to be twice my strength, grunts and shifts. "Too many. We can't keep going like this. They'll kill us all just by wearing us down. They kill ten for each two we extinguish."

"Used to be twenty for each one," I say, turning back to the maps. "They're learning."

"And dying," Talwarth answers in a crisp tone.

"There'll be nothing left of Byron if we keep going like this." This voice belongs to the other warrior guild leader, Fennel, a softer, higher pitch tone.

I drop my leg and stand, turning to face them both. "You're talking about surrender?" There is no answer. I turn to a spirit. "Sordello?"

The spirit shakes its hood at me. "I am Malik."

I blow out air. "I need you to wear different colors or something. Where is Sordello?"

"Friend," A heavily armored hand lands on my shoulder from behind. "We are all as good as the next. Malik is the bravest of us and has studied the most on war."

"I don't fucking care about that," I shrug his hand off before the metal cuts into me, and I spin to face him, crossing my arms. "Ella—" I manage, but stop and clench my jaw.

"Yes, my daughter is still missing. It is good you have returned to us, though. Your troops are weary under our command."

"She is south in Asperheim with Viktor and Erac."

"You are quick to dismiss the lives of your brother and sisters in arms for the life of a murderous—"

I move, rushing at Talwarth, wrapping a hand around his throat and squeezing. The man gapes in shock, his face changing colors from pale to filling with blood constricted in his head. I stare into his bulging eyes and then shove him as hard as I can from my grip.

Talwarth leaves his feet, sailing backward and out of the tent, canvas ripping as his large body bursts through the fabric. I look to Fennel, who holds his hands up and steps away.

I spin, eyeing everyone in the room with fury. "Anyone else want to insult my wife?"

Seth laughs. "Hell no." He stands next to me, putting an arm around my shoulders. It irks me that he is taller and has a bigger build. "You made your point, but you can't blame them."

I turn, slamming a closed fist into his gut. He gasps and doubles over, coughing, and I step away from him. "I can, and I will. You of all of us know what she went through, what she was made to do against her will, and now they call her murderer and monster?" I lower my voice and collect my temper before it worms out of control. "Ella's life matters more than any other for the threat she holds, the power she has, and if we get her back without limiting her to Byron Palace, she can end this. Ella wiped out a legion of demons with magic. Not even a spirit can do that."

Seth stands upright with a hand over his abdomen. "Yeah, I know." He steps out of my reach and holds his hands up. "I'm with you on this."

I snarl, and everyone takes a step away from me. Talwarth steps back through the canvas, brushing dirt off his clothes. "You're a piss poor king," he scoffs. "You took an oath as a warrior, and you're turning your back on it and us." He spits at the ground.

Rage boils in my blood, and I have the urge to rip his throat out. A voice in the back of my mind is encouraging me, whispering tantalizing ways to hurt him. I grit my teeth and my fists, ignoring the words. Blood lust is a tantalizing harbinger of rage and pain. Giving in brings a euphoria until it wears off like a mind-altering drug. Coming down from blood lust leaves a bad taste in my mouth and a lot of guilt in my gut.

"If I am your king, Ella is your queen, and your first priority would be to save her."

Talwarth laughs. "She ain't no queen, and she'll never be *my* queen. She deserves to be put to death."

My vision hazes around me, blood pounding in my ears and vision throbbing in and out of view with each pulsation. I move closer to him, but a hand presses against my chest. Force pushes me back, and I blink, seeing Aron between us, hands out to command the elements.

His thin lips frown at me with something weak in his violet eyes. He is scrawny and average with sand-colored hair. He looks like Erac, aside from the ears that stick out from his round face. "Stop. This will not help."

"It'll make me feel better," I growl, bracing against the force, keeping me at bay. I make attempts to maneuver around Aron's barrier, but he only shifts and moves it with me. "Fuck!" I yell, blasting Aron with a forceful wave of air.

His hands drop, his control broken as he slides in the mud. Talwarth steadies him, and two burly arms wrap around me, hugging me against a massive chest. "Stop, Your Highness," a gruff, deep voice speaks in my ear.

I break free, whirling around and slamming a hand into the male's chest. He takes a few steps back, grimacing. I stare at him, eyes scanning over Lumor.

"Stay the fuck away from me," I say, turning back to stomp toward Talwarth.

Aron puts his hands up with a determined glare. "We need to shift our focus from here to Asperheim. That's where Ella is —" his face screws up "—and my brother, Viktor, our enemies are not those in this tent with us."

"You're mad," Fennel cries.

"No," Sordello says. "We need to root them out. Fighting here is going to wear down your numbers and will not resolve anything."

"The traitor is there as well," Malik declares, "and we want our revenge."

"Asperheim is fortified to withstand attacks." Talwarth steps forward, glaring at me then around the tent. "It's a nine or ten-week trek with this many warriors, hunters, and mages, along with others who help and run this camp."

"At least," Fennel says in his squeaky voice that grates against my ears. "The demons will pursue, and we will lose many in the journey to Asperheim, and you say it is to root out Viktor?" He shakes his head. "I say nay, this is personal."

My brother chuckles. "Of course, it's personal. Whatever would this be? They've got Ella, and no matter your opinion, although it's wrong," he pauses to wink at Talwarth, "Ella is capable of destroying this army probably over the course of a few days with no real trouble."

"And you want to march our army to her doorstep." Fennel shakes his head, running a hand over his face.

Seth stands next to me, and I wonder at his ability to smile like that all the time. "If we can get her back, make sure Viktor isn't controlling her again. She'd be happy to do the same to the demons and him. It's worth the risk."

Talwarth and Fennel don't appear convinced. I check the spirits around the room, but I have a fair guess that they want revenge for their fallen brother and Erac's betrayal as much as I want to filet him to death over an open fire and feed him to pigs. My eyes land on the men I don't know.

"Lumor and Gamal, was it?"

"Aye," the shorter stocky man nods.

"You're warriors?"

"We trained as such, but our mother was a healer, and we have learned that too. We can also track."

I cut my eyes to my own brother. He lifts his eyebrows in response with that stupid smile plastered on his face. "What are you thinking, Dec?"

"Oh, please," Talwarth grunts. "They're dryads, from the south, commoners who—"

"Ella trusted them with her life," Seth interrupts, his face hardening. "I don't care who you are, where you came from, or what the hell your background is. It doesn't matter. Isn't that the warrior's code? We've lost most of your fancy commanders and leads who came from well-off families. When this is over, titles are going to be handed out left and right, or there will be no nobility left. So, fuck your assumptions because they came from a poor family."

"Ella's opinion shouldn't really matter. That woman has a heart that bleeds whenever someone else stubs a toe." I smirk at the thought of her, of being able to talk about her and something other than if she's a murdering monster like Tyle's creations. I breathe easier and refocus on the dryad men. "I need you, and you, Sordello, as well. I cannot command you and yours, but I need help."

"We will help."

"Another step closer to the traitor and going home," Malik says. "We will do whatever you need, friend."

Sordello drops a hand on my shoulder, sharp jagged edges of metal digging into my flesh. "Son, there are things to discuss. Collect yours, and we will meet in Marcus' library after dinner."

I jerk away from him. "I'm not talking. You're taking us to Asperheim."

"The troops—" Fennel starts, but the words die under my glare.

"I don't need the fucking troops, and I don't need you. Aron, you're coming with us. We're going to get Ella." I take a breath in the silence and snarl. "Now."

"You cannot be serious!" Talwarth gapes with a stunned, wide-eyed expression. "To go—"

"Now!" I roar. "Soredello, get me to Ella."

"This will require—" he starts.

"He raped her," I growl. There's a collection of shock around me, and I stare at the footprints entrenched in the mud. "And I felt it. She doesn't know who I am or what the bond is, and she's alone with Erac. Now get me and the rest of us to her in Asperheim. Now."

My words are a low breath, fueled through the air by venom

and hatred, not even I knew was possible. He inclines his hood. "Malik."

"Yes."

Cold rips through me as my elements disperse into the air. I don't know who is responsible. It doesn't really matter. I'm not capable of dissipating myself to Asperheim Palace as I have never been there. The only thing that matters is that I am going to get my wife back.

CHAPTER 4

DECLAN

The tingling sensation of my elements coming back together leaves me shaking out my limbs, trying to get blood to flow and return feeling to my limbs. The longer the distance, the worse dissipating seems to leave me feeling when I'm pieced back together.

My eyes flicker around for points of reference to determine where I am. Heat soaks into my skin, a warm breeze brushing hair in front of my face. I reach up, pushing the strands away to see the others.

Two dryads, my brother, Aron, and two spirits. Those with faces I can see are staring, mouths agape. I glance behind me and then pivot in slow motion, or maybe my senses are overwhelmed.

The Palace of Asperheim is conical and mountainous on maps, usually accompanied by a dragon or two, but those maps are no preparation for seeing it with my own eyes. The structure is a mini-mountain, carved into a functional building, spiraling into the sky.

"Holy shit." Seth lets out a low whistle. "You think he's compensating for something?" Seth asks on a chuckle.

I cut my eyes to him. I'm in no mood for jokes, although I can't disagree with my brother. "Viktor chose it for a reason. It's isolated, a fucking fortress. Fuck..." I trail off and glance back at Sordello.

He inclines his head. "This is the oldest part of your dimension, where the first of your kind came to the unmade space and created life. Your ancestors carved that stone thousands of revolutions ago. It is sturdy, a labyrinth of passages inside. Are you sure of this course of action?"

"Are you asking if we are sure we want to go in there and get Ella back so we can stop Viktor and put an end to this madness?" Seth asks. "Yeah, I think we're pretty fucking sure."

I reach up and shove hair out of my face again as air blows more strands in my line of sight. I need a haircut, but that isn't even in my top fifty priorities right now. Between us and the mountainous castle lays a maze of twisting low sandstone walls. I realize we are in a garden of sorts, a neat stone path beneath my feet and desert plants lining it.

I shouldn't be standing here. My eyes follow the path to where it dead-ends into an intersection further up. "We need to move."

"King Declan." Gamal steps next to me. "We need a plan."

"We go in there, we find Ell, we bring her home. That's the plan," Seth says.

I cock a brow at him. *Sometimes my brother is a fucking idiot.* I shake my head and refocus in front of me. "We need to move." I hold out a hand, forcing the air around us to change and form a short sword. "Keep your eyes open, move fast, and careful."

I head up the path and cut right, almost trotting with the sword in my hand at the ready. The others follow me as I twist back and forth, trying to make my way to the palace. I glance up and realize I have led us even further away.

I stop. "Fuck."

A large, calloused hand lands on my shoulder. "We keep moving," Lumor says. "We find a way in."

I curl a lip and turn back. "Can't you dissipate us *inside*?" I point to the palace. "Running around out here is wasting time."

Both spirits shake their hoods. "We cannot."

"We know the exterior from viewing Asperheim from the seat in Medius," Sordello says. "We do not know the interior of the palace, and we are limited as elementals to dissipating, where we do not know."

"Fuck," I say again and stare at the palace. "Fine. Let's move."

I head to the nearest intersection, turning right toward the palace, and freeze. Two hulking demons continue toward me, black horns protruding from their heads, red fur-covered muscle bulges from beneath the metal and leather armor. Both hold massive battle axes.

"Fuck." I tighten my grip on the sword as Seth comes to stand next to me.

"Run or fight?" he asks.

"Fight."

"Alright, then." He grins at me, drawing the sword from the scabbard on his back. "Let's do this."

I sprint forward. Seth passes by me, heading straight for the beast on the right. I take a different approach, side-stepping and lurching at the wall, pushing off and up to gain altitude. The demon swings and I pull myself apart to miss the attack then reassemble behind it.

I swing, slicing the back of the animalistic legs, a weak spot in the thick hide. It roars, spinning, and I tuck and roll as its ax swings down. As I get to my feet, ready to attack, the head comes off in one clean strike from a spirit.

I spin the sword in my grip, flipping the hilt over the back of my hand to hold it pointy side down. I lift my chin at the spirit and turn to watch the other crash down with a bleat. Gamal and

Lumor stab into the gut through the leather armor as Seth drives his sword through its thick throat. It stops twitching with a last soft bleat.

My brother's eyes meet mine, and he nods. Our wordless acknowledgment that we are okay. I look to the dryads.

"Everyone okay?" I ask.

"Yes," Gamal answers.

"Good. Move," I order and push forward.

CHAPTER 5

MORELLA

I breathe in through my nose, and my rib cage expands. My eyes flutter open, sealed shut with salt and sleep grains peeling back over swollen eyes as if I had been crying. I blink against the stark white light around me. I sit up, pressing a hand against my stomach. Faint white scars littering the knuckles catch my eye as I search myself with blurry eyes, but all I see is seamless pale skin and toned abs.

I hunch forward, and strands of burgundy hair swing forth, the silky, straight strands grazing over my collar bones into view. I breathe out slowly, afraid to move too far or too fast, unsure of where I am. My hands lift, trembling as they rise into view.

I fight against trying to understand how I came to be here, my mind blank. Nothing but a yawning abyss of unknown echoing emptiness exists within me, so instead I turn to check my surroundings. No one is here with me in the glorious room. Ahead of me, straight out, is an open set of double glass doors, arched in a decorative fashion of stonework to a balcony and beyond where I see shimmering sand dunes as far as my gaze can discern. The air dances and shifts, the heat palpable in the air, demanding to be acknowledged.

My eyes drop from beyond to the expansive mattress I lay on, the material soft and yielding beneath my weight, hugging my body as it presses into the plush. As my eyes track back toward my legs, I see dark metal links snaking across the end of the bed, over the edge. I reach out, clumsy fingers working to grip the sheet tangled around my legs, and draw it back to reveal the chain clamped around an ankle.

The band is the same dark material as the links, the skin beneath purple and blue like it was yanked, and my flesh was unyielding. My whole body begins to quake as I direct my toes to wiggle. Horrified, the toes on the chained foot wiggle back at me.

I throw the sheet over the foot, hiding it out of sight, the quivering turning to outright shaking. I try to breathe in deep and am rewarded with a stab of a knife into the center of my skull. I cry out, clutching at my head, and tears prick my eyes.

I whimper, trying to get control of myself, but staving off the inexplicable fear is like trying to stop a wave by standing in front of it. It crashes around the blockade without care for it, almost as if it were not there at all.

I sob, too tired to sit up and not daring to try to lay back. I fight against each breath, terrified of the shooting agony that it causes. The tears flow over my lower lids as unbidden as the horror sinking deep into my marrow. The further the terror sinks, the less the tears come, and the more I quiet, my mind seeming to recede somewhere else, absconding itself away against the pain and confusion and fear.

I find my head listing to the side. Fixating on a single spec of dust in the air as everything else fades. My body settles into a shallow rhythm of pulling in air and pushing it out. My gaze falls out of focus, covered over by tears that burn at first but cocoon me from the world in a swell of protection. Everything stops.

If I do not move...

...then I do not exist...

...and everything will be okay.

The breeze kisses my face, drying the trails of wet down my cheeks into salt trails that pull tight the skin. My eyes burn, drying out and shrinking. I exhale.

The back of my mind begins to buzz, the sound of a single bee bouncing through the air. No feeling or thought breaking through the empty chasm. I do not want to move. All I know is an empty gnawing in my soul as if the horror is far worse than ever imaginable.

I cannot say where I am, who I am, or what happened to me. My mind is a void, so quiet my ears ring, and the pressure of absence threatens to explode. There is something my brain is incapable of knowing.

"Morella."

A word in the air, a brush against my senses from the outside world beyond.

"Morella."

I cannot fight against the layers of comfort and solitude my brain has wrapped itself in. I do not have the energy to even try.

"Morella?" The word is from a soft voice, something strange sounding. Burning contact against my shoulder. I scream and jerk, and then whimper and sob in the back of my throat at the searing spreading through my stomach.

"Morella," the word is breathless and raspy. A face looms in front of my eyes in a pixelated format until all the pieces are in a proper place. Drawn brows and pinched lips, features tight and coated with unsettled concern, materializes.

I gasp for air, never allowing my body to draw in a full lung's worth. I fight for calm, trying to dig back down under the unconscious comfort somewhere deep within myself.

Both of my shoulders are on fire. Hands. Hands are on my shoulders, rubbing and massaging the flesh. The heat fades to a pleasant warmth, and my senses are no longer overwhelmed after being adrift from my mind.

I swallow, closing my mouth and staring at the man before me. His concern melts to a smile of relief, and his hands trail down my arms, delicate fingers dancing over my wrists to take my hands in his. He lifts one, then the other to his lips, pressing little kisses against my knuckles.

"That's it," he murmurs, resting my hands in my lap. "That's it. Just breathe. You're alright. Everything is going to be okay."

He nods, and I find my own head bobbing back at him.

"Good," he continues a slow up and down of his head. "That's good. Breathe and listen to my voice. You are going to be okay. I will help you through this. Just breathe."

I keep nodding at him, begging for him to keep talking with a wordless stare. I need his words, something other than the nothingness in my mind. The horror of truth lies beyond the edge, and his soothing sounds are drawing me away from falling over the ledge.

He smiles and squeezes my hands in his. "Good girl, that's it, breathe and listen. That's all you have to do, okay? Can you say okay for me?"

I swallow and work my tongue around in my mouth, trying to remember its use. "Okay," I manage, the word falling out of my mouth with a bit of drool and no real articulation. I close my mouth and work my throat to try again. "Okay."

He grins at me, the skin at the corners of his eyes crinkling. Those eyes are bright and pulsating, every shade of purple in liquid shards blending into each other to form a beautiful canvas. "Good, that's good, Morella. Morella, that's your name. Can you say your name for me?"

"Morella."

"Very good." He chuckles. "That's good. Breathe, and now can you say Erac? That's my name."

"Er-ac," I try to get the name right. "Erac."

"Yes, so now you know your name and mine." He squeezes my hands again, and I keep my eyes on those bright violet eyes. "That's good, that's very good."

"Good," I repeat. "Okay, good."

He smiles without humor. "Yes." He reaches out and tucks hair behind my ear. "Your mind is strained right now. I wiped it clear, removed your memories to remove a poison from your brain, but it was still there, a piece of it, so I had to do it again. It was dangerous. The mind wasn't meant to ever undergo what I did, and I am afraid a second cleansing might have pushed it too far."

I blink at him. "Too far?"

He chuckles and clasps my face between his hands. "Yes, my little love, too far, but I had to get rid of that poison from your mind. Any little dredge remaining would rot you from the inside out all over again. You forgive me, yes?" He starts nodding again.

I find my head is moving up and down, but I cannot say whether I move it, or he does. His words force inward to my shredded brain. It is ravaged, so I stare at his thin lips instead of trying to focus.

"Here." He pulls back, shifting to the side as I stare ahead, straight through him. "Drink this. It will help you."

I drag my eyes to the goblet dangling from his fingers, gilded and shining gold. He reaches out, taking my hand, forcing it against the basin, and wrapping my fingers around the cup. His large hand remains over mine, and I stare at him, the sandy hair cropped neat on his head.

Releasing my hands, he frowns at me as I sit there holding the thing. "Drink," he says again, an edge to his voice. "It is an antidote against the poison and has something to help your recovery as well. Please, drink."

I retract my arm, drawing the cup to my chest, my chin dropping forward to inspect the contents. The liquid has a fine layer of white froth on the surface, puffs of it clinging to the inner edges of the brim where the liquid laps.

Lifting the concoction to my lips, the scent of bitter floral stings my nasal passages, and I take a small sip. No fluid passes into my mouth, but my tongue laps the dribbles from my lips. I grimace and lift my gaze to him, shaking my head.

He sighs and lifts the goblet toward my mouth with two firm fingers under the wide base at the bottom of the stem. "You need to. I know it doesn't taste the best, but there are far worse things. Come on now, drink."

I do as he says, chugging down the potion to the gritty, dark grains at the bottom. I shudder and shove the cup away, back into his chest even as my body tries to fight the last gulp from going down. The muscles in my abdomen protest as they try to work, so the fluid stays down.

He takes the cup and sets it aside where it topples over, though he seems not to care. "There we go. How do you feel? Better? It will take some time, and you'll drink this twice a day, at least for a while."

I nod with blurry eyes. The task of downing the mouthfuls has stirred up the burning in my gut. "Okay." I swallow, my eyes flickering back and forth between his. They are full of intensity opposite his hushed words. I nod again. "Yes. Okay."

He reaches out and puts a hand on my jaw, stroking my cheek with his thumb. "There's a good girl. You don't need to worry about anything. I'll take care of you. I have waited for this for an awfully long time. Watching you with that animal who poisoned you was a kind of torture." His lips twist to the side in a cold sneer. "But I endured, waited until I had my opportunity, and now you are here, with me, mine to cherish."

His face lowers to the floor, his brow furrowing. He looks up with a lopsided grin, his expression lifting. He kneels on one knee in front of me, taking my hands in his. "Morella, my darling love, I have ached with longing for you these past several revolutions. Watching you with that animal made me violently ill, but now you are here—with me—where you have always belonged and now...”

He beams up at me with hope shining through his face, the soul star’s light beaming through a window as he goes on. “I love you so, so much. You are the dearest part of my soul. We have always been meant for each other. I was not strong enough before, but now that I have been made whole, there is nothing that will come between us. Do you understand, my love? We are destined to be together. I love you, and you love me.”

I remain silent, although I guess I am supposed to return the sentiment. His grip tightens on my fingers to a point of discomfort as I stare down at him. Pursing my lips, I do my best to give him a smile. I wonder if he can tell how forced it is, but if he does, he makes no remark.

There is a knock, and then silence stretches onward. Another knock followed by a muffled voice. “Sir, they’re here.”

Erac’s grip eases, and he sighs, glancing over at the door. My gaze flickers from him to the glossy black painted surface connecting this room to the next. I return my sights to him, seeing his face twist with malice.

Erac faces me, continuing in a hoarse voice ravaged with pain. “Tell me you love me.”

The knocking returns. “Sir? You requested to be informed of their arrival. They are here, in the gardens already.”

I find my voice quivers with trepidation, eyes prickling. “I don’t know.”

He throws my hand from his and scoffs. “Is that what you think?”

His lips twist with a cruel emotion, stuck halfway between a sneer and a smirk. He leans in closer, bringing our faces together, so his warm breath lingers on my lips. My eyes stay on his, widening as my pulse quickens.

The man on the other side of the door begins to knock again, more urgent, and then a sudden stop. "Hello? Sir? Are you there?"

"I'm here! I heard you," Erac snarls, head whipping to the door as he bellows. "Now, be gone." He whips his attention back to me, and I cower beneath his furious gaze.

In slow motion, his hand looms toward me, wrapping around my neck to squeeze. I gasp, my lips parting. He smiles, yanking me closer, his cold lips pressing against mine. His tongue invades me like a slimy snake, and then he pulls back, sliding his mouth back and forth against mine.

"Tell me," he whispers, his flesh whispering over mine as he keeps our heads pressed close. "Tell me you love me." He is almost begging, his voice flagrant with a dark passion that leaves my senses tingling on high alert.

I swallow, my stomach squirming as his grip closes tighter around my throat. "I love you," I manage in a croak, his cruel grip restricting my air supply.

He grins, and I blink my burning eyes. He is gone from me, standing and straightening the collar of his shirt. "Good. Now stay here and rest. I have business to attend to. Take heed not to push your mind too far. Sleep as much as you can. It will do you good."

My head bobs of its own accord, eyes dropping to the shadows outlining my foot beneath the sheet and the hidden chain around my ankle. I stay still and keep my head bent as he slides away.

When he is gone, I lift my head and glance around the room. The furnishings are pretty, silks and satin and fine gauze, and the world is cheery and bright. I stare out beyond the edge of the bed, the gentle breeze drawing pricks of cold along my exposed skin despite the heat. The world may be beautiful and warm, but inside this room is dark and cold, a hollow rotted scent hiding oozing beneath the fragrant air.

I glance at the door, wondering about the man that left. He

says I love him. I said I love him, but then why do my hands shake? The room is pretty, brightly lit, and lavish, but metal links tether me to this room, to this bed, and my body is battered and bruised. My fingers curl as if to grip tight, and a voice stirs deep in a crevice of my mind, whispering and becoming louder until it is an echoing thought.

Am I a prisoner?

CHAPTER 6

DECLAN

I come to another dead end, baring my teeth at the stone wall. I glance to my left, the palace looming closer overhead. I turn and start back, taking the first right. More demons enter the path from further up. I slow, watching them.

One stops, a leg pawing at the ground as its animalistic head lowers. The other trots forward, the hooves clopping against stone. I brace to engage, but the spirits dissipate between the demons and me. One grabs the beast, ready to charge by the horns, and throws it against the wall. It lets out a mixture between mooing and howling, and I grit my teeth, knowing the sound will draw others.

The spirit stomps down on its throat, cutting the cry short, and the other parries to attack with his long sword. Ahead, I catch sight of another pair coming up the path.

"Declan!"

I glance behind to see Gamal and Lumor engaging a pair appearing from behind us. Aron has his hands out, twisted and tense, his face contorted with exertion. I turn to Seth. "Help them," I order with a jerk of my head.

"You can't seriously be thinking of taking on two."

"Go," I direct my sword at the others before pulling my elements apart and rebuilding to meet the demons on their way toward us.

They bleat and swing axes, and I duck and roll, staying low and swinging for the weak spots on the legs of the first. I lurch to my feet behind them, clutching the hilt in both hands to cut through the back of the legs on the second.

An ax swings toward me, and I dive to the side, clambering up and heading for the wall. I run up the surface and push off, backflipping through the air over one. I make contact, grabbing hold of its shoulder on the way down and driving my sword through the open place between its chest armor and neck.

I ride it down as it drops forward, just as a swish of air behind me warns of an incoming attack. I leave my blade embedded and roll away. The second demon's ax cleaves into the wall, sending chunks of sandstone and dust through the air.

The sounds of battle ring through the air, clashing metal and the bleating war calls of demons fill my ears. I dodge a strike, then dissipate to my sword, wrenching it free. My gaze lifts and focuses on the demon, seeing two others standing with it now. One lowers its head, snorting.

"Fuck."

It charges. I grip the hilt of my sword tight and run straight toward it, jumping to miss the attack and using it to catapult myself toward the others. The sensation of being thrown against a stone wall rips through me, and I drop to the ground, landing on my shoulder with a painful pop.

I blink, dazed, and unsure of what happened. The air whistles above me, then I hear as much as feel the thwack of the arrow into my left shoulder. I grunt, hearing another projectile whizzing through the air and scramble to move.

My eyes search behind the demons advancing to see Erac grinning at me. I bare my teeth and wrench the arrow from my shoulder even as others fly toward me from the row of archers behind him. I throw my hand out, commanding air elements together to form a shield, slashing out at a demon preparing to cleave me in two with his ax.

The arrows cut through the air, finding purchase. Two more slide into my healing shoulder, another into my stomach. A couple of arrows or maybe even a few dozen aren't going to kill me, but pulling them out hurts more than I care to experience.

I grit my teeth and growl in the back of my throat, knowing my shield should have held. Erac intervened. He's a stronger mage and capable of forcing the elements out of my control.

"Declan!" Sordello calls, then he stands between me and the attacking forces. He swings two short swords now, cutting a demon in two with synchronized strokes of the blades.

I push away from the wall, attacking another as it pulls back the broad, double-sided ax. I slash at its legs, getting kicked in the gut for my efforts. I lose my grip on the sword and skip along the ground. The arrows snap and break, pushing deeper into me, and I groan.

Pushing up with both hands, I ignore the pulsating warmth of pain in my torso, my gaze searching for my weapon, knowing I won't be able to focus the elements into creating another in this condition. I don't have time to find it, though, so I throw myself out of the way of another demon's ax. The head drives into the stone path, and it wrenches, trying to pull it free.

I scramble away, spying my own sword between the legs of a demon locked in battle with a spirit. I dash forward, diving and somersaulting along the ground to avoid the swing of an ax on my way to collect it. Blood is warm and wet between my shirt and skin, causing the fabric to stick and pull.

Ducking another attack, I panic, throwing a hand up to force a blast of air at the demon. It has little effect, and I'm still within range of its next attack. I lunge, trying to tackle it to the ground, using my elbow in a swing to its face.

It works, and we both hit the ground. I roll to my back, throwing my legs up and using the momentum to throw my body upward and onto my feet. The demon is rising, but its ax is loose on the path between us. I dive for it, snatching it up and doing a tuck and roll with it in my hands once again upright.

The thing is heavy, almost as large as I am. I spin it in my hands, testing the weight, and then inhale deep, swinging it at the previous owner with all my strength, feeling the open wounds in my upper body torque and tear open further.

The ax cleaves through the midsection of the demon. Pain pricks down my left side. I turn my head to see several more arrows sticking out of me. There's a clash of metal, and I face the other way, seeing an ax inches from my head. Seth has his blade locked against the shaft, struggling to keep my head on my body for me.

I heave the demon ax upward. Seth's eyes stretch wide, and he lurches back as I swing. My muscles protest, almost tearing and burning as the beast falls to the ground in two. I let go, the weapon falling to the ground. I can't keep using that thing; it's built for demons three times my size.

Seth yells out, grabbing me and spinning us around. I feel the arrowheads sinking into my back and grind my teeth, my eyes slipping closed for a brief second at the pain. I stand, shaking him off.

"We can't stay here!" he yells.

A spirit steps between us and another barrage of arrows, throwing up a hand. I can see the air in a curved shield shimmering as those arrows rain down on it. I glance around at demon bodies and see Gamal and Lumor supporting each other, limping closer. Aron follows up, his back to me, waving his hands at approaching demons even as the other spirit hacks away with his sword.

"Lumor and I cannot go further," Gamal says, a hand over his stomach. "We do not heal as you do."

I can see the red stain, the blood bubbling past his fingers. I snarl and look back toward the palace. My eyes lock on Erac's gleeful expression. Even from here, I can sense his satisfaction.

"Fuck!" I yell. "Aron, get them out of here." I jerk my head at the dryad brothers.

"What are we doing?" Seth asks. He rubs the back of his neck, staring behind me.

"I don't fucking know, but I'm not leaving her here."

"We need a better plan," Gamal says with labored breathing. "We come back."

"No," I manage.

Seth grabs hold of me. "We'll get her back."

"I'm not leaving," I shove him away. "Ella!" I scream, turning toward the palace. "Ella!"

The spirit turns its hand over my shoulder. "I cannot hold this much longer," he says in a labored voice I recognize as Malik's. "The demons will break through soon. Erac is already fighting my control over the elements."

"Dec." Seth grabs hold of me again. "Stop. You can't get inside, and even if you did, you'd never make it to her right now. You have to leave her here."

I swing a fist at him, achieving square contact with his jaw. My wounds burn and pulse in an angry response. "Fuck you," I spit at my brother. "I'm not leaving."

"We need to go," Gamal says in a stern tone. "Lumor and I need healing."

"Then go. I'm staying." My eyes search through Malik's shield, then I turn away to face further out in the gardens. "There's a way. I just need to find it."

The shield cracks and Malik drops to his knees. I twist to face the incoming hoard of demons, arrows flying. I brace myself, and then the cold rips through me.

I am in a small rectangular room lined with bookshelves

from floor to ceiling all the way around. I take a breath as I realize I am in Marcus' private library and round on Sordello.

"I told you I wasn't leaving." I close my eyes and try to picture Asperheim Palace in my mind, the short sandstone walls and stone path of the garden.

Heavy armored gauntlets land on my shoulders, digging through the fabric of my shirt in an uncomfortable gouging sensation. The air around me presses tight. "Declan, you will do better to derive a plan. We will help you get her back. The entire collective is your family now, and we will aid you in retrieving Ella. Take a second to think."

I can't lift my arms or shrug him off, so I open my eyes and glare. The pressure lessens, and I jerk out of his reach, my movements stiff from the resistance of condensed air around me. "I don't want a second to think, I want my fucking wife!"

My roar rings around the room, and Sordello's pauldrons slump. "I want my daughter safe and happy, but we are going to have to find another way."

I reach up and start pulling arrows out of me. It stings, and as my body begins to heal, I experience the sensation of spiders crawling over my flesh. "I'm going back."

"And you will die for it," Aron says in a flat tone. "No one wants revenge on my brother more than I, but Sordello is right."

I drop my hands to my hips and laugh with a cold bitterness. "I doubt you have as much hatred as I do. I felt it, what he did. He didn't just take my wife or touch her. He fucking hurt her in the sickest possible way. *My* fucking wife, and he fucked her as she begged for it to stop!" I scream.

Aron crosses his arms, but he looks ill. Seth drops into an armchair next to the small round table, home to a chessboard. "Haven," he mutters and hides his face in his hands, elbows on knees.

I inhale sharply through my nose, trying to reel in my

eroding temper. "Haven's not helping us or her. Now I'm going back."

"Declan," Sordello's voice booms. "You will not dissipate to Asperheim. You will not return to Asperheim until we have a plan."

I bare my teeth. "You fucking—" I swing, my fist contacting the armor plate he wears over his torso. I feel the contact radiate through my wrist, up my forearm, and all the way into my shoulder.

Sordello flies backward into the bookshelf, books raining down over him as he drops to the floor in a kneeling position. His hooded face stays on the floor as I pant, and then Malik steps forward, offering a helping hand to him.

I growl in the back of my throat and am wrenched backward by someone else. I round on the individual and snarl. "Get off me. He just—he has fucking runes."

"I know," Seth says, staying a couple of paces away from me with his hands held up. "He has a full set of spirit runes, and you don't, which means he can command you, and you have no choice but to obey." Seth's hands start to lower as he eyes me with weary exhaustion.

"Take it back, recant it, give me a new order and tell me to go," I yell, turning my back on him and facing Sordello, who is back on his feet.

"No. You can punch me, you can yell, you can lose your temper, and still, I will not. You are married to Ella. She is my daughter, which makes you my son, and I'll not lose you too or allow you to throw your life away in a useless attempt to save her. We need a plan. When we have a plan and a way into Asperheim, you will be allowed to return."

"Fuck you," I growl, pointing at him. "Fuck you and you—" I point to Malik, then Aron "—and all of you." Everything is shaking, my legs, my arms, the finger pointing around the room at all of them as I breathe in and out.

Seth steps forward, wrapping his arms around me, and I don't fight back. He has my arms pinned to my sides while arrows protrude from his spine. "We'll get her back."

"Now," I say in a croak, lifting burning eyes to his.

He grimaces. "When we know how to get her, we'll go get her."

I give him a swift punch in the gut and step away. "Rot in the inferno."

CHAPTER 7

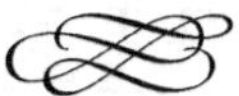

DECLAN

Sitting in Marcus' study, I have claimed my usual seat in a high back chair next to the table and chessboard. I reach out, running my thumb over the white queen.

"Morning," Seth gets past a yawn.

I accept the blood he offers in a glass bottle yanking it away from him. I feel better using brute force, like it matters if I open the cap or rip it off, destroying the metal cage work that allows the cap to be reused to seal the bottle. Seth rolls his eyes and makes some quip that has me glaring with a curled lip.

He laughs at me. "Figured you wouldn't be keeping up with the blood lust."

I take a swig, my nose wrinkling in disgust. "What's this from? Never mind, I don't want to know."

He chuckles as I set the bottle aside. "Sure."

"Seriously, was that from a diseased rat? Ugh." I run a hand over my face and sit up.

"Week old pig, actually."

"You're disgusting," I say under my breath.

He shrugs. "If you fed yourself, you could pick where it comes from."

"Really? I don't need you to take care of me. Are you fucking serious? A week-old pig? Are you mad at me?"

I conjure a glass, forcing the elements to bend into another state, building them together to suit my purpose. The process takes about a minute, and I frown. Ella can manage the task within seconds. I fill the glass half and half with blood and liquor, throwing it all down in one burning gulp. I repeat a second time, then settle to sip on the third round.

"No and no." Seth grins at me while grabbing the decanter. "Can I get a glass," he asks, raising his eyebrows at me. I make another and toss it across the board at him. He catches it. "Thanks."

I grunt in response and look to the suit of armor with cream-colored cloth hood pulled up and obscuring the face. Sordello stands there, arms by his side, hood directed toward the floor in front of the booklined walls. I eye the chest piece of his suit, the dent I left earlier erased.

Marcus sits behind his desk, feet crossed in the middle, lounging back in his chair with a brimming glass of amber liquid. His steady golden gaze comes from beneath craggy, furrowed black brows. Even he has given up on personal grooming, a beard growing in, and his hair too long.

I look around, taking stock of attendees. There's the four of us, and I try to think of who else should be here. "Where's Legia?"

Seth lifts and drops one shoulder. "I checked on her earlier, brought her dinner, managed to get her to eat something for the first time. Chase is dead. Marx has gone back to wherever it is that he goes? Wyatt's locked in a dungeon—we need to talk about that—and well, Ell, we know where she is." He sighs, scrubbing a hand down his face. "So that leaves you, me, Marc. Sordello is a mouthpiece for all the spirits, and thank Haven for that, or we'd never all fit."

I shrug. "Where's Aron?"

Marcus drops his feet from the desk, glaring at me with lines carved in his rich brown skin. "Where is Selene?"

I eye him, taking a drink, debating how much to tell. As the eldest Byron child, he adopted a father-like role to both Ella and Selene. "I dropped her in the infirmary."

"Is she still capable of being queen?"

I smirk. "Selene has never been capable of being queen, but sure, she's mostly intact. I didn't damage her mind, mostly just her body." I take a sip.

Marcus grimaces and gets up, coming around his desk to lean against the front. "Was it worth it?"

I fight the urge to laugh. Marcus is not one to appreciate the response, and I don't want to laugh right now. "What? You want me to feel bad?"

Marcus scowls, but Seth chuckles. My friend's gaze only grows darker, and something akin to fury settles over the features. "Yes, I want you to feel bad. I want you to be miserable, to feel guilty, to at least suffer for what you've done."

I take a drink and decide I like this new Marcus. "I feel bad then."

"No, you don't!" he roars, standing to hurl his glass at me.

I throw my arm up, forcing the air elements together to create a shield. The glass shatters. The depressing part is the waste of whiskey that sprays around me.

Marcus sneers as he plops down in his chair. "You don't feel a damn thing, do you? You aren't sorry in the least. You tortured Selene, the queen, your queen, my sister. –You were going to marry her, you used to be intimate with her, and you can just— Just—"

His words are failing him, and I lift an eyebrow. "Just break bones and cut her open? Just listen to her beg and cry and tell me how much I love her and didn't mean it?" I smirk. "Or better yet, just hear her out on how this will make me happy, how this makes everyone happy?"

I shake my head and down my drink, reaching for the bottle. "No. I didn't just do it. I enjoyed it. She betrayed this court the moment she handed Ella over to Erac, knowing she'd be taken to Viktor. If she had merely handed Ella over to Erac, I still would have done it. That she provided Viktor with Ella? Selene damned herself. Don't blame me, and the court won't hold my actions illegal as I can persuasively argue that my actions were in the betterment of this court while the queen's were to give Viktor what he needs to destroy everyone and everything."

Marcus jerks back. "Ella won't do what Viktor wants. She never has."

"Fuck that," Seth laughs. "She did a lot for Viktor."

"Not when she had a choice."

"Which was when?" I ask. I keep my voice low, my tone even. "When he injected her with his blood and ordered her about? When he threatened you, or me, or Seth and forced her to willingly comply? What do you think will happen with her locked up at the mercy of Viktor and Erac without her memories? She doesn't know about the bond or me, and who knows what else she doesn't know."

The flushed anger of Marcus' face fades from his dark skin. "Ella's strong. She'll fight."

I toy with the empty glass in my hand, staring at it as I spin my wrist in circles. I give myself one long blink to close my eyes and draw my thoughts away from my wife. Thinking of her is only going to cause me agony. I don't need to think about her. I need to go get her. I pinch the bridge of my nose, drawing a deep breath, and then drop my hand.

"Viktor has always tried to break her into what he wants her to be, a perfect, coldblooded weaponized tool which does as told without question or defiance. Erac? Fuck, we don't really know much about Erac and what he wants, but I do know he wants *her*," I stress.

My brother sighs heavily. "He doesn't just want her the way Viktor does."

I grunt, snarling at my liquor. "Viktor and Erac are intelligent. They are determined. They are capable. And together? I am afraid of what they are going to do to get Ella to act as they want—to be who they want. If we leave her in their hands for too long, I don't know what we'll get back."

Marcus blanches and looks away. He knows I am right. I don't need validation. I have avoided those words long enough, wanting to deny the truth of it for as long as possible.

Seth sighs. "If they can control Ella, we're all fucked seven ways to the Inferno and back, so—" he lifts his glass "—cheers, to all the damned good we used to love in this world and to all those whose grim fates are undeserved." He tosses the glass back, then grins, wiggles his eyebrows, and starts to chug the bottle.

My brother is a drunken fool, and my friend is acting like a pissed off woman who wants me to be emotional about things. I glance around the room, knowing Seth is right. No one stands a chance against Ella if she's coming for us, and we are unprepared. "Where's Aron?"

"Aron has been missing from the collective. I do not know where he is now," Sordello says, his hood lifting. "He is in pain. I have not had a chance to speak with him of the events which have brought us here."

Marcus stands, coming around the desk to lean against the front edge. "And where have you been?"

I stare back at him. He's expecting me to feel sorry or something of the like, I suppose. "I've been preoccupied with the loss of my wife, the rightful Queen of Byron, Ella. Your sister? You remember her? What she is capable of?"

"You've been pissing yourself and crying in a corner or torturing Selene for information Wyatt gave willingly. Don't fucking delude yourself into believing this has anything to do with someone or something other than yourself."

I jerk to my feet, fists clenched, teeth bared. "You're right because I don't fucking care about anyone besides Ella. We could win a war with nothing but Ella. She's my fucking wife, the only reason I'm here!" I roar, pointing to the space between my feet. "I came back for her, stayed in this life for her, and when she was gone, when I thought her dead, I stayed king because I thought she'd want me to, to honor her in death, and if I didn't have a spirit keeping me here I'd be finding my way into Asperheim for her right now. Don't fucking delude yourself into thinking anything but."

Marcus leans further away from me, practically laying back on his desk. A hand rests on my shoulder, and I jerk, flinching toward my brother. He stares at me with a pathetic expression. "There has to be more that matters than Ell."

I take a deep breath and drop my volume, my words scratching my throat. "Right now? She is it."

He grins at me, smacking me on the back between my shoulders. "Come on, that's all?"

"Back off, little brother," I say, wondering how I might feel if he were dead. I cannot fathom the event or even begin to imagine how I might feel. I shrug my shoulders.

He puckers up, making wet noises that irritate my ears. "Aw, ease up, big brother," he says, grinning.

I narrow my eyes. "You may be bigger than me, *little* brother, but I will still take you down in a fight."

"Well, sure, but not a fair fight."

I force my lips into a smile, but there's nothing humorous about me right now. "I'd rip your throat out with my teeth even without manipulating the elements."

His grin slips to a smile. "Maybe."

Now I am grinning. The falter in the single word, the eyes stretched a hair wider than usual. My little brother isn't so sure, after all. I shrug his hand off my back and roll my shoulders. "We need a plan." My gaze turns to Sordello. "We know where she is. We can go get her."

The hood shakes back and forth in a slow wag. "The collective has decided. We have lost two already. We will continue to help you fight the demon hordes."

"But you're not going to go get Ella," Seth gasps and starts laughing. "Isn't she one of you? Your daughter?"

His shoulders slump with light clinking. "She is, and yes. We will have to fight our way in, and Asperheim is a fortress. For now, we are surveying the palace and trying to determine the best way. Meanwhile, we will continue to help on the battlefield. I fought to have the collective attack directly and save her, but the risk is too great for our collective, even we are not invincible. We can be killed if we are pulled apart – dismembered – or our runes removed."

"So," I grind out, "elementals are dying left and right in this fucking war."

The hood lifts, and I feel a glare coming from beneath in a bizarre sense. "Your kind die and return to dust, my kind dies, and our enemy uses our runes to become stronger. The risk is too high that one or more of us will die by attacking directly. It is not a fear of dying, but a fear of giving power to those we stand against."

"By doing nothing, they will keep Ella. That's more power than a set of runes." My grip on the glass in my hand tightens.

Marcus clears his throat. "Ella has a set of runes. What is stopping them from taking hers?"

My entire body tenses with anxiety. "Taking those runes from her might kill her."

"And Viktor isn't going to risk killing her." Seth sighs. "He's going to use her. That's worth more than a single set of spirit runes, maybe even every set in existence combined."

"Yes, that is the collective's belief and reasoning behind the disregard of her runes being used against us."

"No, just Ella herself," Seth barks in laughter. "That's so much worse."

"Worse than how a woman was able to command Declan to kneel before her as she slit his throat without him fighting back?" Soredello's voice booms around the room, his finger pointing at my chest. "The runes are not only power to command elements and magic but to control all elementals without resistance. Like Declan unable to proceed on a suicidal mission to get into Asperheim."

"Great," Seth drawls, dragging the word out. He turns, grabbing the bottle from the chessboard for a drink. The glass clinks as it is set harshly on the marble. "Now what?"

I use a hand to force my jaw left, then right to stretch my neck, my eyes scanning the books lining the walls next to me. "Best case, we get Ella back. Worse case, we have to fight Ella. We come up with a plan." I sneer the last words and glare at Sordello.

Seth laughs. "How in Damnatus do you plan against Ella?"

I grit my teeth. My little brother has a point. "How the fuck does one kidnap Ella and hold her against her will?" I snap back. "How does one fucking—fuck—force—" I can't get the words out again. I give up and pour myself another drink.

Marcus puts a hand over his face, then drags it downward, pulling on his features. With a loud sigh, he pushes away from the desk, grabbing a couple of books from the shelving behind his desk. "There are ways of subduing magic, even magic as powerful as Ella's. They proved as much when they took her. I'll go through these," he says, holding up the stack of books.

Seth tips his head back and howls with laughter. "She's deadly even without magic."

"I can handle her without magic." I cross my arms, chest tightening at the thought of going blow to blow. I would win, but I'm not sure how much damage I would do. I hate the thought of hitting her, hurting her. I try to clench my jaw tighter.

"I am far better suited," Sordello rumbles.

"Suited. Ha! That's funny," Seth snickers.

Marcus sets the books on his desk and drops into the chair. He stares at me, a depressed consignment to his features. "We may need to consider the possibility that our only viable option for the least casualties is to..." he winces. "We might have to—"

"No," I grind through bared front teeth. "Absolutely not. I won't." *I can't.*

Seth shakes his head, curly brown hair swaying around his face like a child. "Nope. I'm with Dec. That's not happening. I can't even think that, say those words, not an option. I love her too much."

I don't even turn to face him. I throw my arm straight out, my closed fist making contact with his shoulder. He yelps and moves out of my reach. I cross my arms, focused on Marcus. "Find a way to slow her down, to fuck with her magic."

"Maybe take some of that pent-up aggression out on some demons instead of me," Seth mutters under his breath. "I'll find Aron. He's got more knowledge about magic and Erac."

I shift my weight and exhale. "We find a way to eliminate her use of magic. We figure out a way to get into Asperheim. We expect the worst possible outcome, which means we plan to fight her with her magic, and we figure out how to bring her home." I turn to Sordello. "Is that enough of a plan?"

"No."

I snatch up the bottle of blood and chuck it at his head. He holds a hand up, stopping the bottle midway between us. He collects the spilled blood from the air, manipulating it back into the bottle. The metal cage and cork top are remade, and then he floats the bottle back to me.

"Drink, Declan, your temper is getting the best of you."

"No, really? You think? That prick has Ella, and he's hurting her. I'll just skip through the daisies, shall I?"

Seth smirks. Sordello isn't amused by me. I give him a silent snarl and take the bottle as I dissipate. I head for the kitchens to pilfer a bottle of whiskey to go with my blood and then shred apart to the roof for peace and quiet. I chase the blood with the liquor and close my eyes, trying to reach Ella through the bond. I get nothing but the cold stab from an interrupted bond and take another shot from both bottles.

"Fuck."

CHAPTER 8

MORELLA

The sunken city, the whole thing built in stone and marble, the treetops still full and lush at the surface, the thin leaves trailing from the branches in time with the river's current. The surface is dotted with lush lilies and other water plants around the banks, but further out, the surface of the crystal water is clear, steeped in shadows of the lost world below the surface.

I stare down into it, standing in the middle, the surface of the water like a glass pane beneath my feet. Movement disturbs the shadows, like beings walking in and around the buildings, but every waft of shadows occurs on my peripheral, and when I try to focus, there is nothing there.

I drop to my knees, unable to penetrate the water. I stare down, hungry with a desire to reach through the barrier, to find the shadows moving beyond my reach. Pressing with flat palms, I hope to breach the water. I add more and more force until my arms are shaking with fatigue. The hunger turns to ravenous need, and I slam my fists against the water over and over, causing droplets of back spray to hit my face.

No matter how hard I try, I cannot break through. No amount of force seems to make a difference, and the need overwhelms me until I collapse and lay on my side, bawling and begging for something I do not even have a name for.

~

I slept and dreamed in cryptic messages that left my eyes watering as I awoke. The world turned darker and colder at each lurch back to consciousness, and then the warmth and light returned, bathing me in the hope that it was over.

My stomach rumbles as I lay in the tub, submerged in steaming water. It helps to smooth the ache deep in my core. My leg is still chained to the bed, but the tether is long enough for me to lay back while my ankle dangles over the edge.

The room is full of glass and tiny bottles of fragrant soap on shelves that I took the liberty of emptying into the bath to create a pleasant scent. As I relax, my mind cloisters away from the smells and the heat of the water once more until I am swimming in a blank abyss. It is almost near a pleasant feeling.

Everything is shattered when I feel the quiet is disturbed. I sit up in the tub to grip the edges of the large white basin. Muted clinks and scrapes waft from the adjoining room, and I eye the door partially closed to allow the chain to slither inside.

Erac strolls into the room, pushing the door wide open, and smiles with closed lips. "You seem to be regaining your strength, my love."

I frown up at him. "I guess. My head hurts less today."

"Were you in pain?" He perches on the side of the tub, lifting eyebrows at me. "I did not realize you were hurting. You should have told me."

I purse my lips, casting my eyes down to the surface of the water, glad of the soap suds obscuring my body from view. Something in the back of my mind wonders at the size of his hands as his fingers dip into the water and swirl.

"Morella," he snaps. "What aren't you telling me? Do you still hurt?"

I roll my shoulders back and lift my chin. "I am better. The water has helped."

"Very well." He sighs and stands. "I brought your antidote and breakfast. When I came to see you last night, you were asleep and so beautiful in slumber that I hated the thought of waking you. But you must drink now. Dry off and come out to eat with me."

I watch him go, narrowing my eyes and cocking my jaw. I wait until he is out of sight before standing, wiping bubbles from my skin, and retrieving a towel.

"Erac," I call out, eyeing the dress on the floor that I had removed.

"Yes, my love?"

I wrap myself in the towel and wring my hair over the bath allowing water to drip into the pool in soft trickles. "Do I have another dress?"

"I will be right there."

I wait, eyes locked on the unfamiliar face staring back at me in the mirror. The eyes are bright purple, the color of orchids sharing none of the same inky dark colors of Erac's. Hair that was vibrant shades of red and purple has been darkened by the water, turning a nice shade of blood under the light, almost black in clumps.

I move in for a closer inspection, touching the face, turning to see the thin features, the nose that curves up at the end straight in the middle. A chuckle behind me draws my focus over my shoulder to Erac, hanging a dress on a hook by the door.

"Don't worry, you are very beautiful."

I nod, turning back to meet my gaze in the reflection. My face does seem symmetrical and pleasing. I turn away, reaching for the dress.

"Here," he hands fabric to me and hurries out of the room.

I stare at the undergarments in my hand and sigh, stepping

away from the door and working my way into the clothing, but the dress has a zipper I cannot manage on my own. I exit the bath holding the gown up against my chest.

"Erac?"

He stands from the table set up near the opening to the outside world. "Yes, my love?"

I turn around. "Can you…?"

"Yes, I can."

The warmth of his hands settles against my lower back. The zipper glides with a soft purr. His hands do not stop there but trail further upward over the bare skin between my shoulders to the nape of my neck before parting to run across the tops of my shoulders.

His nose rests against the side of my neck beneath my ear. "You smell sweet, like a flower."

There is a deep husk to his voice, and his hands tighten on my upper arms, fingers digging into my skin. His mouth opens against the side of my neck, the moist breath of heat wafting against the thin skin. A shiver runs down my spine, a reaction to the sensation rooted in no emotion.

"I just used the soap." I wave a hand toward the bathroom, doubting he is watching me anyway.

He chuckles and kisses my neck before pulling away. "Come, drink your antidote and let us eat."

Erac guides me to the closest chair, pulling it away from the table to help me into it. I stare at the gold chalice positioned square in front of me, and with a sigh, I pick it up. I hold my breath and take long gulps until I am forced to breathe. I set the goblet aside, but Erac picks it up and hands it back to me.

"All of it."

I want to say something, to protest about the taste. I grip the stem in a fist and eye the liquid, then turn my face up to him. "What is it?"

"Your antidote."

I bob my head. "What is it made of?" Frowning into the frothing liquid, I move the goblet in circles watching it froth white. "I want to know what I'm drinking."

"It comes from a healer," he grinds out. "There's no need to explain this to you. Drink the antidote."

"Why won't you tell me?"

His voice is tight. "Just drink the damn thing. You need it."

"I want to know what they did to me."

"I've told you. There was poison in you. You don't need to know what it is, just that it is harmful, corrosive, and that it erodes away your power, makes you weak."

"That isn't a lot of information."

Sighing, he runs a hand down his face, pulling on his features. "Drink your antidote, then I will tell you, okay?"

"Okay," I say and throw back the rest of it.

"Good girl." He squeezes my shoulder and takes the cup as he sits across from me. "Now, please eat. You need nourishment to keep up your strength. The body is as important as the mind, and your mind needs to heal."

I wince and stare down at the fruits and bread on the table. "You said—" I lift my eyes to his, "—you'd tell me what happened to me? How did I get poisoned?"

He tilts his head, lips turning to a hard line. He lets out a burst of air, his chest deflating, and he sits forward, leaning on crossed arms. "You were poisoned against your father and me by a pair of brothers determined to use you for their own gains. They used you against your father, to overthrow him, and then they took the power and crown for themselves."

Erac pauses, his face growing darker in the lines around his mouth and nose. "For a while, the brothers controlled you with their poison. They caged you, tarnished you, almost destroyed you." His features take on something dark. "But I saved you from them and their ambitions. I pulled out the poison they put in your head that was rotting your insides."

He sits back with a triumphant grin. I reach out and adjust my fork so that it is straight. "These brothers poisoned me?"

"Yes."

I pull my eyes from the cutlery to his gleeful face. "With what?"

His expression falters. "What?"

"What was the poison?"

He waves a hand in the air and hunches forward, a tad less enthusiastic. "It makes no difference the name of what venomous thing they used. It was damaging you. I removed it, but to do so, I had to remove almost everything from your mind, anything tainted by their poison—knowledge, memories, anything rotted." He licks his lips, eyes shifter to a softer color. "I will not lie to you."

"Okay."

"I removed your memories, but the power of memories is incredible. There are debates posed by great philosophical minds about nature versus nurture, but in truth, no one truly can answer which is more important."

I frown. "I don't understand."

"The magic I used, I didn't remove your memories. I ripped them from your mind. It's damaging, dangerous even, but it was necessary to undo what they did to you, the only way I could save you."

My eyes fall to the plate before me, the silverware glinting in the light. "Is that why my head hurts?"

"Yes," he nods. "But more importantly, and I need you to understand this, without your memories, without all that you have learned, experienced, done, heard, been told, everything you ever came into contact with that has shaped and molded you, is gone. You are going to be and feel hollow until you develop new ones."

"I do feel empty."

"Yes, it's a side effect. Those things that make a person who they are, you don't have those without your memories. Some things may be the same, but I don't want you to expect much from yourself or to understand who you truly are right away. I will guide you, as will your father, to help rebuild you into who you should be." His lip press in a grimace. "What I mean to say is don't push too hard, don't ask too many questions. Your mind is fragile, and for you to ever regain who you were is impossible. The less you know of before, the better you will recover. Knowing from before will only confuse you and make things harder."

I drop my hands into my lap and twist the fingers together. "How did I get here? I don't even know where I am." I glance out the open doorway.

"You are safe," he says, reaching out toward me, laying his arm along the side of the table in my direction. "You are in Asperheim. The rebellious brothers are in another court far from here, and there are miles and miles of desert dunes between us and anything else. You need not worry about anything, my love, I will tell you all you need to know, and I will take care of you."

I bob my head and spin the ornate band on the third finger of my left hand as a distraction. "And—and, I mean, I guess I don't understand."

"I made the proper arrangements with your father for your hand in marriage, and we worked together to bring you here, away from those animals, to where you belong. We are to be married, my love, and your father will bring the rebellious bastards to heel. Everything is as it should be, and in time you will have new memories. We will always have each other."

Light glints off the large yellow stone in the ring as I turn it upright. I lift my hand and show it to him. His eyes flicker toward it, away, and then back to it with an expression of angry surprise. "Is this our engagement ring?" I ask.

"Yes," he snaps. "Yes, I put that ring on your finger when you agreed to marry me."

I frown but turn my hand to stare at it. "It's very pretty."

"It's old," he says in a clipped tone. "From a time before this. I'll get you a new one."

"I like this one." I shrug, dropping my hands below the table once more.

"Are you sure?" He is almost daring me to say yes. "You will not be the same woman you were. Your tastes will change. You may prefer something else. Please, let me get you a new one, a better one that you'll remember when I put it on your finger."

I roll my shoulders back and shake my head. "No. I like it still. Can I keep this one? Something to remind me that I loved you before?"

I swear he almost snarls at me as he takes a drink from his cup, but I blink and tilt my head. When he sets the cup aside, he has a straight face. "Of course. I do not wish to upset you. If you like that old ugly thing, then you shall keep it."

My eyes drop down to the ring, and a strange attachment overcomes me. I lay my other hand over the top of it and lift my chin. "I want to keep it."

He shoves the plate of fruit at me. "You should eat something," he mutters under his breath in a sour tone. "You'll change your mind. After you develop new memories, you will want different things than you once did, and when you do, I'll give you something much better."

Rolling my shoulders back, I sit straighter and try to smile. "Can I ask one more thing?"

"Of course," he drawls.

"Why am I chained? Am I a prisoner?"

The ghost of a smile claims his thin lips. "No. That is for your benefit, not hindrance. It is to deter anyone from stealing you away while I am occupied elsewhere."

CHAPTER 9

MORELLA

I stare at the mirror. The image of a girl with dark burgundy hair cropped close around her shoulders stares back at me. Everything is surreal as if I am watching a stranger move. I don't know who the woman is staring back at me.

Lifting my chin, I watch her move in unison with me, the slender neck stretching and elongating. I run fingers down the side of my neck and over my collarbone, tracing the beautiful black swirling across my skin, eyes following the lines that have no pattern from shoulder to wrist.

The marks twist and writhe over my skin like smoke as I brush fingers along them. An aching need is rooted deep inside of me, longing for answers. A few days have slipped by. I have stood on the balcony to feel the warmth of the soul star and the cool kiss of the breeze but never traveled beyond the limitations of this room.

"Hello, my love."

I turn around, the chain dragging on the floor with a few weak clinks. "Hello," I say, blinking at him.

After a moment, he extends the gold chalice in his hand

toward me. He stares at me as he offers it up, arm stretched out straight, his movements rigid. There is a tension between us, permeating the air with an awkward silence.

"Take your antidote," he says.

His voice is boyish, his sand-colored hair cropped short. His face is a bit rounded with soft curves. While I do not find Erac ugly, I cannot say I find him enticing either.

I realize I am staring at him and step to accept the goblet. I stare down into the dark fluid. It smells like a desert flower, a floral scent of something left to rot in the sun. I wrinkle my nose and lift my eyes. "Do I really have to? Didn't you take my memories to take away the poison?" I sigh as his features pinch with frustration.

"Drink, my love, you must. Please do not make me force you."

Pressing the cup to my lips, I inhale deeply through my nose. Holding my breath, I tip my head back and chug the bitter fluid. The last few gulps are grainy, and I shudder as I finish the concoction. I hold the cup to him, and he takes it, setting it aside on a nearby chest of drawers.

He stands before me in a soft blue buttoned-up shirt that fits over his slender torso. His violet eyes meet mine. I get a hollow feeling in my chest at his melancholy gaze.

"I know." I sigh on a long breath, "Not knowing who I am, not remembering anything, not being me, not really anyone, it hurts."

He gives me a sad smile, only one side pulling up. "I am so very happy you don't have memories. If you did, you wouldn't be here with me."

I bob my head, glancing out the window. "I know. I know you did it to save my life, to get rid of the poison in me. Still," I add, turning back, "this is a miserable experience."

"It is certainly a trying time." He slips his hands into the front pockets of his gray slacks. "We will get through this, though, and you will learn to be happy."

The muscles around my spine shudder in a ripple down my back. I tense, squaring my shoulders. "I am sure you are right. I loved you before, so I'll love you again."

His smile fades, and he sighs, rolling up on the balls of his feet and then rocking back on his heels. "Yes, my love, you will grow to love me." He nods, staring down at the floor. "But for now, would you like to leave this room?"

Fear coils in my stomach. I open and close my mouth, trying to swallow. "Is it safe? Will the brothers find me?"

He shakes his head. "No, and you have been staring out that window for days now. Would you like to go outside? I can take you to the gardens."

Excitement causes me to grin. "Yes," I answer in a breathless rush. "Yes, please."

He smiles, pulling a hand from his pocket to reach out, fingers splayed, palm directed toward the floor before me. The weight of the metal wrapped around my ankle disappears. I drop my chin, gaping downward to see nothing there; no cuff, no chain, nothing tethering me in this room.

"Where did it go?" I ask, my eyes stretching open. I glance around, swaying my hips as I inspect the floor. "What did you—how did you…?"

"My love." He chuckles, and I look to him, seeing his hand offered to me. "Come, I'll take you to the gardens and explain everything to you."

Giddy, I step forward, taking his hand. He pulls me into him, and my body shudders as he presses against me. He smiles down at me, but there's no real life to the expression. There's something off about the way this all feels, and I brush it away as being unfamiliar.

His mouth drops down to mine, and I press back into his. His lips are thin and firm, nothing disgusting or exciting about them. He pulls back, gazing down with those beautiful indigo and violet eyes, flecks of bright purple popping around the iris. They shift back and forth as he studies me.

I clear my throat and drop my chin lower. "Can I go outside now?"

"Yes."

He wraps his arms around me, and I mean to protest, but there's a strange sensation seeping through me. It starts in my extremities, my toes and fingers, working inward to my core. As the feeling grows, so does the cold that comes with it until my insides have turned to ice.

I blink, the feeling leaving as quickly as it had come. My eyes squint against the bright light of the soul star as I pull back from him. He lets me go, but as I take another step, he grabs my wrist. I turn back, stepping closer, nervous he might return me to that room.

"My love, please stay close, where I can keep you safe. Here." He releases my wrist and wiggles his fingers between mine. "We can hold hands."

My hand twitches as our palms connect. "Okay."

He starts forward, and I stay by his side. "I don't know how much memory of the world you have retained. Anything remotely personal was removed, but I did try to leave you the basics. I didn't want you to wake up a baby without the ability to walk or talk or function independently, but I also wanted to be sure to remove every part of the poison."

"Okay."

"A long, long time ago, our ancestors lived in Terra with the mongrels. They call themselves humans. They learned to fear our kind, the fae, and so we attempted to leave Terra and move to the next higher dimension known as Medius."

"How?"

He waves his free hand. "You can read about it later, my love, that's not important. What is important is that we ended up here." He gestures in front of us. "In Caleum. It was the unmade space between dimensions, but with a little blood magic and hard work, it became a world we call home."

"Caleum. Okay," I sigh. "What does this have to—"

"My love, please." He stops, angling in front of me to stare down his nose at me. "Do not ask questions. I will tell you what you need to know. It will be faster if you just listen."

I bite my tongue and bob my head, wary of upsetting him.

"Good girl." He starts walking again, pulling me with him. "The elements of our world can be bent to our will, bound or cursed or manipulated, changed. Only some elementals can manage this skill, and even fewer become masters of the art." He sighs. "Do you remember any of this?"

I shake my head.

He pulls me down to a stone bench in the shade off the way of the path. "Those of us who can command the elements under our control are called mages. I am a mage, and so are you. You were the most powerful of us, able to bend elements at a simple wish, sometimes even without intending to. They simply respond to you on an extraordinary level."

I nod once.

"When I dissolved the chain, I changed the elements from metal, or matter, to another state. In that instance, I shifted them to air, but there are several forms of elements. The first and easiest to manipulate is air, the second is water, then matter, then fire. The last element is life, which requires blood magic, something only advanced mages can manipulate."

He pauses as if waiting for me to answer. I remain silent, despite the hundreds of questions buzzing in my head. So, I nod again and wait for him to go on.

"Each mage has a specific element they most resonate with. Yours tends to be fire, although you have power enough to master all of the different elements." He peers at me. "Your ability, the immense power you have comes from the fact that you are not simply an elemental. You are not a mongrel human plucked from Terra and transformed, but born of a spirit and a dragon."

He beams at me as if he's given some revolutionizing kind of information that I should be in awe of. The problem is, I don't understand what he is saying. My lips peel apart. When he watches me, I take a deep breath. "I don't understand. Is that uncommon?"

He tips his head back and laughs. "There are only two of you, but the other does not have the power you do. He is a rather mundane boy, which is a pity." Erac smiles at me. "Spirits are those who reside in the dimension above this."

I tip my head back, the ends of my hair brushing against my collarbone as I gaze upward. His hand squeezes mine, and I return my sight to him. "How do dimensions work? Can we go there? How are there two of us, me, er—whatever I am? How do you do that?" I ask excitedly, waving my hand. "Can I do that right now? Can you show me?"

He chuckles. "Yes, my love, I can show you. I intend to teach you the way you should have been taught the first time around, but alas..." He sighs, the smile fading.

I stare at him, watching a shadow creep across his features. "Was it the poison?"

"No, I was..." He shakes his head, facing away from me. "I was not in a position where I could teach you, and so it fell to another to train you. Although he was a good mage, he was not the teacher you required." Erac turns back. "This time, things will be different, the way they were meant to be."

There's a strained quietness to his voice, a deep sorrowful tone. I squeeze his hand back, not sure of how I feel inside about all of this. I am not going to be able to comfort him, but I feel like I should at least try. "Things will be different this time," I repeat.

His eyes stare into mine, and a light ignites in them. He

smiles and seems to laugh at himself. "Yes, this time around, I am going to train you, one on one until there is nothing left I can teach you."

"When? Now?" I scoot to the edge of the stone bench and beam at him.

Erac chuckles, his head shaking. "No, but soon. Tomorrow we can start. Right now, there is something else that needs to be done."

"What?"

The mirth in his face slips away as he stares at me. "Your father wishes to see you."

CHAPTER 10

MORELLA

That splinter, freezing experience rips through me, and I blink around in a corridor carved of stone with arched ceilings. I gape as I scan the new surroundings, taking in every detail as Erac knocks on a set of double wood doors. "Where are we?"

"Asperheim," he answers. "Another area of the palace. It was created out of a mountain, carved and crafted into this impenetrable fortress in a time long ago."

A creaking draws my gaze, and the door opens. Erac pulls me inside. I meet the eyes of a young girl who holds the door open from the inside. She is dressed in plain, thick materials with a sigil embroidered over her left breast. I smile at her, and she drops her face to the floor, looking away.

"A servant," Erac tells me, squeezing my hand. "They are of no consequence, existing only to serve us. Pay her no heed."

I nod, glancing around at the rest of the room. Two hulking creatures stand at the far end of the room by another set of double doors. I gasp, clutching Erac's arm and moving closer to him.

"Demons." He chuckles as one snorts, it's snout twitching. "They won't hurt you either. They are here for protection."

Eyeing the deep red-colored creatures, three times the size of Erac, I frown. They each hold double-headed battle axes, black claws wrapping around the handles. "Protection from what?"

He sighs. "Sit, Morella."

I shake my head, trying to get closer to him, holding onto his arm for dear life. He uses his free arm to guide me forward and down onto a couch. "There is a war going on that will determine the course of Caleum. We—" he motions between us with his free hand "—are trying to reclaim the throne for your father and yourself. Stay here." He pries his arm out of my death grip.

He lifts my hands to his lips, pressing them against my knuckles, then drops my hands and turns away. As he approaches the second set of doors, I realize he only measures half the height of the demons. Each horned head turns toward Erac, watching him as he knocks on the second set of doors.

"Viktor?" There's a pause. "I have your daughter."

A door opens, and a man stands in view on the other side. He, too, is small in comparison to the demons. His face is directed at Erac, and then turns, his gaze settling on me. I swallow, nervous about meeting my father. I almost cry at the realization that I am meeting a man who has known me my whole life—that *I* have known my whole life.

A woman who wears a sneer of disgust steps next to him, resting a hand on his arm. Silver and black hair is cropped close about her face, and she tucks it behind one ear as she says, "I will go and deal with him personally."

"Very well, my dear, as you wish. I will leave the matter in your hands, but remember, I do not want him killed."

"I will see to it, my love. Rest assured, I will not fail you."

He bobs his shaved head. "Take demons with you," he turns and takes her hand in his, lifting her knuckles to his lips. "And take care."

She smiles, smoothing the pleated skirt of her navy gown over wide hips. "I will see you tonight for supper." The woman dissolves from sight, and the man grimaces, but his face returns to a bored expression as he fixes his gaze upon me.

He strides across the room, and I watch him, heart racing. He moves with a calm grace. As he gets within a few paces, I stand to greet him. He stops, eyes searching over me. "Morella?"

The tip of my tongue wets my lips as my eyes shift from the man to Erac and back to him. His eyes are green, his scalp bare. "Yes. Hello."

The man stares, and I stare back. He takes another step forward. "Morella, my daughter," he says in a quiet voice, bright green eyes widening with hunger.

I try to smile. "Yes, hello. And who was that woman?"

"Susan," he says waving a hand in dismissal. "My consort. You'll meet her later." He does a quarter turn to look at Erac. "How much does she know?"

Erac steps next to him, and both men slide their hands in the front pockets of their pants and face me. "Very little. Her memories are gone. I've explained to her it was to remove the poison the rebellion used to control her, to keep her from us. She has been resting, her mind coping with the effects of memory loss, headaches mostly." He sighs and turns his attentions to the man next to him. "I've told her of the proper arrangement we made for her hand in marriage, and only this morning did I show her magic and remind her of her own abilities."

"Very well. You may leave."

"When I say she has no memories, I mean the only things I left in her mind are the basic necessities of living."

"I will deal with teaching her what she needs to know."

Erac's face twists. "For the time being, I am the only one she knows. It might be best if I stay. It would make her feel more comfortable."

"My daughter is not a delicate flower, Erac." My father sneers, grinding out the name with vinegar. "I will speak with her, explain what is going on, and then I will take her to her designated rooms." My father angles his body toward my fiancé, and they have a staring contest for a few seconds.

Erac sighs, nodding his head. "Of course."

I blink, and he is gone, using his abilities to command the use of magic. I do my best not to gape and look to the man standing nearby. My mind is racing.

Do I bow? Shake his hand? Hug him? He is my father, after all. How much of a proper greeting should there be?

"Please sit, Morella." He steps to the couch across a low table, waving a hand over the glossy surface as he lowers himself to a cushion.

A tile board appears with two rows of figures on both sides. He reaches out, repositioning a smaller white figurine two squares out, and then rests his elbows on his legs. I stare at the black figurines in front of me and then lift my gaze to his.

Those green eyes are bright, an eerie calculating aloofness to them, the way a predator watches its prey for signs of weakness. I lick my lips again and fold my hands in my lap, spinning my engagement ring on my finger and clear my throat. "I don't know what I am doing."

"The first row, the smallest pieces are called pawns. The back row, starting from your right, is a rook, a knight, a bishop, the king, the queen, and then bishop, knight, rook. Pawns move forward, one or two squares at a time. Bishops may move only on a diagonal, as many paces as are open and you desire. The rook moves in straight lines, forward, back, and side to side. A knight moves in an L shape, two then one." He moves his finger over tiles in an example. "The most precious and important piece is the queen. She can move side to side, forward, back, and diagonally, limited only by available space."

"Oh."

His eyes lift to me, breathing words in a low whisper. "She is the most powerful of them all."

"Okay, so what do I do? Is there an objective?"

The left side of his lips hitches up. "There is always an objective, Morella. In this game, in your life, in this war, you are always working toward something." He taps his white king piece. "You are after the king. Capture the king, and the game is over."

I study the board and the piece he has moved. "How do I do that?"

"Prevent me from capturing your own king. Take as many of my pieces as you can while working to reach my king. Do not be distracted, do not take pieces needlessly. It doesn't matter how many of my pieces you remove if I can capture your king before you take mine." He returns his elbows to his thighs, and his hands dangle between his legs. "You will lose pieces. Do not be afraid to make sacrifices to achieve your objective."

Nodding, I reach forward and push a pawn forward one square, unaware of what I am doing. We exchange moves a few times, and he must correct me on how a knight moves. I lose a few pieces but take one of his. I set the pawn to the side of the board and see he is watching me with a smile.

"The war we are fighting is very much like this game. You have a king—" he pauses and puts a finger on his "—and the enemy has a king." He points at mine. "They are losing pieces, their army no match for ours." He indicates my captured pieces to the side of the board. "But until I can reach their king, this war will go on."

He repositions a bishop, and I move my knight out of danger. I glance up. "Was that right?"

"The pattern in which you moved it was correct." He studies the board with a frown.

We continue our game in silence. I clutch the fabric of my skirt in sweating palms. I cannot determine why I am so nervous and clammy as he removes another of my pieces. His turn has left his queen exposed, so I claim it with my bishop and beam at him.

His lips twitch to one side. Without breaking eye contact, he reaches down, moving a piece. "Checkmate."

I drop my eyes to the board, and my lips peel apart in surprise. "Oh."

"Even the most powerful piece can be sacrificed. No matter how precious she is, if the end goal is achievable at the expense of her, then you must make the sacrifice." There is a strain in his quiet voice, like pain.

I stare down at the white marble queen in my hand, turning her over and running my thumb from top to bottom. I nod, not looking up at him. "The game was hardly fair, my daughter. You didn't know how to play, so you lost."

I set the queen on the table and nod again. "Yes."

"Morella." My gaze lifts to his. "When you lose, evaluate, determine what fault you made, and in the future, do not make the same mistake. That is how you learn." He sits back and checks his watch. "I have duties to return to soon. Come, I will show you to your rooms."

He offers me an arm, and we stroll to the door. The young girl scurries to open it, struggling with the weight, and my father sighs next to me, appearing impatient. I move to help her, but firm fingers retain hold of my arm, stopping me.

"Morella, you will not. It is below your station."

I step back next to my father and take his arm. "Sorry, Father."

"I realize you do not know who you are or how you are supposed to act. I will tell you things only once. Remember what I said about evaluation, and do not repeat a mistake."

"Yes, Father."

He steps out the door with me in tow, and we walk through

corridors, followed by two demons. I glance behind us. "Why are they following us?"

"For safety. Think of them as pawns, yourself as the queen and I as the king. The rebellion will come after us, you for your power and me to end the game. The demons are here to keep you safe. Once Erac has trained you, I doubt you'll require them to follow you around. Until then, I expect them to stay with you no matter where you are."

"Why won't I need them?"

He peers down at me. "You have no idea the power you hold within you. Erac will show you, and I will remind you of who you truly are."

"What do you mean?"

"You have many talents, my daughter." He directs me at a cross-section. "Your power to command the elements is but one. In time I will remind you of the others."

I nod.

"I can only imagine how frustrating this situation must be, the tax on your mind straining it to a point of breaking. Without memories, we are adrift, an empty book with pages yet to be written. For all intents and purposes, your previous self is dead. You are a new person, but consider this an opportunity for you to be whoever you want to be."

I swallow, my dry throat working to bob the grit on the back of my tongue. "Who I was is dead?"

"Not everybody gets the ability to start over, but you do. *We* get this second chance together, and I am looking forward to our new beginning."

We continue in silence, with the occasional snort and grunt echoing around the hall from the overgrown oafs behind us. He brings us to a stop at the end of a hallway in front of a dark wood door.

"This will be your rooms. When you were younger, when you could decide your living quarters, you chose one for the view it provided. I often found you gazing out the window. I hope the view from this room is satisfactory."

Reaching out, he turns the silver knob, twisting and pushing. The door swings inward to an expansive room. A massive four-poster bed sits in the middle, and to the left is an opening in the wall, a generous window without glass that leads to an open terrace.

I drop his arm, stepping inside, mouth open as my eyes take in the beauty. I head for the open expanse, staring out across the stone balcony at the crystal waters of an open sea and white sand beach. Turning back, I smile at my father. "The view is gorgeous."

He inclines his head, standing just a few paces inside my room. "This room is the most difficult to reach from the outside. There are miles of gardens surrounding the palace in a maze, and the beach you see is difficult to access. For now, do not leave this palace, which means you are not to go to the beach. Erac and I will decide when it is safe for you to travel beyond the walls of safety. Do I make myself clear?"

"Yes."

"Very well. I have things to attend to." He turns.

"Father," I say.

Pivoting on his polished dress shoes, he frowns at me. "Yes?"

I step forward, hugging him. "Thank you."

He is stiff and then relaxes, putting his arms around me. He squeezes me tight, inhaling deeply. "My daughter. I intend to give you the world, and you will be able to pick any view you desire in all of Caleum, but for now, I have work to do. I will see you as often as I can, but if you need something, talk to Erac."

CHAPTER 11

DECLAN

Sitting on the roof again, I take a shot of whiskey and chase it with a mouthful of blood. I review, in short, everything that got me to this point. How I used to sit here when I thought Ella was dead. How I screwed up so bad, how things got so fucked.

From my perch on the roof, I spy demons in the gardens, screams drawing my eye there in the first place. I chug whiskey, drain the rest of the blood, and leave the bottles, dissipating to the gardens. I use a shock wave to push the demon back a few inches from the boy.

"It's just a fucking kid!" I roar, pulling a sword from the air.

The demon grunts. It doesn't respond. They don't talk. I have no idea how Viktor manages to communicate with these things to force them to obey him. I take its head off after a skirmish, then keep moving, taking down a few more, running into a few warriors. I shout directions, get them into a movable unit, then kill another, and we keep going until the gardens are cleared.

I am exhausted, panting for breath like a fucking dog.

There's decimation everywhere. I think I hear a woman crying. The tent next to me is in shambles and smoking.

Fucking demons.

I toss the sword aside and dissipate to my rooms to wash the demon blood off. I drop onto the couch, pulling at the laces on my steel toe boots. They're heavier but useful for kicking demons. A scent wafts across my nose, and I jerk to my feet, whirling around and snarling at my mother. "Thought you were in Asperheim. What the fuck are you doing here?"

She tucks a lock of hair behind her ear. The action irks me. Her hair won't stay there, and she'll repeat it a dozen times, a useless gesture, like an annoying tick. She always chastised me for pinching my nose, the hypocrite.

"Why do you even bother? You know it's not going to stay there? Your hair's been that way for as long as I can remember, and you're always fighting with it. Give up already. Fuck, let it grow another inch. Something. Anything."

She does one of those half-chuckles, snorts through her nose with a reacting smile. "The prodigal son, my eldest and biggest disappointment. Such a waste your life has been."

"Sorry about that," I say with a smirk. "Perfection was just a little too hard to achieve, and then, someone tried to have me killed, and it all went bad from there."

"Declan, do not sass me. I am your mother."

I purse my lips and cross my arms. "You tried to kill me," I pause for emphasis. "Twice. You want to tell me why, at least?"

She smiles. "Oh, dear." She clasps her hands in front of her. "Everything was set up perfectly, like a chessboard where all you had to do was make one move, and you still couldn't do that right. You had one, tiny, easy thing to do."

"Yeah, marry Ella."

"You were engaged to Morella, so your idiot father would hand over that book to Viktor, and I wanted my son, my blood, to reach the pinnacle of power. All you had to do was let things be, but then you went and ruined everything. Really? Having feelings for Morella? I assumed you'd have higher standards. I certainly raised you better and never did understand what you could possibly see in her that would be worth threatening Viktor for."

"She didn't deserve—"

"Morella had a job to do," she snarls, one finger jabbing the air toward me as she moves one foot forward. Her usual perfect composure deteriorates to rage, and then she steps back, clearing her throat and regaining her mask of innocence. "You interfered, prevented Viktor from utilizing her to do what was needed."

"So, I was expendable? Awesome. What about that having your son and blood at the pinnacle of power thing?"

She tucks her hair again and sighs. "It was a goal, but so was assisting Viktor. Getting rid of you and your father opened avenues for me. But then after we were rid of you, when she should have been available, that brat lost her mind. She was useless to us, still pining after your brother even at what was your funeral. I often wondered if she was disturbed by your death or just the loss of your protection."

Irked, I roll my eyes to the ceiling and then back to hers. "It was definitely me. She didn't have a fucking clue what I threatened Viktor with or over until that prick told her."

"Well, Morella certainly didn't wait before latching back onto Seth," she says. There is a quiet malice to her expression despite the smile plastered to her face.

"My wife and my brother have a complicated relationship, and I'm the only one with a right to be pissy about it," I tell her, dropping my arms to my sides. "You killed me because I was in your way. I always knew you were a bitch; I just didn't realize you were that cold-hearted too."

"Declan," she shoves through clenched teeth, her cheeks

turning pink. "You will show respect to the woman who raised you. I am your mother, and you will do as you are told."

"I think we covered that already," I say with a smirk.

"Look at you." She flourishes a hand at me. "When is the last time you looked in the mirror. Your hair, that beard," she says aghast, shaking her head and then trying to tuck her hair behind her ear again. "A proper gentleman would be clean-shaven, have a neat appearance. You look like you've been homeless in the city for cycles, not like you're the King of Byron."

I'm getting a lecture? Like this woman has any right to dictate anything in my life or how I act. "Fuck off," I mutter. "I'm fighting a war."

"You are throwing a tantrum like a petulant child." My mother shows visible signs of fatigue. "Do not force my hand in this matter. Give up. Let go of that stupid girl and bend your knee to our Emperor, Viktor. You've managed to survive twice on miracles. There won't be anyone here to save you this time."

I pull a sword from the air, twirling it in my hand, testing the weight. "You make me sound like a damsel in distress."

My mother wrings her hands together. "Viktor did warn me you would not see reason."

I laugh. "You slit my throat and took my wife."

She tilts her head. "Morella is needed. Will you allow—"

"Fuck no. I want her back, and the rest of you and Caleum can fuck right off after that. I don't care what you do, but it won't involve us."

"My dear son, no." She tries to tuck her short brown and gray hair behind one ear. "That woman made you weak. She is no longer a burden to you, although I do wish I could say the same." She turns her nose up at me.

I adjust my sword and roll to the balls of my feet. "If she's such a burden, I'll take her off your hands."

Something dark and scary slithers over my mother, her skin

going white, her eyes widening, dark abysses that reflect no light. I stand at the ready, but she smooths her skirt down over her hips and stays where she is. "That little girl has rotted you from the inside. You have two choices. Give up, or I will lock you up in darkness for the rest of your life."

"You know what they say." I sigh. "Third time's the charm."

My mother shrugs and lets out a long breath. "You stubborn, foolish boy. I'm not here to kill you this time. No, that wouldn't help us, but I cannot save you if you will not help yourself."

"I don't need saving, Mother," I twist the word. "What I need is my wife back and then to disappear somewhere in this fucked world where no one ever finds her again. Do you have any idea what Erac is doing to her?"

She chortles, eyes sparkling. "Whatever he wants, dear. It's his right to do as he pleases with her so long as he does not disrupt Viktor's plans and use of her."

"She's a fucking woman, not an object," I snarl, drawing a small dagger from the air with my free hand and then chucking it at her face. It stops before it makes contact.

Shit. She has spirit runes. I forgot.

Her face contorts with rancid rage as she plucks the blade from the air. "I gave you every chance this time, but I'll not have you undo everything Viktor and I have worked so hard for. We've made sacrifices. We've come this far, and I'm not letting my disappointing offspring get in my way now."

I roll to the balls of my feet, not ready to give up, but this is going to suck. There's no way I can win. Gripping the hilt of my sword in both hands, I force a smirk. "Well, if that's all then?"

She narrows her eyes, and I rush forward, pulling back to strike. She holds up a hand. "Stop."

My body listens despite my mind screaming at it to move. She smiles, reaching out to pat the side of my face with a couple of stinging slaps. "That's a good boy. Get on your knees now."

I bare my teeth as my muscles bunch and coil to obey. *Why is it on my knees? Why can't they leave a little bit of dignity in my life and at least let me stand on my feet like a fucking man?*

She toys with the blade, inspecting it, and then slices my shoulder down over my heart in a slow, intentional movement. The pressure of the weapon leaves behind a sharp, throbbing heat followed by the feeling of my flesh knitting back together behind its destructive wake.

She stares down at my torso. "What is it like," she asks in a hushed voice. "How does healing feel?"

It's fucking weird. It doesn't hurt. It doesn't feel good. I'd almost say it feels like nothing, but that isn't right either. I always feel it. It's like my body saying, "don't do that again, dumbass." I glare up at her, not saying a word.

"I've always wondered what it's like, being a shade, why I wasn't blessed with the change even though the strain runs in my blood." She drives the dagger through my shoulder above my heart.

I groan, clenching my jaw against letting her know how bad that hurts. I tip my head back. "Probably because Haven knew you were enough of a psychotic cunt without the bloodlust."

She rips the blade from me, kicking me in the chest to knock me over on the floor. I stare up at the ceiling, blinking away bright white dots. I don't get long to catch my breath.

"Get up. Get back on your knees. Stay still and stay silent until I have had enough fun."

Well, fuck.

There's a knock on my door, followed by the sound of it opening. "Dec," Marcus calls out.

I clench my jaw, my heart-rate ratcheting up. I want to yell out and warn him off, but under the direct order of my mother and her set of spirit runes, I am incapable of doing anything. Rage burns through my veins, the bloodlust thrashing against being helpless.

My vision grows hazy as she grins down at me, everything

throbbing in and out of focus in time with my heartbeats. I struggle to hear anything she says over the rush of blood and clunking of my heart. Still, my body obeys, taking the dagger from her and standing.

I turn to face Marcus, who gapes at me. Part of me wants him to run, to fight back. The other half of me is lost to the bloodlust and desire to kill. I grab his shoulder with my available hand and stab with my other, twisting the blade in his gut, horror and awe in his eyes, staring right back into mine. I bare my teeth.

Haven is a sick son of a bitch for this shit show.

I rip the blade out, and he stumbles a step back, still gaping at me in shock as red stains his shirt. He puts a hand to the wound, his dark skin turning ashy on his face. We stare at each other in abhorrence, frozen in the moment as blood begins to pool and drip from between his fingers.

"Make it quicker, Declan. That rat has caused enough trouble for us. He's worthless without Ravenna."

I try to fight, straining against the order. Every muscle in my body tenses as I growl in the back of my throat to show my displeasure.

"Don't worry about it, son. You'll only have the rest of your life to live with it on your conscience."

I jerk, limbs shaking and burning as I try to stop them. I've lived this nightmare dozens of times through Ella's memories, but it's worse, so much worse than I ever comprehended. My eyes find Marcus' in terror, even as the blade approaches his throat.

He manages a cocked smile. "It's alright, my friend. I don't blame you."

I let go of the blade, stepping away from Marcus, and catching him as he falls to his knees.

Fuck.

His blood is hot against my skin, drenching me as I grab

him, lowering to the floor with him. My eyes are prickling with rage and fury, blurring even as I reach out to close his dark, clouded eyes with trembling fingers. The scent of fresh, perfectly good blood makes me queasy for the first time in my life. Not even the curse inside of me wanted this.

"Such a mess." My mother *tsks* behind me. I draw in a ragged, breaking breath. "Oh, grow up. You said it yourself, this is war. I gave you your chance, but my, that is a lot of blood. I forgot how much blood there is when you slit a throat, and this gown is new. I'd hate to ruin it. I'll just make sure it's your hand when we find your useless brother before I leave. No one is going to miss him."

I squeeze my eyes shut, trying to reach Ella one last time. I'd give anything to feel her for even a moment. *"I'm sorry, lover."*

I hear a crack and a muted noise, something between a gasp and a grunt. I pick my head up, turning to glance over my shoulder. A spirit stands over my mother's body sprawled on the floor.

"Sordello?"

"Yes, my son." He approaches and kneels, putting a hand on Marcus' chest. I hear the heavy exhale. "We were looking for you."

His voice that booms is low and soft. I shake my head. "Can you…?"

"No. He is gone."

I am unable to find words. My eyes fall shut, and my head droops forward. I try to fight the agony, but the noises that rip from my throat hurt. I sit in that hell, incapable of doing anything.

~

"Dec? Declan? Oh, shit." Hands land on my shoulders, shaking me. "Dec!"

"He is alright. He is just grieving."

I lift my head, my eyes fluttering open. My skin pulls against the dried blood, and I blink into the dim light at my brother's face. I startle, unsure of how long I've sat here holding onto a dead body.

Seth appears concerned. He doesn't look at me with horror or disgust. Not yet. He will when he learns the truth.

I jerk away from his hands and move the body to the floor, off of my numb legs. Seth grimaces, offering me a hand up. I smack it away and get to my feet on my own.

"What happened?" Seth asks, but his face is directed at Sordello.

The spirit shrugs, his armor clinking in the quiet. "I found them on the floor. Your mother was standing over there, and I knocked her out."

"What?" I ask in a hoarse whisper. "She's still alive?"

Sordello tilts his head. "Perhaps to clarify, I broke her neck, but she will heal and come back in her current state."

I step over to her, grabbing my sword off the ground. Seth is blathering, but the words wash over me without registering. Taking the sword in both hands, I strike down at her, the blade sinking into her neck.

Fuck. I can't even take a head off properly right now. Ella's gone. He raped her, hurt her. Marcus... I killed Marcus.

I wrench the blade free and try again, and again, and again. There's something wet on my face. Hands grab me, turning me, pulling the sword away. My fingers are too numb to hold onto it, and I hear it clatter to the ground.

"Haven, Dec." Seth grabs me against him. "It's going to be okay, big brother. It's going to be okay."

I shove him away from me and swipe at my nose with the

back of my hand. I blink away the salt in my eyes and grit my teeth. "I did it."

There's a deep, dark laugh emitting from the suit of armor nearby. I turn my head to glare at Sordello.

"The blade may have been in your hand, but what happened wasn't you. You had your control taken away. At that point, you are a vessel for the will and deeds of another."

Seth claps me on the shoulder. "I think he's trying to say it's not your fault."

I silently snarl at him. "It sure fucking feels that way."

"I get that. I dealt with Ella after all the times Viktor made her do things like this."

I dig the heels of my palms into my eyes hard enough to see colored spots. "I relived those memories," I croak, dropping my hands. "Knowing and living are two different things."

Seth gives me a lopsided grin. "Sure, but how many times have we told Ell it wasn't her fault? How many times did we have to remind her that she didn't have control over her actions and how that means it wasn't her doing those things? Same thing."

I want to growl at him, but he has a point. I've tried a thousand times to convince her it wasn't ever her fault. "Fuck." I scrub a hand down my face and grimace. "I get why she didn't listen."

Sordello hums. "I watched my daughter all her life. I saw the effects of removing control long ago. You are furious that we won't endanger our lives to get Ella back, but do you see now our deliberation?"

"Shut up," I snap.

"No, and you cannot make me," Sordello chuckles. "Take your shirt off."

Without thought, I pull my long-sleeved black shirt over my head. I eye the material in my hand and then cut my eyes to the spirit. "Fucking really?"

"I should have worded my request differently. My apologies." He steps to me, and the tingling sensation of eyes searching over my chest and stomach prickles my skin. "What in Haven's name did Marx do to you?"

I clamp my jaw shut, not volunteering any information. Instead, I toss the shirt to the floor behind me. "Did you want me to take my shirt off for a show, or...?"

"Shades commanding the elements are rare, but I never realized your control wasn't natural."

Every muscle in my body tenses. I stare at the wall over his shoulder. I never think about the runes, never relive what they did. The searing agony burning through flesh and bone to the very core of my soul is one of the more excruciating experiences Marx gave to me.

Sordello moves around me, and I remain stationary, refusing to blink or breathe. "Your back is clear." He sighs. "You'll want to lay down."

I move, stiff-jointed, lowering myself to lie face down. "Now what?"

"I pull the runes off your mother to prevent her recovery."

"And I'm on the floor for this?"

He gives a laugh. "I cannot destroy the runes, and it seems a waste to leave them locked away on scraps of leather."

The bottom of my stomach drops out, and my mouth goes dry. "You're going to put those things on me?" Trepidation causes my limbs to quell, and I lift myself enough to gape at Sordello.

He shrugs. "You married Ella, didn't you? As the collective is a unit, and you are her mate, that makes you family. Who else should wear them?"

"Wait, hold up." Seth puts a finger in the air, his other hand on his hip. "Family? As in, you and Ella and Erac are related?" He stresses the words. "Like, Erac's obsession isn't sick enough, he's fucking related to her and—"

As Seth struggles for words, I drop my forehead to the cold stone floor and focus on breathing. The last time runes were seared into my flesh was an experience I never wanted to undergo again.

Sordello sighs. "By your standards, Aron, Erac, and Ella are cousins."

"I think I just threw up in my mouth." Seth makes a retching sound. I lift my head to eye him. "They're family?" He's staring at me.

"What do you want me to do about it?" I snap, pushing myself to my knees. "I'm going to kill him. Isn't that enough?"

My brother shudders. "Doesn't seem like it really, no."

I lower my torso to the ground again. "Let's get this over with." The stone is cold against my bare chest, making my skin pucker.

"Any chance you can somehow divide that two ways," Seth asks? "Be cool if I could get a set of those too."

"These runes belonged to Orso. Declan has every right to wear them, and he will bring honor to Orso's life and energy in our collective, a good replacement to his seat on the council. These runes are not for you." Metal clinks, and an armored hand presses against my upper back. "The collective wants you to have the runes."

I nod, not responding. My palms are sweating as I lay flat on the stone, ready to push up. There's a lot of weight in Sordello's words, expectations of the collective. Acid stirs in my gut and lungs.

"Yeah, but I'm his brother and Ell… I'm family too," Seth whines. "I need a set of those runes too."

"I will discuss it with the collective," Sordello says.

"Hey. Remember me lying on the floor? Can you just do it?" My voice is thick and gruff, anxiety thumping my heart violently against my chest bones.

"What was done to you before must have been terrible."

"Get on with it."

He sighs. "Sleep, Declan."

I guess there is a blessing in that I won't be conscious this time but being incapacitated gives me heartburn. My eyes flutter shut even as I try to fight the order, wanting to stay alert, willing myself to be awake. I fail.

CHAPTER 12

MORELLA

I stand in my rooms.

Mine.

Something that belongs to me. I have become acquainted with every corner, every detail, running my hands over the decorative trim carved into the stone surrounding the opening to the terrace. Everything belongs to me, and I have memorized it all.

A couple of days have slipped by as I learned my way through the maze of corridors, committing to memory the turns and passageways that lead between my suite to the main hall where dinner is held each evening and to the library where I am allowed to go as often as I want whenever I want. It is the heavenly escape from my rooms.

Most mornings, I have stood on my terrace, leaning against the balustrade, gazing down at the beach. Erac and Viktor have been clear about the threat to my safety, that I must stay within the realm of protection because of the treasonous, traitorous bastards that poisoned my mind. Fury ebbs in my veins like an incoming tide at being reduced to relearn magic and who I am.

I run my fingers over the rows of pink scars on my right forearm. I study the markings along my left arm, a finger trailing across the white scar left between twisting black lines. The marks are the only signs I have of what I once was. These are only truths about me that I can merely guess at the meanings of.

I drop my arms to my sides and tip my head back, breathing deep through my nose. Rain. The scent is heavy in the air of the coming storm. Dark clouds on the horizon, gray and hazy light already here. I can make out the shoreline, a sandy white beach, jade waters darkened by the storm at sea. I listen to the waves crash, wondering how many times I was beaten down, how long I withstood against the assaults on my life before I succumbed to those brothers who poisoned me.

I clench my fists and feel them tremble with fury. I will take my revenge. I will take back Caleum from those who stole my crown from me. There is nothing that will be able to stand in the path of my rage. There is no one who will be left alive in my wake.

I will be repaid in blood.

I draw a deep breath and relax my hands, turning to glance at the one entering my chambers. The boy is as tall as I and still growing, a gangly, thin scrappy early teen. His wide-set dark eyes meet mine, and he smiles. The expression is hesitant, with no light to the act.

"Oh," I say, inclining my head at him. "I thought you were Erac."

His nose wrinkles as he curls his lip back. "I came to fetch you for him. He wants you to come to dinner."

"Hmm," I hum, turning back to face the gathering storm. I lean against a pillar, and the boy steps next to me. I cut my eyes to the kid, daring to stand at my side as an equal.

He takes a step back, muttering words I cannot make out, a soft sigh under his breath.

My focus snaps to him. "What?"

He winces and stares away from me. "Sorry, Majesty."

I turn from leaning against the opening to fix him with a

stern expression. He kicks at the floor and shoves balled fists into the front pockets of a dirty, tattered orange robe. "What is it? Do you have something else to say?"

His startled face lifts to meet my gaze. "No." He shakes his head rapidly, his hair swinging freely about his face. "No, Majesty, that is."

I reach up and prop a hand under my jaw, bracing my elbow on my other arm bent across my midsection, studying him. "What is your name?"

The boy perks up at that, his eyes wide, head cocked to the side. His mouth drops open with surprise that I would inquire to a servant's name. "George."

I force my lips to curl. "George. Tell Erac I will not be joining him for dinner."

"Oh." His crestfallen expression matches the tone. He starts to turn, getting a quarter of the way before he turns back, scrunching up his face. "You could at least say please, you know."

My eyebrows shoot straight up, and I balk at him. "Excuse me?" Drawing my eyebrows down, I let my features pull together, pursing my lips.

His shoulders slump, his head drops to the floor. "I'm sorry, Your Majesty. I'll go." He turns.

"George, come back here."

He stops and about faces, stomping back to me. He is pouting, his face scrunched. He stops in front of me and glares. "What?"

I pull the hand from under my jaw and hold up a single finger. "I am the princess of Caleum and—"

"Yeah, so?" He stands his ground, spreading his feet and putting his hands on his hips. "You used to be the crown princess of Byron, and you were a lot nicer then."

Shock peels my lips apart, and my heart skips a beat.

"What?" I snarl in a deep growl I never imagined I was capable of.

It is his turn to look dazed. "What, what?"

I reach out and grab the front of his robe, pulling him closer to me, leaning over to bring our faces close together. "I used to be what?"

The kid tries to stare at the tip of his nose, or maybe mine. "Uh, the crown princess of Byron?" He reaches up and rubs the back of his neck. "Least, when you were here last time."

"What?" I roar, ready to breathe fire like the enormous dragons that fly through the sky.

He tilts his head and peers at me. "How come you don't know any of this? I mean, it's one thing to forget me or my name, but..." He rubs the back of his neck as he diverts his eyes.

There is pressure building behind my eyes, ready to burst. My ears are warming, and a whisper in my blood flushes my skin and causes me to itch. "I want to know what you know."

He lifts his chin in defiance, eyes snapping to mine. "Say, please."

When my pulse stops racing hard enough to wreak havoc on my vision, I let go of the front of his robes, unsure when I grabbed him. He takes a step back and tries to smooth the fabric. I clear my throat and toss my hair over my shoulder. The short strands sway right back in place against my neck, silky and cool.

"Please," I say. "Please tell me what you know. What do you mean before? Before this," I extend my scarred right forearm at him. "Their poison?"

George gives me a skeptical death eye. He points at my arm. "Don't know about poison, or what that is. I just mean before, when you came here to get away from your dead fiancé. I was yay high." He holds a hand level in the middle of his chest. "Like, three revolutions ago? You were the crown princess at Byron."

I dart my gaze around to check we are alone. Erac has a nasty habit of showing up unannounced and from thin air. I lean over and crook a finger at George. He steps closer, and I smile.

"What else can you tell me?"

George shrugs. "I was a kid, so I didn't get to know much."

I snort through my nose. "You're still just a kid."

"I'm not a kid." He glares.

I smirk. "Yes, you are. I was here three revolutions ago?"

He nods. "You were. You came after your betrothed died, only he didn't really die, but you didn't know that at the time." George shrugs.

I pull back and study him down my nose, raising one eyebrow. "I don't remember any of this, but I want to... Please."

George gives me a funny look. "Lady, you're crazy. You wanted to forget all about stuff before, and now you want to remember it. Make up your mind."

I am dizzy with desire, craving answers. Lurching toward him, I grab him by the shoulders and shake him. When I get no response, I drop down to a knee, crouching to see his face. "Tell me about when I was here before." My voice is taut, strung tight like a tendon, ready to tear. "Tell me about before their poison."

George gives me a strange expression. All the lightness drains from his voice. "You were a lot nicer, didn't want to be called majesty or yer highness. You'd flinch when dad would talk about you being a princess. You liked reading, spent all day around books. Dad said you lost someone you love. When I got older, I learned you had been trying to recover from the death of your husband-to-be, but then it turned out he wasn't really dead after all." George shrugs his shoulders. "Whaddya want to know, Majesty?"

"Erac was my husband-to-be? Why did I think he was dead? It was them, wasn't it, those bastard brothers that poisoned me, they tried to kill Erac? To keep us apart? What about my father?" My heart is racing.

The boy's eyebrows lift and push together. "Erac wasn't your husband-to-be." He blinks. "I don't remember his name, it was...uh...it started with a D? Maybe it was a B? I'll have to ask."

I frown and run my tongue between my upper lip and teeth. "Was this before the war?" His head bobs. "And before I was poisoned?"

He shrugs again. "I didn't know you got poisoned."

"My father says I was poisoned, turned against him, and the rest of us, used as a weapon to hurt him, kept away from him and my betrothed."

George tilts his head and gives me a baffled look. He kicks at the stone beneath our feet, his head tipped down to his chest. Lifting his head, his dark, round eyes meet mine. He rolls his shoulders back and drops his hands into the pockets of his robes. "I can tell you all of this, but I'm supposed to be bringing you to dinner. Erac sent me to make sure you went."

I draw a deep breath and wave a hand. "Erac can wait. I want to know more."

"More about what?" a furious voice whispers behind me.

I glance behind me at Erac. He becomes a bit more pleasing to the eye in a mundane sort of way every time I see him. I smile sweetly, the way I have learned to do to please him. "Oh, nothing, dear, we were speaking about things." I meet George's gaze with an intense gaze.

He bobs his head. "Yes, Her Majesty was learning of her home's history." He points to the crest over his left breast. "She was asking about this symbol, and I was telling her it meant I was part of the Keepers, which don't exist no more."

I return to smiling at Erac. "Is it dinner time already?" The wind is picking up, blowing my short, auburn hair about. I hold out a hand, forcing air together to create a barrier and cease the gusts from mussing my appearance. "I had not noticed the time. I've been enjoying watching the storm approach us."

Erac steps forward, hands sliding up my arms to my shoulders. He grips hard, fingers digging into my flesh. "You must come drink your antidote. We wouldn't want our princess to fall ill, now would we, George?"

George shakes his head. "No, Sir."

"Then why have you delayed?" Erac's voice is low and tense like he's half holding his words in with a clenched stomach.

George drops his chin all the way against his chest and bows at the waist. "Sir, forgive me. I meant only to serve."

"Erac, dear, please, there is no need to frighten the boy. I delayed myself with curiosity." I turn, prying myself from his grip to face him.

Erac scowls at me, grabbing my upper arms and holding fast. "What have I told you?" He shakes me slightly. "Stop asking questions. Take your antidote every morning and every night." He pulls back, grabbing my jaw in one hand, forcing me to stare back into his violet eyes. "Do I need to take your magic away?"

"No." His grip on my jaw is painful, but I don't try to pull away. He'll only get angry if I do. "I will do better."

He shoves my face from his hand and steps back, expecting me to take the hand he offers. "Then come to dinner and behave yourself, or I will take away your magic and lock you up again."

I incline my head, clenching my jaw as my face is toward the floor. Cold seeps through me, and I blink, staring around the great hall in the middle of the palace. I roll a shoulder, trying to shake off the feeling of dissipation. Having my elements pulled apart and rebuilt by another always leaves a pit in my stomach.

I exhale, taking my seat at the high table. I sit to the right of my father, one chair over to allow Erac to sit directly at Viktor's right hand.

Erac sets a goblet down in front of me. Gold, brimming to the top with blue, frothing liquid. "Drink your antidote, Morella."

I raise the liquid to my lips, tasting the warm, bitter fluid beading against my lips and tongue. I inhale deeply through my nose and chug as quick as I can to get the floral aroma drink down. I set the goblet to the side, and Erac puts his hand on my shoulder, grabbing the cup and inspecting the dribble left in the bottom.

He squeezes my shoulder and sets the goblet between us. He spins the stem in his fingers with a frown. "How are you feeling? Anything odd happening to your mind? You took this late today."

I shrug, and his hand falls away. "Fine. Nothing is different." I shift in my seat. "What is the antidote made of?"

He sighs heavily, eyes narrowing. "We have talked about this, time and time again. Why do you insist on causing trouble?"

I lift an eyebrow at him. "To know what I drink every day is troubling you?" I shift and turn in the chair, resting my elbow on the armrest. "I want to know what happened to me, what was done to me."

Erac faces forward with a putrid expression. "You do not need to know those answers. What was done to you was a vulgar corruption of your mind. Your father and I have worked hard to rid you of their poison. Why do you insist on inquiring about it?"

I turn forward and stare across the room at the elementals strewn about. There are demons posted around the perimeter, a line burned in the middle of the walls, and columns all the way around the room.

"What made that?" I ask, pointing toward the burned indent in the column closest to us.

Erac sighs. "Magic. The ancient kind. There is a high price to pay for magic like that. Many lives were paid for that spell, but it was to save you, so worth the cost." He takes a drink of wine. "Are you going to eat something?"

I rest back in the chair, slouching against the high velvet

back with my elbows resting outward. “Yes, I will, when I am hungry.”

He glances at me with a frown. “Morella,” he sighs, his face softening. “My love, what are you doing? Please,” he says, drawing a finger down my cheek, “eat something. You need to keep up your strength. An attack can come at any time from anywhere. There have been scouts spotted all around us over the last few cycles. The rebels are planning to attack.”

I bob my head, staring at the blackened slice in the pillar. “Yes, I know. The antidote makes me nauseous. Perhaps if I knew what was in it…?”

“Enough, Morella,” he snarls, smacking the table. Several others glance over, including my father. I meet his eyes beyond Erac’s and then focus on my husband-to-be. His violet eyes shift back and forth as he glares at me.

He keeps his voice low, but it shakes with anger. “Why do you insist on this? The matter is closed. Do as you are told.” He motions with two fingers, his gaze beyond me, and a servant moves forward with a plate of meat and gravy. “Now eat. You need your strength for the spell tomorrow.” He takes a gulp of wine and faces forward with fury etched in the lines of his scowl.

I straighten my back and pick up a fork. My other hand rests over a knife, and my eyes slide toward Erac. He turns away from me toward Viktor to whisper. I can hear them, but not enough to understand. I grip the knife, wondering if I could ever figure out how to stab my own future husband. A voice is whispering to me in the back of my mind, encouraging the idea until it is the only thought in my head.

I start cutting meat staring out at those in the great hall. There is light music playing from a band at the far end, the sounds of conversation and laughter in the air. I saw at the meat, working out my aggression. I violently stab at the meat, scarfing down a few bites, but the antidote has set my stomach churning, and the meat tosses like a ship at sea in the worst of storms.

I down my own glass of wine, set my utensils on the plate, and shove it away from me. I clean my mouth and stand.

Erac grabs my wrist, looking angry. "Where do you think you are going?"

I rip myself free of his grasp, grabbing at the skirt of my dress. "I am the most powerful being in all of Caleum, not a child to be told what to do."

His lips twist. "You may have power, but I have more knowledge than you, and you will not win a fight against me."

Dark whispers swirl, warmth spreading through my limbs. I narrow my eyes, daring him to try.

Erac sighs, and his face softens. "I want to spend time with you."

"And I want to go to the library." I turn and stride out of the room with my back to him, straight up the middle of the room, nose in the air.

I could dissipate, and it would have been faster, but I am making my point. This is a display for my dear husband-to-be, and I add a swing to my hips. I am no one's pawn, and I will not be controlled. I am a queen, the most powerful piece in play, and I will do as I damn well please.

Out of view, I dissipate to the library. Most history books are written as afterwords, only after the great deeds and life are over, but maybe I can find records of my life. Perhaps I can learn the name of the man I was betrothed to before Erac, not daring to ask him for that information and not willing to wait on George to provide it.

CHAPTER 13

DECLAN

I wake up, coming to in a groggy state. In a haze, I remember Sordello was giving me runes. I do my best to get my fingers on the skin of my back, but nothing is there. I rub the mark over my heart and several more down my left arm. The runes are all raised and rough black scars. I wonder if the runes wouldn't transfer, if I was somehow unworthy of them or if Sordello changed his mind.

I shower and clean up, then dry off, catching my reflection, seeing swirling black runes down my spine. The spirit runes. I run fingers over them, trying to feel them, but there is seamless skin. I stare.

My brain pieces together what is happening, what I am now. A spirit. Like Ella, my wife. I can live forever with her, here in Caleum or in Medius. I am one of them too now.

I want to tell her, and then I remember she's gone, taken away from me. I squeeze my eyes shut and pull my elements apart, dissipating to her rooms, wanting to be as close as possible to her.

Pieced together, I draw in a shaking breath, trying to get a grip on my sanity. Everything here reminds me of her or something about her.

I inhale, wanting to catch a whiff of her scent still lingering in the air here. Instead, I catch a nose full of sugary flowers. My eyes pop open, and I stare around. Everything has been moved, boxes litter the area in front of the door, the walls are painted bright yellow, something glaring even in the dim light of the moon.

My stomach churns, and I breathe out the acidic bile rising to the back of my throat as I stare around at the gold details, the glass tabletop, the floral upholstery. All things Ella dislikes. I move to the window seat, looking out across the view to confirm I have the right room.

"Declan?"

My spine crawls, and I turn, meeting Selene's baffled features. We stare at each other, and then she smiles, coming closer. My feet are rooted to the floor as she steps to me, her hand pressing against my bare chest.

"You came to me," she whispers, standing on her tiptoes.

Her mouth almost touches mine before my dazed brain can process what is happening. I jerk away from her, leaving her to stumble forward. I keep moving backward until the window seat contacts the back of my legs.

"What are you doing?" I manage. "This is Ella's room."

Selene's stance hardens. "Ella is never coming back."

Yes, she is. She will. I'll bring her back. She has to come back.

I shake my head. "What are you doing?"

She glances around. "Do you like it? It was dreary in here, no color. I brightened it up, used finer things." She runs a hand over the stiff back of the new couch. "It's so much prettier in here now. Morella never deserved a suite this nice anyway."

I drop onto the cushioned bench and drop my head in my hands. I can't smell her in this room anymore. There is nothing left about my wife in this room. Lifting my head, I stare at Selene. She watches me with a soft face.

My voice croaks out of me in a weak question. "Where are her things?"

"Burned. I am removing every last stench of her from this palace."

Nausea makes my head spin. "Why are you doing this?"

She tosses her hair and looks around. "She was never going to use this suite again, and it's a beautiful set of rooms. I wasn't about to let it go to waste."

"She's not dead," I whisper. "These are her rooms."

Selene clicks her tongue and moves around the couch to sit on it, curling her legs up and leaning on the armrest to face me. "Ella is never going to come back to Byron, and if she does, she'll be put to death."

My eyes stare at her, straight ahead, not really seeing. I am trying to remember the way this room looked before with dark wood furnishings, a shaggy white carpet that felt good against my bare back as Ella straddled my hips. My eyes slip closed, and I fight through the emotions threatening to spill out of me.

I reach up and pinch the bridge of my nose, breathing out slow, then I open my eyes to glare at Selene. "I want anything left of hers."

She blinks back at me like an innocent child. "It's gone. All of it." She lifts and drops one shoulder. "Anything Morella has ever touched was destroyed. Even the jewelry, which was a waste. It was a crime, really." She clicks her tongue against her teeth.

"Why?" My voice is low and shaking. "Why are you doing this?"

She lets out a soft laugh that tinkers like the broken pieces of my heart. "It's time to move on, Declan. Morella is dead or as good as in this court. I am not. I am very much alive and thriving, and I am taking what should have always been mine, including you."

I gape at her. There's something hard and dark in her eyes, a conviction or a spine I did not realize she had. I thought torturing her would kill any desire she had for me, leave her broken and afraid. It seems to have resolved something in her.

"I was always meant to be the heir, the next queen of Byron. Morella was a mistake, an abomination of life. I should have been the one betrothed to you from the start and crowned after Viktor was declared dead. I should have been the one everyone fawned over and adored."

She collects her golden curls together and drapes them over her shoulder, brushing her fingers through them so they lay in a perfect cascade. She glances up at me from the tops of her eyes and bites her lower lip. My balls crawl into the pit of my stomach.

"Won't you love me now?" she whispers through the dark. "I am your queen."

"No." It's all I can manage with my shredded brain. The word hangs in the air between us.

She scoffs and leans further over the armrest to give me a full view down her low-cut gown. I keep my eyes on hers, but she smirks. "Declan Dean Bard—" she starts.

"Byron," I tell her. "Declan Dean Byron. I married Ella."

She snarls, purring like a cat. "She has no claim to that name, and you are going to renounce that marriage, or so help you Haven." Her words come out as a harsh growl.

"When we get her back—"

"The next time the court meets, you will refute the marriage, annul it," Selene snarls as she lurches to her feet and takes a step toward me. "I don't care how you do it, but you are going to do it. Your marriage to Morella is going to end, or I will strip you of the crown."

I scoff, leaning back against the window, staring at the spot on the floor before her bare feet. The cool glass feels good against my sweating skin. "I don't care about the crown."

"Yes, you have said that, but I think you do. Without the crown, you will not control the army. There will be no war against Viktor. The guild leaders are dissatisfied with you and your choices. Without the crown, you have no leverage to continue this fight."

I frown. "You'd surrender to Viktor?" I shrug and sit up, resting my elbows on my knees. "He'll kill you for it."

She crosses her arms. "I'll be his loyal subject that saves him the grief of war against Byron. He'll give me the court of Byron in his service."

I narrow my eyes. "You're a fool. Viktor isn't fond of you."

"You'll give me what I want, or I'll take away everything *you* want."

I glance up at her, my eyebrows pushing together. "You already helped take away the thing I wanted, so go fuck yourself."

Tearing my elements apart, I dissipate back to my room. I grab a tumbler, emptying the contents down my throat before hurling it against the wall. It shatters, shards flying back at me.

I dig around my room, looking for anything Ella might have left here. We spent most of the time in her rooms, though, so my search turns up empty. There's nothing left of her but a ghost in my memory. I reach out for her through the bond, pain stabbing in my temples. I try harder, needing to feel her, to know she was real.

My skull feels like it is splitting in half, and I collapse onto my bed, reaching for a pillow. I cuddle it against my chest, pretending it is her, trying to remember how she felt and smelled when I held her close. I keep my eyes shut and dig through my memories until I am a rabid animal.

I dissipate to Asperheim in search of her. I move like a shadow, dissipating through the gardens, hopping over walls on a direct route inside. I dissipate myself to a balcony and break glass to reach through and unlatch a closed door.

Creeping through halls, there is a brushing sensation in my chest being this close to her, the pieces of our souls searching for each other, demanding to be brought together. I exhale until my lungs are empty. Even with the interrupted bond, souls will still yearn and strive to be whole.

The feeling makes me queasy, knowing I can do nothing to alleviate the tugging within me.

Lurking in shadows, I step and dissipate through a maze of passageways. I have no idea what I am looking for, where I am going. I focus on the tugging in my chest, hoping it will lead me to her.

I stumble through a door. Inside are book-lined walls, three stories high. Almost laughing at myself, I stalk around the perimeter of the library. They can kidnap her, hurt her, and my lover is still going to bury her nose in books.

Weaving through smaller shelving, working my way toward the middle of the room, the feeling in my chest grows, my need and anxiety notching up until I find her asleep at a table, her head on an arm, her eyes closed. I am frozen in shock and longing, then reach out for her, but I cannot touch her.

"Ella!" I yell. I punch at the blockade of air. My knuckles crack on contact as if I punched marble. "Ella!"

Erac appears at my side. I turn, punching him before he can get a word out of his mouth. I lunge at him and get thrown backward. My trajectory changes, and I shoot upward.

Fuck.

I try to breathe as I rush down to the ground with a lot more force than falling generates. I slam into the floor, feeling the stone crack, or maybe that was bone. I groan and shove up. Drawing air in tastes like blood and my chest burns with agony at the motion.

Erac stalks toward me with a chuckle. "I could make this so

easy and command you to slit your own throat, but I want you to know I really am better than you in every way."

I stumble to my feet toward him, happy to see blood trickling from a crooked nose. With as much force as I can manage, I try another hook. He dodges, grabbing my wrist, and I end up on my knees. His other hand comes up, sending a shock wave through my arm.

I snarl and growl, trying to pull away from him as the bones fracture. "You sick fuck. You raped her, and you're family."

Erac twists my arm. I groan at the pain, and in part, at watching as my arm acts as though it is made of rubber. "Yes, I tasted her, felt her, claimed her," he says. "She belongs to me now as she always should have. She cried at first, but then she liked it."

He draws a blade from the air. Ignoring my injuries as best as possible, I push up, getting a leg free to kick his from underneath him. He topples, and I use the momentum to end up on top of him. My damaged arm hangs at my side, useless but tingling as it heals. I get one hand around his throat, squeezing.

"You're fucking delusional," I snarl. "She begged for it to stop. I heard it. I fucking felt it."

My fingers are pried off his throat by nothing. He sneers at me. "She doesn't know that. She doesn't even know who you are anymore. She tells me she loves me now."

"Fuck, lover, what have they done to you?" My eyes cut toward her, seeing her still snoozing away, her face at rest. A shimmering bubble is around her, elements protecting her, probably blocking the sound of this fight or if I yell out to her.

In my momentary mental lapse, I get thrown backward again, and this time I am crushed to the ground by force. I concentrate on the elements, trying to break free, but even with his attentions divided, I'm not strong enough to force the elements out of his control.

He gets on top of me, a knee in my chest, grinning down at

me. The tip of the blade presses against my neck, cold metal biting into my skin. "Thank you for coming. You've been a pesky problem I needed to be rid of, and I've waited a long time for this." The blade slips toward one ear, stinging in its path. I glare up at him, and he smirks. "So long, Declan."

The blade rips through my thin skin. It stings and burns, my blood spilling out warm against my skin. I choke, drowning in it, my senses drowning in the tangy metallic fluid. My vision grays and fades. The last thing I see is Erac, beaming down at me victorious.

CHAPTER 14

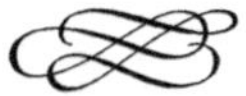

MORELLA

I stare down into it, standing in the middle, the surface of the water like a glass pane beneath my feet. Movement disturbs the shadows beneath, like beings walking in and around the buildings, but every waft of inky color occurs on my peripheral, and when I try to focus, there is nothing there.

The sunken city built in stone and marble is submerged deep under the veneer. Treetops full and lush with vegetation reach from the depths to breach and sway in the river, the thin leaves trailing from the branches in time with the current. The expanse is dotted with lush lilies and other plants around the banks, but here in the middle where I stand, the crystal water is clear, steeped in shadows of the lost world below the surface.

I drop to my knees, unable to penetrate the water. I stare down, hungry with a desire to reach through the barrier, to find what moves beyond my reach. Pressing with flat palms, I hope to push through to the other side. I add my weight, then try to add more and more force until my arms are shaking with fatigue. The hunger turns to ravenous need, and I slam my fists against the water over and over, droplets of back spray hitting my face.

Each hit sends cracks spreading across the surface. As they advance, the city begins to crumble, lost to the darkness swirling below. The water fractures like a mirror, the image of the beautiful city scattering to blackness, and I fall through, clawing at the air above me to try and stop myself from being plunged downward as I take one last gulp of air.

Something pulls me down, further into the inky nothingness. The monster below latches on tighter as I try to kick free. My hands reach up, fingers grabbing at bubbles. I pray for the surface even as I plunge deeper into the void.

I open my mouth to scream, icy water flooding inside even as I hear the high-pitched wail released from my lungs. The liquid burns my throat and lungs leaving the metallic taste of blood on my tongue.

I startle awake, my eyes flying open wide, my heart pounding with violent force within my chest. Trying to catch my breath, I stare, my head craned to one side, at book-lined shelves as silent witnesses. The reoccurring dream has plagued me from the day I woke with no memories, but this time it was different. This time I broke through.

Lifting my head, the top page sticks to my cheek, glued to me by drool. With caution, I peel it away from my skin, then rub my face and smooth the folio in place. My tongue runs along my gums, searching for that metal flavor. I wince, then lap at my lower lip.

I lift a hand and touch it, pulling back to see the blood on my fingertips. I suck on my lower lip, checking my surroundings. The library stands solemn and mum, blanketed in thick shadows, and the throws of monachopsis grip me.

My eyes lower to the book I drooled all over, seeking signs of permanent damage before sweeping the area. There are so many leather-bound pages for me to hope to read them all in a single lifetime. I have scanned multiple medicinal tomes in search of what the antidote I drink might be but to no avail. Without a name or ingredients, which are refused to my knowledge, the effort is futile.

With an expel of air, I shove the chair back and stand, still suckling my bleeding lip. I lick at the wound and turn, my eyes searching for anything out of place to explain the brush of unfamiliarity against my senses. There is something out of reach, on the peripheral of my ability to comprehend, a hair tickling my arm, stuck to my shirt that I cannot find.

I peer at the darkness, and then my eyes rivet on a dark splotch on the stone before me. I crouch down to the floor, balancing low on the balls of my feet, for a closer inspection.

"Morella."

I glance up, Erac stepping from the shadows. I point at the space in front of me. "Blood?"

He frowns and stops opposite the blotted puddle. "Yes." He crosses his arms and casts his eyes at the primal stain.

"Why is there blood on the floor?" I ask in a hushed voice, my skin prickling with pimples, the little hairs on my body standing to attention. "Who did this come from?"

Erac tilts his head, eyes still fixated on the floor. His lips purse and push out, then he sighs. "There are dozens of hearts beating deep within Caleum." He shrugs. "They are planted here, in the south, through one of the hundreds of caves along the shoreline."

My face freezes in a twist of confusion. "Er, um, okay, like hearts? Like, real, actual elemental hearts?" I blink up at him. "What does that have to do with blood on our library floor?"

His eyebrows lift, and his face is full of boredom and fatigue. "Yes, Morella, real hearts." He waves a hand at the space between us. "One probably bled up through the ground. It's no matter. I came to fetch you for bed."

I fixate on the blood, reaching out to touch the spot. "Can you tell me about the hearts?" My eyes lift to his, and I lick my lips, wetting them in anticipation of knowledge.

Erac smirks. "Of course." He offers me a hand to help me to my feet, and I accept, being pulled up and forward into him. His nose nuzzles my hair, inhaling deeply until his chest swells. With my ear pressed against his chest, I can hear the heavy strums within.

I pull back, meeting his deep indigo eyes. “What’s wrong?”

With a smile, he presses his lips to mine, his hands clasping my head to tilt my mouth for him. His fingers twine into the strands of my hair. “Nothing. Nothing at all now, my love." His words are like a sigh of pleasure.

Cocking an eyebrow, I ask, “What changed?”

The sadistic twist of his lips warns me to pull away, but I know better. When in proximity, I yield to him. I have learned that much.

“Oh, nothing,” he muses with a pleasant ring. “Nothing you need to worry about, or I anymore. I fixed the magic. You’ll never have to drink that horrible antidote again.” His dark chuckle is an eerie mix with his bubbly mood and sing-song voice.

I clear my throat, my mouth dry. “Oh, that’s good. What did you do?” I ask in a hushed voice?

He snickers and pulls me away from that place. “I broke the magic. You are mine, Morella, from here until the end of time you belong to me.” He tucks me against him as we walk arm in arm. “And there is absolutely nothing that is able to take you away from me anymore.”

“Well, can you tell me what the poison was then?”

He stiffens as he pulls me out of the library and into the corridor. “Morella,” he warns. “It doesn’t matter what it is.”

“Why won’t you tell me?”

“You need to leave it alone and stop asking questions. It will only hinder your recovery, and you’ve been progressing well. Now, let us be done with this tiresome thing and go to bed.”

CHAPTER 15

DECLAN

Air rushes up around me like I am flung through it, being sucked back to consciousness after a long sleep. I squeeze my eyes shut and roll to my back, then peel my lids back over dry eyes. I blink to focus my vision, closing one eye to focus on the ceiling and then switching to the other before getting both eyes to work in unison.

I jerk up, positioned in the middle of my bed, a sheet tangled in my legs. Stretching my head side to side, one of my hands comes up, wrapping around the back of my jaw and throat, making sure all the bits are attached and healed. When I pull back, I glance at my palm, making sure there's no blood.

Holy fucking Haven, so that's what this is like? Waking up?

I scrub a hand down my face and shake the sleep away. Flipping the sheet off, I slide off the bed and land on my feet. Standing upright, I shove my jaw to the side and crack my neck.

"Dec?"

I have enough time to glance at the door between my bedroom and sitting room before it flies open, and my brother rushes in. I grin at his mouth, hanging open.

"Don't you dare look at me like that," he yelps. "What in

Damnatus were you thinking?”

I guffaw at him and roll my shoulders. “I don’t know what your problem is, but I feel great.”

“Yeah?” His face drags in on itself as he glares at me. “You feel great? I’ve been worrying myself into an early grave.”

I shake my head and stare out the window at the orchards beyond. “I have spirit runes.” I roll my shoulders in a half shrug.

“And? What the hell did you even do?”

I glance over with a single lifted brow. “Better question, how did I end up here?” I point to the ground with both hands.

Seth lifts his eyebrows. “Here being in this room, or here being naked? And will you please stop pointing at your dick? Because I don’t want to see it.”

My eyes drop down to find I am, in fact, directing toward my naked lower body. “Who the fuck took my pants off?”

Seth crosses his arms and leans against the bed. “Healers? Probably. Maybe Selene snuck in. I don’t know, just put some pants on.”

My lip curls back at him. “That’s…” I cannot find a word strong enough to respond with. Grimacing, I move to the chest of drawers and grab a pair of jeans. “How did I get here? As in Byron.”

“Better question, where were you?” He stares me down with daggers in his eyes.

“Asperheim.”

“Idiot.” Seth bobs his head from side to side. “No idea. Selene found you in the throne room.”

I give him a skeptical glance as I button the jeans on. “What?”

“You were on the throne,” he says again, shrugging at me. “It was weird. You were propped up like you were just sitting there, eyes open, throat slit, and there was a crown on your head. Selene found you right before a session started. I think my ears are still ringing.”

"Yeah?" I sigh out. "Why's that?"

"She screamed. I heard it in my room."

I scrunch one side of my face trying to figure the distance between his room and the throne room. "Eh."

"What happened?"

I stop moving, a sweater half pulled on, my face falling. "I went to get Ella," I say, eyes directed at the ground between us. "I saw her. I almost had her. I hesitated. It won't happen again."

My brother laughs. "Yeah, damn right, it's not happening again. Sordello told you to stay here, to wait for us to figure out—"

"That fucker has my wife," I snarl. The muscles in my neck strain as I roar at Seth.

He holds his hands up and takes a half step away. "Dec, I get it, I do. Calm the fuck down."

I turn away from him, clamping my jaw down tight, and take a long draught of air in through my nose. "Fuck, I'm sorry," I manage through clenched teeth. I face him again, and he gives me a half-smile.

"Yeah, I know. Sordello wasn't sure you'd actually come back, runes or not, so you're damn lucky."

"Why?"

He leans against the door. "You didn't have a drop of blood left in you, like you were drained, bled dry. Aron said there's a spell for it."

My heart stutters, and I try to stay calm. "How long was I out?"

He glances over his shoulder, eyes rolling to the ceiling. "Uh, a day shy of two cycles. What the hell were you thinking?" He holds a hand up. "Nope, never mind. You weren't, were you?"

My shoulders drop. "I just want her back." The words are low, my eyes focused on his boots.

Seth sighs, heaving out a heavy, long breath. "Yeah, I know."

We stand in silence, my heart squelching in my ears as

seconds tick by. I lift my gaze to meet his and wince. One side of his mouth pulls back.

He almost laughs at me. “So, who kicked your ass?”

Disgust sweeps through me. “Erac.” The fucker giggles at me, and I narrow my eyes. “Little brother,” I warn. He bursts into laughter, and I have the urge to clock him in the face. I grip my fists and cock my head at him, glaring.

He snorts through his nose and leans against the doorframe. “I’m almost sad I didn’t get to see it. I bet you just looked pathetic.”

I breathe through my nose, reaching up to pinch the bridge. “It was hardly a fair fight.”

“Bet it wasn’t a fight at all,” he answers, smirking. I take one step toward him, and he shakes his head. “You can kick my ass all you want, but you know damn well that Erac, Aron, Ella, any of the spirits, any of them can take you down in seconds or less with the elements. We need their help.”

I grind my teeth and throw my hands in the air. “I thought I could get in, get her, and get the fuck out before anyone noticed.”

He purses his lips. “You said you saw her?”

I step to him, gauging the distance, and then stop, waving a hand between us. “This far. I was this close.”

Seth reaches out to put a hand on my shoulder. He turns a bit green around the gills and gives me puppy dog eyes. “How’d she look?”

I shake my head. “Like she was asleep on a stack of books.”

“So, not like she’s being tortured?”

My right eye starts to twitch. “Erac raped her. That’s not torture enough?”

“Well, yeah, but…” Seth trails off, staring at me with eyes stretched wide.

“No, she’s not locked in a dungeon beaten and bloody.” I cross my arms and kick at the ground.

"Then why hasn't she come home?" His voice sounds the way my chest feels when I think about her, constricted under enough pressure that it might snap and break.

I manage to swallow. "Erac said something."

"Yeah?" Seth's leaning in toward me, hanging on for my next words with a desperation that's palpable.

"He said," I grind out, "she doesn't even know who I am anymore. I didn't think about it then, but…"

"But what?" he snaps. "What?"

I lift my eyes to his, holding my scarred forearm out. "I didn't know who she was either after Marx took my memories."

Seth's eyes drop to my arm, and he reaches out, grabbing my wrist. "Bearings," he whispers. "You think?"

"I think the only way Ella doesn't fight back, the only way she wouldn't come back to me is if she didn't know I exist, that she doesn't know about the bond or—" I stop, lips tightening together and twisting.

"Doesn't know she loves you," Seth says for me.

Burning bile rises in my throat, the putrid taste lingering on the back of my tongue. "Yes," I say on exhale.

He nods. "Makes sense."

I grimace. "Memories. I had mine ripped out and replaced with new ones. They changed me. I'm not going to hide that or pretend it isn't real. She's gone, Ella, she's not her anymore. They killed her even if she's upright walking around."

The grip he holds on me tightens, my bones cracking under the pressure. "No. She's not dead, and I got you back. I'll get her back too."

"It'll take a fucking miracle, you know that, right?"

"I am a miracle." He winks and lets go of my wrist. "You should probably let everyone know you're still alive—er, alive again? Dunno, but definitely let the court know you're still here, still king. I think there is session this morning."

I eye him. "And what are you doing?"

He grins. "Moving the camp to Asperheim."

"I'm not going to waste time on smiling and shaking hands while—"

"You are," Seth says in a direct order, cutting me off. "This isn't going after Ell or fighting demons even. This is setting up camp which doesn't require any of your particular talents."

I breathe out my nose and narrow my eyes. He smirks, and I look away. "Fine."

"I'm serious. You need to show your pretty face around, let everyone know you're breathing."

"Yeah, I got it," I snap at him. He thinks he's so clever. I consider rolling my eyes like Ella, and all the air is squeezed from my lungs as I am gutted at the thought. I stare at him, struggling to breathe.

He knocks a fist against my shoulder, grinning at me. "I'll get the camp set up, and then we'll figure a way to get her back. We can't really afford for you to lose the crown right now."

I bob my head, eyes burning. "Yeah, okay."

"Oh." His face grows dark and scrunches up. "Marcus... We made it look like he died in the gardens. No one's asking too many questions. It wasn't a hard sell, but just so you know and, you know, don't say anything."

I clench my jaw and turn my face away from Seth. *Fuck, I hadn't thought about that.* Turning back to him, I exhale through my nose and nod again. "Yeah."

"You missed the funeral being dead and all."

I squeeze my eyes and hands shut. "Great," I manage. "Anything else?"

"Nope, just let the court know you're alive, and I'll move the camp. It's going to be okay."

With a scoff, I turn away for the bathroom and a shower. "Right."

"It's going to be okay!" he yells after me.

CHAPTER 16

DECLAN

I sit on a black silk-covered cushion and sip on cold, congealed blood left over from a boar. The taste is revolting, the fluid thick and hard to get down. Selene comes striding into the room, her heeled shoes clacking on the marble floors and echoing around in the still air. She stops in front of me, staring with wide yellow eyes and lips parted.

I lift my bottle at her in a gesture of greeting and then take another drink. She picks up her skirt and moves to take a seat next to me. "You're alive?" Her voice is a breathless whisper. She reaches out, trying to take my face in her hands, but I jerk away.

"Yes, I survived." I twist the word, fury rising when I think about how pathetically I flopped in that fight.

Her eyes are stretched open wide, a bit too large and wide-set in her face. "How?"

"Spirit runes. Sordello gave them to me. Woke up this morning." I hold up the bottle of blood in a sort of acknowledgment.

"Would you like something better tasting? Fresh?" She holds an arm out, offering her wrist.

I take another drink and look her dead in the eye. "Week old blood from a toad tastes better than you."

Her eyes flash at me as her mouth pinches, and she drops her arm back to her side. "Why are you being so cruel? This isn't like you, Declan."

I raise an eyebrow. "Are you really that stupid, or have you managed to convince yourself of it because it's what you want?"

She picks up her skirt, stepping to my side and lowering down onto her own cushion. "I am neither stupid nor delusional."

I snort into the open bottle and smile. "Then, you're insane."

"No." She draws the word out like she did when begging me not to hurt her anymore. "I know what I want, and I'm not afraid to get my hands dirty to get it." She turns to face me. "Just like you."

I sit straighter at the remark and clench my jaw. "Not like me," I manage.

She tips her head back, her blonde hair spills over her shoulders, and she laughs faintly. "I had fractures in my face, my ribs, my wrists, and that doesn't begin to cover the lesions." She shakes her head. "You hurt me to know about Ella. Willing to do what needed to be done to get what you wanted."

I smirk. "I didn't need to hurt you. I wanted to. Wyatt told us everything without being coerced."

She blanches. "Well, you're a shade, so it's only natural."

"There is nothing natural about my desire to inflict pain upon you," I snarl under my breath. "You helped hand Ella, the most powerful being in all of Caleum, to Viktor. Not only did you help take my wife away from me, but you gave Viktor what he needs to win."

"You wanted her to live. Now she will. She is out of reach of this court, beyond our laws, and Haven only knows why, but Viktor absolutely adores her, so she'll be safe with him. I helped you get what you wanted, too."

I roar with laughter, honest mirth clenching my stomach and lifting my spirit. "Yes, I absolutely wanted to never see my wife again. I wanted Viktor to win this war and rule over us all. I especially wanted her to be back under Viktor's control, to be beaten, whipped, coerced into atrocious acts of violence to further his agenda." I take a drink. "How very kind of you."

She bristles. "You can't have her in this court and alive."

I shrug. "Then, I'd leave the court with her."

Her jaw drops. "You can't. You're the king."

"So?"

"You have to be here." Her voice is shrill as it lifts. "You have to attend court, to preside and rule. There are obligations, appearances."

"Then, I won't be king."

"You'd give up the crown for her?"

"Yes."

"I don't believe you."

I turn my torso toward her with a bored expression. Her face is turning pink, her eyes are glassy as if she might cry. I believe the thought of walking away from the throne is enough to bring her to a sobbing mess.

I smirk. "I don't care if you believe me or not. I don't give a fuck about being king."

"Yes, you do. You fought for it when you came back." Her hands clench her skirt. "I remember how you went around trying to convince the court."

"Yes," I hum. "I tried very hard to persuade them to reinstate me to my betrothal to Ella."

She releases her hands and fluffs her skirt. "Why? Why would you work so hard for her?" She twists the last word with venom. "What is so damn special about her that causes everyone to make such a fuss?"

I smirk. "She's beautiful. She's powerful. She's kind, polite to servants and anyone else who crosses her path for no ulterior motives other than to be nice. Because she values it. She's compassionate and fair in all of her rulings, and those who call on this court love her for it."

Selene scoffs. "I'm fair and compassionate. I'm beautiful. I can be nice. Why not fuss over me?"

I stare her down. "You are vain, not very bright, and your considerations to others go only as far as it works for you and at your convenience."

"Ella isn't perfect!" Selene's scream echoes around us, only making me smile wider.

"Nope. She's got a wicked temper and has little discipline. She lacks forethought or even a cohesive, singular logical mind-set. She loses interest in most things quickly unless it's a fighting combo or a book. She's terrible at being on time or even making an appearance for things she doesn't want to do." I snicker. "Trying to get her to do something she doesn't want to is a task and a half."

"Then, why?" Selene asks in a pitiful whine. "Why would you want her?"

I turn away, facing the double doors and wishing someone else would show up to end this conversation. I don't want to think about all the reasons why I love Ella. It's going to gut me. I sigh and take a drink, wiping my mouth on the back of my hand.

"Ella..." I stop and suck in a deep breath. "She's more likely to hurt herself to help someone than to walk away. The only things she wants are me and to help everyone." I smile, although nothing is amusing. "And she'd sacrifice me to save everyone else because that's who she is. I couldn't do it, but she would. Because she doesn't give a fuck about the crown for any reason other than to make others happy. Because everyone that meets her falls in love with her because of who she is..." I trail off, trying very hard to keep my composure.

"I miss you," I tell her, getting no response. I freeze, bottle

part way to my lips. I think my heart stops for that single second. The bond is gone.

"And she's killed, tortured others," Selene grits out through clenched teeth, "done despicable things, things that make normal men shudder. She's a monster and a murderer." I shake my head, but she keeps going. "She's never coming back. I can learn to fight with you. I can be nice. I can be like her."

"You are nothing like her," I snarl. "And I'm never going to love you."

Fuck. The bond. Sweat beads along my scalp, and then I relax. *She'll have half her soul back, the half that was in me, she'll have it back, and she might get memories back.*

"You are king, and I am queen. You'll learn to love me after we are married," she says. Her tone is rather decided.

I laugh. "I am already married—"

"That isn't valid."

"Like hell, it isn't. I had the King of Spirits and her own father marry us in accordance with her spirit heritage." It sounds good, even if I don't know if it's true. The spirits all share a collective thought. I doubt any of them ever get married. Sordello has spoken of love as an abnormality amongst the spirits.

Selene draws in a breath that sounds like a hiss. "The court is not going to be happy."

I shrug and lean back on my hands, staring at the doors and willing someone to come through them. "Not my problem. I don't care if the court is happy. That's Ella's job." The words are out of my mouth before I realize.

Selene twists to glare at me. "Ella has no job or place at this court. If you wish to maintain this charade, you'll need to accept the consequences of your actions. If Ella ever returns here, she will be put to death."

I curl my lip. "She won't stay dead even if you managed to

somehow kill her. She'd have to let you kill her, and that's never going to happen."

"You should renounce your marriage before the court realizes the legitimacy of it and takes issue with you."

"You should go stick your head up a pig's ass." Her mouth opens in shock, but I shrug at her. "I'm not recanting my vows."

I twist the sapphire around my third finger of my left hand. The band spins easy enough, the inside smooth against my skin. Ella used the large sapphire, condensed it, creating the ring through the manipulation of the elements. I don't know why, but sapphires give mages amplified powers, and somehow what she did made the amplification higher.

It still wasn't enough to beat Erac, that fucking voice whispers to me in the back of my mind.

The dark blue gem gleams at me as I spin it, remembering the way she beamed at me when I put it on instead of dwelling on that thought. The doors at the end of the hall open, and I glance up to see others entering the room. I let out a sigh of relief through my nose and rise. Stupid small talk is better than dealing with Selene.

One of them is Spaulding, the charismatic youngest of the Byron siblings. I should check on him. Walking straight for him, I hold his gaze. He stares at me with bright blue eyes that seem to have none of their typical spark of humor, his square face a high gossip topic among the women of the court, but it's strained and gaunt. This entire family has been royally fucked—pun intended.

CHAPTER 17

MORELLA

I press two fingers to a leather-bound book. The flesh is dark red, and the ridges line horizontally from top to bottom. In the middle is a pressed symbol I am unfamiliar with. I sigh, touching the one next to it, an exposed paper binding that is tattered, the top corner peeling back.

Our library is massive, and for the last couple of cycles, I have spent days exploring the shelves, itching to touch every spine of every book in this room, craving for the knowledge within. There are hundreds of rows of shelves reaching high up to a glass dome that glitters when the soul star shines through it. I love this room, adore roaming the various levels, just putting my hands on the spines of books as I pass by.

There are so many, and I wonder if they hold the answers I seek. Without knowing the right questions to ask, it's hard to decide which volumes to select. The search for a book about my previous betrothal was in vain, but I have little information to go on. Isolated with only Erac and my father here in Asperheim, I am limited in what I can learn.

George hasn't been to see me again, and word sent for him is ignored. Briefly, I consider leaving, but I don't know where I would go, who to find. Then there is the threat to my safety to worry about.

A hand covers mine, and I glance up to see Erac. His face is tight, his ears pulled back and low. I tilt my head and frown in a silent question. Shaking his head, he pulls me in toward him, hugging me close so that my ear presses over his chest.

A rapid hard clunk comes from within his center. I tip my head back and snake my arms around him. "What's wrong?"

"The rebelling pricks showed up." His words are stretched tight, like the leather over book spines. "Again."

I glance to the side and over my shoulder. "Are they still here?" I narrow my eyes as I reclaim eye contact. "What do you mean 'again?'"

He shakes his head. "They tried before, right after you regained consciousness after my second try to remove their poison."

I grit my teeth, indignant that they continue to try to hurt me. "Where are they?"

He cups my jaw and tips my head back. "Outside the palace's defensive walls. I wanted to make sure you were safe, but I must deal with this." He kisses my forehead.

I put my hands in the middle of his torso and push away. "We," I stress. "I am coming too."

"No." He reaches out, wrapping his hand around my wrist. The pressure draws my eye, and I remember the dark bruises when I woke up in his suite.

"They poisoned me, my mind…" I direct a finger at my temple. "They did this to me. They hurt me, destroyed me. I don't remember anything about my life, about who I am."

I am not sure when I started yelling, but Erac's eyes have grown wide, and he leans away from me on his heels. Inhaling, I lower my voice and shake my head, searching for some semblance of inner calm.

"My love, I understand." He runs his hands up my arms,

from elbow to shoulder. "This is a trying time. I long desperately for you to genuinely love me as you are supposed to."

I roll my eyes. Loving him is at the bottom of my concerns. "I don't even know who I am. Not one single thing about myself when you and my father and everyone else knows everything about me." I am yelling again, my eyes burning. "Everyone knows me, my name, and you are fighting over me, and I don't even know why. They did that. They did that, and I want them to pay for it."

Erac's eyes light up, the corners of his mouth pulling back in a sly smile like the cat that ate the mouse. His hand extends in an open offering. "Then we will make them pay for it."

My hand slaps down into his as I hurry to accept. My eyes meet his, and he chuckles, eyes crinkling and dancing at me. I narrow mine back, setting my jaw and squeezing his hand beneath my fingers.

They will repay in blood what they took from me.

Lifting my hand to his lips, he says, "Burn them. Burn them all and everything you see. But listen, my love, and listen close." His free hand tucks hair behind my ear and cups the back of my neck. "If you see a shade, those with gray or black eyes, they are the most dangerous of all. They are bloodthirsty, ruthless, filthy animals, and if you see one, it must die immediately. If you hesitate, it will kill you instead."

I would ask about shades later. Right now, I do not want answers. I want revenge. A white-hot need burns through me, spreading from my core and through my limbs. It pulsates, slinking further with every beat of my heart.

I. Want. Blood.

A whisper purrs in the back of my mind. *Break. Burn. Hurt them. Make them pay.*

My eyes burn as they lift to his, and one side of my lips curls. He grins just as evilly back at me, and then cold pressure against my skin leaves a blistered feeling.

I glare out against the soul star's blazing heat shimmering off the sand dunes. White tents have popped up, elementals are strewn over the area in small clumps. I glance over my shoulder to see a conical palace stretching high in the sky.

"So close," I breathe. "They dare to come this close?" My blood boils at the audacity of them setting up camp here.

I blink as brilliant stars form on the horizon, then see glints from some beings made of metal as they materialize, another hoard of elementals and crates appearing with them. The heat in the air mingles with the steam pouring out of me.

This ends now.

Throwing a hand out, I set the sand swirling through the air, commanding the elements to unleash a sandstorm raging across the land to destroy their tents. The twisters raze through their ranks, ripping and flinging. I grin, contorting my hand to merge the swirling storms together into one ravenous cloud, spinning ferociously.

I twist my hand, grappling with the air, force it and the sand to obey, traveling in a circle, rounding them all together. I roll my wrist, closing my fist to enclose them in a ring of sand.

I storm across the desert, down the dune, keeping my fist closed and my eye on the prizes locked away. Erac follows, but I cannot hear him over the whispering in the back of my mind. I need to destroy. It's begging for a massacre.

I part the sand, striding through the grains with hell on my mind and a kiss of chaos on my lips. A suit of armor stands before me, holding gauntlets out as if to ward off my storm. I sneer at it, trying to see below the shadowed hood of thick white cloth.

Destroy it.

I throw a hand from one side of my body to the other with all the fury in my veins. It rolls through me, that dark whisper drinking in the fear radiating toward me. The armor flies away, hurled to the side to expose the elementals beyond huddled together.

They should be afraid. They should all be afraid of me.

I will bend them and break them, return them all to the sand from which we came. A scream of rage rips from me as I extend my hand, commanding them to be dust. Several of them disintegrate, the grains whisking away to join the turbulence around us.

They scatter like rodents, scurrying away from me to hide. But there is nowhere for them to go. I grin ear to ear, stepping further into the storm. Turning one after the other to sand to join with the others in the storm.

Another suit of armor steps before me, the massive silver gauntlets blackened at the edges. I step into throwing both hands forward at it. It slides back an inch, the air between us shattering. The force wave explodes, sending the armor backward, out of sight in the swirling sand ripping around me.

"L!" A single elemental is moving toward me, a hand in front of his face. "L, stop!"

I square up to him, holding out a hand, but he keeps running toward me, the sand shifting under his feet, causing him to stumble.

He did this to you. Make him pay.

I grip at the air, ready to turn him to sand. Instead, the air between us crystalizes, hardening like geometric ice that glints. Snarling like a rapid creature in pain that only wants to inflict pain on others, I fixate on the armor. My vision turns narrow, forgetting everything else.

One hand lifts and starts to clench the air. The metal armor constricts, hands coming up, trying to stop the air from crashing down around it. I tense up through my arm, through my fingers, commanding the air elements to pull inward, to pulverize that thing.

"L!" the muffled cry carries around the barrier. I glance over, seeing the man through the solid air, banging fists with a distorted face.

He is tall, so much taller than any elemental I have ever seen by inches, long brown hair billowing around his face. I peer at him, wondering why he is not afraid of me. A flick of my fingers could turn him to nothing but grains of sand.

With a smirk, I use my other hand to dissolve that wall. Glancing over, I see the armor forced into an awkward position.

"Ella," the man roars, almost upon me, reaching out for me. The face is screwed up with emotion, yet I feel as if I should know something about those features. They are familiar and wrong at the same time. I press my lips together in a frown, trying to grasp the feeling at the back of my mind. The sense slips away as quickly as it came.

I scream, closing my fist, but another armored being cuts between us. It holds both hands up, pressed palms out, stacked together, and a force rips through the air throwing me backward. I roll along the dune, getting a mouthful of dirt. I struggle, clawing at the shifting substance, crawling back to the surface, getting on my knees.

Erac is there, helping me. I swipe at the drool and debris on my face, the sand scratching against my skin, clinging to my lashes. I bat him away, trying to get back to those vermin. The storm is gone. All that remains are canvas and poles poking out of ridges of the dune.

They are gone, all of them. Whatever was left of them and the metal armored beings with them have vanished. There is no one left for me to destroy, no one left to pay for what was done.

I want my pound of flesh, my dues in blood.

The rage dwindles to a swirling smoke in my veins, and sour ash lingers on the back of my tongue as I scan the horizon.

CHAPTER 18

MORELLA

The hollow ache in me builds until it ruptures, and I scream at the empty space until I have no air left in my lungs. Erac grabs me from behind, wrapping his arms around me, pulling me away as the sand roars into a sinking pit, dragging whatever was left behind to depths where they will never see light again.

I struggle, fighting against him. "Let me go!"

"Hush, love, my beautiful queen, hush now. They are gone."

I need to destroy them, destroy everything.

I squirm. I kick. I scream at Erac, the sand, and the sky. "They will repay in blood what they took from me!" My voice sounds like a blood-curdling wail far away from my own ears as wet clings to my cheeks and lashes.

Erac's voice is quiet, too soft and delicate to break through the storm and lust for blood raging inside of me. "You have done well. Calm down now."

I rage against him until I am exhausted. Together we collapsed on the desert floor, and I lay half on top of him sobbing for breath, sinking in grief. "They did this to me," I whisper, blinking out tears that roll down the sides of my face into my hair.

"I know," he pants, almost chuckling. "And you will make them all pay. I promise you, you will have your chance to destroy them when the time comes."

Nodding, I lose myself in his arms like solid cage work around me, holding me down, keeping me confined. I need that right now as the burning rage ebbs away, leaving a wake of raw agony.

Catching my breath, I reach up, swiping at the dirt and tears on my face. I clear my throat, pulling his arms away. I sit up, rolling off him and getting to my feet, dragging the heels of my palms under my blurry eyes. They are full of grit as I try to blink away the excess to see right.

"My love." He presses my hands together, raising the tips of my fingers against his mouth. "You did well."

I sniffle and shake my head. "The armored ones—"

"Spirits," Erac scowls. "Yes, they are strong like you and me, but you can handle them. When you've learned, when I have taught you all there is to teach you, you'll cut through them with ease."

I nod. "I want to learn more."

He chuckles, drawing me against him. "I will teach you everything I know. It has only been a few cycles, hardly enough time, but you are excelling through the basics quickly."

My soul is heavy, dropping through my body and settling in my feet. Erac steps away from me, and I cannot move. The void inside of me is a vacuum, drawing all life out of me. I crumple forward into the empty space where he was.

Erac turns back, frowning. "You barely tapped into your energy."

I stare up at him from my knees, lost in this turbulent sea. He purses his lips and turns back with a disgusted sigh, crouching in front of me. Reaching out, he grabs my chin in one hand, jerking my face toward his.

His eyes shift back and forth, and he clicks his tongue against his teeth. "Let's go."

The air constricts, freezing cold around me, and we are in my rooms. I manage to get on my feet as he watches me with a forlorn expression. I shake my head, keeping my eyes on the floor.

"Are you really so defeated by such a small act? The expenditure should have been insignificant for you."

I exhale with restraint, not wanting to let him know the fatigue within my core. "I am fine."

He jerks his chin down and stares at me from the tops of his eyes. "Perhaps it is... Nevermind. Yes, you need to rest, that's all." His head lifts, and he smiles. "How did it feel?"

My shoulders twitch as if to roll back or shrug. There is a pitiful slug writhing in my stomach. "I don't know," I whisper, staring at him with fatigue. "It felt good, and now I feel tired."

Exhaustion is plaguing me, but I don't know that magic is what drained me. The rage, the need for destruction, that dark calling, begging softly in my mind, pleading with me to unleash chaos, to bathe in blood... All of it has faded away and left me weak.

"Erac," I meet his gaze. "There was one who ran toward me, yelling."

"What?" he snarls, lurching toward me on stiff legs.

I shake my head again. "It is nothing. I thought it was strange. I thought they would all be afraid of me."

He puts his hands on his hips, feet spread. "Did you destroy him?"

I tilt my head. "I didn't say it was a man?"

Erac steps toward me, fire in his eyes. "Do not toy with me. Did you kill him?"

I take a step back as his face contorts. "I–I tried. One of the armored interfered."

He sneers. "You hesitated. I should have known there'd still be something left, even after I wiped you clean twice." He curls his lip at me, his voice raised and edged like the skin around an open wound. "I never should have trusted. Should have known better."

My skin crawls, my heart sinking. "Are you going to try again? To remove their poison?"

"No," he snaps. "Once is bad, twice is worse, and a third time…" He smirks with rancor. "A third time would likely shatter your mind. You'd be ruined. Maybe you'd recover how to speak, but you'd be almost a living marionette, your mind destroyed beyond repair. I am already surprised at how well you are recovering from a second clearing."

"Oh." I frown. "Who was that man?"

He grins at me. "One of the brothers that rotted your mind. Do you see now? The poison is still affecting you. You hesitated when you saw him, some remnants of loyalty."

My heart skips. "It was one of them?" My eyebrows crease together. "Why would I be loyal?"

"Because of what they did to you."

"But what did they—"

"Enough," he yells, stomping his foot and clenching his fists at his side as he leans forward. "The next time you see that man, you will kill him. Do you understand me? No more hesitating, no more questions!"

We stare at each other, then he dissolves into the air before my eyes. With his absence, I can breathe again, gasping gulps of air, hiccupping as I fall back against the wall. My body sags and slides to the floor, grains digging into my skin beneath my clothes as I am dragged down, reduced to an empty ball of flesh.

I lay there a long time before I can move. The world grows dark around me before I pick myself up off that cold stone.

When I do move, I go slow. I cannot shake the memory of the man rushing toward me with desperation. I wonder who he is, the tickle in the back of my head like a hair stuck to my shirt, whispering against my arm when I move that I cannot locate.

The idea that their poison is still in my veins leaves me filled with angst. My stomach twists in knots. An urge to split my own skin and dump my insides out to be rid of their contamination once and for all. If it is still there, inside of me, then Erac might try a third time to remove that toxin and leave me as a mindless object, a pretty doll.

I grip my fists and grit my teeth. *No. I will not allow Erac to destroy me.*

CHAPTER 19

DECLAN

When court is over, I walk through the halls of the palace. Several are blackened by fire with gouges in the stone walls left behind by demon claws, evidence of demons being in the palace from that night my mother slit my throat, and Ella was taken. Or maybe when my mother came to kill me yet again. I wonder about what happened that night while I laid incapacitated and bleeding out. The only things I know for sure are Chase died to save everyone and destroy the demons, Ella was taken, and I was a useless sack of flesh.

I grit my teeth, fury slithering through my veins, the voice in my head begging for me to let loose and sniff out blood to gorge on.

A spirit materializes in front of me, dropping an elemental I realize is Samuel at my feet. It kneels, breathing heavy, metal clinking. "Declan," the voice wheezes.

"Sordello?"

It shakes its hooded head. "Malik."

I put a hand on its shoulder, not sure if he can feel the touch. "What happened?"

"We made a few trips, the camp to Asperheim." He draws in

a deep breath and stands. My hand slides off his armor. "Erac and Ella attacked. They destroyed what we brought. We tried to save as many as we could. Sordello and Lerlie are still fighting, our two strongest in magic."

"Of course, Sordello's the strongest and her father." I kneel, lifting Samuel by his shoulder and rolling him to his back. There's blood on my hand when I pull back, the stench of it building in the air around me. "Fuck. He's hurt but alive."

I stand as two more spirits appear. "Which are you?"

"Sordello, my son, and Lerlie." He waves at the other.

"Can't you all wear different colored hoods or something?" I ask, irritated with not knowing one from the other. Not even the females are smaller than males. Maybe they don't all have a designated one or the other definition. I roll my shoulders and scowl at Sordello. "What the fuck happened?"

"Malik has told you of the events."

I grip my fists and breath out my nose. "Ella," I stress, "and Erac? They were together?"

"She fought against us. I held her off with Lerlie's help for as long as possible as the others transported your kind back whence we had come." He waves a hand. "We did not save everyone there, and everything else was destroyed. We concerned ourselves only with the living."

I bare my teeth. "Ella attacked you?"

"She did," Lerlie answers. The voice sounds female. "Along with the traitor. She killed many before we could react."

I run fingers and thumb of one hand into my closed eyes and rub until I see spots. "Fuck." I drop my hand to my side. "Fuck!" I scream. "Where—is everyone still alive back at camp?"

"Yes, I will take us there."

I motion at Samuel. "Get him to the infirmary before he bleeds to death."

I dissipate to the camp, finding a mass horde of angry elementals surrounding Seth. They are a deafening mob, and I try to push through to my brother before giving up and dissipating to his side. He glances at me with a pale face.

I nod and then roar for silence at the top of my lungs. Fennel and Talwarth step inside the ring to face me. They wear masks of fury, and I square off with them.

"You cost the lives of dozens!" Talwarth roars, wagging a finger in my face. "Good men, warriors, dead. This is your fault. Your war."

"*My*," I emphasize, "war? This isn't my war. This war isn't about me at all. This is about Viktor."

"This isn't about Viktor. This was about getting that murdering bitch you call wife."

I swing, my fist contacting the side of his face with the intention of breaking his jaw. I never want to hear him spew vulgar lies about Ella again, and if that means he can never speak again, then so be it. He hits the ground and Fennel leaps between us.

"Enough!" he screams. "You are king and a warrior. Show respect to your guild leader and your subject."

I snarl, showing teeth. "Then respect my wife."

"Your wife attacked the camp and killed who knows how many. Talwarth has every right to be upset."

"All the more reason we need to fight and take Ella back."

Seth elbows Fennel away from me. "We can't win a war against her."

Talwarth has not moved, not so much as stirred. I wonder if I killed him and nudge his body with the toe of my boot. "I took offense at Talwarth calling her a murderer."

"She is! She attacked our warriors in broad soul light without hesitation. She is working for Viktor."

"Against her will," I snap.

There are dull roars from the hoard around me.

"It didn't look that way."

"She didn't hesitate."

"She turned my brother to ash right next to me."

"She looked dead set on it."

"You didn't see her. See her eyes."

"Enough!" Seth screams. "All of you. Shut up. Now."

The crowd goes silent, and I smirk. "Didn't know you had it in you."

"You shut up too," he says in a snippy tone. "I think you just killed Talwarth. Ella clearly isn't in her right— Don't fucking say anything," he breaks off to warn the others. "Ella attacked me too, and anyone who knows anything at all would know that isn't her."

I turn to Seth, my mouth going dry, ears pulling back with horror. "She went after you?"

His face loses its color, and he shudders. "I went straight for her. I thought I could get her back. If one of the spirits hadn't gotten to me, I'd have been turned to ash with the others."

My hands grip into fists. The word fuck doesn't seem to carry enough weight to describe my feelings. I exhale and relax. I stare around at the contorted faces and silently curse Haven. There is no coming back from this for her. I can't fix this one. Worse, dozens more—whatever the real number—of our precious army are gone.

"Okay, we need a plan."

"We need a miracle," Seth mutters.

I scoff. "No, we need a better plan to get her."

"What?" Fennel yelps. "You're mad. She destroyed supplies, killed dozens."

"How many?" I ask, putting my hands on my hips. "How many did she kill? Do your job. Take inventory and a census. I want to know how many we lost."

There are disgruntled responses and mutters from the crowd. My eyes flick over their faces of malice. They are all ready and willing to call for Ella's head regardless of what has been done to her.

"This is war," I snarl. "This isn't going to be easy, and not everyone is going to survive. We have all lost friends and brothers before, sisters, hunters, and mages. We will again."

There are more comments made from fury and disgust. Three spirits materialize inside the ring of angry elementals. One places its armored hand on my shoulder.

I look to the spirits. One wears a black hood, and I realize the other is dark blue, the third with its hand on me is purple, the color of Ella's eyes. I nod. "Sordello?"

"Yes, son, we have taken your advice to wear colors. Not all may follow us, though." He drops his hand. "What would you have us do?"

"I don't know." I reach up and pinch the bridge of my nose. "I need to think."

His hood inclines. "I understand."

"A suggestion," Malik says, his deep voice recognizable from the black hood. "We cannot move your camp to Asperheim in such a visible place, if at all. Your kind is no match for Ella and Erac. We can barely manage them ourselves."

"Manage them?" someone from the crowd screams. "You have to kill them." There are similar supporting comments.

"No," I yell. "No one is killing Ella."

Talwarth stirs and sits up. He looks around, and Fennel kneels beside him. After a brief inspection, he glances up at me. "You'd still protect her life? If you defend her and will not kill her, then you stand by our enemy, one who has killed our brothers and sisters in arms. I'll see you executed as a traitor."

A snort through my nose answers him. "I'm not defending anyone but my wife."

Talwarth reacts with rage, features twisting, and a blotchy red splotch forms on his forehead. "Your wife is a murderer, a traitor, a monster who has defied the laws of this world and of this court. Now she stands against us. She'll be killed along with the others."

A laugh gurgles out of Seth. "You lot are welcome to try." I glare at him, and he snickers harder. "What? Like this lot—" he gestures around "—is capable of even coming close?"

I scowl and shake my head. "No, but letting them try is sending them to their death." I exhale and glance south over my shoulder. "We can't send the army to Asperheim, visible or not. I'll not waste their lives."

"Agreed." Malik steps forward. "Ella is far too powerful for us to contend with. There must be another way. Your army will dissolve to dust within a day if you bring them to her."

Sweat beads along my scalp. No one can stand against her and survive in a head-on fight. Any advantage I thought we had in the army is gone. I look to Seth, who looks like a kicked puppy who just wanted attention, and then back to Malik.

"We need to get her back."

"You've lost your mind." Talwarth takes a step toward me, his fists clenching.

I tilt my head and stare down my nose, ready for an attack. "Ella is a weapon. As long as Viktor has her, we have no hope of winning. If we can get her back, we can use her against Viktor and his demons."

Talwarth spits at my feet. "I'll never fight at her side."

"Yeah."

"No way."

"She needs to die."

My blood starts to boil. "Enough. None of you know what Viktor is capable of. None of you know what Viktor has done to her. She is under his control, acting against her own desires. I am king, and I have declared this, therefore it stands as truth."

"So be it." Fennel sneers, turns, and pushes through the crowd.

Talwarth eyes me. "We will see how long you are king. The warriors will not stand with you anymore." He turns to the crowd. "Your king has chosen the murdering bitch over you. He has turned his back on your life in exchange for a woman. Go, rest, lick your wounds. I will speak with the true queen."

The crowd begins to disperse with muttering. I watch them go with a knot in my stomach, twisting tighter like a noose around my neck. Talwarth turns back to me.

I stare back at him with fury snaking through me, my limbs starting to tremble. He gives me a cold smile, one side of his mouth curling back. "Remember this moment, King." He twists the title with malice. "You'll rot in a cell for treason until I bring you her head."

Seth moves, and I grab him, shoving him back. I face Talwarth, leaning in close and breathing fire under my breath. "Stay away from my wife, or she'll be hoisting *your* head."

Talwarth scoffs. "You're no king at all. Just a boy with a crown."

He walks away, and I glare after him, my hands gripped in fists tight enough to make my fingers tingle.

"That's fair," Seth mumbles. "You get to hit him, but I don't?"

I cut my eyes to Seth as he steps next to me, both of us watching Talwarth leave. "One of us accused of treason is bad enough. If I lose control of this, you need to take over."

There's the sound of a deep chuckle, and I glance to the spirits. The black hood of Malik sways side to side. "They do not know what they face in Ella and the traitor."

I frown. "But you do. You all do."

"Yes," Sordello crosses his arms. "We will evaluate the situation. Your army cannot face them, and we cannot go home until Viktor is dead."

"Wait, what? You're stuck here?" Seth lets a low whistle fly.

"Until we have completed the reason we were called upon, we will never see our home in Medius again," Lerlie says. She sounds melancholy. "Viktor must die. We accepted the call and so have bound ourselves in duty to do so."

"We will have to take the risk," Malik answers. "There is no other way."

"Our death will only increase their strength." Sordello drops his arms.

They all fall silent, hoods and figures shifting with muted metal clinks. Seth lifts his eyebrows. "Guess this is a collective thing. Seems a lot like a bond where they all have a conversation inside their head."

I nod and sigh. "Yeah, I haven't felt the collective yet, though."

"You are not at peace within and will be unable to do so until you are," Malik says. "You're as bad as Ella was when she first got her runes, an annoyance we will have to contend with."

Sordello's hood lifts and shifts in my direction. "You may wear our runes, but you are not truly a spirit until you are part of the collective. The runes will work for you, grant you their power, but not all of our gifts will be available to you until you are one of us."

I roll my shoulders. "Is Ella part of the collective? Can't you reach her?"

"No," Sordello answers me. "She has never achieved that state."

"So, if she does achieve that state, does she get more powerful?"

There is a long pause before Malik speaks. "Yes, but do not fear for this. Her love for you is stronger than anything they might do to her. We have all felt it, and until she is reunited with you, she will never gain the ability necessary to reach true peace."

I grip my fists and stare off into the distance. The spirits return to their internal discussions or maybe stand in silence for all I know. I kick at rocks, wanting to break something.

Seth grins. "As much as it sucks that Ella attacked us, it

might work out for the best. Maybe we don't need the army after all."

I roll my shoulders. "If the spirits fight, we have an army, but we won't need Byron."

"We're still fighting, though, right?"

I smirk. "Yes."

"Awesome," he chuckles. "This is going to be the coolest thing I've ever done."

CHAPTER 20

DECLAN

I sit in Marcus' study, holding the white queen chess piece in my hand, running my thumb over the nubs at the top, signifying her crown. I sip on bourbon and place the piece back on the board. I stare around the room with blurry eyes. Somewhere high over the palace, a bell rings seven times.

The night passed by in misery, locked in my own hell of replaying memories and getting little sleep. I know I need to sleep, I need a clear mind, but I can't get any real rest. All these things are eating away at my brain, every memory like a tiny maggot worming through tissue. It hurts. It makes me sick.

She promised.

Seth walks into the room. I stare up at him with my mouth open, trying to comprehend him.

He stops and screws up his face on one side. "You look as good as I feel."

I take a drink and set the empty glass on the chessboard with a clink. He steps closer and drops into the chair across the table. We stare at each other.

My brother eyes the glass. "Are you drunk?"

I lift and drop one shoulder. "I don't know."

He rubs his hands over his face and then up into his hair, grabbing at it and stretching his eyes open wide at me. "What's going on?"

"I spent all night tearing apart my room, trying to find something that used to belong to Ella."

"Did you find it?"

I shake my head in slow motion. "No."

"What were you looking for?"

"Anything at all."

He laughs. "Just go to her room then."

I bare my front teeth at Marcus' old desk. "I can't. Selene moved in."

Seth curls a lip. "That's gross."

One side of my mouth twitches. "She's redecorated, painted, burned everything of Ella's."

"Bitch."

I sigh and tip my head back against the chair, staring at the ceiling, my eyes switching in and out of focus. "I can't even smell her scent anymore. She's gone."

Seth sighs, and I listen to him pour two drinks. "Here." I pick my head up and see him offering me a full glass. "Just take it. Drink. I think I've got something somewhere of hers."

I bare my teeth at him as I accept the glass. He waves a hand and takes a drink. We sit in silence for a while.

"What are we doing?" he asks.

"Drinking, like you said to."

"About the war, Ell, this whole mess?"

"I don't know. The spirits are still deliberating." I shrug. "I don't know what to do next, and Selene said I have to recant my marriage, or she's going to strip me of the crown, so it might be out of our hands soon."

He groans. "What the hell is her problem?" He laughs in a bitter fashion. "You really made a monster."

I turn my head to face him, frowning even as he smirks at me. "What?"

"She sunk her teeth into you and the crown, everything Ell had when she was queen."

I twitch at his words. "What?" I repeat louder, a bit more awake.

He takes a drink, chuckling at me. "That thing I am not to mention, reference, imply? I'm talking about that."

I curse under my breath and drain my glass. "Selene has always been jealous, always wanted what Ella had, was—is always thinking she should have been the heir."

"She's got the crown now, and sure, she's trying to keep it, but she's coming straight for you too. You must be damn good. Maybe you can give me pointers."

The urge to throw up overcomes me. My stomach shoves bile into my throat, and I force myself to swallow the burning phlegm. "Figure it out yourself, little brother."

He shrugs, wiggling his eyebrows. "Maybe one day I'll get a chance to."

I stare at him in confusion. "What?"

"What, what?" He sighs and shakes his head.

I gape at him. "You aren't fucking serious?"

He shrugs again. "As serious as I can be." I roar with laughter, and he frowns. "What? Like you've had loads of women?"

I try to get myself under control but keep chuckling as I pour myself another drink. "Ella, Skylar, and I used to frequent brothels in my time away." He looks disgusted, and I sit back with my glass, grinning. "We need to get you laid."

"Oh, shut it," he mutters. "What are you going to do about Selene?"

"I'm not annulling my marriage if that's what you're asking."

He scoffs. "No kidding. Don't want you to. What else are you doing?"

"No idea," I say, still smirking at my brother's condition.

"We really need to find you a woman, though. I still remember where the brothels are."

"No," he says loudly. "Why the Damnatus didn't you just visit those instead of screwing Selene in the first place?"

That sobers me. I breathe out through my nose and stare at the bookshelves. "She was convenient, easy, and I didn't have to pay." I glance over at him. "I really thought Ella was dead." The words come out constricted and thick.

"Yeah, I know. We all did." He crosses his arms and leans them on the table facing me. "But she's alive, and she's with Viktor and that bastard Erac, so what are we doing about that?" He jabs a finger in the middle of the chessboard. "Right here, right now, what's done is done. What are we doing now?"

"Finding you a woman," I smirk.

He gives me an exasperated gape. "Dec, I am serious."

"Me too." I set my drink aside and get to my feet. I sway a bit as the alcohol hits me. "The spirits haven't made a decision about attacking Asperheim directly or indirectly or what they are doing now that we aren't fighting demons in an open field. I'm not recanting my marriage, so I'm done being king, and we have no idea how to get to Ella."

"Sit down," Seth groans. "I'm not having sex just to have sex, and I'm not going to one of your brothels. How much sleep have you gotten?"

"A couple of hours." I shrug, dropping back into the chair without needing encouragement. The room is spinning around me. "I can't do this." I breathe out and shut my eyes. The whirling gets worse, and I open my eyes to stare.

"If you don't, I will. I'm not giving up." There's heat in his words that draw my eyes to his. They sparkle black, and I lift my head to study his intensity.

"Fuck," I mutter, dropping my face into my hands and rubbing hard.

There's a knock on the door, and Samuel steps into the

room. "I thought we could set up headquarters here for now." He lifts his arms full of rolled parchment.

"That's a great idea," Seth says, moving to Marcus' desk. "Set everything here. Marc will be fine with—" He stops.

I drop my head between my knees and groan. "He's dead."

My brother sighs. "Yeah, so, I guess, it's fine. Yeah, let's set up here. You look good, Samuel. I was worried. Heard you were in the infirmary healing."

"Yeah, some flying debris almost took my arm off." He holds his arm out, rolling it as he presses fingers into the place where chest and arm meet. "Healers managed to let me keep it, so there's a silver lining."

I stand and pace as Seth and Samuel set up the maps. I'm doing laps around the room, feeling caged and helpless.

"Is there a problem, Dec—er, Your Majesty? Sorry, still getting used to that." He rubs the back of his neck and gives a sheepish grin.

I stop, cocking an eyebrow. "Do you think I give a fuck about that title?" He seems to tense. I cross my arms and roll to the balls of my feet. I swallow hard and look around, then drop flat-footed and eye him. "It's just a question. I don't fucking care about being king. I don't care what you call me, just help me kill Viktor and get Ella back."

Samuel's lips twitch, and he shoves his hands in his pockets. "Can I ask…?" he hesitates.

His eyes roll to mine. It makes me think of Ella, and I grit my teeth. "I am not going to cause bodily harm for asking a question."

"Haven, you already look pissed off."

"I am. I want Ella back. I'm going to be pissed until I get her back."

He takes a half step away. "What if you don't?"

"Then, everyone responsible is going to pay in blood."

He clears his throat and shifts his weight around. "The

things Selene has said about her, that she's a murderer and worked with Viktor all her life, basically helping him get to this point, and that she's been a thief, and has tortured elementals…" he trails off.

I take a deep breath and drop my hands to my hips. "She did it if that's what you're asking."

Samuel jerks his chin up, and his face contorts. "And you still love her?"

I let out a short bark of laughter. "I do. You've met her. You know how she is."

"I thought I did, but—"

"There's no but," I grind through clenched teeth. "You have no idea how she fought against it. You don't know that she was always missing because she was recovering from beatings that should have killed her when she made him mad or recovering from what she'd done. She hated it. She hated Viktor for it. She didn't want to do those things. He made her. She had no choice in them. I know it. I felt it, witnessed it through the bond. I knew what he'd done before anyone. Before he told her—"

"He told her he used his blood," Samuel whispers.

I sneer. "In the same breath he used to tell her he had me killed right after my funeral."

Samuel blanches, going white with shock. "Haven, that's cruel. She was devastated when you were declared dead."

Seth laughs. "That's Viktor. He was as awful to his children as he was to this land, and don't think for one fucking second Selene didn't do things for Viktor too. But she wasn't under his complete control, and she isn't fessing up. Marcus knew. He'd been taking care of his siblings and himself his whole life. He knew all the secrets."

"Sounds like you two do too." Samuel's face pulls in on itself. "So, who she pretended—or how she acted with me, us in class and… That's how she really is?"

"Yes. Ella has the best of intentions and hates to hurt

anyone, something Viktor tried hard to beat out of her growing up," Seth explains. "Haven, the things I saw her put through. We were just kids still."

My stomach twists at the memories I experienced through our bond. I breathe out slowly and cock my jaw. "Sam, she doesn't deserve what Selene's done. That bitch has gone out of her way to slander and destroy Ella in every way she can because she's only letting go of the crown if it's pried from her cold, dead fingers. It wasn't done for right and wrong. It was for power, and who is going to have it."

He steps next to the desk, fingers brushing over the map. He picks the king piece up we use to mark Viktor. "When she showed up half dead and bloody, I thought she'd gotten what she deserved."

A growl rumbles in the back of my throat, echoed by Seth.

Samuel sets the piece back down and meets my gaze. "But that was because she went after Viktor, wasn't it?"

I cross my arms. "Yes, she went after him."

"What happened to her that night?"

I shrug. "She went after him, and she lost. Going against Viktor, if you lose, it ends badly."

Seth hops on the desk. "She went to kill him. He cast some crazy magic so she couldn't control the elements and then forced her into a chess game. If she won… Well, she didn't and never mind. It ended badly."

Samuel gives us a confused look. "What was the game for?"

"It was bad enough that she lost and got the shit beat out of her, and that was the better option. Let's leave it at that."

Samuel's scowl deepens. "No. I want to know."

Seth stares at me with terror, but I shrug. "I don't know. I never got the chance to ask. I had all of five or six hours with her before everything went to hell again, and that wasn't what I was discussing."

"What was the game for?" Samuel repeats with venom. "Why won't you tell me?"

Seth stands and lays a hand on Samuel's shoulder. "Because it doesn't matter. She lost rather than joining Viktor."

"She played a game of chess on whether or not to join him?" Samuel gives me a skeptical look, then glares at Seth. "That's why she attacked us?"

"Er..." My brother looks to me like he needs help. "No, this is different. She lost the game, so she didn't join him."

Samuel cocks a stance, legs apart, hands on his hips. "What was it for then?"

Seth gives me a pleading look. "It doesn't matter what it was for. You've seen what happens if Viktor gets control of Ella. There's no price too high to pay—"

"What was it for?" he yells.

I grit my teeth, having an inkling of what Seth is trying to hide. I breathe out through my nose sharply. "Fuck."

Samuel glances at me. "You know."

"I have a guess, knowing Viktor and Ella."

"Tell me."

I shake my head. "No. Trust me, if Ella lost willingly, she did it with remorse and a whole ton of guilt."

"Why would she feel guilty if it was the right choice?"

Seth snorts through his nose and gets to his feet. "Because Viktor doesn't give anyone a right choice. He gives you the option to do what he wants or to lose. In this case, Ella chose to lose."

"But he has her anyway!" Samuel screams, his face blotchy red. "She's under his control now, so whatever choice she made, it wasn't worth it. What was the game for?"

I move to the desk and pick up the king piece. The white marble has red and black veins running through it. As I breathe in, I hang my head. "Viktor would use someone else against Ella, counting on her saving someone else rather than herself, and he would have used a friend, someone she cares about, to make it personal."

"Gemma," he says on an exhale of breath. "But Gemma turned her back on Ella after she learned the truth. They weren't friends anymore."

I set the king down and turn to face him. Denial is scrawled in his features. I shrug.

"That's worse." Seth sighs. "Viktor's twisted. He played that card, calling out Gemma's betrayal, trying to use it against Ella, to make her believe that everyone in this court that is calling for her death doesn't care about her, that she shouldn't want to protect them. He wanted her to give up and join him willingly."

"She should have," Samuel grinds out through clenched teeth. "If she would have joined him, Gemma would still be alive, and nothing would be different from now but that."

His words ring around the room, and I wince. He moves to storm out, and Seth grabs hold of him. "If you think for one second that Viktor would have let Gemma live, given her betrayal of Ella in the first place, you need to think twice. Viktor, for all his fucking madness, will do anything to protect Ella. He sees her as his daughter."

Samuel tries to rip free, and Seth lets go of him. "You don't know that. You just won't admit Ella is a monster." His eyes dart between my brother and me. "You two are sick. You can't see what is right in front of you, the forest through the trees. Ella let Gemma die to save herself."

"She got the life beat out of her," Seth yelps with laughter.

"But she's alive, and Gemma's not."

I snatch the king off the desk and hurl it at Samuel's head. Damn his shade reflexes because he manages to duck out of the way. It hits the wall and snaps in half as it falls to the floor. "Viktor won't ever kill her no matter what she refuses to do for him," I growl. "He'll just hurt her until she does it."

He stands and glowers at me. "Maybe he won't kill her, but

he should. Someone should. She deserves to die, and I hope to Haven that he is hurting her, over and over, and so bad she can't take it, begging for death."

He turns on his heels and storms out of the library. I turn to Seth, who snarls with silent ferocity. "That's going to be a problem," I tell him. I scrub a hand down my face and stare at him, trying to sober up.

"Everything's a problem," he says in his stupid, cheerful voice.

CHAPTER 21

MORELLA

I have a sense something is out of place, a nagging in the back of my mind that my world is off-kilter. Staring down toward the beach, I watch a dragon play over the crystal green waters, rolling through the air and dragging the tips of wings through the water, leaving white foam streaks across the surface. It seems happy, carefree.

There are so many questions in my mind. I need a distraction. I need answers.

I stalk to the door and stick my head through, barking orders at the men waiting there. "Find the servant boy George and bring him here." I pull back inside and then lean out, whispering to the guard as I eye the demons across the way. "Please, I just want to talk."

~

I sit next to George, licking an ice cream cone in the gardens. It was his idea, not mine. I question giving the boy sugar. He says we did this before, and sometimes doing something again will bring back memories. I think the kid might be stupid but agreed, anyway. I do not have any better ideas, and desperation is taking hold.

The soul star overhead is burning bright white, and the warmth feels blissful against my skin. I close my eyes and stretch my neck as cold, sugary vanilla melts on my tongue. My fingers run down one side of the rope-like tendons, pushing on aching muscles as I relish in the heat and flavor.

A grunt and a heavy puff of air expelled in a snort draw my eyes open. I drop my free hand, lift the ice cream cone to my lips, and glare at the demon. Massive horns sprout from its head, and its wide-set yellow eyes stare back.

"Why are the horns black and the tusks white," George asks, eyeing the demon across from us.

I cut my eyes to him, then back to the demon. "Why does it have bristles like hair? Why is it red?" I smile at George. "Why are your teeth white and your hair black?" I reach out and ruffle the strands.

He leans away, glowering at me, and licks his cone. "I'm not a kid. You can't do that anymore."

"Yes, I can. I just did." I reach out, but he's quick, standing and dodging my reach, skipping back a few paces. I chuckle and drag at the frozen crystals that taste wonderful against my tongue. A shadow passes over us, and we both glance up at the dragon flying overhead. "I wish I could see one up close," I confess under my breath.

"You have," George says, and I raise my eyebrows at him. He shrugs. "You've seen one. You got invited to the Red Crosse Keep and got an inking. There's always a dragon involved with that. You just don't remember." He twists his lips to the side and studies me with narrowed eyes. "Why don't you remember anything?"

I incline my head and give him a look. "Poison, George. I had my mind poisoned, and my father and Erac saved me by taking everything out of my mind, which means my memories too." I hold up my right forearm with the row of pink scars from my wrist to the crease of my elbow. "See? That's how they got it out of me."

George mashes the rest of his ice cream into his mouth and chucks the cone over the hedge wall. I cock my jaw to the side, but he shrugs. "Something will eat it," he says through a mouthful of frozen deliciousness. Melted chocolate is dripping from the corners of his lips. He gets the blob down his throat and wipes his hands on the front of his robe. "Can I see?"

I hold my arm out, and he grabs it in clammy palms. He stares at the marks, pulling my skin close enough to his face that I can feel the moist warmth of his breath. A little shiver runs down my spine, but I smile at him when he looks up. He releases my arm, and I cross it over my stomach as if I could shield it.

I take a final lick of my ice cream and then bite into the cone. "What do you think?"

He shrugs, hands in his pockets, and kicking at the ground. "That's weird." He lifts his head. "You're weird, you know that? Every time I see you, you're a new kind of weird."

I raise my eyebrows. "That is not polite, George." I give him a warning with an edge to my tone and stern expression. "I expect an apology."

He shrugs. "You never used to care about that. You were really nice, even to servants, saying please and thank you all the time."

"I am nice by being polite." I narrow my eyes. "Now, apologize."

He snaps upright. "I apologize," he says in a flat tone. His eyes grow wide. "What? How did you…?"

I tilt my head, batting my eyelashes. "Magic," I say with a smile, but I have no clue. I can surmise the boy did not intend to refute his words, and somehow my command forced him to. I don't want to alarm him, though. He is my only link to who I was before. At least, the only link willing to answer my questions.

He narrows his eyes. "Must be that control rune."

I cock my head, moving my ear toward him. "What rune?"

"The control rune, on your forearm," he says in the disbelieving tone of a child who wants candy and knows I have it, despite being told otherwise. "The rune you got when you were here the first time." He groans, watching me expectantly as if I'll have an epiphany and remember something.

He sighs, rolls his eyes, and huffs as he sits down on my left side. He points to my heavily marred left arm with flourishing black lines. "I don't know which lines they are 'cause you have too many now, but the last time you were here, you went to the Red Crosse keep and met with the monks for an inking. Dad took you, said you were the only noble who managed the hike. Most give up, or complain, or stop a thousand times." George gives me a disgusted look, his eyes rolling up to the sky with a huff.

"Anyway," he says drawing the word out, "it was right before you left. You showed me the rune after breakfast when you told me you were leaving. Said it was going to free you from your father, and you could go home now. You could face him, move on, or whatever."

I glance at the demon who is watching over me, never far from reach. They have names, apparently, and you can tell males and females apart from their horns, but they all look the same to me. Leaning toward George, I whisper, "What do you mean about being free?"

George leans back, eyes on the demon as well, but he keeps his voice low. "All I remember is you said you couldn't go home and face your father, couldn't take the things he asked you to do. You said you didn't have a choice in them, and it made you sick inside, but with that rune, you could."

"Tell me," I beg. "Tell me about before, about me, about my

husband-to-be. Did you figure out his name? About an inking—Tell me all about all of it. I want to know—to remember."

He clears his throat. "And that's why dragons stay in the south. The sands are where they like to nest. It helps them stay warm," he says, bellowing in my ear.

I bolt upright, putting a finger in my ear and wiggling it, glaring at him. I shift my gaze beyond George to see both my father and his coming toward us. I smile at them and nudge George's foot with mine.

Standing, I smooth wrinkling from my shimmering gold dress, the lightweight fabric a loose-fitting fashion with a plunging neckline and open back to cope with the heat. "Hello, Father," I beam at him. I incline my head. "Pedro."

Pedro is a fat man, sweat beading up on his brow and his ruddy cheeks working double-time as he pants in the afternoon heat. "Majesty," he mumbles breathless as he tries to touch his nose to the ground in a generous bow.

I turn to my father. "What a pleasant surprise to find you in the gardens."

Viktor stares at me, his thin lips curling together in a closed smile. He runs a hand over his bare scalp, eyeing the watch on his other wrist. "Yes, my daughter, all creatures need fresh air from time to time." He drops both hands to his side. "Should you not be with Erac? You have much to learn yet. I need you to complete your training. I have use of you."

A bead of sweat rolls down my spine. The words echo in my mind, and my eyes cut to George. I roll my shoulders back and stand tall, giving my father a closed-lip smile to mirror his own. "Of course. I lost track of time. How foolish of me?" I try to chortle, laughing away the error.

My father fixates on George. "Why did you not perform your duty? You are a servant, here to keep my daughter on schedule. That is the only reason you exist in this world." His tone is scathing.

"Father, hardly," I say, frowning at him and glancing at George. "He's just a kid."

George looks to me, and then the ground. He mumbles an apology, toeing at the gravel along the path. He lifts his head and stares back at my father. "It won't happen again, Majesty."

My father's green eyes sparkle in the light with malice. "You are right about that, boy. Your failing will be reprimanded."

"Father," I say with a forced smile, placing a hand on George's shoulder. "George and I were—"

"Silence." There is fury carved in the lines around my father's mouth and the way his eyes stare me down. "You are late and growing later. We do not tolerate behavior like this, Morella. Now go."

I let my hand fall away from George. I meet his eyes, moving on to his father, who has gone a bit pale, and smile at Viktor again. "Of course, Father."

I turn away, gathering my skirt in my hands. I close my eyes and inhale deeply through my nose. I picture the library, pulling myself apart to reassemble there. I open my eyes, looking up as I stand in the middle of the room, beneath decoratively cast metal squares, each one depicting dragons and magic.

This room could be my tomb, and I'd die grateful to waste away locked inside, forever trying to decipher the tiles, reading the stories they tell. I inhale, swelling up and searching the space for Erac.

"Hello?" My voice carries through empty air and dies against stationary shelves. I raise my voice. "Erac?"

"You're late."

I turn on my heels to face him. He stands behind me, violet eyes clear and fixated on me. They flicker, scanning down my body before returning to mine. He reaches out, snaking an arm around my waist, and pulls me against him.

His nose finds my neck, and he inhales as he drags the tip up to the hollow where my jaw and ear meet. "You are absolutely breathtaking."

I stay malleable in his arm and close my eyes, waiting. "I'm sorry I was late."

"I was worried," he whispers against me, his lips brushing over the thin skin.

My body shudders, and I tense up to fight the reaction. "I didn't mean to worry you." I resist the urge to step back. "I don't know why you insist on worrying over me. It's not like anyone can get to me here or that anyone can hurt me."

He smiles. I can feel the expression on his face. "Yes, my love, you are powerful, but not invincible."

He pulls back, and I let out a breath I didn't realize I was holding. Despite the tenderness he shows, I cannot forget my very first memory. He develops rage without warning, his soft disposition changing in the blink of an eye, and I woke up in agony with dark bruises around my wrists. I shudder.

"Are you cold, love," he asks in a soft, low voice, brushing his hand beneath the edge of my hair and over my shoulder. "You do look lovely, but perhaps you should wear more." He trails fingers down my sternum, and my body twitches of its own accord.

I purse my lips and turn them up. "I was out in the gardens with George. We were eating ice cream under the soul star, and I lost track of time."

"I want you to wear more, cover yourself." He grips my shoulders firmly, but not enough to cause pain. "And I want you to stop spending time with George. He is a servant, beneath you, and he's always sneaking about. I question if he is up to no good."

I tip my head back and shake with mirth. "Dear, you cannot be serious. The boy is a child, twelve, thirteen, maybe? What could he possibly be doing other than shirking his duties?"

Erac shakes his head, hands tightening. "I mean it, Morella. I do not want you to speak with him again."

I frown at him. "He's nice to me."

"Everyone is nice to you," Erac tells me in a terse voice. He gives me an exhausted glare. "They have no choice in it, and if someone mistreats you, you will tell me, and I will deal with it. Yes?" He bobs his head, running a thumb over my cheek, staring into my eyes.

I sigh as he pulls me against him again. "I know everyone has manners and is nice." I twist the word, rolling my eyes. "But George is different, he isn't afraid of me, and he knew me, before, from before I—"

"Morella, stop," Erac snaps, jerking a step back, grabbing my upper arms in a grip hard enough to bruise. He glares from beneath drawn brows with a hard-set mouth. He jerks me back and forward a few times. "Listen to me. You are not going to see George again, and if you do, you will ignore him."

I frown. "Why?"

"If he tells you things from before, if you keep asking questions, it's going to hurt you. Trying to get old memories, learning things, it could damage the magic we used to block the poison."

"I thought you removed the poison? That's why you took my memories. You took everything."

"Yes, we did, but we couldn't remove it all."

"So, what if I get some of my memories back?"

"Morella," he groans. "Stop." The word comes out as a hoarse roar. "Stop asking questions. Stop making problems. I literally pulled the memories from your mind, like ripping muscles from your arm. It's damaged, still healing, and no good will come from learning of the past."

"What are you hiding from me?" The words are a thought unformed, whispering past my lips as a subconscious ghost.

He jerks back as if I slapped him. His fingers dig into my

flesh, nails cutting the skin, leaving a burning sensation beneath his grip. "Morella."

"What are you hiding from me?" I ask louder, shoving at his chest.

He reaches out, taking both my wrists in hand and wrenching them, twisting them outward. "This is for your own good. Everything I have done, what I am doing is to keep you safe. Wiping your mind again could be catastrophic."

"I want answers. I want to know what happened to me." His hands squeeze, and I gasp with pain. I lower my voice, letting him see the tears forming in my eyes. "I just want to know, to stop asking so many questions. I don't understand. I don't... I can't remember anything, and I feel like I'm going crazy. I can't... I need to know. I have so many questions, and my mind feels so empty and too full. Please. I just... I can't take this anymore," I whisper and add a sniffle at the end. I stop, blinking, glad when a single tear is pushed out and down my cheek.

His grip and face soften, and he pulls me in close against him. I press my face against his chest, and he gives me a gentle squeeze, wrapping me in his arms. "Please don't cry. I understand, my love, but this is for the best, yes?" He leans his torso away from mine, peeking down at my face. I look up at him and blink again. He gives me a tender smile, the skin around his eyes crinkling. "Yes," he says, wrapping me tightly in his arms again, then proceeds to sway us, rocking me calmly.

I let my eyes close, and the motion lulls me into relaxation. I inhale deeply through my nose and slowly out through my mouth. I turn my face to the side, staring at the books. So many stories. I want to read them all.

How many of them are lies too? The voice is a silky whisper.

I am reminded there is still poison in my mind, that voice in my head speaking to me. I have not dared to tell Erac or my father, fearful of what they may do to me. The voice is not an internal reason, far from it. It must be remnants of the poison, what they could not root out.

I pull away, stepping back and clearing my throat to recompose myself. "Are we going to have a lesson today?"

He watches me, reaching out a hand to rest on my hip. "If, and only if," he says with a smile, "you feel up to the challenge, my love. I do not wish to push you too hard."

I give a genuine smile. "I don't think magic is ever going to be too much for me." I hold a hand out, twisting it this way and that, watching flames dance in the air above my movements. "I love this feeling when I control the elements, a kind of warm hum through my veins, almost like my body is purring." I laugh at myself and extinguish the flames, facing him.

He is watching me with adoration, a smile toying with his lips, tugging on the ends. I watch them twitch, then lift my eyes to his. "You are incredible," he whispers, leaning closer, eyes dropping to my lips.

I grin, swatting at the air between us and stepping back. "Well, come on then, what are you teaching me today?" I put my hands on my hips and strike a pose. "You've taught me the basics, how to control the elements. The slightly more advanced, controlling the elements to control something else. What now?"

"Would you like to know how to wield magic to protect yourself?"

I drop my stance and stand upright, beaming and clapping my hands together rapidly. "Really?" I squeal with excitement, biting my tongue between my teeth and hopping in place. "Really, really?"

He laughs, stepping forward to take my hands between his and cease the clapping. "Really, really, my love."

With excitement, I shove thoughts of lies and whispers to the back of my mind and focus on Erac. At times like this, I can see why I fell in love with him. The way he speaks of magic and wields the elements without effort is breathtaking.

He walks me through several steps of twisting my hands and forcing the elements to change. Passion burns in his gaze as he stares at me, explaining magic, and I stare back, wondering if this is how we fell in love the first time around.

You've never loved him and never will.

I falter in the way I twist my hands and build elements together as energy. The spell slips from my control, bursting with an ear-splitting screech and shattering the air around us to dust. I cough, spluttering and sitting up, waving a hand in front of my face, peering through ash glittering in the air.

Erac kneels next to me, eyebrows and mouth drawn together. "My love?"

I reach out, putting a hand in his, and allow him to draw me to my feet. I stare around us. Nothing is worse for wear. I meet his gaze and wince. "Sorry."

His lips twist to the side. "Perhaps we should reconsider where you practice." He brushes hair behind my ear. "I'd hate for you to ruin the library."

I glance around. "What did I do?"

He shrugs. "Froze the air and shattered it. If you can master the spell and keep the elements under control, you can create copious damage." He frowns, his head tilting to the side. "It is unusual for you to lose control. What broke your concentration?"

I give him a closed-lip smile and squeeze his hand. "You didn't tell me what we were doing, just what to do." I let my lips peel apart and show him my teeth, keeping eye contact. "I got a little too excited to see what was going to happen."

He hums, brushing fingers down my arm. "I will be more thorough in explaining what we are doing from now on."

I nod, letting go of his hand. I turn away, taking a deep breath with my back against him, and stare with wide eyes at nothing. The voice is increasing, a nasty tone I cannot control. I may have to confess to Erac soon, even as I loathe the idea of being wiped clean again.

"My love?"

I turn, grinning as much as I can force myself to. "The beach, perhaps? To continue?"

He nods, offering me a hand. "I think it prudent. You will be devastated to destroy all these books," he teases, "and I'd hate for you to be upset and sulk through dinner this evening."

CHAPTER 22

DECLAN

I stare across the table, the unfinished game between Marcus and I still littering the checkered squares. I remember watching Marcus study the chessboard so many nights. He's been my voice of reason for revolutions, and I'm adrift without him now.

Lifting the crystal tumbler to my lips, I take a sip of whiskey. The tang burns across my lips and stings through my nose as I exhale. My friend, a second brother, and I killed him. His face is stuck in my head, his last words a curse ringing in my ears. I groan, draining my glass.

On the couch, at the far end of the room, Seth is trying to convince Legia to eat something. My brother coaxing her with a low voice, almost begging. Legia keeps sniffling, a sound grating on my nerves. I lift the glass for another drink and pause, eyeing the door as someone knocks.

My eyes lock with Seth, and he sighs, pushing up and shuffling to the door. The door swings inward as he opens it, and his shoulders roll back, his posture stiffening. "Not now. What do you want?"

My ears pull back as a familiar voice pushes past him into the room. “May I come in?”

The skin on the bridge of my nose wrinkles with disgust, and I try to drain my glass. “Let him in.”

Seth steps to the side, and King Marx waltzes inside, an unfamiliar woman trailing behind him. I watch the way she moves, head held high, dark eyes surveying the room. I cock a brow at her as she meets my gaze and gives me a dazzling smile.

Marx comes to a stop, and the woman stays at his shoulder. “Declan, my boy, how are you?”

I glare at him. He grins back, his face and scalp shaved bare. His eyes fixate on me, blue eyes I have an urge to dig out with my fingers every time I see them.

I clench my fists. “Why are you here?”

Seth crosses his arms and glares. “Yeah, why? Because the way I see it, we don’t owe you a thing.”

I question if I should have told my brother the truth about Marx. I didn’t give him the full details, but I did at least fess up to who put the bearings in me from all his pestering.

Marx steps to the side and indicates the woman. “May I introduce you to my daughter and heir, Asena?”

Shrugging, I settle back in the chair. “Sure.”

The woman grins at me. “It is a pleasure to meet you as well, Mr. Bard.”

“Byron,” I say, one side of my face wincing. My voice is constricted around the name.

“Of course, my apologies.” She nods, wrapping her arms across her middle. “My father was present for your vows and did mention them to me. It slipped my mind among everything else.”

Seth laughs. “Hardly blame you there. It’s not like that’s the biggest news you’ve heard lately, I’m sure.”

My face twists with disgusted shock as my head rotates to

him. His gaze is pegged straight ahead on Asena, a big, dumb, goofy grin plastered across his face. I blink and let my features return to normal as I turn back to her.

"It's fine," I say, trying to take a drink from my empty glass. I curse under my breath.

"I'm Seth," my brother says, stepping forward and giving a bow. "Dec's brother."

Asena's large, dark eyes are wide-set, and they roam down to his toes, one of her thick black eyebrows lifting ever so slightly. "And you are his *little* brother?"

"He's bigger than me," I snap, "but I'll still beat his ass in a fight."

"Well, I mean," my brother breaks off with a laugh, "I'm still bigger and stronger." He's grinning like a lunatic.

I shift my gaze back to Asena. She's pretty, with golden-brown skin and thick, shining dark hair that matches the dark brown of her eyes and hangs loose about a face with bold features. Smirking, I sit up and reach for the decanter.

The glass clinks in the silence, and I stand, taking my drink with me. My eyes return to Marx, a man I should never have taken my sights off. He winks at me, and I bare my teeth. "What are you doing here?" I ask again.

Marx chuckles. "I see we still haven't moved past things. May I remind you of the consequences my actions wrought?"

"You can fuck right off," I snap. "What are you doing in my court? The Clemm court has maintained plausible deniability and neutrality in this mess, and yet you continue to pop up here."

Marx crosses his arms, muscles bulging. For a fae, he has strength, but I could still beat him to a bloody pulp. The only reason I don't are the inevitable questions like why I killed the King of Clemm, why I felt it necessary to rip his limbs off and keep his skull as a trophy. I cross my arms and stare him down.

Asena clears her throat as she puts a hand on her father's shoulder. She's as tall as he is, stepping next to him. "I understand you and my father may not see eye to eye."

A laugh bursts out of my brother, and he throws an arm around my shoulders. "That's one way to put it, sweetheart."

"You'll excuse us if we don't act impulsively," she says in a quiet voice.

"I am playing the long game, I am afraid." Marx reaches up, pulling from the air a starch-white envelope, which appears in his hand. "One that alludes to benefits." He offers it to me.

I snatch it, the parchment thick and crumbling beneath my fingers. Downing the contents of my glass, I toss it aside, letting it skitter across the surface of the table and snap against the marble chessboard. I stare down at the broken wax seal, a king piece stamped in a blood-red circle. I tear the card from inside, flipping it over as my eyes scour the flourished scrawl.

Seth reads over my shoulder, the proximity and position making my closest shoulder drop and twitch. "It's an invitation to meet," he says with disbelief. He nabs the card from my fingers, bringing it closer to his face.

"Yes." Marx inclines his head. "One I received from an old friend, an attempted seduction to surrender."

"That's gross," Legia's soft voice carries through the air.

I glance over at her. From here, I can see the red in her eyes and nose, the way she curls in on herself, hunched over and arms wrapping around her stomach. When our eyes meet, she drops her gaze to the untouched food in front of her.

Turning back to Marx, I cross my arms. "I'm going to ask again. Why are you here?"

Marx's face drops the smile, and I'm reminded of how brilliant, methodical, and evil he can be. His lips twist. "This is a game of chess. I need to be sure of where all the pieces are on my board."

"To hell with that," I snarl. "You're not playing chess with thousands of lives."

Marx chuckles. "Of course, it's a game of chess. You're playing with Viktor."

I scowl but drop my arms. As much as I hate to admit it, Marx is right. Reaching up, I pinch the bridge of my nose as I sigh out my nostrils. "Fine. We can work together."

"Hang on," Seth cuts in. "You're not serious? You can't be. Not after…" he trails off as my eyes meet his. We stare at each other, and his face screws up on one side.

"After what?" Asena asks. "After we didn't come to help Byron the moment you declared war on Viktor? We've done nothing to show a stance against you."

I face her, scoffing and watching her wide eyes flicker between Seth, her father, and me. Shifting my gaze, I eye Marx. "She doesn't know?"

He shakes his head. "While everyone seems to have the need to compare Viktor and me, let me add another difference. I do not embroil my daughter in my plans. She is a young woman with the right to her own life." There's a warning in his voice for me to not push the issue.

I smirk and shake my head. "Fine. I don't need everyone in Caleum knowing anyway."

"Knowing what?" Asena snaps. There's a quiet fury to her expression.

"That your father's an ass," Seth says with a smile. "That he hates being compared to Viktor, but really, they're a lot alike."

Asena pivots, staring down my brother.

He wiggles his eyebrows at her. "Can we move this along?"

"No," Asena says. "I want to know what is being discussed. Father," she turns to face him, so her back is to me. "I deserve to know if this is going to complicate things."

Marx contemplates her, and I reclaim my seat. I snort through my nose into my glass as I take a drink. "Marx interfered with Viktor and my mother's plan to have me killed. Instead, he kept me away from Byron for his personal use."

Asena pivots on her heels to face me, hands on her wide hips. She's not lean and thin like Ella but has an hourglass shape with full curves. "What are you talking about?"

"The time Dec was thought dead?" Seth asks, lifting his eyebrows.

She glances at him and then fixates eyes dark with intensity on me again. I stare back until she swings her body back to her father. "What did you do?"

"Declan was to be killed by a group of mercenaries. I paid to have him delivered to me instead, thinking I could use him as leverage against Viktor. Alas," he begins, running a hand over his scalp, "the information wasn't what I thought, so I found another use for him."

Asena throws her hands in the air. "You had him that whole time? Haven, Dad, he was supposed to be the next king of Byron."

Marx chuckles. "Yes, and everything worked itself out. I didn't interfere with his return. I even tipped off the Gammet brothers to the magic I used."

My ears perk up. "That's how they knew?"

He fixates on me. "Yes. I wrote a letter to them after I heard they were being called upon to assist in the matter of your identity. Anonymously, of course."

"I just thought they were smart," Seth mutters. "Figures. Guess they aren't that smart."

I shake my head. "Yeah, I'm starting to wonder about that."

"No wonder you don't want our help," Asena says. She collects her hair and drops all of it over one shoulder. "Nonetheless, we should work together on this."

Seth laughs. "We're doing fine on our own."

My eyes flicker to him with a raised eyebrow. "What world are you living in?"

"Come on." He shakes his head. "We don't need their help. We can't even trust them."

"We can give a bit," I say. "He's never going to give up his crown to Viktor. It's the one thing we can count on."

Marx chuckles, stepping forward and taking the seat across from me. He shifts and gets comfortable, eyeing the board. He turns to Seth. "You were going to lose."

My brother gapes. "What?"

"The game." Marx indicates the board. "You were playing, yes?"

"No," I say, my throat getting thick again. "It's an old game."

Sitting back, Marx meets my eyes. "I see. The eldest boy, Marcus, wasn't it? This was his personal library, a gift from Viktor when he turned sixteen." His gaze sweeps around the room.

I scrub a hand down my face. "How do you even know that?"

He rests bent elbows on the armrests and frowns. He lifts his hands, fingers pressing together. "Let's see what I know. You tried to get Ella back and died for your troubles, which means the bond is broken. You were thought dead without a drop of blood in you and staged with a flare of the dramatic, which means Erac likely is the culprit, not Viktor."

I grunt, kicking my leg up on the table's support pole. "He's a mage with spirit runes and revolutions of practice controlling the elements. I got my ass kicked if you really want to know."

Marx smiles with closed lips. "Yes, I imagine, but you didn't stay dead, which means you have a set of spirit runes."

"I do," I say, on edge. The bastard was after a set, and I'm not comfortable admitting to him that I have one. He knows how to remove runes and can perform the magic. "I took my mother's head off for them."

"Interesting," Marx muses. "So you killed your mother? I wasn't aware of that. However, the bond could have been useful, and you're no match for Erac even if he can't control you, so your actions were rather stupid. I thought I taught you better?"

I exhale through my nose and glare at him, not responding.

He laughs and drops his hands. "You're losing your support around Byron as king after Ella attacked your troops but also because the ones willing to fight and support are dropping dead like flies. Then there's the matter of Selene's interest in you, and she's very interested. I wonder about your brief engagement to her…" He trails off with a light air of humor.

"Fuck off," I mutter, my eyes dropping to the unfinished chess game.

Seth roars with laughter. "Yeah, it's what you think."

"Shut up," I yell at him. "Just shut up for once."

Marx's blue eyes are dancing, but he doesn't laugh. "She's trying to make you recant your marriage, which I'm presuming you'll refute."

"I am."

"So, you're on the edge of losing the crown, still have no hope of getting Ella back, and you're losing the open war on the battlefields. How am I doing?"

I cock my jaw off to the side and glare. He's right, and he knows it. I'm not going to pat him on the head for it.

He chuckles and turns away. "Marcus, as I understood it, was rather involved with his family, yes?"

"Sure was," Seth chirps up. "He always knew what was going on with Ell, helped her out when he could, and I know Selene would go to him for help when we were engaged."

Marx nods, getting up to wander behind Marcus' old desk. He shuffles papers around, then stops and lifts his gaze to me. "Did he keep journals?"

My eyes move to the desk, recalling the way he would sit and write for hours. "Yeah."

Marx nods, then turns to his daughter, giving a forced smile.

"Your mother and I were good friends, but she was not my first love."

Asena looks a bit shocked.

"When I was younger," he stops and shakes his head, "the fall out between Viktor and me was complicated, but a large part was Chloe. When I met her, she was the heir to Byron, not yet queen, and although I intended to ask for her hand, Viktor became engaged to her first."

"That sucks," Seth mutters darkly. I curl my lip at him.

"You would know the experience," Marx answers, lips twisting with cruelty. "At least it wasn't to my own brother."

"No," Seth snaps. "I never intended to ask Ell to marry me. I never thought I'd marry her, and we never had that kind of relationship." He turns his gaze to me.

I smirk. "You wanted to."

He makes a face of annoyance. "Maybe, but that's all in the past. I'm not in love with her anymore." I tilt my head and narrow my eyes at my brother. He stands his ground, eyes not wavering from mine. "I'm serious, Dec."

I sigh through my nose. "You two have a thing. I hate it, but I try not to punch you in the face when it comes up, so it's fine."

"We don't have a thing," he insists. "Really, we're friends."

There's a broken laugh, and we all turn to Legia. She walks on shaky legs and then drops in the chair opposite of me. "No, Ella and I are friends. You two are something else."

I press my lips together and turn to Marx. "The point of this?"

He is inspecting the bookshelf behind the desk, hands clasped behind his back. At my words, he turns, almost surprised. "When Chloe died, I didn't trust it. She had been writing to me, re-establishing our relationship. She was afraid of Viktor; she said as much in her last letter. I brought my own shaman to examine the body, paid off servants." He waves a hand. "Her death was ruled as natural to the court, but the truth is she was poisoned."

Asena gasps. "What? The Queen of Byron was murdered?"

I shrug, settling back. "That's hardly surprising."

"Yes," Marx says, his voice oddly subdued. "I wonder if Marcus kept records of everything? Judging by his desk, he was fond of doing just that."

Seth shrugs. "Great. The queen was murdered. Who cares? This doesn't help us."

"Ella wasn't here when the queen died," Legia says. She sniffs and runs fingers beneath her eyes. "She came back for the funeral."

"Precisely," Marx says, nodding. "Smart girl."

My eyes widen. "You think one of the others did it?"

Seth lets out a low whistle. "I didn't know the others were involved."

"If we can find journals or records kept—if Marcus was as involved as I've always suspected, perhaps we can help you keep the crown."

I cross my arms. "Why are you helping? And why is she here?" I jerk my chin at Asena.

Marx eyes his daughter with a melancholy gaze. "I brought her here because the worst place for her to be is in Clemm. Viktor will use anything he can to try and take my crown. She's part of this, as much as I detest to admit that. Viktor knows she'll be a pressure point for me."

I gaze at her, watching her shift, uncomfortable in her skin. "Anywhere near me, Seth, or her," I jerk my head at Legia, "isn't safe either. Probably not with you too."

"I am aware, dear boy, I am aware. But she needs to know what she is up against. She needs to get to know you three in case…" He stops, frowning down.

Asena moves around the desk to give him a hug. "It's okay,

Dad. I promise if something happens to you, I won't give him Clemm."

Marx's lips pull back in a forced smile, and he kisses the top of her head. "I detest the idea of you having to deal with this. This is far too personal between Viktor and me for you to be anywhere near this situation." He clears his throat and directs his attention to me. "And I am here because the last thing in the world I am going to do is hand over Caleum to Viktor or let anyone else do it. Now, are you going to help me find Marcus' notes?"

CHAPTER 23

DECLAN

I spent all yesterday talking. I think my throat is about to come apart, but at least there's a new plan. At least, a plan to keep me king. The spirits haven't delivered a verdict yet, so until then, this is the course of action.

I'm done talking for now, and without fighting demons, I need another way to let out my pent up rage before I give in to blood lust, so I head for the practice field. I start with hand to hand combat, moving slow, building up the pace until my muscles are warm and my blood is pumping. I step and jab, step, and swing harder. The post cracks, and I keep whacking it until it breaks.

I move to the sandstone wall, pummeling my fists against it, welcoming the radiating pain through knuckles and up to my elbows until I am breathing hard. I stop, inspecting my bloody hands, feeling the bones in my wrist fill with healing warmth. I work them in circles, rubbing my forearms as my flesh mends.

"Excuse me, Sir. Your Majesty."

I glance over at a young dryad. Her green hair hangs in a thick braid over her shoulder. It reminds me of Ella, and I punch the wall again. "What?"

"You've been summoned to court, Your Majesty."

I sigh and stare at the cracked stone. "Thanks."

I catch sight of a curtsy in my peripheral vision and watch her skip away. Someone should do something about children being used as servants. I don't mind ripping apart another adult, but something about kids gets to me. I close my eyes and pinch the bridge of my nose.

Maybe when this is over, I can channel my inner Ella. Fuck that. Ella can fix it herself when she is queen again.

I dissipate to my rooms for a quick shower and trade the grunge clothes for a button-down shirt and slacks. Instead of walking, I dissipate to the middle of the throne room as a reminder of what I am capable of. Selene dons a shocked expression, glancing around before narrowing her eyes at me.

I smirk, moving to sit beside her. "We had court the day before yesterday."

"This isn't a typical procession. This is about the war. I had an interesting conversation with Talwarth and Fennel yesterday afternoon. Ella is standing with Viktor against the army. You, yourself, have made the claim that with her on his side, there is no chance of winning."

I hum, staring straight ahead.

She puts a hand on my shoulder, her voice softening. "Have you made your decision?"

"Yes."

"Let us all hope you have made the right choice." She clears her throat and stands. "Are we still waiting on anyone for this emergency call to session?"

There is silence. I look around the ring of courtiers before me. Seth catches my eye and shakes his head, making an inappropriate gesture as his eyes move to Selene. I smirk back at him, and he winks.

Next to him, Asena leans close and whispers in his ear. He grins, blushing, and then he turns his head in the direction of

Marx on the other side of Asena. I narrow my eyes at them but don't have time to give it much thought.

"Then let us begin. This session is being called to address the war and the choices this court is facing. Resolutions must be made for the betterment of everyone," Selene stresses, "so we will call on you to take a vote after arguments are made on these decisions."

She pauses, turning to face me. "But first, there is one individual that needs to make his own choice. Declan, you were named king of this court, and there are those who believe you are not performing your duties."

I lift my eyebrows and lean back on my hands. "How so? Have I betrayed this court?"

"You knowingly did in your marriage to Morella Rowena Annabelle Byron."

I smirk, knowing Ella hates that pretentious name. She'd be rolling her eyes and muttering under her breath at the announcement. I lift my chin and smile. "I fail to comprehend how my marriage is a discredit to this court."

"Morella was determined by this court to be a murderer, guilty of several crimes, including torture, theft, and of being tainted by male blood. Do you dare argue these crimes?" Selene waves her hands out in front of her, offering me the floor. "Do you dare stand with her after she attacked our army, killing dozens of warriors, exactly forty-seven of our army?"

I push off my hands and get to my feet. "The argument is the same for all crimes you see fit to accuse her of. Ella was being controlled by Viktor then the same as she is now. Any elemental injected with the blood of a male has an obedience to the sire, an unholy removal of free will."

"We all know this," Selene snaps, "and by the laws of this land, of Caleum, not Byron, any elemental injected with male blood is to be put to death."

Sliding my hands in my front pockets, I step down to meet her. "We are conversing about the creation of shades."

She tenses. "We are not discussing shades as a race."

I grin to expose my pointed canines. "Aren't we?" I ask in a silky whisper, eyes narrowing. "Shades were born of elementals injected with male blood. Are you prepared to declare all shades must be put to death for our nature?"

She bristles. "No, of course not. Shades are an accepted race in high and low society."

"Where do we make the distinction?"

"Morella is not a shade." Selene's voice is sharp, louder.

"She isn't?" I raise my eyebrows. "We have established that the act of using male blood to create an elemental makes a shade, by law. I wonder the response from every other shade in society if you kill one simply for what she is?"

There is a murmur through the room. One voice lifts above the others. "You're talking about riots of shades?"

"Possibly. If we feel threatened, unsafe, it starts with one, but how soon until you find fault with others?"

"This isn't about her being a shade. This is about her killing other elementals."

"She did not have a choice in what she did because of what she is. Viktor has absolute control over her actions simply by speaking. I personally witnessed this, as has Seth and Marcus."

"You and your brother are corroborations from biased sources who will say anything to save Morella. Marcus is no longer here to support this claim, either."

I rock on the balls of my feet. "Fair point, although I would like to point out that Ella is not the only child of Viktor who was coerced into less favorable actions." The color drains from her face. "Are you willing to admit your own actions?"

"I am." I glance over and see Spaulding on his feet, hands wringing together before him. "Your Majesty, that is. I'll tell."

Startled, I blink. I never considered that the last prince

would be willing to speak up. My eyes flicker to Marx, who lifts and drops a shoulder. "Thank you, Spaulding," I say.

He nods and drops down to his cushion. I pull my attention back in front of me.

Whispers are flying around the room, but Selene stands tall. "I have nothing to hide."

I grin. "No?" I step around her, putting her to my back to face the court. "For far too long, this court has operated on lies. If this court wants to condemn Ella for the lies being exposed, then I suggest we expose them all."

"This is about Morella being a murderer," Selene yells at my back.

"This is about proving whether or not Ella should be put to death."

"No, this is about your choice to marry Morella and betray this court."

I pivot and face her, raising my eyebrows. "And my betrayal is based on the damning of my wife." I pace around Selene, making her pivot to face me again. "So, let's have a fair trial for Ella."

"She has killed dozens of our warriors." Selene's face flushes pink to match the gown she wears. "She was a murderer before, confined to this palace under pain of death, which you, yourself, decreed."

I stare at her. "Maybe I didn't make my point clear enough to you."

Selene jerks back a step. "She was to be killed for her crimes, killed for leaving the palace, and now she's added dozens more to her body count," she shrieks. "Morella is not coming back."

I spare a glance around the court. Most gazes drop away or look to the ceiling when I make eye contact. I sneer. "Ella is capable of—"

"I don't care," Selene snaps. "She is not coming back. She is never going to be welcomed back to court, and she will not be your queen."

"I brought Ella out of this palace myself to see what she could do on the battlefield to help us. She's capable of destroying demons with magic. A highly valuable skill set, and if you hadn't helped hand her over to Viktor in the first place—" There are shocked responses around the room. I keep my face straight despite my urge to grin, knowing I played that piece at the best moment. "—then this conversation wouldn't need to happen. If you never betrayed the crown of Byron, this war would be over. Those lives would never have been lost. Ella wouldn't be under Viktor's control, being used against this court and others around Caleum. Ella would still be here."

I realize I am yelling. I take a breath and get a grip. "Take responsibility, Your Highness, for what you've done before you condemn Ella."

There is silence around me. I stare her down. The bitch is never going to have what she wants. I will go out of my way to systematically destroy her for the rest of my life for her part in this.

Her lower lip trembles at me in a pout. "I did what I had to."

"You want to see Ella dead for what she has done? You killed your own mother, Queen of Byron."

There's a buzz around me, but I focus on Selene's stupid face that she is so proud of and smile. Her mouth flaps open and closed, eyes welling up.

"No!" she shrieks at last. "No, you don't understand, I didn't."

"You didn't?"

"No," her voice trembles.

I hold out a hand, and Marx stands, bringing me the journal we found in Marcus' library. It was hard to find, in a secret compartment of his desk. It was unmarked, nothing on the leather cover to indicate all the secrets held within. There are records and entries dating back to when Ella was eight. It was the first entry. I assumed it was something hidden that Marcus wanted to document the truth about. What started his obsession with denoting everything he and his siblings did for Viktor.

She stares at the book. "No, I didn't do it. I didn't do anything."

"You went to Marcus, looking for poison."

"No."

"Later that cycle, you attended tea with Chloe, your mother."

"I had tea with my mother all the time."

"Your mother died after ingesting her tea. The cause of her death was never officially known." I smile. "At least, it was declared to be of natural causes."

Selene rounds on the court. "These are lies, slander—"

"Marcus knew every secret. Ella's, his, mine, Spaulding's, yours." I grin, holding the journal up. "This was his. He recorded everything he knew about what Viktor did or had himself or a sibling do. You acted on Viktor's orders, killing your mother."

"I didn't."

"You did." I toss the journal at the Duke of Devereaux for safekeeping. "It's even noted that you cried on Marcus' shoulder for hours after you did it, blubbering about how Viktor made you do it, and you didn't have a choice. Would you like to see the entry? It's dated."

"They are lying!" she screams. "Marcus has killed too. That book isn't real. You just made it."

"Interesting that you haven't mentioned that before." I look around at all the shocked faces. "But you were so quick to expose Ella's actions."

"She wasn't supposed to be queen." Selene is spinning in circles, glancing around the room on the verge of tears. She looks back to me, her lower lip trembling. She stares at me, eyes welling up. I smile, tight-lipped, and back away from her. I pull my hands out of my pockets and gesture at her.

"So," I say, "you have killed for Viktor, and you betrayed the court by aiding in the abduction of Ella, knowing full well she would be taken to Viktor. Exactly who isn't fit for the crown?" I rub a finger back and forth across my chin in contemplation.

"I am the blood heir of this court. You will renounce your marriage and reinstate your betrothal to me or forfeit the crown."

"I'll not recant my vows."

"Then, you are no longer King of Byron."

CHAPTER 24

DECLAN

The courtroom implodes, and I stare straight at Selene as her face contorts. A single tear runs down her cheek. "You could have had everything with me."

"I'd rather have nothing with Ella than anything at all with you." I chuckle and shake my head. I stare around at everyone on their feet, faces of bewilderment and fury. "Enough. Everyone, sit down," I yell, and the room falls quiet.

Selene might have announced I am no longer king, but everyone still scurries to obey, taking their seats and staring at me. I scratch my jaw, where it itches under the beard, then focus on the woman before me.

She huffs and stomps her foot like a child throwing a tantrum. "You have no authority here."

"You are as guilty as Ella is of anything."

"You tortured me." She pokes me in the chest and whips around to yell at the court. "He tortured me for hours without end."

"Yes," I say in a dull tone. "You betrayed the court. I was acting in service to this court to provide information."

Her mouth flaps, then she screws up her face. "I did what had to be done, to be rid of Morella."

"You handed a weapon over to Viktor to use against this land because of your jealousy. That is treason." I do my best to say the words without emotion.

"I–I…" she flounders, grasping for words before she screams at me.

I take a step back and stare, half in amazement and half in amusement. My lips twist to the side, and I shrug. "My marriage is of little consequence to this court at this time. You caused the death of Queen Chloe and aided Viktor in his pursuits."

"I didn't have a choice," she manages to get out. "I couldn't say no to Viktor. He was going to hurt me if I didn't do it."

I snarl at her, stepping close. "Do you know how many times Viktor beat Ella for finding a way to ignore his orders? Do you know the scars he left behind? I've seen them all, counted them, tried to kiss them away." My voice is low, but the words carry through the air, every courtier holding their breath. "Ella fought back against his control. Sometimes she'd win, and she knew each time she angered him what the consequences would be."

Selene's cheeks are stained pink, her eyes puffy and red. She sniffs, wiping fingers under her eyes, smearing black marks along her skin. She pushes past me and stands at the front of the room. She takes a breath and composes herself.

Folding her hands together in front of her stomach, she smiles around the room. "Well, that certainly was exciting, wasn't it?"

I stare, my brows pinching together, my lips pursing. "You're not seriously going to just act like none of this was said?"

She clears her throat and makes a flourish with her hand. "Take your seat, Mr. Bard."

I take a single step forward, muttering. "Fine, let's play make-believe in your fucking head."

Her hand lifts, palm toward me. "As your station requires, no more than related to the Duke of Kennelton."

I smirk, sliding my hands in my pockets. "As Sordello has made it clear that he is King of the Spirits, and his daughter is Morella, and I am her husband, I am far more than a relation to the Duke of Kennelton. And actually, I have a set of spirit runes."

Her eyebrows pinch together. "Yes, this court is aware."

My lips curl. "Tell me the truth, Selene. Tell me if you killed your mother."

Her eyes grow wide, her mouth moving. "Yes, I poisoned my mother." She slaps a hand over her mouth as the room fills with whispers.

I spin on my heel and take a seat next to Seth. "Probably should have just started with that." I scratch at my jaw.

He leans in close. "Well, it worked about as well as me trying to get laid anyway."

I wrangle to keep my laugh inside and end up choking. He stands. "I'm sorry, Your Majesty, but now that we have no king and you're not fit to be queen, who is ruling over this court?"

"Sit down, Seth," Selene hisses.

Another man stands, the Duke of Deveraux, Legia's father. He holds the journal up. "This will need to be reviewed. Already the first entry is bothersome enough, but I will inquire the same, Selene."

She looks around the room with a face of confusion. "I had no choice."

The Duke shakes his head. "That is the same excuse Morella has presented. You cannot condone your behavior and condemn another's with the same excuse."

I have never kissed a man, but I could kiss the Duke. Seth and I exchange glances, and then I wait for the inevitable.

Spaulding walks out to the middle of the floor with a drawn expression. "May I have the floor to speak?" There are no objections from the room, but the Duke remains on his feet. "Thank you. My family, our father, caused quite the mess, not only in the land or this court but also for his children. Each of us has blood on our hands. My character and my choices have never once been questioned, but even I have acted in the name of our father, coerced into atrocities."

He stops, hanging his head and covering his eyes. After a moment, he drops his hand, glancing around the room as if he has forgotten where he is. "Ella… I can only imagine what he used her to do if he maintained absolute control over her. It may be true, she carried out cruelties and sickening acts, but whenever she has had a choice, she has shown a heart of gold. I am asking you to forgive all of us, not only Ella, but Selene, and myself for the things we did to protect ourselves and those we care about, and those things we had no choice in. Please, excuse the acts we were forced into and let us be defined from our actions going forward, or you'll be forced to hold each of us accountable and execute us all."

I take in a breath and count the seconds. I get to six before Elizabeth stands. "I motion to excuse all of the Byron children from acts committed under the control of Viktor in the past, obviously excluding Morella's current behavior."

There is a murmur of agreement around the room, although Seth's is the loudest. I stare in shock at Spaulding as he bows to the court. "Thank you. From the bottom of my heart, I apologize for the wrongdoings my siblings and I have done. Your ability to show mercy is beyond generous."

He meets my eyes from across the room. I drop my chin, and he nods before turning to resume his seat.

Seth turns to me. "Didn't expect that."

I shrug.

"Who was that," Asena whispers on his other side.

"Spaulding, Ell's brother."

"How old is he?"

"Young," Seth says in a hurry. "I don't know if he's even eighteen."

"Shame," Asena sighs. "He's well-spoken, would be a fine king."

"I can be well-spoken," Seth whispers back.

I elbow him in the side. "Shut it and pay attention."

Talwarth and Fennel march into the room. They stop in the middle of the floor and bow to Selene. "Your Majesty," Fennel says. "Thank you for having us."

"You have been called to give evidence on the progress of this war and the likelihood of our chances to win. Please, the floor is yours." She gestures with open arms and then plops down on her cushion.

"Well, shit," Seth mutters.

I cut my eyes to him and sigh through my nose before giving my attention to Talwarth and Fennel. They drone on and on until I think my ears might bleed. Numbers are thrown out on the dead and of the cost of the war.

"In summary," Fennel says in his high-pitched voice, "we have a small chance to win this war, but the costs are incredibly high. Our warriors, the hunters, mages are all dying rapidly, far more so than our enemy."

Talwarth points at me. "With Morella and Erac standing with Viktor, even Declan has declared we have no hope of winning."

I grit my teeth and get to my feet. "Then we take Ella back and get her to fight with us. If we do that, Erac, Viktor, demons, none of them stand a chance."

"The men won't fight with that traitorous bitch." Talwarth turns to face me.

Seth stands next to me. "With Ella and Declan, there might be no one else that has to fight."

I clench my fists at my side, knowing full well he believes what he is saying, but I doubt he knows what he is asking of us. Ella would be a helpful asset, but I have no intention of her doing this on her own. I grit my teeth and stay silent. They need to believe she can save them.

Fennel puts a hand on Talwarth's shoulder. "You are saying that if we can swing Morella back to our side, there is no need for another warrior, hunter, or mage to be involved?"

"Yes," Seth bobs his head. "Absolutely."

I resist the urge to take him to the ground and beat him to a bloody pulp. "Ella is incredibly useful when it comes to weaving spells and manipulating the elements."

My brother chuckles and nods. "Yeah, she dissolved a handful of elementals with a snap of her fingers."

I pinch the bridge of my nose. "Not helpful," I snarl under my breath.

"The court will vote on the war," Selene says. "There will be a deliberation period, let us say one cycle, during which no activities against or for our enemy will be taken. Talwarth, Fennel, thank you for your cooperation."

The court dissolves, and I bare my teeth at Seth. "You just promised them Ella and I would end this on our own."

He grins. "Sure did, and you can. She can." I grind my teeth, and his smile fades. "What? You know she can."

I look away at all the faces moving past. "I have a lot of work to do to remind these idiots of who Viktor is, why he isn't king, and just what Ella is capable of if we leave her in his hands, regardless of personal feelings. You," I give him a fist in the shoulder, "don't promise anything else, got it?"

He laughs and side steps someone to stand next to Asena. "Hey, how about I show you around Byron?"

She beams at him, accepting his arm. She's pressed close to him as they saunter off into the crowd milling about. I watch them go.

Marx speaks at my shoulder. "You need to get control of your brother."

I turn to scowl at Marx. "He's my brother. I don't tell him what to do."

Marx chuckles, patting me on the shoulder as he moves by. "Yes, and that is my daughter. You know full well I can make him disappear."

I roll my eyes to the ceiling, sighing through my nose. *Why am I responsible for everything?*

CHAPTER 25

MORELLA

Bright, warm light soaks my skin with a blissful heat as I lounge under the soul star. A book is propped open in my lap, held in place with a bent-up knee. My gaze is off to the distance, watching waves lapping against the shore.

George is absent. I have asked after him to be told by servants they do not know which boy I inquire about. He's either hiding, or the others are protecting him after he was punished by my father.

My fingers strum on the open pages of an ancient tome. The boy is a link to my past, and I have more questions now than ever. I dare not ask Erac, and my father is always so busy, but my list of queries is only getting longer.

Who was my betrothed, if not Erac? And why was I free of my father? Why did I want *to be free of him?*

Laying out on the chaise, I stare at the ocean, wondering if I could ever go to the beach, along with every other fervid question. The codex in my lap lies forgotten, pages baking in the warmth of the soul star. I long to dissipate to the shore and feel the sand beneath my feet and between my toes. Erac has been very firm with me that I am not to leave the safety of the palace, but that has not stopped me from daydreaming.

A shadow looms over me, blocking the light, so I tip my head back and glance up into a familiar face. I smile, close the book, and sit up. "Father."

His chin drops and lifts, his bare scalp showing a sheen of reflected light. "My daughter, how are you?"

I shrug and glance toward the beach. "I'd love to be able to go out there."

"In time. In time you will be able to do anything you desire, and there will be no one to interfere or impede you. May I?" His eyes drop to the seat next to me.

I scoot over and pat the spot. "I made it," I say with a triumphant grin. "Just this morning."

"Your skills are advancing." He turns in a stiff manner, then lowers down to sit next to me. He leans arms braced on his thighs, fingers steepled together before him.

"What do you need me for?" I stare into eyes a sparkling green that suggests a hint of malice in the light of the soul star. "How can I help?" I reach out and put a hand on his forearm.

He pats my hand with his own and gives me a tight smile. "You have done enough already. The rebels who were setting up camp, you and Erac handled that nicely for me."

"Of course." I laugh. "I will make them pay for what they did to me."

He turns his head, fixating me with a stare. There is no emotion in his face for me to discern. The contrast between how my betrothed and my father handle their thoughts is stark. He stares forward again, down the length of the palace toward the gardens obscured by shimmering mirages from the heat.

"I will be gone for the rest of today. I am traveling to Clemm. I intend to start there to bring the remaining courts to heel."

"There are four courts, right?" I beam at him. "The court in the north, Roget, the court to the east in forests of jade and crystal ruled by the elves, the Clemm court," I wrinkle my nose and laugh, "which is the most unremarkable aside from Erac's home, and then the–the Byron court, right? Those who are rebelling?"

"You have been reading again, I see," he drawls.

I frown, sure he would have been proud of my efforts. "Yes."

"Do not sound so disappointed, daughter. You are doing well. Keep reading, learn from Erac everything you can of magic, and controlling the elements."

"Yes, Father."

"I am going to garner abject subservience of the remaining courts. Our forces have been busy proving our ability, and it is time to negotiate their surrender."

I frown, pulling my lips inward and together. "Negotiate?"

"Yes, they will surrender, or I will use what power I have to destroy them. They may try to make exceptions. I am certain they will."

"Then why negotiate at all?"

A wry smile plays with his lips. "I have the power to command them to submit, to control them, force them into obedience. Many revolutions ago, I learned the errors of forcing submission and expecting subservience." His eyes dance at me with suppressed mirth. "You taught me that, my daughter."

A bit stunned, I pull back to peer at him. "Me? How did I teach you such a thing?"

He smiles with closed lips. "While you were growing up, you were an unruly child, not always a woman."

I tilt my head back, eyes closing. "I don't understand. If you can force them to surrender, then why not do so?"

"I can make them bow, but if they do not willingly drop to their knees, I will have to continually bring them down." He reaches out, putting a hand on my shoulder. "We, you and I daughter, and Erac, we are blessed with runes from Medius, which grant power. None who are barren of the runes may ignore our commands. They must and will listen to an order. Using the runes to force their submission will bring only temporary peace. I cannot be everywhere all the time, constantly commanding their obedience. They must choose, willingly accept my rule, or a cycle of obedience and disobedience will follow."

I hold up my forearm, heavy with black decorative flourishes. "Do you mean these?"

"Yes." He reaches out, tapping my collarbone. "The mark here is your power rune. Know this rune keeps you alive. Never allow one to damage this rune above all others. No matter the wounds inflicted upon you, it can always bring you back to life, to heal even the most grievous of injuries. Always protect this rune."

I nod, and his finger drops away. He leans forward again, frowning at the stone. My mind drifts to George, the way he snapped to apologize when I commanded, and how he pouted about it afterward. Drawing fingers over the marred skin, I nod to my father. "I understand."

"Good. I need you, my daughter, not only to understand but to help me. When we have won Caleum, we will then claim Medius. That is the dimension above us from which spirits hale. There are spirits here, our own kind, fighting against our right to rule, called upon by our enemies to vanquish us, and I intend to bring any who stand against us to heel."

"Why do they fight us?"

He turns, eyes settling on mine. "There will always be those who fight against you, those who want the power you hold for themselves." He turns away, speaking in a melancholy tone. "This war is no different."

There is a long pause, and a dragon flies overhead, wings spread, sun glinting off scales as it soars close to the soul star. My father leans back, gazing up. "Someday, Morella, and someday very soon, you are going to rule over Caleum. We will take control of Medius, and one day when I am tired and too old to continue, you will inherit everything. The greatest legacy there has ever been, and it all starts with you."

"Me?"

"When the time is right, we will destroy the rebellion's army. You'll be able to wipe them away from this world, return them to ash and dust with the easiest wave of your hand. You are that powerful."

I stare down at my hands, flipping them over and then up to meet his gaze, which has returned to me. One side of his lips pulls back ever so slightly.

"With your powers and my intelligence, there is nothing that will be able to stand in our way. We will take back what was stolen from us and create a new and better world, one of elemental and spirit."

I bob my head. "And that starts with you leaving to deal with those courts?"

"It started the moment you were returned to me."

"Oh." He faces forward and sits upright. My father does not usually move so much. I lean over and nudge him with my shoulder. "Are you alright, Father?"

He laughs a bit and rubs a hand over his mouth. "The Clemm Court was my home a long time ago. The king is an old friend turned against me, and my father is a nobleman there, neither do I wish to see."

I chew my lower lip. "Can you not fix the friendship?"

He scowls at me. "No, and I have no wish to. I am polite when social etiquette dictates, but I will never forgive. Remember, my daughter, forgiveness is a weakness. An evil man will wrong you, and if you forgive, they will wrong you over and over. Never forgive, and you will protect yourself."

I bob my head and sigh. "And your father? Was he an evil man who wronged you?"

A darkness crawls down over my father's features, and I

shiver with an unnerved sensation sliding through me. "I came to say goodbye before I left." His tone is harsh. "I did not wish to leave you and allow you to believe you had been abandoned or discarded. I never wish for you to feel such a thing that your own blood has turned away from you." He turns to me, pressing his lips to my forehead.

He pulls back and stares down at me with a grave face. "I do have one request of you."

My spine straightens as I perk up with excitement. "Oh?" The word is an audible gasp.

I think he almost smiles at me. "The spirits are a problem for us. They were conjured to be weapons against us and something difficult to contend with. Erac has a spell to send them away, somewhere they will wither and rot and not interfere. Can you help him?"

I nod my head in rapid succession until I am dizzy and beaming.

"Good. Do as Erac says to complete the spell. He will need your power. I will ask very little else of you right, Erac has mentioned your questions, and I understand why you ask them, but you cannot know of what was before. I've been assured this is too much for your mind to handle, and I would detest seeing you damaged beyond repair. The only other thing is: Stay here. Do not stray beyond our walls, and Erac will keep you safe from the rebellious scum."

He stands, and I tip my head back again to stare up at him. "Yes, Father, I will. Please be careful."

With a curt nod, he grabs my face and presses a kiss to my forehead. "You are very precious to me."

My father dissolves, and I gaze around with wide eyes as if I could trace his elements disassembling into the air. Exhaling, my fingers run over the edge of the dark olive bound cover. The texture beneath my finger is smooth, almost slimy, as if the skin were still alive. The middle of the cover has an imprinted design, something intricate with interlocking circles, the impression of a droplet repeated a dozen times around the symbol.

Getting to my feet, I dissolve the chaise to air and pad barefoot back into the room to set the book on the stand next to my bed before dissipating in search of Erac. It takes a few tries as I check the gardens and the library before hesitatingly dissolving to air and piecing myself together in front of his door.

I knock. "Erac?" No answer, so I try the knob. The door is locked. It takes a simple twist of elements, and the door pops open. I stick my head through and double-check to confirm the space is empty.

Deciding to wait for him, I slip into the room. This place haunts me. I have so few memories, and waking up in this room is prominent, a harrowing experience I cannot get out of my mind at times. An echo of the immense pain in my stomach twangs through me as I sit on the edge of the bed.

There is nothing about the room that indicates the horror it inspires in me. The silks are shades of blue and violet, the room full of gold details. I glance around and see a small gold box on the stand next to the headboard.

I move closer, picking up the box. Something shifts inside. I grip the lid and pop it open, staring at the tiny silver balls filling the bottom. Some of them have black burn marks, a burnished discoloration. I pluck one up, surprised at the weight, and drop it into my palm, rolling the smooth, warm ball around, studying the surface.

A hand streaks in front of my eyes, covering my fingers and squeezing. Immediately fear slithers through me, turning my muscles to stone, petrified into immobility. My eyes lift to Erac's furious gaze.

I do my best to smile. "Hi, darling."

"What. Are. You. Doing?" His jaw is clenched. His lips do not even move.

"I was looking for you."

"My door was locked."

Wincing, I try to pull my hand back, but his fingers tighten. "Ow, you're hurting me."

"You broke into my room. You have touched things that do not belong to you." My wrist is throbbing as he glares, impossibly tightening down further on me. "You are prying into my things."

"Please," I whisper, "that really hurts," my voice warbles.

"Then don't touch things that don't belong to you!" he bellows.

Erac wrenches the box from my other hand and releases me, snatching the metal ball out of my hand. He drops it into the box, and the lid snaps shut, a ringing sound in the silence.

I watch him set the box back on his nightstand as I cradle my aching wrist against my chest. He moves stiffly then kicks my feet apart to stand between my knees. He grips my face, jerks my head back by my hair, and frowns down at me.

"Really," he sighs. "Why do you do these things?"

My eyes drop down toward the floor, and I try very hard to keep them off his crotch at the same time. "I'm sorry. I was trying to find you."

"Are you stupid?"

I shake my head as best as I can in his grip.

"Then why would you be looking for me in a box that wouldn't even fit my foot?"

"I thought I'd just wait here for you, and I was curious about your things."

"My door stays locked. I am the only one who comes and goes from this room unless I invite you. Do you understand me?"

"Yes."

His grip relaxes, and he presses his lips to my forehead. "My love." He sighs and pulls back, grabbing me under the jaw, forcing my eyes up to him. We stare at each other, and then he tilts his head, his eyes flutter, the lashes lowering until his gaze is focused on my lips.

I tip my head further back and sit up straight to press my mouth to his. His lips part, the tip of his tongue touching my lips, so I part them, letting him inside my mouth. He deepens the kiss and pushes me back onto the bed.

One of his arms is underneath me, wrapped around my body, the other supporting some of his weight off me as he lays on top of me. He rips his arm from beneath me, grappling with the skirt of my dress and forcing it up.

I lay there, staring at the ceiling as he moves on top of me, his thin lips clammy as they drag down my neck and over the tops of my breasts exposed above the material of my gown. My hands fall above my head, and I lay there, letting him do what he wants.

There are pleasant feelings, some sensations that I enjoy, but when he thrusts in and out, I close my eyes and bite my lower lip against the uncomfortable pressure, waiting for this to be over. When it is, his fingers dig into my hips with brutal force as he grunts, then he flops down on top of me, his weight making it hard to breathe.

I stay there, eyes opening to the heavens, and praying to Haven that he moves soon. He nuzzles his face into the side of my neck and presses a small kiss against me.

"Why must you make me crazy?" he asks, his usually boyish voice thick with pleasure and sleep. "Don't you know how much I love you?"

CHAPTER 26

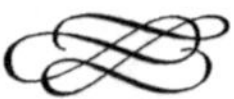

MORELLA

Waking up tucked against Erac, I'm wrapped in silk sheets. The light of the soul star is flowing through the air, brushing warmth across my face. I stir. He snorts and shoves his nose against my ear before breathing out hot air against my neck.

Sitting up, I elbow him off me and sit up, wiping sleep from my eyes. Erac stirs, rolling to his back, and smirks up at me with a lazy hitch of his mouth. He tucks one arm behind his head and reaches out for me with the other. I reach back, and he laces his fingers in mine.

"Morning," I mumble, meeting his indigo eyes.

"You need to eat."

I nod, turning away and pulling my hand from his. "Okay."

I leave his bed, dissipating to my rooms for a shower. Standing in front of the mirror, I check my face and rub my wrist, then shift the elements around me into a beautiful dress. I pull the water from my hair and brush the knots loose, twisting pieces together into a low knot at the base of my skull, pulling pins from the air to secure it all in place.

Next, I focus on lining my eyes in shimmering gold, my lips

in muted red. When I am finished, I step back to inspect my work. Standing there, I see myself in a floor-length gown of shimmering white material, low cut down the front, the skirt loose around my legs with a high slit. I lean against the glass, palms flat, and my eyes welling up.

I sob, pulling back and covering my mouth with a hand. A tear rolls over my lower lashes, down onto my fingers. Something cracks in my core, and I scream at myself, reaching out to the mirror and shattering it. The shards fling around as I sob again. They freeze midair and float around me.

Something else wells up inside of me, a burning lust to destroy, a dark whisper tantalizing my senses, dancing in the shadows of my mind. I hold my hand out, shattering the sink basin, then the large white tub. I decimate the windows, and everything else I can lay eyes on that can be obliterated to pieces as I scream and cry.

But then, everything bursts inside of me, and I fall to my knees, sobbing and hiccupping and giving into the raging grief in my soul. My forehead rests on the cold stone floor, the cool calming me. I get to my feet, wiping away the wetness on my face and lift my hand. All the broken pieces lift from the ground. Closing my eyes, I reimagine the room as it was. The hum of energy pulsing out of my skin and into the room around me is a source of relief, a sort of contention settled.

With everything back together, I lean forward, fixing my makeup with a few changes of elements and touch-ups of fresh materials. I check myself in the mirror again, my lips twisting and pulling to one side back at me.

I snap my fingers, changing the dress to black and the shimmer around my eyes to something dark and smoky. The red on my lips becomes the color of blood, and the nagging pull at the back of my mind recedes, banished with the change of attire.

"Ella?" I glance over at George in the doorway of my bathroom. His eyes widen. "Whoa, you look scary."

"Good." I turn away from the looking glass and move toward him. "Erac sent you to fetch me for breakfast?"

He kicks at the ground. "Yeah–no, he sent Tabit, but I asked Tabit to let me do it instead." He lifts his eyes to me again. "They don't want me to talk to you no more, and the other servants keep trying to stop me from getting involved."

My spine ripples and straightens as I clench my fists. "Erac says remembering things—things you can tell me—will damage the magic that removed their poison."

George scoffs and shoves his balled fists into the pockets of his robes. "I don't know about that, but at least you kinda look like you again."

I pull back a bit, my breath catching in the back of my throat. "What do you mean?"

"You always wore black before."

I nod. "I feel good in black. What else did I do before?"

It is his turn to tilt his head. "You weren't like other nobles and fancy folk. Never saw you in a dress before. Mostly you looked like you were a thief, but you were nice and smiled and said please. You weren't like the others, you were honest and stuff, and you treated me and my dad like normal elementals with feelings. And you were always crying and reading. I remembered his name, your betrothed. Kinda stupid of me to forget it." George's face scrunches up on one side like a wince.

"What was his name?" I ask, breathless for more. "Who was he?"

My father materializes further in my rooms behind George. The boy shrugs at me, shoving his hands into the pockets of his robes. Time crawls, my heart beating once in my ears like a hammer striking against rock.

"Declan," George says before I can open my mouth to stop him.

Something shifts in my father's gaze, an indiscernible twitch of his features, and then he is upon George, grabbing him by the arm. All the color drains from the boy's face, his dark complexion turning ashen.

"Father, you're back!" I exclaim, doing my best to beam at him as if my heart is not about to race right out of my chest.

"Yes," he says, his voice tight, the poison in his eyes burning like livid green flames. "Are you conversing with this servant?"

George tips his head up and gapes. "Yer Majesty, I—"

"You will be silent." He gives George a violent shake. "And you, my daughter, have you eaten breakfast? I expect you to join me in the main hall."

I nod. "Yes, of course, Father, I am glad you're back. Why don't we walk together, and you can tell me about your travels?"

His eyes cut to George. "No, this miscreant seems to have forgotten himself, and I will remind him of his place." I open my mouth to argue that George has done nothing wrong, but my father holds out a hand. "Leave us, Morella. Now. Do as you are told."

My lips press shut, and I nod, eyes locking with George's. His gaze is wide. I can see all the way around the brown orbs, and his lips are sucked between his teeth.

Smiling to reassure the boy, I give a curtsy to him and my father. "Of course. I will see you at breakfast." My eyes linger on George's before I dissipate to the main hall.

I take my seat next to Erac, reaching for a piece of dragons' food, a chartreuse, thick hide fruit with a watery, sweet interior. It is my favorite snack and the best treat for breakfast.

My betrothed scowls at me, eyes narrowing. "What took you so long?"

I turn in my seat, giving him a full grin. "It takes a while for me to look so beautiful for you."

He eyes me, his line of sight dropping from my face down my torso. He smirks and picks up a gold goblet. He frowns. "Are you alright, my love?"

"Fine."

He shifts, turning to face me. "You seem tense."

I narrow my eyes, looking out across the room. Demons stand with large axes in hand, flanking all entrances. There are not many others in the room, a handful of elementals dressed finely, talking amongst their small ranks. I am contemplating asking who Declan is.

"Morella," my father's voice cuts through my thoughts, and I turn toward him. He takes his seat on the other side of Erac. The seat to his left remains vacant. "How many times—"

"Where is your consort," I ask. "I haven't been able to meet her properly."

My father's mouth turns down at the corners, something soft overcoming him. "Susan is no longer with us." He reaches out, his fingers trembling as they pluck up his drink. "How many times must I remind you, you are Princess of Caleum, and you do not converse with servants?"

Erac turns to me with disgruntled surprise. "Who was it this time?"

"George, again," my father says.

Both men glare at me with death in their eyes. "Did I not tell you that you were never to speak with him again?" Erac snarls.

"I have taken care to see to it that George stays away from her from now on," my father tells him.

"What?" I gasp. "Father!"

"Do not dare defy me, my daughter." He twists the words with a soft cruelty. "Honestly, speaking with a boy of his rank as if you two were equals. I will hear no more of this, I warn you. You were told once before to stay away from George or to ignore his presence. The boy was reprimanded already for his indiscretions, and I now have been forced to take further measures."

"What did you do?" I cry in dismay.

My father's lips purse and his eyes gleam mean before he answers. "You will not see him again, and you will not search for the boy. Do I make myself clear?"

My stomach knots, a sickness settling in my gut like acid eroding my flesh. I face out across the room with a set expression as my insides turn to a molten disease, and my ears begin to ring. "Yes, Father."

"Very well then. Erac, where are we with getting rid of the spirits?"

He reaches out and picks up an unsliced piece of dragons' food. "Morella and I can tend to that this morning."

"Why was it not done yesterday?"

My face heats up. I hope Erac will not confess our physical activities to my father. I suppose they are not forbidden as we are engaged, but the idea that my father would hear of them makes me squirm.

"Morella and I were working on our relationship," he says dully. "The spell will only take a few moments to complete."

"Something so important?" My father directs his gaze to meet Erac's. "Should something this important be done so simply."

Erac sneers and pushes his chair away from the table to stand. "Sometimes, the simplest solutions are the best, Viktor. You might do to remember that. Come, Morella." He offers me a hand, and my eyes travel over the food before me that I have yet to touch. "Now."

With a huff, I put my hand in his. "Yes, dear," I snarl under my breath.

His hand tightens to the point of discomfort, but the fury in my gut turns the pain to mere pressure. I narrow my eyes at him, and his lips press together hard enough to be a white line on his face. We stare at each other, and I wait for him to lash out. I want him to. I want an excuse.

Cold pressure squeezes me, and I blink against the bright white light of the soul star. Heat blazes my skin and sucks the moisture from my lips. I wet them with the tip of my tongue and glance around.

"The gardens?" I ask, looking to Erac.

"Yes." He holds the piece of fruit up. "All we need is this and a knife. Can you make me a knife?"

I hold out a hand, palm flat, and close my eyes, trying to picture a knife. Cool metal kisses against my skin, and I glance at my creation. The blade is small, with a black leather-wrapped handle and a loop at the end.

Erac and I both stare at it, and then I lift my eyes to his. The thought to move quick, to draw blood from him, rips through me. I wonder what it would taste like, the air soaked in his fear.

He frowns. "Did you intend to make that?"

I shrug, holding the blade aloft to inspect. "I didn't really intend much, just thought about a small blade, and this is what formed."

He plucks it up. "Fine. Yes. Here." He hands fruit to me. "Take this too. I'll walk you through the spell."

My heart skips a beat, but not in fear. "Really?"

He laughs. "Yes, really, my love." He tucks a stray hair behind my ear. "I will tell you what to do, and we will do this together."

I cannot wait. All the thoughts of pain and rage whisk away at the notion of learning new magic. I squeeze the leather-bound handle tight in my hand and hold up the fruit. "What do I do?"

"Cut the fruit in half with the knife."

I do as he says.

"Very good," he says, taking the two halves from me. "Now, cut your finger."

The tip of the blade hesitates over my left pointer. I let my hand fall away. "Why?"

He sighs, inspecting the two halves with modest interest. "Just do it. Why must you always question everything? I tell you what you need to know. It doesn't have to be a big cut, you don't even need to use the knife if you don't want to, or even cut yourself, but we need your blood."

"What?"

Erac glances up, a bit startled, and blinks at me. "Manipulate the elements. You can split flesh, draw blood through unbroken skin, or you can dissipate your blood out of your own body if you so chose. You've never needed a knife to draw blood."

I twirl the blade on my finger by the little loop and ask, "How much blood do we need?"

"Enough to create a version of our runes on here." He shows me the exposed interior of the dragons' food.

I stop spinning the blade and use it to split the tip of my finger down to the knuckle. The bite stings, but watching the blood bead up is oddly satisfying. Throwing the knife tip first, it embeds in the ground to await future use.

"Now what?" I ask, offering my finger to Erac.

He frowns at my finger as several drops of blood bubble and then rise into the air. I gape with an open mouth.

"How?" I ask in a whisper.

His brows knit together, his eyes fixating on the churning droplets. "You don't need your hands if your mental will is strong enough. The elements are being controlled by you, your mind, your intent. The hand motions are given for fledgling mages to help them harness and focus their commands, and most mages use them as a reflex they've developed even long after they've stopped needing the movements."

The blood is thinning into long wisps. It spins in a helical fashion, forming delicate lines and flecks against the open span of the fruit in Erac's hand. The symbols bear a resemblance to the twists and turns of the black lines on my left arm.

"The spirit runes," I say, forehead wrinkling.

"Yes, our runes, our legacy we have earned with our blood. It is the same blood that runs through those spirits that stand against us. We use this blood as an offering and the power within to banish those we share the most primal fluids with."

"Beneath the armor, they look like us?"

The blood is laid out, and having finished painting the symbols, Erac gives me his attention. "They are beings of light. They have wings too, though they keep them pent up and out of sight most of the time."

"Do we have wings?" I ask, unable to contain my excitement.

He gives me a look of disbelief. "No."

"Oh."

"Now, focus, I need you."

I nod. "Okay."

"Good girl. Now" he offers both halves of the fruit to me "—take these. There. Good, and now put them together, gently, don't damage them. Yes, right."

His hands rest on top of mine. I smile at him, anxious to continue. I long for the hum of energy burning through me as a living breath of magic exhaled from my soul after holding it in for too long.

He rests his forehead to mine and smiles, his eyes now a bright violet. "When we finish this spell, we are going to end up somewhere else."

I suck my lips between my teeth and stretch my eyes open wide, asking without words.

He chuckles. "Blood creates a bond." He moves his hands over mine, covering the fruit. "Our blood contains the same blood of spirits. Your blood has more power than mine, which is why we are using yours. So, blood creates a bond, and you used the blood of spirits to draw the runes they wear to the flesh of the fruit. You have bound all those with this blood and those marks to this very piece of fruit."

"By drawing with blood?"

"Yes, and no. There is very little blood magic that can be done without intent. When you play with blood, you need to keep a clear mind to know what you intend. The intention of how you use the blood is more important than even the spell you weave."

“We’re all bound to that thing?” I ask, a bit horrified. “What happens if it’s destroyed?”

“That’s why I told you to be careful,” he snaps, pulling the pieces away from me. He cradles them close to his stomach, pouting at me like a petulant child. “We have the same blood, we wear the same marks, destroying it would destroy them and us too.”

My brow furrows as I watch his thumbs caress the seam between the two pieces. “Why the hell would you ever create something like that?” I point an accusatory finger at him and it.

“We have been bound, but also bind all of those with the same blood and the runes to this fruit. Where it goes, we go. Viktor wants the spirits gone, and not even you and I together can dissipate the spirits to another dimension, but we can dissipate this.” He holds the fruit aloft.

I cock an eyebrow and shy away. “And once we have sent it to another dimension, all those bound to it go where it goes?”

“Yes.” He smiles like this is a great accomplishment.

I think he is crazy, but I sigh and drop my arms. “What dimension are we sending them to?”

“Damnatus. The spirits cannot return home until they have done what they were called upon and accepted to do.”

“Which was?”

He purses his lips. “Kill Viktor, your father.”

My lips peel apart. “How dare they?”

Erac smirks as if I said something funny and moves on. “I don’t know if we can override that magic, so we are going to send them further down.”

“Um, wait, what?” I hold a finger up. “You plan on sending us to a lower dimension?”

He shakes his head with the ghost of a smile. “Traveling up is harder than traveling down. The amount of energy it will take to send this,” he lifts the fruits between both hands, “to another dimension along with those bound to it will be difficult for you enough by going down. Again, without trying to combat the magic that tethers the spirits to Caleum, going up is more strenuous and will undoubtedly be impossible for you to achieve."

"Yeah," I massage a temple. "So, we're going to Damnatus with that thing, right?"

"Yes, Morella." His voice is full of worn patience.

"And they're going with us?"

"Yes."

I narrow my eyes. "What happens to the fruit once we get there?"

"We destroy the bond of the blood and dissipate back here." He jerks his head at our surroundings.

"Didn't you just say going up is harder?"

"There should be no concern about trying to return. You will be bringing only us and Viktor, something I imagine you're capable of."

Everything sounds simple enough. "Okay," I take a deep breath in. "What next?"

"Now," he holds the fruit out between both palms, and he exhales slowly. "Close your eyes and visualize Damnatus. The dimension is dark, lit only by a blood moon, and the air is full of smoke and ash, the ground hard with pools of boiling silver pitch. Clear your mind and picture a world that looks like that, and see the dragons' food there, see me holding it there, want to be there with me."

My eyes drift shut as I listen to him describe the world. The magic builds up inside of me, and I exhale, everything around me shattering like shards of ice against my skin. The pressure mounts and builds until I am crushed, and then it fades.

I cough, the air burning my mouth and lungs as I draw it in, the taste of burnt air singeing my nose. I blink, and the air is visible with ash that falls from the sky like blackened snow, the craggy surface illuminated by pale pink light. Nearby a silver pit of fluid shimmers and bubbles in the ground.

"Welcome to Damnatus," Erac says.

My eyes track to the sound of his voice. My father swats at the air in front of his face and scowls. Erac pulls the fruit apart and winks at me. "Quick now, pull the blood off the surface."

I do as he says, the blood wafts, catching flakes of ash in the air.

"Pull it back into yourself, remake it apart of you and break the bond it shares with everything else."

I hold out a hand, grabbing the droplets from the air. They stain my skin, and I focus on them, forcing the blood back underneath. The stain disappears beneath the surface of my palm like a reversal of bleeding.

Erac tosses the fruit aside and holds his hand out to me. "Now, take us home."

CHAPTER 27

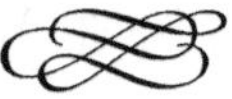

DECLAN

I go looking for the spirits. I stroll through the gardens, but none are present. I head for Ella's rooms and then knock on the door across the way. There is no answer, so I grant myself entry. The suite is empty.

I curse and dissipate to my suite. I have no idea how to find them. I pace in my rooms for any other ideas. The only thing that comes to mind is Dis, located in the middle of Caleum and part of the Clemm Court territory. It's where Erac and Aron called home for hundreds of revolutions and large enough to house the spirits.

The sound of electricity in the air sizzles, turning blistering cold around me as pressure builds.

As I stand there, my elements shred apart, and I go blind. I give in under the weight of freezing pressure until I reform. I blink, the air burning my lungs. The scent and taste of rotten bodies fill the air, and I blink against ash falling through the sky.

I cough, pulling the fabric of my shirt over my nose and mouth, peering around. The world is black, rough stalagmites everywhere. Overhead a pink orb hangs in the sky, giving off a faint light.

A heavy metal hand lands on my shoulder, and I spin, taking a step back. I trip and fall back, my body stopping in midair.

The spirit reaches out, and I take its hand, letting it pull me to my feet. "Where are we?" I yell, a gust of wind pelting my face with the black ash falling.

"Damnatus," it says, a female. "Do watch your step." It points to a puddle of bubbling silver fluid.

"Why?" I growl.

"Come, let us meet with the others. They are nearby. Keep your eyes open, as there are still demons in Damnatus, and do not step in the pits of quicksilver, it will burn you and suck you below the crust of this plane to the underneath."

I trudge, avoiding the puddles on the rough surface. Keeping my head down and holding a hand in front of my face, I do my best to protect my eyes from the falling ash and random gusts that fling it against my skin. We approach the others, and across the landscape, I see more of the others wandering toward the group.

One of them steps away, approaching us in a hurry. "Declan."

"Sordello," I splutter. "What is going on?"

"We've been removed from Caleum," another spirit who stands with us explains.

I peer up at him, registering the hood as Malik. "Why?" There's no answer, and I grunt. "Right, Erac and Viktor."

"Likely with the help of Sordello's daughter," the female spirit says. The hood bows forward.

I grit my teeth. "Am I stuck here?"

"You are not, my son. Come, let us find Aron. As a collective, we should have the power to send you home."

I take a few steps, following. "What about the rest of you?"

"We cannot go up," Malik says. "We cannot go to Medius until we have completed the reason we left, and we cannot travel to Caleum as we are not of Caleum."

I stop, scowling, and facing him. "What? But you're not in Caleum where you were called, and you aren't in Medius, so you're not stuck in those two dimensions."

Malik puts a hand on my shoulder and shakes his hooded face at me. "We are bound as elementals are not. It is the burden of our runes. Because our runes can control beings lower than us, we are not permitted to move freely. Only magic can move us between dimensions, and not magic we are able to perform."

I wrench away from him, heart hammering. Without the spirits, my chances of getting Ella back just dropped to null. I gape behind my shirt, eyes wide, stinging as ash falls into them. "No. There's a way. They brought you here. Aron and I, we can do the same magic they did."

"You aren't strong enough."

"But with Aron," I repeat, "we can. We'll do it together, whatever it is."

Behind me, Sordello chuckles. "I appreciate the enthusiasm. Damnatus is not favorable, but there is no use in trying. Moving to a lower dimension is less difficult, and they've moved us two dimensions below Caleum. It will take all the power we have as a collective to send you and Aron home."

My head is shaking. "No, there has to be a way. I can't—we can't do this without your help. The demons—Viktor—Ella—" my voice breaks.

"My son," Sordello comes around to face me. He grips my shoulders, kneeling before me.

"Don't fucking look at me like that!" I yell. "I can't do this—this whole fucking war—getting past Erac. I can't get past him."

Another gust of wind blows me a half step forward, and Sordello holds me steady. His hood slips back, revealing a glow beneath. He reaches up, correcting the hood and the light dims. "We need to hurry. Getting you and Aron back is our priority, but

Damnatus is dangerous. We have precious little time before demons realize we are here, then it will be a war to survive, and the collective will not have time to focus on returning you to Caleum."

"Fuck," I say in a hoarse whisper, the air making my throat raw. "There has to be a different way, something to do."

"There is not," the female says. "Please hurry."

I hang my head and squeeze my eyes shut. I take a deep breath and regret it, coughing and spluttering, my eyes watering as they fix on Sordello again. "When you get us back to Caleum, can I do what Ella did and call you to Caleum?"

"No, my son," Sordello shakes his hood. "We will not hear the call so far from our home."

My chest tightens with anxiety. "I can't do this alone. What am I supposed to do? Erac is too strong for me."

"Trust Aron. He is the second son of Virgil, and he will be able to help you. Now we must return you, or we have lost all hope." Sordello releases me, rises to his feet, and moves on.

The other two follow, but my legs won't work. I can't get the muscles to cooperate, and I stumble along. There's already no hope.

~

The return trip is excruciating. My lungs are frozen and pressurized. I suffocate in darkness until I blink in bright light. I squint, trying to determine where I am. The great room comes into focus, the pieces filling in as I stare around the courtroom.

My legs are shaking beneath me, and I start to sway.

"Declan."

I whirl, fists up, and pause. "Aron?" I lower my fists.

He inclines his head, blood trickling from his nose and the right corner of his mouth. With a wheeze and wince, he leans back against the wall. He slides down until he is a crumpled mess of limbs on the floor.

"You look like shit," I tell him, crouching down to his level.

"Ha." He gives a weak laugh and then rubs a dirty hand over his face, smearing black crud over his features. He holds his hand up, showing me the grime over his flesh. "You don't look much better."

"Why Damnatus?" I limp to him and join him on the floor, panting a bit. I check my own nose, my hand pulling back with blood. "And why am I so fucking tired?"

He waves me off. "Travel between dimensions is difficult."

I glance around. "Yeah, I'm realizing that."

He chuckles. "Ella jumped from Caleum to Medius. She let out so much energy that she destroyed the Byron family estate. She made space in the new dimension and built a whole room in their palace, a part of existence that never was, willed into life because of her." He waves a hand about with a grin like a drunk man entertained, and then drops it against his stomach. "She had every right to sleep it off for a few days."

I ignore the words coming out of his mouth for various reasons, one of which is that I do not understand a single one. "Aron," I grind through clenched teeth, my patience already tested for the day, "I feel like a fucking idiot every single time you talk to me. I know enough to manipulate the elements, but that's the bottom of the barrel. I know magic becomes more advanced and complex, and I know nothing about any of it. So, talk to me like I am stupid."

He snickers and sighs long and slow. "You are neither idiot nor stupid, although perhaps ignorant of magic, I'll grant. The spirits were trapped in Medius until Ella called them forth, and then the spirits were trapped here, in Caleum, until their purpose was finished. Erac used this knowledge, casting a spell to send them into an even lower dimension. They are not able to travel through dimensions unless called or sent." Aron is breathing normally again and pushes himself into a sitting position. "And no one is going to be strong enough to bring the spirits back from Damnatus. Well, maybe Ella."

"So, us and them aren't bound like the spirits are." I run a hand down my face. "And Erac trapped the spirits in Damnatus?"

Aron bobs his head, chin nearly bouncing off his chest. "Yes. Certainly, Ella helped. Erac, for all his vanity, is not as powerful as she, despite what he believes." He breathes out long and slow, then turns his face to me. "Even if we collect all of the mages in Byron, I doubt we'll have enough power, and they will only send them back again."

I stare at the cracks of mortar between the stones in the opposing wall as adrenaline starts to course through my veins. A voice is whispering like silk tendrils through my mind, soft and alluring.

I take a deep breath. "So, we've lost the spirits, and I've lost the crown of Byron."

"How?"

"Mistakes were made." I get off the floor, running hands over my thighs and then straightening my shirt, functioning mechanically to keep from losing my temper.

Aron fumbles to his feet and glares. "That's an awfully big mistake."

I cut my eyes to him and snarl. "Don't follow me." I start up the hall.

He ignores my warning, trailing after me. "Declan, wait."

I spin, throwing compressed air elements at him. He fumbles backward and stops, gaping at me. I keep my hand out. "Stay away from me."

He closes his mouth, frowning. "You're angry."

"Fucking furious," I snarl under my breath to assure him I am in no mood to be around. "I've lost my wife. Again. I failed to protect her. Now I've lost the crown, and the war hangs in the balance. Without the spirits, I have no chance at convincing these delusional dimwits that surrender is asinine. Ella is helping Viktor, apparently willingly, and Haven above, I am going to rip out every throat responsible the first chance I get."

Aron shifts his weight and twitches. "This is not your fault or your responsibility alone."

A laugh rips out of my chest. "And yet my brother has promised the court Ella and I will clean up this mess for them, without the aid of the army."

Aron winces. "That is not likely."

"You don't think I fucking know that? You think I still believe I am going to get my wife back? We don't even know what those bastards have done to her."

The whispers are slithering into my marrow, and I'm grasping at my sanity, fumbling at the hope that this has a happy ending. I ram my fingers into my eyes, half tempted to rip them out to feel something other than the endless weight of lonely misery. I grip my fists and take a breath.

I stare at him, and he frowns back. "Stay away from me," I repeat, my voice hoarse with fury and too much talking. "I have never talked so much in my life, and I am done talking about things."

I shred my elements apart and reassemble them in the practice field. I command the others present to leave and rip my shirt off, buttons flying. I am already starting to punch the closest object as they hurry to leave.

My fist contacts a solid element, my hand, or the thing crunching, maybe both. I pull back and slam my fist into the thing again, wanting the throbbing heat, needing the feeling of hitting something as hard as I can.

CHAPTER 28

DECLAN

With nothing left to do but convince the court to continue the war, I leave my rooms in search of courtiers in need of persuasion. Talking is the last thing I want to do, and while I am no longer king of Byron, I am a prince or something of Medius, and I can throw that around in my favor.

Time crawls by as disparities gnaw away hope. Another cycle passes by. I have lost track of time as I have lost my temper, blinded by rage more and more after each conversation in favor of continuing this war against Viktor.

For their part, I know Legia, Seth, and Aron are fighting the same losing battle. The absence of the spirits is being noted and questioned, although I offer no valid reasons for their loss. I remind them all what Viktor did, but they are citing death tolls and expenditures as an excuse for their fear.

I hate them all.

Seth collects me to attend the session with black eyes and no smile. I stare at him on the other side of my door. "No Asena?" I ask.

"They left yesterday to go back to Clemm."

I nod and exit my room, struggling to breathe. He doesn't

joke or flip sarcasm or even say another word. We walk in silence to our fate, sealed in the hands of cowards.

When we reach the courtroom, everyone is milling about. Aron and Legia approach, keeping a notable distance from me. Legia dances in place, wringing her hands together and twirling a loose piece of hair at the nape of her neck. "You two look rather grim. We don't know the verdict yet. We've all done what we can."

I stare at her and blink. Seth hangs his head and shuffles his feet. Crossing his arms, he hangs his head. "Things don't look good, Gia."

"Haven, but I know that." The words are a breathless whisper. "I stood there and listened to Lady Maine tell me I am still young, and I'll find a new husband, no sense in having the next die in this war as well. As if." She rolls her eyes and makes a rude gesture with her hand. "Chase died to save these spineless arses, and they're acting as if that's somehow justified because their precious lives are *so* valuable."

Seth bobs his head. I stare around the room. Elementals are smiling and making conversation. My hands twitch as my sight flashes red. They deserve to hand their heads over to Viktor.

A hand lands on my shoulder, and I jerk, facing my brother's somber gaze. "You were growling."

I wrench my body away from his touch. He drops his hands into his front pockets. Legia whines, "Oh, I hate this. I hate this waiting part. This is too much. I think I am going to be sick."

If I had eaten anything in days, I might feel the same. I roll my shoulders back, pressing the blades together and clench my jaw.

"Maybe you should offer to marry Selene, get the crown back," Seth mutters, kicking at the marble with the sole of his dress shoe. "Not like you can't go back on that again. Get to keep the crown."

"I'm not renouncing my fucking marriage, and I'm tired of

fucking saying it. I married Ella, and it took too fucking long to do it. I'm going to stay married to her until we are both fucking dead." My harsh announcement draws the eyes of others around the room. I snarl at them and turn to sit down on the floor.

I cross my legs and prop my elbow and head on one knee, strumming my fingers on the other. Legia is right; waiting has become uncomfortable. I reach up and loosen the top button on my shirt to breathe easier.

For all the times I have waited things out, mostly under insufferable conditions, this must be one of the worst. I strum my fingers faster, ignoring the building pressure in my chest. Selene comes strolling into the room, smiling and greeting everyone in an obnoxious sparkling gown. My lip curls back as I watch her move past, and everything moves around me in slow motion, colors dulling, and sound fading as my heart rate jacks up.

Ghosts of Ella flicker around the room, like shadows of our past coming to life. The mass in my chest rolls over in my ears until everything snaps back. I feel like ice water has been thrown over my head and shoulders. I sit up, shaking the feeling off and blinking, startled like a rat in the light.

I try to focus on what is around me. Talwarth standing next to Selene and their annoying droning. The only thing on my mind is the memory of Ella dragging me in here one night after a ball, a little drunk and giggling. I spun her in circles, even without music. It was the only time she'd ever managed a dance without stepping on my toes, and the first time I didn't hate being in this room. I got her out of her dress and laid her down on the cushions, and I've had a hard time paying attention in this room ever since.

I sigh. These memories are killing me, drowning me in longing.

Seth glances over at me with concern. "You okay?"

"No." My eyes search the room for any sign she was here,

but there is none. She is gone from this palace, every little trace of her.

I grit my teeth as Selene spins on her heel, moving out of the way as servants roll forth scales. She gestures around the room and smiles. "This is such an important decision that only the truth of blood can tip the scales."

Aron stands, his cry ringing out. "This is a highly unreliable determination."

She turns on him with a smile on her lips and hardened features. "Excuse me? The scales of truth are a long-standing tradition in this court and every other when deciding matters of war."

He puts his hands on his hips. "As the high mage—"

"Are you?" she asks, interrupting him with a sugar-sweet tone. "Are you the highest mage?"

Aron's face takes on a mask of cruelty. "Don't question me, girl. Scales like these have not been used since Tyle's reign, and for good reason. Blood is unpredictable and holds no logic. Fear alone is enough to tip the scales."

She draws herself up. "This is a matter of war, a decision that needs to be made based upon honesty, not on promises that can skew results."

I recall Seth's words, promising Ella and I could end this war on our own. My eyes cut to him, and I curl a lip back. He shrugs at me. "Seemed like a reasonable promise."

Aron stands his ground. "The scales of choice are highly dubious in how they function. Any little thing can trigger a response against what the caster would choose. The weight of blood alone will be different for each voter. Are you prepared to follow these scales, given how unreliable the results will be?"

"Blood is the lifeforce driving through us all. Blood reveals the truths we may not wish to see."

Aron shakes his head. "You're a fool. Those scales will call upon ghosts of the past, shadows of what is and was, and could be manipulated to determine your vote. No one will have any say in how their blood falls, and I will repeat again, not every drop of blood will weigh the same."

"The very same reason I am using them." She is losing her composure. "This is my court. I wear the crown. I will make the decisions." Her shriek rings in the silence, and I almost smile. She clears her throat and adjusts her crown. "The voting will begin now."

She backs away from the scales, and Spaulding stands. He walks toward them with a drawn face, but his gaze flickers my way before he turns his attentions to the scale. Facing the court for all to see, he lifts his thumb, piercing his skin with the sharp point at the top of the shaft.

His blood bubbles up, rolling down the right side of the beam, and drops into the pan. There are a few gasps as Spaulding covers his face, shaking his head. Even from here, I can see his body trembling. After a moment, he collects himself and moves away from the scales.

"In favor," Selene drawls, glaring at Spaulding as he shuffles back to his seat.

We go around the ring, one after the other. Most votes are against, and my stomach is twisting like snakes. No one walks away from the scales with a smile, some on the verge of tears. Legia burst into sobs as soon as her thumb contacts the spindle at the top of the shaft. Her vote in favor resounds the loudest from the stone walls.

Seth stands, walking with squared shoulders to the scales to cast his vote. He hesitates, staring at me before pricking his thumb. His eyes squeeze shut, and the color drains from his face. He lifts his head and pulls his thumb back.

Blood pools and swirls, lifting above the spindle, then drops and rolls down the right beam and into the pan in favor. I start to breathe again and push myself off the floor, wiping my hands together as I pass by him on his way to resume his seat.

Our eyes catch for a second, and I see the red ring of fury burning around black orbs. I frown, leaning away and continue to the middle of the room. I stare at the scales as I walk around, putting my back to Selene and facing the court.

I can hear hearts pumping in the quiet room. The gilded shaft twists upward to an arrowhead. The beams angled down to thin chains supporting the rounded discs hanging on either side. I swallow my nerves and ram my thumb down on the spindle.

Warmth blossoms in the calloused, flat pad. The world turns bright. The whole world rushes over my shoulders, loud and bright, sucking me back into a void through a veil of ice, and then my wife stands before me.

"Ella." Her name tumbles from my lips as a strangled groan as I reach for her, pulling her close, inhaling the scent of honey.

She presses against me, nuzzling her small nose against my neck, her head tips back. Her hair tickles my arms as they close around her, and I hold onto her with every fiber of my body, mind, and soul.

She sniffles as if she is crying, and it wrenches something I didn't realize was so broken inside of me. "You would fight for me?"

"Yes."

"You would die for me?"

"Haven," I manage. "Yes. A thousand times, yes."

The world comes screaming back for me, and I blink, coming to on my knees, moisture on my face. "No," I growl. "Ella!" I yell, whipping around, searching for what I know isn't there.

I stop, putting a hand over my eyes and catching my breath. I hear the clang of my blood dropping in the pan, followed by gasps around the room, and look to see the scales tipped in favor of the war. I step to it, frowning, the scale never having wavered once for all the votes.

My eyes scan for my drop of blood, but there is no visible

difference in any of the few scattered there. There are whispers around the room.

"Cheater!" Selene's shrill cry draws my gaze over my shoulder at her.

"No!" Aron is on his feet, yelling back. "That is the weight of love and not something that can be manipulated. I warned you of the consequences of blood."

She glares, her eyes searching my face. I turn back to the scales so heavily weighed down in favor that the pan skims the surface of its perch.

A thousand times over, lover. I'll follow you to the inferno if I have to. I rub my temple and step back to my seat.

No matter the other votes, the scale never moves again. I breathe easier with each passing vote, whether for or against.

Selene stands, moving to the scales with her skirt clenched in her fists. She throws them down and holds her thumb over the tip. She bites her lip and screws up her face, her hand shaking.

"Oh, come on, Your Highness, it's just a little, tiny prick," Seth calls out, hands held around his mouth. Her face jerks up, and she narrows her eyes. He gives a thumbs up. "You can do it, buttercup."

She presses her thumb down then pulls back, checking it. I raise my eyebrows, no sign or scent of blood to be found.

"Gonna have to do better than that," Seth roars with laughter.

"Seth," she hisses.

"Need help? I'll be more than happy to draw blood for you."

Her face turns pink, and I clamp my jaw down on a laugh. "Be quiet. I am the queen. I am capable of doing this myself."

"Not from what I'm seeing," he spits back with a grin.

There is a smattering of muted chortles and strangled coughs. I smirk with the strange urge to hug my brother. I toss my arm over his shoulder and chuckle. "You fucking ass."

She screws up her face, scrunching her eyes shut as she taps her thumb on the spindle. She peeks from one eye and frowns before trying to squeeze a drop of blood out of her skin.

"Haven," Seth mutters, shrugging me off him, getting up and striding across the room. "This is going to take all day."

"Seth," she yells, "don't you dare touch—" He grabs hold of her wrist and impales the point into her thumb. She squeals and pulls back. "I hate you!" she screams.

No one says anything, and Seth points at the drop of blood rolling down the beam of against, falling with a chink against the others. "I don't really care. We could have grown old waiting for you to stick yourself hard enough."

She glares. "I wasn't talking to you."

He shrugs, kicking at the floor and crossing his arms. "Shame." He jerks his chin at the scales. "Looks like we have a verdict."

"Yes," she responds in a brisk voice. "The majority vote stands. We are no longer at war."

Seth drops his arms, pointing at the scale. "It's tipped in favor of."

Her chin lifts. "Declan cheated."

I get to my feet. "I poked my thumb and let the blood fall, the same as everyone else."

"You did something, manipulated the elements. You had to. There aren't enough votes in favor to outweigh all of those against."

"I told you, I didn't."

"And we are to trust your word?" She sneers at me, grabbing her skirt and stepping down to the main floor. "You, the husband of a traitor and murderous witch?"

I clench my fists. "Careful, Selene. Monarchs are losing their crown quickly these days."

"Was that a threat?"

I smile, rocking onto my heels. "A fact. Byron has lost two kings and two queens in the last few revolutions."

She opens and closes her mouth, then huffs and sticks her nose in the air. "The *majority* vote wins, regardless of how the scales tipped. Byron Court will no longer war with Viktor. Any," she glares at me, "who go against the court will be found guilty of treason and treated as such."

My eyes sweep the room. Most duck their heads or turn away from me, refusing to meet my gaze. Not many voted in favor of. They are cowards, tucking chins to their chest rather than fighting. I turn to Seth, scowling in irritation.

"You know damn good and well we aren't giving up." My brother chuckles, shaking his head.

"Then you'll be put to death," Selene snaps back. "Is she worth your head?"

I glance around the room, all eyes staring at me. My eyes find Selene's. "Of course not." *She's worth so much more than that.*

Seth's jaw drops. I narrow my eyes and turn my face ever so slightly to the right. His brows furrow, and he turns back to Selene. "My mistake, Your Royal Fucking Majesty."

"If anyone ever interferes with Viktor, stands against him, it will go against this court's decision," Selene repeats.

I stare at her, daring her to try to arrest me right here and now. "We understand."

"Will you accept surrender?"

I hitch one side of my mouth back, not sure if she expects me to answer that question. Either way, I keep my lips pressed together.

"Answer your queen," Talwarth snarls, coming to stand beside her. "Will you stand with this court?"

I cut my eyes to Aron, making eye contact for a heartbeat, then shift my eyes to Legia and onto my brother. I let my sight linger on each of them then shake my head. "No."

"Guards! Arrest the Bard brothers."

"What," Seth yelps. "I didn't—"

My elements shred apart with a blistering cold force I haven't felt since Ella moved me two dimensions down. I shake my body and limbs, staring around a dismal room of red and wood coated in the grime of a hundred revolutions.

The walls are lined with crude wooden shelves, and a few tattered red tapestries faded and threadbare. A few curtains hang at the ends of shelves that look like they're designed to hide them from sight, stained with holes eaten through the material.

Seth runs his hands over his torso, then down his legs. "Thank Haven, I'm in one piece."

"Do not be absurd," Aron gives him a dirty look. "Not high mage," he mutters. "Who does she think she is? Not high mage," he scoffs.

"Where the blazing inferno are we?" Legia whines. "It smells bad, like rotten air, and it— Haven, is that a rat? Was that vermin? No, no, no! I am not staying here. This place is awful." She wraps her arms around her torso and glares around as if she is daring the dirt and dust to even try to touch her.

"Where are we?" I ask, inhaling enough dust to coat my throat. I cough.

Aron stands back and smiles, spreading his arms. Stacks of books collecting dust are everywhere in the dim light, covering the surfaces of several desks and a single couch in the middle of the enormous room. "Welcome to Dis."

Legia shivers and hops in place. "It's darned cold in here, and there's like, no light? Or some? Where is that even coming from? And I'm serious, I think that was a rat, but it looks a hundred revolutions old, a big, fat hairy one, and I'm not staying here."

Aron's face is drawn in on itself. I glance around with a raised eyebrow, lifting and dropping one shoulder. I have survived in worse conditions. "It'll work."

“No. No, it will not. This absolutely will not work.”

I fix my gaze on her. “And you’d rather be locked in a cell back in Byron?”

Her mouth puckers as small as she can make it, and she wrinkles her nose.

“That’s what I thought. How long will you let us stay?” I turn back to Aron.

“As long as you need.” He shrugs. “Or want. This is my home. I am offering it to you.”

CHAPTER 29

MORELLA

Nearly two cycles have crawled by since Erac and I sent our biggest threat away. I have been chock-full of expectations that there will be retaliation. The expectancy is idiotic according to my betrothed, but I have this nagging in the back of my mind that somehow we screwed up, that something went wrong.

Erac rolled his eyes and walked away when I tried to explain to him my concern, so from then on, I have kept quiet. I am not certain I can be honest with him, and I have yet to talk about that whispering in the back of my mind that begs me to do dark things.

On the bright side of it all, I'm free to wander the beach now. The sand is warm and shifts under my bare feet as I walk above the tide line. The salt in the air clings to my skin and lingers as a taste on my lips like the world is kissing me for coming to see it.

I stretch my arms out wide and spin in circles, eyes closed and face tipped toward the soul star, basking in the warmth until I am laughing and dizzy. I collapse back, laying in the soft grains as they meld around me like a warm hug.

A shadow looms over me, and I blink, squinting up into my

father's face. I grin at him. "Have you come to enjoy the beach with me?"

"No, I have not, although the idea is a nice one. We have visitors."

I prop up on my elbows. "Oh?"

"Yes. I thought you may want to greet them with me. I suspect this is the fruit of your labors, and you deserve to see your reward."

"Okay." I sigh, laying back. "When do I have to go?"

There is the slightest hitch to his breath, and peeking one eye open, I see a corner of his mouth is pulled back. "We are Emperor and Princess of Caleum. We can make them wait as long as you would like."

I sit up and cock my head at him. "Then, you can enjoy the beach with me for a little while, can't you?"

For a moment, he is still and silent then settles down on the sand next to me. "I dislike the sand."

I scrunch my nose at him and laugh. "How can anyone hate the sand?"

He wipes his hands together and frowns at them, inspecting his open palms. "It gets everywhere."

I snicker, picking up a handful of sand and tossing it at him. He jerks away and glares. I wince. "Sorry."

His green eyes are brilliant in the light, the brightest shade of green found in new grass or fresh snakeskin. The left corner of his mouth pulls back high, curling. My father grabs a handful of sand, letting it flow through his fingers, then plucks another and lobs it toward me.

I hold my hands up, laughing and ducking my face to shield it, but I never feel the contact. I glance up, seeing he has frozen the sand in the air before me. He smiles with a closed mouth, and I grin back at him.

He stands, brushing sand from his trousers, and offers me his hand. "Come, I am ready."

With a sigh, I take his hand. Pulled to my feet, I use my free hand to shield my eyes from the light as I tip my head back and meet his gaze. "Where to?"

"The throne room, please."

I close my eyes and picture us in the room. Cold seeps through me, and when I open my eyes, I stand in the same room with my father's hand in mine.

Erac turns to us, his hands on his hips. When he sees us, his eyebrows lift, his eyes on my father. "Viktor." He motions toward the others present.

My father releases my hand, tucking it in his arm, and turns us, stepping away from them to the throne. He drops my hand and sits on the throne, so I move to sit in the open seat next to him.

Erac motions for the visitors to come forward, and I watch them with a weary expression. There are three, one a boy with a timid smile and a lightness dancing in his eyes. He appears young, maybe a few revolutions less than me. The other two are women near the same age as myself, both fair of hair and light of eye.

The woman in the middle has beautiful blonde curls hanging loose around her shoulders, and she steps one pace ahead of the others as they come to a stop. Her features are delicate, her beauty radiating, and I seethe with jealousy, wishing to be so beautiful.

"Hey, Ella," the boy says with a small wave.

I give him a tight smile, the nickname giving me a pang in my head, a reminder I have not seen George in a while. "Hello."

"You will address me, boy," Viktor snaps.

He hangs his head. "Yes, Father."

"You will address me as Emperor or Your Majesty. I have no blood relation to you. Your parent died a couple of revolutions ago, killed by the idiot on your left with poison." Viktor lifts a hand to indicate the beautiful woman in the middle. "Why have you come, Selene?"

The woman in the middle gives a deep curtsy to my father and then stands, clasping her hands in front of her. "The Byron Court has ruled in favor of relinquishing its rule to you."

My father sits back, his arms resting, his fingers steepled in front of him. I watch him, his features drawing closed in contemplation. I hold my breath, wondering why he delays. We have wanted this for cycles.

"Very well." He pushes up and steps toward her, hands behind his back. "I accept your surrender and will take control of the court immediately."

"Thank you," Selene gives him another curtsy. "I will return and be your ever-faithful queen, serving you."

She turns away, and my father slides his hands into his front pockets. "I did not dismiss you."

"Oh." She pivots on her heels and faces him.

"I did not name you queen in Byron."

"But I'm…" she tries to smile. "I am a Byron. Who else…?" Her eyes travel toward me.

I raise a brow and my chin at her, staring back without fear.

"Spaulding." Father nods toward the boy who waved at me. "Will you serve me?"

The boy looks a bit confused, eyes cutting toward Selene before he rolls his shoulders back and puffs out his chest. "If that is what you require."

"Good boy." Father's head turns the other way, and with his back to me, I can only assume he is looking at the second woman. "Skylar Blackburn, your family has always been loyal. How would you like to be queen?"

She stammers, eyes flickering to her right at the others. She shifts her weight from one foot to the other and smiles with pursed lips. "Of course, Your Majesty, but—"

"Then you will marry Spaulding. I expect good things from the two of you."

"You can't do this!" Selene shrieks, her cheeks tinged pink now. "I am Queen of Byron. I brought the court to heel. I am the reason the Byron Court is surrendering to you at all."

My father glances back at me. I tilt my head, and he turns to face the three of them once more. "The crown you wore belonged to my daughter and heir, Morella."

"*Morella*?"

I wince at the shrill scream of my name.

"She is a murderer! The court—"

"You will be silent and remain so unless I request you to answer me." My father's voice is low, cutting through the air like smoke, smooth and dangerous.

I slide out of the throne and step next to my father, eyebrows pulled together, lips turned down at the ends. "Father?"

He holds a hand up to stay my words and turns to me. "This girl has betrayed you. She slandered your name, wanted you dead."

My heart rolls in my chest, and something slithers awake inside of me, crawling through my chest as silky desire. I inhale deeply through my nose, the scent of coppery blood hanging onto my senses. "Why?" I manage, my shaking hands curling into fists.

My father smirks and turns forward. "From what I can surmise, jealousy played a role in it, but she is conniving, vying for power as all the others and too stupid to do it any other way than steal it from you."

The girl's mouth drops open as if she wants to scream, but no sound comes out. Her eyes turn glassy, and her heart-shaped face turns bright red.

"She spilled my secrets and yours for her own gains, putting your life in grave danger in the process."

I twist my lips into a sideways sneer of joy. "Maybe she should fear for her life then."

"A valid concept of retribution, my daughter," he says with an airy lightness to the words. "Spaulding, Skylar, you are both excused. We will talk terms and negotiations of the Byron Court ruling over dinner this evening." He lifts a hand and snaps. Two servants hurry forth. "Take these two to a room. They should get acquainted. I want them to remain there until I call on them for dinner. Any deviation from my decisions will result in punishment. Am I understood?"

Spaulding and Skylar exchange glances and bow their heads. They echo agreements and turn to follow the servants out of the hall. My father turns his back and strides toward the throne. I listen to him settle in his seat as I glare at the woman who would see me dead.

The voice in my mind is whispering tantalizing ideas. She will pay. I will make her repay in blood. I will taste it as it spills from her skin and laugh as she screams for mercy.

I turn my head to direct my words to my father. "Did she show me any mercy?"

"Answer the question, Selene. Did you show my daughter any modicum of mercy on your way to taking her place?"

Her face screws up, and she turns red, ready to burst as she struggles against the order. "No." The word tears from her lips like an angry growl of a wounded animal.

I throw out a hand, picturing the small blade I conjured in the gardens. The small, thin diamond-shaped blade and black leather-wrapped hilt with a loop on the end materializes in my hand, and I throw it. The metal glints as it cuts through the air and embeds in her shoulder.

She screams, her body twisting back from the force of impact. Her hand slaps toward it, then she whips around to face me with bared teeth and murder in her eyes.

I smile at her, batting my lashes with faux innocence, and

use the elements to draw the blade back out of her so I can grab it from the air. She whimpers and falls to her knees, scrambling toward me on all fours to bow down at my feet.

I glance over my shoulder at my father, who shakes his head at me with pinched lips. I turn back and consider kicking her in the face. Barefoot as I am, that might hurt, so I crouch down, grabbing her face and lifting it toward me.

Tears are falling from her buttercup yellow eyes, set wide in her face. Her pretty pink lower lip trembles, her beauty somewhat tarnished by the red splotches on her cheeks and the snot dribbling from her nose.

I caress her cheek, aching to break that pretty, doll-like face. "I bet you're so proud of your looks, aren't you?" I whisper. "I bet you'd just hate it if someone were to leave ugly scars all over it, wouldn't you?"

I press the tip of the blade against her cheek. She is pleading with her eyes, fighting back a sob. The power I hold over her is intoxicating.

"Answer me," I command her.

She shakes her head and blubbers, "Yes."

"I thought so."

She tries to pull away, and I grab her by those gold strands at the scalp and yank. She yelps and I grin, slashing at the side of her face.

"No," she wails, scratching at the weapon in my hand with one hand, the other covering the bloody line I left behind.

"Yes," I breathe, pressing the blade over her lips. I curl a lip as snot leaks onto it. "Beg, bitch. Beg for me to forgive you, beg for your face." The words are hushed, tumbling from my lips before I even register them as a thought, that dark whisper flowing through my veins like a cheer released.

"Please," she sobs. "Please, Morella, Ella, please," she hiccups.

I flip the blade in my grip, and this time slash upward from her jaw toward her nose on the other side. She screams, squirming to get away, throwing her hands over her face. I just tighten my fingers to the point of numb pain in her hair and do my best to rip the strands out and give her a nice bald patch to go with her scars.

With the lump of hair in my hand, she makes another shrill squeal of pain and kicks, writhing out of my grip. I relax my fingers, wiggling the hair loose and blood back into the digits as I watch her slither on the floor away from me, an arm trying to cover her bleeding face, her eyes stretched open wide and fixated on me.

I smirk, tossing the small blade aside as I stomp my way toward her and stand over her. I drop down, a knee in the middle of her chest, grabbing her by the shoulders and forcing them flat on the floor.

She spits in my face, and I pull back, ball my fist and swing. The action surprises me as much as it does her, and she gapes at me, dazed. My hand throbs, and I check it, not seeing evidence of damage done to myself. I grin, repeating the motion a few times, the burn in my chest through my shoulder and arm familiar yet strange and oh so good.

Selene lays on the ground, blood splattered across her porcelain skin. Her chest is fighting against my body weight in uneven gulps, her face turned away. The whisper caresses my mind, dulling my senses, my vision blurry around the edges.

I stand, staring down at her with ragged breathing and a clenched jaw. "Are you afraid?" I ask between heaving breaths. When she doesn't answer, I kick her in the side and scream, "Answer me, you fucking bitch, are you afraid yet?"

She recoils and sobs. "Yes," she whimpers.

"Good." I lean over and spit in her face for good measure.

Her eyes sparkle with fury. She is bleeding and crying. She says she is afraid, but she is not broken. I haven't done enough.

I stand over her, splaying a hand out, palm directed at her

face. The skin splits straight down her face, and she screams, eyes clenching shut. I spread the fissure further, down her throat and torso, watching the blood seep to the surface and spill out in dribbles. It is not enough. She needs to hurt more, to truly be afraid of me.

I kneel over her and grip the split skin in the middle of her neck and peel it apart. Warm fluid squirts out, spraying my face. My fingers fumble to find purchase in the slippery flesh, so I dig my nails into it for grip. I hear as much as I feel her screaming, the tissue around my fingers trembling and flexing.

The skin will not tear further, so I grab the loose pieces at the base of her neck and tug. My right hand peels back a strip, and I reach for her face next. I keep pulling and tearing until my fingers are refusing to work anymore.

I snarl at her, one eye frozen wide open in terror, the light gone from it. I try to catch my breath, my lips curling back in a grin even as I gulp in air. My legs shake as I get them to work, lifting me off her ugly corpse and turning to face my father.

I try to wipe away drops of blood on my face but only smear warm fluid across my cheek. I glance down at my hands, coated with sticky red so thick that my skin is obscured. I wrinkle my nose and let my hands fall to my sides, lifting my eyes to my father again.

He watches me with a straight face, no hint of emotion discernible. My breathing has evened out by the time he stirs. He gets to his feet, approaches me, and pats a hand on my shoulder as he moves past.

I turn to watch him walk out of the room in silence. I lift my hands, staring down at them, and nausea settles in my gut. They clench into fists, the congealing blood pulling the skin tight where my skin flexes. When I look up again, my father is gone.

CHAPTER 30

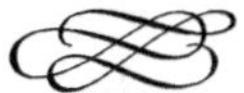

MORELLA

I stare out at the stars over the sea as I lean on the balustrade. The breeze wafts my drying hair around my face. A sickness is gnawing in my gut, and I check again that there is no blood left on my hands. Another presence draws my eye. I startle and stand upright. "Father?"

He inclines his head. "You did not attend dinner. Erac was going to come, but I felt you may be overwhelmed enough."

I snort through my nose and accept the goblet he hands me. I chug the wine and make a face of disgust. I glance at the dribble in the bottom and then turn and hurl the cup toward the sea, the pull of sore muscles in my shoulder twinging and reminding me of what I did earlier.

I lean forward, bracing my forearms on the railing and resting my forehead against the cool stone. I curse under my breath and squeeze my eyes shut.

"Morella, she deserved her fate and tenfold. You have always been skilled in such ways."

I curl my lip at the balcony floor, not bothering to lift my head. "Skilled?" I scoff. "I literally ripped her flesh off her body because I wanted her to be afraid."

He chuckles. "I would say she was terrified."

My head whips up to glare at him. "You didn't even say anything. You just walked away from me."

My father tilts his head and contemplates me. The left side of his mouth twitches. "She would have done much worse to you, given the chance."

"Worse than death?" I scoff again, rolling my eyes. "I'm pretty sure death is final. What is worse than that?"

"To have your own daughter despise you? What about Erac watching the woman he loves slowly destroyed and having little chance to save her?"

I wince and turn, leaning against the banister and crossing my arms. He has a point. "Having no idea who you are because you were poisoned? Struggling every day to try and remember something you'll never know again and having to learn everything, even who you are once more?"

We stare at each other, the wind blowing hair into my face as the silence between us stretches on for ages. Motion stirs around us, and together we turn to face Erac as he approaches us.

He gives me that lopsided, goofy grin he uses when he feels bad about something and shoves his hands in his front pockets. "I came to see if you were alright."

"I made it clear to you that my daughter would need this evening to recover," my father says in a scathing tone. I feel the venom dripping off his words as they waft through the air.

Erac's shoulders square up. "She is my betrothed. I am allowed to see her when I want. If she is upset, I should tend to her."

My father swells up, his stance shifting, his feet spreading further, and his arms crossing. "I am her father, and I know what my daughter needs."

My future husband sneers. "She's recovering because of what you allowed to happen."

I roll my eyes. "I am going to walk on the beach and leave you two to fight it out without me since you're going to talk like I'm not even here anyway."

"Morella." My father's voice carries a warning. "Before you go, know that tomorrow you should rest and collect yourself. The day after, we are leaving."

I gasp, eyes fluttering open wider. "What?"

"Excuse me?" Erac steps forward, his mouth settling in a hard line. Erac's face pinches white with fury. "I did not give her permission to leave the safety of our walls."

My father holds a hand up, eyes cutting to him as he stops in his track. "No, I did, when the threat to her was removed." He pauses a heartbeat and then lowers his arms to his sides and gives me a smile. "Enough time has passed. I believe you are ready. I am due to visit the last two remaining courts to arrange their surrender along with the others now that Byron has given up their pathetic little war against us. I would like to show them that you stand with me."

I nod. "Of course, yes."

"Very well. Then you may go to the beach or the library or wherever it is you go to enjoy your evenings. Erac, I will have words with you."

"Just a moment," he says, grabbing my wrist with fingers that dig into my skin and grind the bones together in discomfort. "The spirits are gone, but there are still threats present."

My father gives a rare indication that he finds something humorous, one side of his mouth pulling back, a slight hitch of breath forced through his nose. "Hardly, boy. You killed the one, but he didn't stay dead. He wears the runes and was exiled with the rest of them. The other is an ignorant buffoon with more jokes than sense between his ears. There is nothing my daughter cannot handle."

Things talked about in riddles in my presence irritates me, and asking questions will only unite them against me with dark glares and words of warning against remembering things I shouldn't. I grind my teeth and try to pull free of Erac's grasp. He holds firm, even adding pressure until my wrist throbs.

"Let go," I say through a clenched jaw.

He sneers. "Remember what I have said about shades."

I roll my eyes, having heard this speech a million times. "Shades are animals, unable to control their urges for blood. They are mindless creatures, barely human, and if I see one, I need to kill it before it kills me. If I ever see gray or black eyes on a man or woman, I don't ask questions. I kill them before they have the chance to kill me. Yes, I know."

Erac scowls at me. "This is for your own good."

"I can take care of myself." I dissipate to the beach, not caring what other matters my father and betrothed will discuss. The empty ache in my chest has been lessened with the news that the day after tomorrow, I get to leave this palace and go out into the world for the first time in my life.

At least the life you remember, that snarling whisper laughs at me.

CHAPTER 31

MORELLA

Laying in the middle of my bed, I turn over a page with delicate care. The binding of the history book is rotting away, the pages yellowed, wrinkled with age and decay. I inhale the scent as I move on to the other side and continue reading. I run shaking fingers over the image of a shadowy elemental with blazing red eyes.

I frown at the image. Erac warned me against shades, stating they have gray eyes that change in color with temperament and would rip my throat out on sight. The image shows red eyes, though, and I make a mental note to ask about that later, focusing on the words on the next page.

A young, idealistic emperor took the throne in 7,404. His name was David, and his even younger wife, Elibeth, bled for two children. Their firstborn was a son, Tyle, and their second was their heir, Princess Kari. David abolished harsh laws against commoners. He believed to restore peace, the majority of the population needed to be content in their lives. If he could bring about changes to ensure happiness in their lives, he believed balance, and therefore peace would be restored.

David's younger brother, Richard, did not share in those beliefs. Richard murdered his brother and took Elibeth as his wife. Tyle was a mere eight revolutions old but was established as emperor until the crown princess would come of age.

Tyle grew up in a terrible situation and was poisoned by Richard. On his eighteenth name day, Tyle staged a celebration, which resulted in a public execution of Richard for the amusement of the court.

Tyle became worse than his uncle. The nobles were pitted against each other, and the commoners slaughtered for entertainment. Caleum started to wither. Portions of the land fell off into the northern black ocean and the crystal sea.

The process of creating new life fell on women and not men. As part of nature, women are soft and nurturing, maternal, if you will, while men are hard, strong, and, most importantly, dominating. Our ancestors realized to further the existence of our species, we had to inject our elemental blood into human babies. During the learning process, it was discovered that offspring injected with a male's blood were prone to violence, had authority issues, and altogether were unable to partake normally in society.

Tyle did not care to read about those days but went so far as to experiment. He injected human babies and elementals alike with his blood in repetitive and cruel experiments, creating a volatile and uncontrollable species we now call shades. He used them as personal guard dogs, unbeknownst to the court.

When the crown princess was nearing her eighteenth name day, Tyle took her into the gardens on the evening of her celebration. While they were in the gardens, the poor girl was ripped to pieces by Tyle's guards. The court was shocked at the mutilation, and when pressed for answers, Tyle confessed to his creation. The exposure of this species' existence, and the mysterious death of the princess, pushed the court to imprison Tyle.

His daughter was crowned, and a revolution slipped by with the land on a tipping point. When his daughter flew into a rage and massacred hundreds of elementals, the court realized Tyle's experimentations went far beyond a few bodyguards.

Elibeth took charge of the kingdom and sentenced her granddaughter to death. After the execution of Tyle's daughter, he was forced through a rift to the lowest dimension, the Inferno, exiled there for the remainder of his life as punishment. For a brief time, Elibeth served as queen and took up where David had left off, trying to restore peace. All too soon, Tyle returned from the pit he was thrown into, with an army of kangers in tow.

With his army of kangers, Tyle quickly began to overrun the land. Soon the elementals were ready to surrender. At Tyle's demand, all daughters who were to inherit from their fathers were to be sent to a gathering. This gathering was to be an attempt to reach terms of surrender and sign a peace treaty.

During the convergence, Tyle passed around wine, and the nervous girls drank much in hopes of calming their nerves. After he signed the treaty of his own surrender, he revealed the wine was mixed with the blood of shades, and the noble bloodlines would forever be tainted. He sent the girls home to tell their fathers so that they would know his torment. The treaty of Tyle's surrender lasted merely a fortnight, broken when the enraged fathers attacked. The battle that ensued lasted cycles. Worst, the elementals were losing.

All hope was lost until a young elf, Lilith, sacrificed herself to the spirits in Medius. Her sacrifice brought about our salvation. The spirits descended and rescued us. With the spirits in Caleum, the kangers were defeated and sent back to their hovel.

With care, I lift the edge of the page, using both hands to move further into the book without damaging it. Time has done that enough. I settle down to read the next two pages, my eyes trailing over words.

My door bursts open, and I jerk up, my content relaxation disappearing as I kneel in the middle of the bed. Erac storms into my room, grabbing at me. "Where are they?"

"What?"

"Where, Morella?" he bellows, pinning my wrists together in one hand and glaring around the room.

"Where is what?" I yell, not backing down.

He lets go of my wrists, grabbing the book, throwing it behind him toward my bedroom door. Pages fly and waft to the stone flooring in a dizzying storm of parchment. I stare, horrified that I'll never know how to get the book back together in proper order.

I tear my eyes away from the heartbreaking mess and see Erac rooting around the room, destroying my pillows, ripping dresses as he tears them from the wardrobe and flings them to the floor. He up-ends every container, opens every drawer, all the while muttering under his breath.

"Erac," I snap, floundering to get off the bed and to my feet. I put my hands on my hips and glare at him. "What in Haven's name are you doing?"

He slams a drawer shut and whips around to face me. "Did you take anything from me, things that belong to me?"

I gape at him with lips parted and eyebrows pulled together. "What things?"

"Answer me!" he roars, a vein popping out in his neck and forehead. "Did you find things in my room and take them?"

"What things?" I ask, leaning back on my heels. "I haven't taken anything from you."

"No one else goes in my rooms," he snaps, stalking toward me. "Not even servants."

I can see the way his face is twisted with rage, and I start to tremble as I hold my hands up, compressing air together to form a barrier and shield myself. "I didn't take anything from you."

"Liar!" he roars, throwing a hand out. The barrier vibrates but holds. "Hiding from me only proves my suspicions."

"You can search this room all you want. I won't stop you. I didn't take anything. I don't even know what you're looking for."

He dissipates behind my shield, and before I can react, he grabs me by the throat and a wrist. His eyes are blazing as they search my face. "Where are they?" he growls in a low voice that leaves me tense with fear.

I use my free hand low and by my side out of his sight, pooling energy in my palm. "I–don't–know," I manage. I feel the elements condensed in a burning ball, and I swing, slamming the energy into his chest.

He jerks back, yelping, his fingers slipping from the chokehold. I use both my hands, forming a triangle and pushing forward, then rip my hands apart outward. A blazing blast of air forces him against the wall. I command it to remain as I watch him struggle. The voice in the back of my mind is whispering in a feverish pitch, hissing to see him bleed.

I ease the elements from my control, glance around, then back to see him getting upright. I sneer at him, keeping my hands at the ready. "I didn't take anything from you." My own voice sounds strange to my ears, twisted and low, like a snarl or a growl of warning from an animal. "You can search this room all you'd like, but you're not going to touch me."

He stares at me, a bit paler than usual, perhaps. It is hard to say with how pale his skin is, to begin with. There's a difference in the way he regards me. He seems a bit more hesitant to approach.

He nods, and I cross my arms. "What are you looking for? What was taken?" I demand to know.

He shies away, narrowing his eyes. "This is not for you to meddle in."

I stand back on one heel, spread my arms, and splay my palms. "Tell me," I warn, the stream of energy prickling through my veins, tensing my muscles.

"Morella, darling…" He goes slack-jawed and wide-eyed. "Don't."

"I am so sick of the way you treat me. The way you hurt me

and try to scare me, and I'm done letting you. I'm the most powerful being in Caleum?" My hands press close together, and I strain, arms shaking with the effort to compress the raw magic together, a blinding bright ball of heat forming and expanding between my palms. "Time to find out."

He throws an arm up to protect his head, turning to the side and dropping to a knee as I turn my palms outward. The energy sails toward him, exploding on contact, its brilliant light leaving me squinting and blinking. The world quakes and a deafening boom leaves my ears ringing.

Erac pushes himself off the ground, blood dribbling from both corners of his mouth, nostrils, ears, and eyes. He is breathing raggedly, but a small smile plays on my lips.

He dusts off his chest with both hands and stares at me like I might have hurt him in more ways than to simply cause bleeding. "There are things not even you are powerful enough to overcome. You will do well to remember that. Remember that I am here to help you because you couldn't save yourself."

His voice is low, chipped away to raw pain instead of the usual fury. I open my mouth to argue that he came here accusing me of theft and attacked me, but he dissipates, dissolving out of sight. I stare around my room and fume, clenching my fists and holding them up to see them shake. I have the urge to hit something and make a swing at the air in front of me.

My shoulder wrenches and I nearly lose my balance, but there was something about the motion that is comforting. I repeat, making a few swings with my right arm and then one with my left. I let out a deep breath through my nose and allow my eyes to close. I focus on my rooms, feeling the energy pour out of me as I control the elements, forcing things back into place as they were before Erac arrived.

I open my eyes and turn to fetch the book from the floor. It isn't there. Instead, the book is in the middle of my bed, all pages neatly nestled against the spine and tucked away. I move to close my door and meet George's gaze as he peeks around the jam.

His eyes drop to the floor. "Are you okay?"

I raise my eyebrows at him. He winces and steps into the doorway. He looks a bit pale and clammy, and I frown, eyes running over him. "Are you sick?"

He moves to shake his head and grimaces. "No, Your Majesty."

I purse my lips and narrow my eyes. I am done with their rules. "Morella will work. What's wrong with you?"

He stands still and blinks at me. "Nothing, Your Majesty."

I frown. "George," I draw his name out through clenched teeth.

"Are you okay?" he asks again in a small voice, eyes cast to the floor.

I nod, cross my arms, and lean against the doorframe. "I will be fine. What's wrong with you?"

"I'm not supposed to talk to you, nor come near you anymore. Not to tell you stuff." He keeps his head down, mumbling at the floor. I expect him to kick at the ground and shove his hands in his pockets, but he doesn't move. "But Erac was mad, and I was thinking he might come after you. I'm sorry."

I push away from the door and drop to one knee to get low enough to look him in his big, dark eyes. "George, are you okay?" I keep my voice to a whisper, then glance down the hall leading to my room in both directions. "What happened? Why did you think Erac was going to come after me?"

There's a noise, another door opening and closing. I glance in the direction of the sound, and when I look up, George is scampering down the hall. I frown after him but decide whatever he'd been through to encourage him to keep his distance or stay silent wasn't something I want to be repeated. The kid looked miserable enough.

I sigh and close the door, leaning my back against it and stare around the room. I let my fingers strum against the wood behind me as I focus on the open expanse leading to my balcony. George knows me from before I lost my memories, my mind. He was willing to answer my questions, even if it was just to say he didn't know, and now he's stolen something from Erac. I lift a questioning eyebrow at the horizon, feeling a quiet fury slithering through my veins.

Erac is hiding things.

CHAPTER 32

DECLAN

As it turns out, Dis is more than a big, cold room. Aron brought us to his personal library, twice the size of the Byron courtroom and about five hundred revolutions older. The place is massive. It's an entire underground mansion, possibly bigger than the City of Cato outside Byron.

At least we each have our own room. I could have twenty rooms, which leaves at least one open for me to use for working out, plenty of spare furniture for me to destroy. Aron has assured me no one will miss it.

I pace through the halls, needing something to do. The size of Dis makes this easy. I stop in a crossway, staring around.

Ella would love this.

I groan and crouch down on the floor, using one hand to steady myself.

"Drop something, Mr. Bard?"

The voice grates on my ears like fingernails over eyeballs. I stand and stare at Marx. "What are you doing here?"

"I hated that question when we were in Byron; I am even less fond of it while you are in my court, boy."

I stand tall and cross my arms. "Why are you in Dis, in a random hallway?"

"I have fugitives hiding under my rule. I have every right to be concerned." He smiles. "I came to see how you are holding up."

My left eyebrow and a corner of my mouth both hitch up. "You suddenly care about my mental state?"

"I heard you and Ella could put an end to all of this while I was in Byron."

Scowling, I turn my face to the ceiling. "Yeah, you can thank Seth for that. Those are his words, not mine."

"Ah." Marx chuckles and rubs a hand over his bare scalp, staring at the floor. "That brother of yours is something."

"Yes."

"He has a mouth on him." Marx eyes me with humor. "Something he got from you?"

I stare with a furrowed brow. "Maybe my quips and back talking were all shoved in my head by you."

"Doubtful. We have a way of emulating those we look up to. Knowing Seth tells me all I need to know about whose comments I was graced with."

I fight back a smile and look away. "You're giving me too much credit."

He laughs. "How are you? You've lost the crown of Byron, your court is surrendering to Viktor, and you've been accused of treason." He adjusts the rolled-up sleeves on his button-down shirt that strain to encapsulate his forearms.

"Fine."

"I'll let the lack of respect slide as you are under a lot of strain."

"Fine, you useless dick."

He puts a hand over where a heart should be and feigns shock. "Useless?"

I smirk. "How are you doing? Does Asena know that we are here?"

His humor slides away. "At present, no. She remains blissfully unaware, and I'd like to keep it that way."

I smirk. "Then don't piss me off, and I won't tell her Seth is close by. What do you want?"

"I told you I'd let you know when I was meeting with Viktor. You've made it more convenient by coming to me."

"Well, you're still a dick, but maybe not useless." My head bobs, my gaze on the floor. "When?"

"Tomorrow. I have reason to believe he is bringing Ella."

My breath catches. "Don't screw with my head. I'm in no mood."

He reaches out, and I jerk away. He sighs, steps, and places both hands on my shoulders. "Declan, my boy, I have no intention of doing anything of the kind. I was sincere in my inquiry. How are you doing?"

I stare long enough into his bright blue eyes as my own fog over with moisture. I shrug him off and pull away. "I'm fabulous."

He shakes his head. "Stubborn as ever."

"It's part of my charm."

He sighs with a smile. "I have a place for you in the palace if you want. Being here must not be easy."

I lean back on my heels and stare down my nose. "Why would you ever think that?"

"Ella would have loved this, wouldn't she? Dis?" He jerks his chin at our surroundings.

My stomach hurts. "Yes."

"Has she ever made it here before?"

My chest aches and my stomach turns to stone. "No."

"Perhaps there's enough of her in there," he muses and gives me a knowing smile. "Wouldn't it be lovely if you got to show her around on her visit?"

I think I throw up in my mouth. I'm not sure. My throat burns, and there's an awful taste on my tongue. "Dis? You want me to show her Dis? If I sink my teeth into her—"

"Interesting turn of phrase. Do you want her back?"

"I'm not dignifying that with an answer."

Marx gives me a long look. "You need to earn her trust. If you ever want her to believe you over them, you need to give her a reason to. You can't beat this into submission, and if you piss that woman off, you'll end up dead." He rubs the back of his neck. "The bond is no longer intact, and if I understand bonds, that would mean she got half her soul back when it broke. That is going to give Viktor grief. She's still here, somewhere. You'll just have to give it a push, but trying to force this isn't going to help."

"Great pep talk. Want to rub salt in any other wounds?"

"Get a map." He claps me on the shoulder. "Learn your way around. I'll be sure to introduce you." He walks away with a chuckle.

"Fuck!" I scream, throwing a hook at the wall. Stone cracks, chips flying. Dust dances through the air. I pant, putting my hands flat against the wall, pressing my forehead to the cool surface. My eyes slip closed against emotions I cannot name. "Fuck."

CHAPTER 33

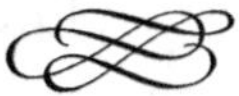

MORELLA

"Do you like the view?"

I peel my nose from the glass and turn to gape at my father, seeing double. I blink and realize there is a man standing next to my father who looks similar. I fixate on my father, and he gives me a stern expression as I sigh and stand upright from leaning on the window sill. The view from Clemm Palace out over the city is intriguing, and I lost track of the time I have spent staring.

"Sorry, Father." I clasp my hands and stand at attention, waiting for what comes next.

"This is Marx." My father jerks his head at the man.

My eyes travel over him. They are the same height, both bald, but Marx has more bulk to his build. My eyes flicker back and forth, noticing the man has blue eyes instead of green, and the way they carry themselves is different. My father has a quiet intellectualism to him, whereas Marx stands with legs apart and arms crossed in an aggressive stance.

I incline my head and force a smile. "Hello, Marx. I am Morella."

He smiles back and offers me a hand. "It's nice to meet you, Morella. Morella? May I call you Ella?"

"No, you may not," my father says in a harsh tone. "My daughter deserves respect, not a childish nickname."

I lift my eyebrows but maintain my smile.

Marx winks at me.

I give him a quick curtsy. "It's lovely to meet you."

"Of course," he says. "How foolish of me to refer to her in such a manner. Shall I show you around Clemm as we speak?" He offers an arm out to me.

"There is no need for you to do any such thing," my father says. "We are not here for entertainment, and I am more than capable of showing her around if she would like to see the palace later."

"Oh, come off it, old friend," Marx laughs, clapping him on the back.

My father looks like he has laid an egg, but the expression lasts only a moment before his mouth becomes a hard line so that his lips lose all color and seem to disappear.

I grin in genuine mirth at my father's displeasure and even giggle, holding a hand up to my lips as if I could hide the noise. My father's eyes fixate on me, and I drop my hand, clearing my throat. "If it would please you, Sir—"

"A title of formality is wasted on the man," my father grumbles.

I roll my eyes and tilt my head at Marx, smiling ear to ear. "Perhaps you can tell me about Clemm?"

"Of course, of course, yes, but don't you recall your lessons from childhood?" His face never changes from a grin, but something is slithering behind that mask of friendliness.

I purse my lips, and it is my turn to glare at him. "Answer the question, please."

He holds his hands up. "I see I have crossed a line I did not know existed. Please, let us sit. I have tea prepared."

He offers me his arm again and sweeps me across the room to a round table with three place settings. He helps me down into the chair and even pushes me in with a doting manner.

"Thank you."

When he sits, we turn to look at my father, who has not moved. Marx laughs. "It's not poisoned, and I'll eat or drink everything you find suitable." He waves a hand in the air and turns back to me. "Clemm is in the middle of Caleum. We have many farmlands, and most of our exports are crops for the rest of the land. We are known here in our court for our friendly natures and common sense, but the most remarkable thing about Clemm is that Dis lays just outside our city."

"Dis?" I ask, the name plucking a string in the depths of my mind, no doubt something I have read before.

"Yes, Dis, home of the Gammet brothers and our mage leaders, the council of mages that assist them."

My heart leaps in my chest. "The home of magic," I say, sitting up, leaning toward him. "I've read about it. That's Erac's home, isn't it?" I turn to my father with a grin.

He almost seems to huff as he stalks toward the table. "Yes, Erac lived in Dis for some time."

"Your father is part of the warrior's guild, so he won't know much about Dis, but being a mage and on the mage's council," Marx says, drawing the words out, "perhaps there is something I can show you that he can't."

"No," my father says, taking a seat. "I'll not trust you to take my daughter anywhere with you."

I snort through my nose and hold my father's gaze. "As if he is capable of hurting me?" I laugh with an exaggerated eye roll. "Please."

"Yes, the female is the more deadly of the species," Marx says, his voice quiet.

"It is out of the question," my father says, pouring himself a cup of tea. "Perhaps you would like to focus on the point of this meeting?"

Marx sighs, giving me a mock glance of disbelief. "Viktor's been a bit of a stick in the mud for revolutions now, but you'd never believe he used to be the life of the party."

My father looks ready to murder. "Byron Court has surrendered."

"Did they?" Marx slathers cream on a scone. "I hadn't heard."

"They have."

Marx shoves the scone past his teeth and proceeds to talk through the mouthful. "Does that mean you'll be returning home then?"

"I expect your cooperation," my father says in a quiet tone.

Marx takes a drink of tea and shrugs. "I believe I said when Damnatus freezes over, old friend."

"Morella can make that happen." The words are solid, and Marx stutters in his movements. "Would you care to reconsider?"

Marx glances at me. "You're not really going to freeze Damnatus, are you?"

I rest back in my chair and frown. "I don't think I would mind freezing it. It is a horrible place."

"Hmm." He eats another scone.

I flick the end of the knife on the table as we wait. I look to my father, who sips the tea, and bored and restless, I strum my fingers, commanding the elements to lift the pot and pour a cup for myself. Marx watches me with a mixture of excited contemplation and bewilderment.

The pot clinks back onto the small china plate, and I pick up my cup with one hand. "Is there something you want to ask?" I say to Marx.

He shakes his head. "No, Morella, not at all. If that is all, though, I am a remarkably busy man."

"Please sit down," I tell him as he rises from his seat. He drops back into the chair, and I smile. "Thank you. Now, I'd like to discuss terms with you."

"You're a right old bastard," Marx says, laughing at Viktor. Shaking his head and running a hand over his scalp, he fixates those blue eyes on me. "Okay, Morella, I'll hear you out."

I give him a look of surprise, batting my lashes and staring. The man was ready to walk away from my father, but now he is giving me his undivided attention, scones and tea forgotten, the humor gone from his features.

"We—" I start, but he cuts me off.

"You," he says. "If I'm going to surrender my court, it would be to you, not this old prick." He jerks a thumb at my father.

My ears warm and I clench my fists in my lap. "You will do very well to remember that I am capable of turning you to sand with a single thought and will have no qualms in doing so if you insult my father again." I bat my lashes at him with a smile.

His ears pull back, and his features pinch. "You would do well to remember that I am twice your age and have known your father—" he twists the words with a sour taste "—my whole life. You hold the power at this table, and so I will hear your proposal because I am aware of what you are capable of, and I am aware of precisely how this situation is working. Are you even aware of that?"

"The terms are simple. You will remain in charge of day to day operations here at Clemm, swearing fealty to my father," I indicate him with a hand, "and you will honor and obey him."

"Sounds like you want me to marry him," Marx scoffs. "I'm not interested in that."

"All taxes will be paid annually, and all final decisions will rest with my father and me. For all intents and purposes, think of yourself as a Duke of Caleum instead of King of Clemm." I finish with a sweet smile as if he never interrupted me.

He shakes his head. "Again, I am not interested. I appreciate your time."

"Marx," I warn. "We need your cooperation, or we will be forced to take action."

"And I might be inkling to toss my hat in with the Bard Brothers."

I hiss at him, setting my teacup down with a sharp snap. "That court surrendered."

"Yes, I heard." He stares at me with indifference.

"I will deal with the brothers soon enough."

He sits back with a smile teasing at his lips. "Deal with them how?"

"They are going to repay me in blood for what they did to me."

Marx raises his eyebrows, evidence of shock on his face. He blinks at me and then tips his head back and laughs from deep in his chest.

"Precisely what is humorous?" my father asks, sipping his tea and waiting for Marx to calm down.

Shaking his head, Marx grins, running a hand over his bare scalp. "You are playing a game that you haven't even glimpsed the rule book for. And you," he stares at me, "are playing a game you can't see all the pieces to."

I cross my arms and one leg over the other. "I'm not playing games. I expect your full surrender, or there will be consequences, actions taken."

The man has the audacity to smile. "And what action would that be?"

My eyes cut to my father.

"By all means," Marx begins with a chuckle, "ask Daddy for help." My ears burn and ring, and the teapot explodes as I focus my rage on it. Marx shakes his head and stands. "It was good to see you, old friend." He sighs, clapping my father on the shoulder as he saunters away.

My father's lips twist and curl back to one side. "Your daughter, Asena, how is she?"

I glare at Marx's back as he comes to a halt. "My daughter is not currently in Clemm."

"I see. I wonder if her future is here," my father says with a smile, picking up the cup of tea. "I would send my regards."

Marx's hands curl into fists at his sides as he turns his head. His face is in sharp profile to me, his eye settled on my father. "Asena is much like her mother. Good day."

I stand to stop him, but my father stays me with a hand. "Let him go, my daughter. He will come around soon enough."

I settle back, the door closing behind Marx with a soft click. "Why are we letting him walk away?"

Father gives me a smile that vanishes as quickly as it came. "He and I have our ways. I expect nothing less from him at this point."

I frown and finish my tea. "Will you show me around Clemm then? Or perhaps Dis? I would much rather see Dis."

"Erac can take you to Dis another time. When all of this is finished, you will have plenty of time to explore anywhere in this world you desire. Clemm, I can show you." He stands.

We wander the halls, and he explains artwork, the tapestries, telling stories of old. We find our way to the heart of the palace and the throne room, where a large bell hangs in the middle, suspended from a beautiful stained-glass dome. Passing around the bell, I cannot help but to reach out and touch the reflective surface.

There is a piece of me that aches when I touch it longing to recall something at the edge of my mind. I frown. "Father, have I been here before?"

"Are you remembering something?" His voice is tight.

I shake my head. "No, just a feeling. I get them sometimes. I don't even know what they mean, but a strange feeling."

"You would do well to ignore them. They are no doubt pointless ramblings of your own mind trying to make sense of things you have never seen." He turns away, drawing me out of the room. "This way, there is more to see."

CHAPTER 34

MORELLA

We pass through a long corridor with open windows on one side and mirrors massive in width from floor to ceiling along the other. I cling to my father's arm at his side as he shows me around his home. There is a light that comes to him, a glimmer beneath the surface of eyes I have not seen before as he recounts small stories from his past. His childhood was full of friends and laughter, it would seem, and my heart aches for what he has lost.

As we approach the other end, my father tenses. I shift my gaze from the splendor around me to the man coming to a halt before us.

He leans on a cane made of red-stained wood, polished from age and use. He has a head full of dark hair, a touch of gray at the temples, the long strands on top combed to one side. He scowls with a surly and sour expression but carries the airs of an extinguished gentleman.

"Eh?" One side of his mouth pulls back. It is not a half-grin of joy, but instead, a twist of cruelty. "What are you doing here, boy?"

My eyes travel from the man to my father. Boy is not the

most accurate word for him. I press my lips into a frown. "He is showing me around Clemm Court."

Neither man acts as if I spoke at all. My eyes shift between them, the pulse in my neck twitching with aggravation. A few heartbeats tick by, and I prepare to open my mouth to make sure they heard me when my father speaks.

"Morella, allow me to introduce you to Francis Taldor." The words are frosty, the air rigidly cold between the men. "Francis, meet my daughter Morella."

Francis never moves his eyes away from my father, his expression lackluster. "You've come to introduce me to my granddaughter, finally? She's rather thin, a bit frail looking."

Heat pipes into my ears as they pull back. I blink a few times. "We've never met?" I ask. "But we're family."

"Ha," Francis scoffs, straightening his spine, rolling his shoulders back. The cane shifts in front of him, his hands overlaid to rest on the top. The handle is decorative, carved as the bust of a wolf, the front legs carved into the length of the walking stick, the body stretching out to form the grip.

"Family is an obscenity. He knows not the meaning of the word," my father answers.

Francis' face twitches at the seam of his nose as he curls his lip. "Family is defined as descendants of a common ancestor."

"I could not agree more. Which begs the question, why would you claim my daughter as your relation?"

"Don't be petulant, boy."

Viktor pulls me closer, and my fingers tighten on his bicep. His free hand comes up, covering my grip. "Good day."

Francis chuckles. His gaze is on his cane, swinging back and forth with a slow grace to the disbelief he conveys. "You would do well to remember that anger is the greatest poison of them all. This silly grudge you hold does me no harm." Francis fixes his steel-blue eyes on my father.

My father gives a wry smile. "There are far worse poisons to the souls than anger."

"Your mind was never sharp enough to reach achievements like mine is," Francis says, his voice cutting the air like a razor, paper-thin but sharp.

"My father is Emperor of Caleum, and you would do well to remember that and show him some respect," I spit out with venom.

"Yes, so I have heard. A hollow title rightfully mocked in my circles. I handed you success on a silver platter, and you've managed to take a piss on it." Francis lifts his hand, and my father flinches, the barest of movements betrayed only by the dozens of mirrors and brilliant light in the hall. Francis scratches the side of his face under his dark, groomed beard. "Utter humiliation you've brought down upon me and my name once more."

My father recovers by sliding his hands into the front pockets of his pressed black suit pants and clearing his throat. "There is nothing hollow or deserving of mockery."

"You aren't an emperor until all the courts have bowed to you," Francis says, eyes sparkling with danger.

"The courts will kneel to me."

Francis bursts with laughter. "You are here in Clemm to beg for our fealty?"

"I don't beg." My father twists that word with malice. "I am—"

"You're begging, like a dog for scraps."

My father's mouth pulls tight. "If there is a dog in this room, it is you."

Francis moves quick, the crack of flesh against flesh stretching my eyes open wide. My lips peel apart as the blood in my veins fills with sizzling rage. That dark, whispering desire prickles to life between my ears, soft hissing I cannot understand.

"Your mother wasted nothing so much as the blood she

poured into you. She had many faults, that woman, but you were the greatest mistake she ever made by far."

My father rocks back on his heels, a pink stain on his cheek where Francis had backhanded him. I step forward, reaching out to rip the cane from Francis' grip. I lock the handle behind his neck, wrenching him forward, and drive the palm of my hand into his nose in an upward fashion. He flails backward, eyes wide and watering with a trickle of blood down his lips. For my part, I gape, not sure where the knowledge on how to do that came from.

As I stare with wide eyes, Francis changes from a cynical gentleman to a wounded animal. "Why, you little bitch." He blots fingers at his nostrils and pulls back, the glistening red evidence on his fingertips.

My father steps before us, a firm hand at Francis' throat. He leans his weight back on one foot and snarls. "I think not."

Unlike Marx's insinuations, I don't need him to protect me or tell me what to do. With narrowed eyes, I send Francis flying to the side. His body slams into the mirror. The glass fractures, cracks emanating from an epicenter of staggered, broken ripples.

Francis teeters, eyes and mouth open in consternation, and I smile at him, my lips pressed tight and twisted. The whisper inside my head is becoming an incipient compulsion to draw blood. It is easy for me to force the broken shards of the mirror to separate, hanging in the air like harbingers of death directed at Francis. A burning need rolls through me.

"That's enough, Morella," my father says in a quiet voice, holding up a hand. He takes a step forward, inclining his head and breathing fire as he speaks in a furious hiss. "I promise you this. Before this is over, you will be on your knees."

Francis laughs, a sneer contorting his features with dark passion. "Never could beat the stupid out of you, could I?" He spits in my father's face, dribble lingering on his lips, a bit of drool glistening from the middle of his lower lip.

The whisper in me becomes an inky shadow in my mind, thrashing and hissing like an animal caught in a trap at being denied. *Make him bleed, make him beg like the vain girl.*

My father wipes his face and glances over his shoulder at me with burning green flames in his eyes. "Not yet, Morella. I expect him to attend my coronation."

Rolling my eyes, I release the elements of air, allowing all the broken pieces to fall where they may with a look of discontent. The cracking of rupturing glass fills the air for a split second, and I feed my frustration at the lack of drawing blood into one word. "Fine."

Francis turns to my father with skepticism. "You're a useless bitch." His voice shifts from snarling to a soft caress. "Now, my granddaughter..."

My skin crawls as his eyes wash over me with veneration. I wrinkle my nose, my upper lip curling back to expose teeth of disgust. I want to gouge his eyes out for eyeing me in that way.

Make him afraid. Make him respect.

In a sudden flash of agility and speed, my father grabs one of the pieces of mirror, driving it under Francis' jaw. His other hand curls into the pressed button-down, and he pulls and shoves with a threatening growl. "My daughter is none of your concern, and you'll take care in how you speak to her."

"I could help you, you know?" Francis doesn't seem to be talking to my father, his tone silk once again. "Teach you things. I can give you what you need. I have control over this court."

"Marx is King of Clemm," I say, lifting one eyebrow.

Francis chuckles. "Marx is an idiot. Grew up with this ignorant schmuck." He jerks his head at my father. "They were two peas in a pod. Every time one did something dumb, the other just couldn't wait to do something dumber still. Trivial pranks and unintelligent jokes for revolutions. Always looking for someone's approval."

With a growl, my father impales the sliver of glass into Francis' shoulder. "I'm not looking for your approval."

The color of Francis' eyes darkens with apoplectic pain as he grunts. "Says the child lashing out."

My father shoves him away. "You're the one who taught me actions have consequences."

Francis steps forward, throwing an uppercut into my father's face. "You're right, I did."

The blazing indignation ripping through my veins urges me as much as the whisper begging for another taste of stealing life. I hiss, narrowing my eyes, my vision hazing red as I give in to the cacoethes. With swift concentration, I lift the broken, scattered shards and send them sailing. They whizz, slicing the air with phantom cries.

The dozens of sharp-edged slivers sink into Francis, littering his torso. The only sound is his gurgle of life, blood bubbling at the corners of his mouth. The pleasure at watching the blood seep around the reflective fragments is exquisite, and my lips curl at the ends as his dimming sight locks with mine.

"Actions do have consequences," I purr, my voice cruel and strange to my ears.

In slow motion, he stumbles back a pace, and then he twists as he falls, collapsing to the ground with a soft thump. I grin wider as my father turns to meet my eyes, but the smugness fades as his fury radiates like the heat from sand dunes baked golden under the soul star. His thin face turns white, his lips vanishing as he quakes. Something akin to volatility rages in his eyes as he draws a ragged breath through his nose, the only sound in the room disturbing the air.

If I could cower and hide in thin air, I would. As I speak, he takes two steps toward me. "Father, I'm—"

Before I can finish the words, his backhand cracks against the side of my face hard enough to snap my neck. My body twists and pulls in on itself in recoil, and then I stand, tangy heat filling my mouth and permeating my palate. Shock detonates in my chest like a reverse explosion, sucking all the whispering and blistering need into my core where it vanishes. All that remains in the wake of the vacuum inside me is cold disbelief.

Stunned in place, tears blister over my eyes as I watch him walk away. I let out a whimper, putting a hand to the side of my face with care. The skin over my cheek is warm against my cold fingers.

He does not look back as he says, "Return to your room and stay there." He continues to walk away, leaving me to stare with blurry vision as he leaves me there alone.

~

The soul star sets, and still, Viktor has not returned to our suite. I shuffle back to my bedroom and stop in the doorway. Turning, I take in the grand sitting room that sits between his room and mine. Standing there, left behind and abandoned, I study the space bathed in dusty shadows.

The hollow sickness in my chest has faded as the shock wears off. I frown at the cream couches with stiff backs and armrests embellished with gold rivets.

His father was blatantly disrespecting him and deserved what he got. If my father couldn't see that, then that's his problem. I'm not locking myself in a suite to appease him.

The trouble is, I have no idea what else to do. I glance at the door of our massive suite and chew on my lower lip, picking at the chapped skin between my teeth. The thought that Dis is nearby trickles into my mind.

I could go.

Leaning against the open door, I sigh, my gaze lifting to the ceiling. I tip my head to the side, my eyes closing, and concentrate on Dis. The name repeats in my mind a thousand times, my desire strong. I mean only to conjure a book from the library at Asperheim, but instead, the cold disintegration of my elements tears through me.

I gasp with surprise as my elements collide, rebuilding with abrupt collision. My mind reels, and I blink, stretching watering eyes open wide. Around me stretches gray stone in long corridors, with pitch mortar and moss growing in the cracks of the walls.

Lights are strung along the ceiling like fire that gives no warmth or smoke. I stand at a cross-section, gaping about at them when something solid collides into me. I rock back on my heels in recoil, teetering off balance. I would fall if not for the strong hands that clasp my shoulders.

The strength in them is easy, firm without hurting. They are warm and calloused, the hands of a man who knows physical labor, with long fingers that hold me steady. The grip relaxes and withdraws.

I blink, tipping my head back to gaze up at the man. He frowns down at me with a furrowed brow and a heavy weight in the lines around his mouth. His dark gray eyes fixate on me, staring for a moment. They flicker and stretch open wider.

His jaw goes slack, the tension melting from his features in exchange for something softer. I focus my sight on his charcoal-colored irises hidden behind strands of bronze hair hanging in front of his face, brushing against the bridge of his nose.

I stare right into the heart and soul of a shade. My heart lurches in my throat, my fingers curling at my side, ready to obliterate him.

The heat of his hands leaves my shoulders as he draws back and upright. For an animal, he has immaculate posture and is impeccably dressed even if he emits raw power in droves. I swallow the ball of fear on the back of my tongue and relax my hands.

"Hello."

CHAPTER 35

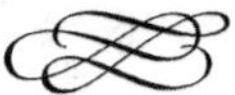

DECLAN

Marx arranged the meeting with Viktor, having me wait in this room until he could wrangle Ella away from her father and bring her here. I am going to pass out. Maybe I am going to throw up. It is too hot in this room. My skin is stretched too tight.

I hear everything. My heartbeat. The clock on the wall. The servants moving through the walls. The elementals one room down and across the hall. They are having an affair. She's worried her husband has found out. He's taking his clothes off. Someone is walking in the corridor, getting closer.

I pinch the bridge of my nose, and the door opens behind me. I freeze, and then in a painfully slow fashion, I turn around. My eyes lock onto Marx.

He shakes his head and steps further inside, closing the door behind him. "I wasn't able to get her away from Viktor."

A tidal wave of emotions slides through my chest. I can't decide if seeing her or not is the better option.

"I am sorry. I tried."

I nod and take a deep breath, staring at the navy-blue couch. "She is here, though."

"Have you seen her?"

"No." I put my hands in my front pockets to keep from clenching them.

He drops his hands on his hips. "My suspicions are confirmed. She has no memory. I don't know what they took or what they left, if anything. She had no idea of who I am, or she has learned how to tell a convincing lie."

I snort through my nose. "This is Ella we are talking about, right?"

"It would appear to be, although a skilled mage is capable of manipulating the elements of themselves or another individual to change an appearance."

I roll my shoulders back. I run a hand down my face and turn my back on him to stare out the window.

Clemm Palace sits at the base of the northern mountains. A gray haze for miles in the distance lifts into the sky. I focus on the stone garden paths below me.

"We will get her back to you." I glance over my shoulder, his face a rare soft mask of honest emotion. His lips press and pull back, more Viktor's style than Marx's flashy grin. "If nothing else, trust that I am never going to let Viktor win."

My eyes shift back to the window. "Funny way of showing it, but I believe you." My shoulders droop, and I collapse down on myself, barely upright.

His hands clap down on my shoulders, jostling me. He squeezes, and then they drop away. "My boy," he begins with almost a sort of affection to his voice, "keep your head down. I have received paperwork for you to be arrested on sight. I am the only one in this court aware of your presence, so if you are seen—"

"Yeah, I got it."

"Good. Get back to Dis. Give me time to collect information we can use."

I do a quarter turn toward him. "Sit, stay, good boy." The joke lacks any real tinge of emotion.

I shred myself apart and rebuild in my room at Dis. I pace back and forth and grab at my hair. My wife is here, and all I want to do is go to her. The feeling is maddening, and I need something to keep busy before I get weak or act irrationally.

I stalk through the halls until I am lost. *Maybe it's a good thing I didn't try to show her around.*

I turn a corner and walk straight into something smaller than me. I shuffle, latching onto it to keep us both upright. I ease my grip and take a step back.

My brain processes. She's the right height, and the hair color is reddish-purple. Her hair is chopped short around her shoulders, and there's an intelligence to her eyes with a playful light.

Damn, she looks good.

I fight the instinct to call out her name and grab hold of her. She blinks, those violet eyes I know so well, and then smiles at me.

"Hello."

I do my best to smile. "Hi."

Should I have gone with hello? Shit.

"Do you work here?"

I manage to shake my head, not daring to blink. I can't stop staring.

Fuck, she's beautiful.

"Oh." Her face falls. "Marx offered to show me around, but my father didn't like it. I decided I didn't care; I just had to see Dis. I've read so much about it."

She still loves to read. My heart does a flip in my chest. *She's still in there somewhere.*

"Are you a mage? Can you show me around?"

"I am not a mage, but I can try." I look around, trying to figure out where I am.

She gives a skeptical look. "Are you certain? You seem lost."

I flash my teeth in a grin. "I am."

"Well, then I suppose we are both without hope." She laughs. It's music to my ears.

I offer her my arm. "How about we wander lost together? I can at least tell you what I know."

"I will accept what I can." She takes my arm, and all the hairs on my body tingle and raise. "May I ask, if you're not a mage, and you aren't a servant, why are you in Dis?"

"I recently moved in."

"Oh."

Clearing my throat and taking a deep breath, I brace myself. I need answers, information, so I ask, "May I ask why your father didn't want you to see Dis?"

She keeps her gaze on the walls around us, seeming to bask in the moldy air and moss-covered stones. She hums, "If I tell you, I'll want something in return."

The lump in my throat bobs as I swallow hard. "Anything. I'll give you anything you want."

She turns, peering at me with suspicion. I fight to keep my features blank, staring at the corner of her eye where it meets her nose. "Alright, because there are those who would hurt me. He is protecting me."

"Why would anyone want to hurt you?" My palms are clammy, every part of me exuding in a nervous sweat.

"There are some who would hurt me because my father is the one true Emperor of Caleum, and there are those who oppose him." Her voice is low, almost indifferent. She shrugs. "There are these two brothers who tried to turn me from my father and betrothed, and my father worries they might try again."

"What did they tell you these brothers did to you?"

She sighs and shakes her head. "They poisoned my mind. They are why I have no memories, because of what they did to me." She pauses, and I try to keep my composure at being assigned blame for what Erac and Viktor did to her. "I decided I'm not hiding anymore. They can try to come for me again, and I will make them pay for what they did."

Every single time I watched her dissolve something to ash flitters through my memory. My heart is pulsating hard with pressure, but I do my best to hide it. "Pay?" I manage.

"Yes." She brushes her short hair away from her neck. "They are going to repay in blood what they took from me."

Well, fuck me.

We move on in silence, my heart racing. Marx's warning to earn her trust pops in my head, and I take a deep breath. I'll work on giving her a reason to trust me when I tell her those bastards are lying. "Was there somewhere you wanted to see specifically?"

"Oh, yes, actually." She hesitates, and I smirk.

"I can't read your mind," I tease but saying the words is like taking a knife to the gut.

"You may think it's silly."

I cock my head at her, staring down my nose. "I promise I will not laugh."

She takes a deep breath and sighs. "There is a record book, the guild ledger, where everyone signs their name when they join."

"There is."

"I've read about the ceremony. How each court hosts the guilds over an entire cycle of light, a celebration and carnival, and how at the end there's the declaration of elementals coming of age to announce their choice."

"Yes."

She glances up at me, eyes searching my face. "I wrote my name in the mage guild book, or so I am told."

"Told?"

"Yes, told." There's a hard edge to her voice.

I wince. "You want to see your name."

"Yes."

I nod. "I think I know where that is."

"It'll be a start. I don't think I'll ever remember it, but at least I'll know I did it."

There's pain in her voice, and I react by trying to reach through the link. I twitch, knowing the bond is gone.

"Are you alright?"

"Just a headache. What else have you read?"

She tips her head back and laughs. "Everything. Did you know this was the original court? The last emperor, before my father to rule over all Caleum, lived here with his courtiers. We are walking through history. There was so much that happened here, and the gardens above." Her eyes travel upward, and I glance that way, too, at the ornate stonework above us.

"I knew. I didn't think much of it."

"Have you found Tyle's secret study? Or the bloodstains of his sister? I'd love to see those."

I chuckle. "No. I've not found any of those, but you do love your histories."

"You have no idea."

Oh, I think I do. Outwardly, I grin. "We should turn left up here, I think."

"I hope you're right." She eyes me. "I can turn you to dust faster than you can hurt me."

A laugh pops up my throat. "I am never going to hurt you."

She fixates on me, narrowing her eyes. I breathe in through my nose and catch her scent. Her eyes scan mine, and then she laughs. "Haven, you look terrified now."

I'm face to face with my wife, and I have no idea what to say. She doesn't know me. You know me. Please know me.

I tear my eyes away from her to focus on where we are going. "You'd be first on a list of things that terrify me."

I am not joking, but she laughs anyway. "By the look of you, you don't scare easy."

I turn to the right and breathe out a sigh. The massive oak doors ahead mean I managed to find the grand library. I give a wry smile. "There are fifty-seven libraries here in Dis."

She sighs longingly. "I know. I wish I had time to see them all, but I think I'd need a hundred revolutions."

I wonder if she knows she has that time; if she knows about the spirit runes at all. "I think if you put your mind to it, you could. I know you'll always be welcome here."

I move to grab the door handle, and she flicks her hand, commanding it open with no sign of effort. I narrow my eyes. "How am I supposed to be a gentleman when you do that?"

She lets go of my arm, slipping inside. I follow her, sliding my hands in my front pockets. As she gapes around the room, I watch the way she lights up in a room full of dusty old tomes filled with words strung together in long-forgotten moments. I've never understood, but watching her turn to me with a grin across her face means I don't need to, just let her enjoy it.

I miss this, listening to your thoughts as you read, the feelings you have when you hold a book, the way you will just test the pages, feeling them between your fingers.

All those things that used to make me twitch with irritation are haunting me, coming back in droves of agony. I clear my throat and point to the podium at the far end. "That's what you want."

I blink, and she is there. I follow suit, piecing myself together by her side in front of the decorative stand. The shaft is a wooden carved spirit, the flat base upon which the book sits are the wings. The likeness is terrible—the wings of feathers and armor replaced with a robe. Maybe it isn't supposed to be a spirit at all, but if not, I have no idea what it is.

She runs a hand over the book, her features frozen, eyes staring. I crane my neck to see her face, the way light glints on the liquid bubbling over her eyes. I reach out to her hand, placing mine over hers.

She jerks to life, head whipping to glare at me. I don't care. "You're going to be okay," I whisper. "In the end, after everything is done and over, you're going to be okay."

Ella's features soften, the corners of her mouth turning down ever so slightly. She pulls her hand from beneath mine and opens the cover. Her fingers run over the colored fabric markers, each dedicated to a single revolution of new members.

"You'll want this one," I find the right tab, opening the pages for her.

She reads the tab. "14,107. How do you know which one I need?" She cocks a hip with a hand on it.

"Lucky guess?" I raise my eyebrows, pushing them together, staring down my nose with honest innocence. I have no idea if it was 106 or 107.

She narrows her eyes then turns back to the book, running a finger down the line of names. It stops. I glance over her shoulder to see the looping scrawl, halfway between neat and pretty, and a scrawled mess.

"That's it." She looks up at me, lips parted, eyes wide. "That's me. I wrote this."

Oh fuck, lover, don't look at me like this. I can't fix it. I can't.

Her eyes drop back down to the book. "Morella Rowena Annabelle Byron," she recites on a long breathes. She wrinkles her nose and looks up. "That's a serious name."

I laugh. "Yes, that is quite a name you have."

She brushes her fingers over the edges of the pages as she studies me. "So, now you know who I am."

"Do you?" There is no malice in my voice. I don't mean to upset her, yet she sniffs and blinks, turning away. "Lo—" I stop and clear my throat. "What's wrong?"

"Nothing." Her voice is a fragile whisper.

I hum and step around her, pulling her hands away from her face. "Was this not what you had hoped for?"

"It was. I saw it. My name. I wrote it, at some point," she

mutters, blinking a few times and looking to the ceiling. "I just wish I could remember. I want to know what the festival is like, and the displays and plays and all the magic in the air when the mages would stand on stage."

Those stupid ceremonies are nothing like she is fantasizing about at all, but I am not going to burst that bubble for her. I run a thumb over one set of her knuckles.

"I wrote my name. I joined this guild, and I can't remember it. I'm told they give pins. I can't recall receiving it. I want to know if I was happy. I must have been happy."

Oh, hell, lover. You weren't happy. You weren't allowed to be happy or given the chance.

I recall that day, catching sight of her in the crowd. I had disliked her, but there was something so broken in her eyes as she tried to push back to the palace that I had just grabbed hold of her wanting to make it better.

I take a deep breath. "Maybe you were happy, maybe not being able to remember means you can believe you were happy, even if you weren't."

"I know it's stupid, but..." she stops, and her mouth twists to one side, her eyes glued to the floor.

Same old Ella, stopping mid-sentence and holding back. That is familiar territory. It's as good as I am going to get right now. As much as I want to chain her up and keep her here, I can't do that, and she'd kill me for trying.

"But what?" I whisper.

"I kind of... It's really stupid, but even if I had the pin, like, something to hold onto, something concrete that I was there, that I lived it."

I smile, letting go of her hands. I place mine together, eyes closing, and I concentrate. When I pull them apart, a mage's pin rests in my palms, five copper circles with a twinkling blue sapphire in the middle.

Her eyes stretch wide, and she reaches for it, stopping, eyes lifting to mine. I nod, the right side of my mouth pulling back.

She squeals and snatches it up. "Is this...? This is what they look like? I've seen them drawn, but it's always black ink. They're this orange color? And that, is that a sapphire?" She glances up at me. "I thought you said you weren't a mage."

I shrug. "I'm not."

"Then how'd you manage a sapphire?"

"I have no fucking clue," I tell her, rubbing two fingers against my chin with a stupid smirk. "Sheer desire to give you what you wanted?"

She gives me a baffled expression and then plays with the pin. "Thank you," she says on a breathless sigh. "Thank you, thank you, thank you."

Rage begins to boil in my veins. There is no reason something so stupid should make her this happy.

What the fuck did they do to you?

She holds the pin close against her chest, and something else catches my eye. My ring. There isn't another like it. Ornate silver band, big yellow sapphire.

I grit my teeth and clamp my jaw as tight as I can, my fingers curling into fists. My arms start to shake, and I try to squeeze harder. Whispers tempt me to break bones and rip flesh. I won't hurt her, though.

She beams at me. "I should go." The words are soft. "But thank you for this. It means so much to me."

I manage to nod, still staring at her hands, the pin clutched in one, my ring on the other.

"It was a pleasure to meet you." She clasps one side of her skirt and does an awkward little curtsy.

Nice to meet you? That's fucked up. I'm your fucking husband. I can't move, can't blink, can't breathe.

"I'm sorry, I'm not very good at that."

"No," I snap, jerking to life. She pulls back, looking appalled.

"No," I say with a smile, a softer tone. "Please, don't apologize. I should." I give a bow and then stand tall. "You did fine."

She wrinkles her nose. "You are a gentleman, aren't you?"

"Sometimes." I force one side of my mouth into what I hope is a smile.

"Thank you."

She dissolves from my sight. I don't know how long I stand there, staring at where she had been. I stay still until I quit shaking. The only thought in my head as I walk away from that place is the look on her face when I gave her that stupid, worthless pin.

CHAPTER 36

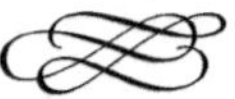

MORELLA

Silence can be deafening. The absence of words can speak louder than any screaming voice. Sometimes the most gut-wrenching thing that can be said is nothing.

I can sense the anger simmering beneath my father's skin in the same way I can feel the exuding heat from a fire. We have not spoken a single word, and I'm not sure if he is aware of my visit to Dis. Thinking about the city underground and the handsome stranger brings heat to my cheeks. I do my best to contain the smile on my lips and cut my eyes to my father.

He is reading a book, sipping his tea, still ignoring me. I roll my eyes and shift to turn away from him so I can daydream about my sexy stranger without notice. The strength in his hands, the veins pulsing on his forearms, the biceps flexing. All that brawn, and yet, when he grabbed hold of me, it didn't hurt.

I ring my own wrist in a light grasp and let myself smile. I want to see him again. The thought sings through me, and I sit up straighter. I'm engaged to Erac, and I want to see another man. All the same, perhaps I can sneak away again today.

The pin he gave me, I used to clasp a sash around my waist,

and I trace the circles over and over again as I let my mind wander.

"Morella, we are leaving. Let's go."

Startled from my daydreams, I get to my feet. "Father?"

He is on his feet, fixing his brilliant green eyes on mine, and I flinch. The left side of his lips twitch, the minutest flex of muscles. "I have cleaned up your mess."

I stand, brushing the skirt of my dress. "But–but Marx didn't, he–we—"

"We?" He cuts me off, swelling in posture as if a string pulls his head upward. "You lost your head. You allowed your emotions to sway your actions. It was sloppy."

My face warms as I cast my eyes down. I contemplate telling him about the whispering. It's becoming more persistent, snarling even at him and Erac at times. Oddly it didn't snarl at the stranger yesterday.

"We are leaving." He touches the buttons at the collar of his white dress shirt.

"But why?" I demand. "Clemm Court has not agreed to a peaceful surrender."

The corner of his left eye twitches, narrowing his gaze for a split second. "Enough, Morella."

"No," I say, raising my voice. "No, we aren't leaving Clemm."

He scowls. "I see." The air grows cold and dark around me as he bores into me with those poisonous eyes. Something slithers alive in them, slimy and cruel. "You think you know best?"

I lift my head, turning my profile to him to stare out the windows of our sitting room. I squeeze my teeth together, the muscles in my jaw jumping. I don't know why I'm fighting to leave here other than the unexplainable sense that I should be here.

When I don't answer, he chuckles, the noise full of malice. "You have forgotten everything I taught you."

My lips peel back from my teeth as I turn to glare. "I don't have a single memory from before."

"No? Whose fault is that?" The question is a dangerous silky inquiry.

My ears burn and ring. "Theirs, those brothers you talk about, they poisoned me."

He grins, his face splitting into the sneering expression that twists his features with something cruel. "Not at first. At first, it was you. You and your vapid emotional reactions. You gave them the opportunity. You let them in, showed them weakness that they capitalized on."

I stare back at my father's callous gaze. "So, I did it to myself, is that it?"

He looks pleased, checking his watch. "You let your emotions control you far too often. Come, let me show you." He extends his hand to me. "I have secured an audience with Miritarath."

The name is a stranger to my ears. "Who?"

"Miritarath precedes over the elven court, Gummurssevi." My father's words are paper thin. "For all the reading you've done, I would have suspected you would have acquainted yourself with important knowledge."

I roll one shoulder and reach out with sweating fingers to take his hand. He crushes my limbs in a cruel grasp and cold ripples through me. It leaves my limbs tingling as my elements rebuild.

A hundred pairs of eyes fixate on me as I glance around. Everything is graceful curves, and a bubbling fountain meets my ears. My father stands next to me, releasing his grip and throwing my hand from his.

He straightens his sleeves, checking the buttons at the cuffs, but I turn away, taking in the breathtaking beauty around me. The hall is marble with gold and rust-colored veins, but instead of walls, there are only trees. Their trunks are thick, the bark moving in organic patterns filled with moss and glittering gold.

A throat clears, drawing my eyes to the front. A flight of wide steps leads in dully gleaming arches up to a platform where two gilded thrones sit. A man and woman occupy those thrones, staring down their noses at my father and me as if we are worms eating through their gorgeous floors.

"Viktor," the man says, struggling to rise from his chair.

I straighten my back and ignore those around me, standing at attention by my father's side.

The man gets to his feet, his labored breathing the only noise in the hall. "We of Gummurssevi welcome you and your daughter to our court." He gives a meager bow. I imagine it might be all he can manage.

"Thank you, Miritarath."

"I would graciously invite you to stay with us as my esteemed guest. Gummurssevi would be honored."

"Yes, so you said in your letter." My father slides his hands into the front pockets of his trousers.

Miritarath wheezes with a grin coloring his cheeks. "Yes, yes," he says, shuffling forward.

A younger man steps forward, light of foot, without sound in the quiet air. He helps Miritarath forward without words. My eyes cut to my father as the men work their way down the steps for what feels like an eternity.

The two men arrive at the bottom of the steps, and my father has not so much as twitched, but I have shifted my weight, crossed my arms, chewed my lip, dropped my arms to my side, switched legs, looked around the room at least twice, and stretched my hands. I wonder at his patience if this is the point he is trying to make. Not that my fidgeting is an emotional response, but I cannot fathom what else he could mean.

Miritarath stops a few paces before us, his long ears drooping away from his head. He chuckles, leaning much of his weight on his younger companion. “I am an old man,” he wheezes. “I do not move as well as I used to.”

I smile big with closed lips, having nothing to respond with. Instead, I eye the man with him. His long ears are tucked close to his short hair, a color of rust between red and brown with dark green streaks. His eyes are a dark jade in a thin face pinched with a quiet wisdom.

“My grandson,” Miritarath says, using his free hand to pat the hands latched to his other arm in order to hold him up. “Ayelorn.”

I raise an eyebrow at Ayelorn as he does his best to bow around his grandfather. I incline my head. “It’s a pleasure to meet you.”

Ayelorn’s eyes twinkle at me as he gives me a boring smile. “The pleasure is mine, Morella. The world has heard of your beauty and power, although I will be hard-pressed to say which is greater.”

The words are flat, a necessary pleasantry he was forced to endure. I suspect the words may have been rehearsed. I almost laugh, my lips parting in genuine mirth. “You seem hard-pressed to declare that much.”

He gives me a sheepish grin, eyes cutting to Miritarath. “Ah, you have caught me. Pap-pap has often told me my strengths do not lie in words.”

“No?” I ask with open interest. “Then, where do they lie?”

“In gestures, mainly, and intellect.” His cheeks tinge pink at his boast. “Undoubtedly, I will be known as King Ayelorn the Quiet when I am notated in history.”

“Is that so?” I ask. “I wonder how I may be remembered. I will have to ask my subjects to decide if it shall be by beauty or power as you are unable to say.”

Miritarath laughs as Ayelorn stammers, his pale skin blushing red. “I do believe you have bested him, dear. Come, come, let us have tea and treats as friends.”

"No, thank you," my father says. "My daughter and I ate breakfast shortly before our arrival. Let us get down to business."

"Come, now, the children do seem to be enjoying themselves. Let them get to know each other, and we can speak of what you came here for."

"I would like to see more of Gummurssevi," I admit. "This hall—if it is even a hall—it is beautiful. Is all of your land built in such a manner?"

"This is our court hall, yes," Miritarath says. "Our lands are all fashioned in a similar sense, but they are living and growing. We embrace the nature of all things."

Miritarath shuffles forward, but my father stands steadfast. "I have come to accept your submission. The whole of Caleum will be united once more."

"Eh?" Miritarath stops, glancing up. "Is that what you've come to discuss?" He begins to cackle.

Ayelorn's eyes flash, the innocence in his gaze replaced with displeased concern. They move from me to my father. "My family has tended to these lands and our people for revolutions. Ours is the blood used to form the unmade space and create Caleum. We allowed your kind to rule once. It was a grave mistake on our part. We will never bow to you."

When his eyes return to mine, they are hardened. I stare back with a sweet smile on my face. "Are you sure about that?" I lift my hand, elbow bent and palm facing upward. Energy pools and swarms as a warm glowing ball of swarming tiny lights.

Meeting his gaze again, it betrays his fear. He clamps his jaw, his chest swelling as he draws air. "Perhaps we can discuss this further. I am certain we can come to some arrangement."

I allow the energy to release back into the air. The skin of my palm remains full of heat, and I stretch my hand, the rosy skin pulling tight. I close my fingers to a fist and let it drop to my side.

"The only arrangement I will accept is your sworn fealty," my father says in a low but firm voice.

Miritarath shakes his head. He does his best to stand on his own, but Ayelorn doesn't release him. "You come to my court and demand my crown? I've heard the rumors, heard what you've done." He eyes me. "No. The answer is no. Our world and people are ours and ours alone."

"Morella," my father says, "what is the foundation on which every civilization rests?"

My eyebrows pull together with my lips. "I don't know?" I turn to meet his gaze.

"Children."

My eyes stretch, and I glance around the room, spotting several grabbing hold of the young, holding them close with fear sprawled across their features. I look back to my father with fear tying my insides in ugly bows.

Miritarath draws in a shaking breath. His voice booms and quakes around the hall. "You'd harm the most innocent?"

"If you will not serve beneath me, then you have no future." My father speaks as if we were all still discussing if we will have tea. There is not the barest hint of care to his voice for what he speaks of.

I swallow, wide, dry eyes fixating on Ayelorn. He stares back at me with ears pulled back, the skin on his face pearl white now.

My heart beats several times as we all wait in utter silence, the air as quiet and still as death. I wonder if Viktor's threat is earnest and why he would not extend the same words to Marx. Cutting my eyes to the side, I study his face, but his features betray nothing.

Miritarath recovers first. "You're as bad as they said. They warned me, told me what you had been willing to do to your own daughter." He curls his lip. "I'll not let you treat my people this way."

"Morella," my father says, "please remove all children in this room, including Ayelorn."

"What?" I gasp, turning a bit to gape at him with absolute horror. "You're not serious? You want me to—"

"I did warn you," he says, not bothering to even glance my way. The words are low, as if meant only for me.

You let your emotions control you far too often. Let me show you. His words echo in my mind.

He is right. I am letting my feelings dictate how I act. I lift a shaking hand into the air, ready to snap my fingers.

I allowed my feelings to open me to a weakness once before, and for that, I have paid dearly. I must learn from my mistakes. I won't be so easy to corrupt this time. I cannot allow my emotions to get the best of me.

My eyes close, and I concentrate on the children I saw about the room. My heart stutters, and a queasy sensation slips and writhes in my stomach. I breathe out.

"No, wait!" Ayelorn roars, but it is too late.

My middle finger strikes against my thumb and down against the knuckle. The loud pop resonates around the room. For a single heartbeat, the energy pours out of me, and then there is silence. The quiet doesn't last long before the air fills with mournful screams and wails of fury fueled by agony.

Opening my eyes, I see Miritarath on the floor, collapsed with Ayelorn gone. I hold my breath and wait, the cries quieting around the court as my eyes scan the room. My gaze is met with hatred from those on the sidelines. Rolling my shoulders, I cross my arms and pull them in close.

My father steps forward, towering over the king with a frown. "I will offer once more. Will you accept me as your emperor?"

I suck in a breath and hold it, hoping Miritarath will see reason.

He stays a crumpled mess on the floor as he lifts one hand to grab the elegant crown from his head. Tossing it at my father's feet, he mutters, "For my people, I bow to you."

Exhaling in relief, I close my eyes and tip my head back. Energy releases from my core in shock waves as I return all the children.

"Pap-pap!"

I meet Ayelorn's gaze as he kneels, starting to help Miritarath off the floor. His jade eyes focus on me with lines at the corners as they pinch with contemplation. I purse my lips and look to my feet, shuffling in place.

On the edge of my vision, they move, standing together in shadowed blurs. I sigh, stepping forward and plucking up the discarded crown. Turning, I offer it to my father.

He snatches it out of my hands, inspecting it between his. He compresses the metal, reforming it into something else. Rather than watch, I face Miritarath and Ayelorn once more.

Miritarath reaches up, a hand on his grandson's face. "My boy." He grins, his face radiant.

I smile at his joy, disregarding my father's aggravation. Something whistles by my ear, a gilded dagger blooms in Ayelorn's eye, embedded to the hilt. A woman screams and rushes forward, faltering on the steps and falling to the bottom. My lips peel apart, and I stumble back a step. An iron hand clamps down on my shoulder.

"Ayelorn! Ayelorn!" the woman cries, crawling along the floor on all fours in a scamper until she reaches his body. She shakes him, sobbing and calling his name. "My boy. My sweet boy."

"You gained our mercy this time, Miritarath," my father says, his voice dripping with fury. "Next time, punishment will be swift, and your children will not be returned."

CHAPTER 37

MORELLA

Alone in the throne room at Asperheim, we stand squared up. I shake my head, using my fingers to work the underside of my hair to remove knots.

"How dare you," my father snarls, the muscles in his neck straining. The corner of his left eye is twitching.

I stand my ground, dropping my hands on my hips. "You wanted me to kill all those children?"

"You showed them mercy. You let your emotions control you."

"Leniency, and you killed Ayelorn." I scoff and cross my arms. "That's punishment enough for asking twice."

"It was a sign of weakness to let them live. It will only encourage them to push back. They will not believe the next time I tell them the consequences."

A laugh bursts from me. "You killed Ayelorn! And you got what you wanted."

"Morella, you will do as I say."

"Or what? You'll scold me like a child?" I cock my head to the side.

"I will—" he stops abruptly, something registering in his

eyes. I can see it. I just don't know what it is. He clears his throat. "You have always been stubborn."

"Well," I say with a sneer, "it is nice to know that some things don't change even after you ripped away everything I was."

He steps to me, reaching out to backhand me. This time I see the blow coming and hold my hand up, blasting him in the chest. I dialed back. He winces and is a few feet away from me, but I'm out of reach again.

I drop my hand, lifting my chin. "I am a grown woman, not your little princess. I'm going to have an attitude, an opinion, and, yes, emotions. Deal with it."

I glare at him as I dissipate to my rooms. Standing at the foot of my bed, I let out a noise of frustration and grab at the air in front of me. My fingers curl into the nothing before me, and then I sigh, tipping my head back and running my fingers through my hair.

Collecting the strands, I braid them. Dropping my head forward, the glint of the pin at my waist catches my eye. I carefully loosen the securing needle to hold it in my hands.

I dive face-first onto my bed and then roll over and stare at the ceiling. In my hands, I toy with my pin. My thumb runs in circles over the rings from the outside to the sapphire chip in the middle. Trying to think of something other than my father or the genocide of children, the handsome stranger takes over my mind.

I sit up, frowning down at the trinket. With the sense of something strange, I close a fist around it and stand, striding to my door. I wrench it open and slide my head out, meeting the gaze of the guard there.

"I want to see George." I pull back and then jut my torso through the open doorway again. "And I don't want my father or Erac to know about it."

The two men on either side of me exchange sideways glances.

"Please," I plead with them. "They'll be angry with me, and they might hurt him. I don't want them to hurt him."

One of them shifts his weight from one foot to the other, looking straight ahead. "Yes, Your Majesty."

Closing the door, I hold the pin close to my heart and inhale. I return to the bed, flopping down and play with the pin, gray eyes filling my daydreams. Wondering who he is, I fall asleep, cuddling his gift to my chest.

CHAPTER 38

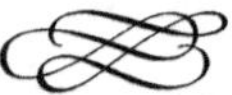

DECLAN

I squeeze my eyes shut and smack the wall of the shower. It's been close to a cycle since I saw Ella, and I haven't had much to do but punch things. I never said anything to her, didn't tell her the truth. I should have told her instead of staring at her. I wrench the knob on the shower, and the metal crumples and breaks free of the wall in my hand.

Freezing water rains over my shoulders, blistering my skin. I stand there, snarling at the wall. Punching through the tile, the bones in my fingers crackle and snap. I don't care. I work them around until they heal enough for me to clasp the pipes and squeeze them shut. I'll find a way to fix it later.

I stand in front of the mirror, staring into my black eyes. My upper lip curls back at my too-long hair. Wet, it's dark, sticking to my head. I glare at the muscles jumping at my movements. It doesn't matter how they bulge and are cut in clear lines; I don't have enough strength to go through this shit again.

I punch the mirror, leaving fractures in the glass and my blood at the epicenter. Someone is knocking on my door. I grab a towel and stalk toward it as the knocking transitions to banging.

Seth starts yelling. "Dec, answer the damn door, or I'm breaking it down."

I twist the lock and glare at my little brother on the other side. "What?" I grind out through a clenched jaw.

He raises eyebrows into messy brown hair. "You look like hell."

I move to close the door, but he slaps a palm against it, keeping it open. I cock a brow. Seth is bigger than me, but he is not stronger. He drops his hand, standing upright. "You need to come with me. Marx tracked me down. A man and his son are here, with Wyoma and some other guy, Archi–Archimage, Archimake?"

His attempts to remember an inconsequential detail irk me. "Get to the fucking point."

"The point?" He crosses his arms. "They have news about Ell."

My heart drops into my stomach. "Why didn't you just say so?" I grab sweat pants, ramming my legs into them. "Where?"

Seth crosses his arms. "Aren't you going—"

"Where?" I repeat louder.

"Clemm Court."

His words are clipped. I've upset him. I don't care. I grab his shoulder and dissipate us to the room.

My eyes take in the room; the massive bell hung in the middle. That comes with memories of Ella, the night I met her for the second time in my life. We fought over the spirit rune on the bell, and I followed her through the palace as she ran from guards.

Court is in session, the room filled with courtiers in fancy clothes. A grouping to my right here to see the crown. I cross my arms over my bare chest and glare at Seth. "Asshole."

He shrugs. "Tried to tell you, you didn't want to hear it."

I breathe in deep and pinch the bridge of my nose. "Who knows about Ella?"

Seth points to the grouping to our right. I scrutinize them closer. A woman stands next to a short, fat man and a little boy. The man and boy are medium skinned, golems, one fat, one too small, neither is a threat. The woman looks sturdy, possibly a fighter. She is fae with red hair. The fourth member is a cloaked and hooded figure. I measure him visually, familiar with the Gammet brothers wearing cloaks.

I take a step toward them, and the hooded figure holds out a hand. It's normal flesh and bone, albeit frail in appearance. He reaches up, pulling the hood back to expose a bare head and the face of a corpse. I think it looks at me. My skin crawls at the milky, empty eyes.

"King Declan."

I cock my jaw to the side, not debating the title. "Who are you?" Marx walks toward us, standing at my elbow. This close, I can feel him, and it makes me want to rip his throat out. I meet his blue eyes.

He gives me a tight smile. "Declan, you are in a fine mood this morning, I see. Please, allow me to introduce you to Archimago. He is a Redcrosse monk. And Pedro, the leader, er, used to be the leader of the Keepers of Asperheim." He sighs. "And his son, George."

I eye the group and clench my jaw. "What about Ella?"

The younger boy steps forward, maybe fourteen at the most. He stares at me with a hard gaze. I lift a brow at him. It's a kid, and I need to dial back.

"You need to fix Ella. Something is wrong with her."

No shit, kid. Arms still crossed, I squeeze my hands into fists and remind myself if Ella ever does come back, and I ripped the head off a child, she is going to be upset. I exhale. "Yes, something is very wrong with her."

He leans back, large dark eyes running up and down me like he is eyeing me up for a fight. He looks back at Archimago. "I don't know about this. He doesn't look very tough."

There are a couple of laughs, and I glance around the room. They cease quickly under my sharp gaze, and I lean down toward the boy. "Kid, I can pull your head off and rip your spine out of your body with it, and I'm going to if—"

"Excuse my son." The short, fat man steps forward, moving the boy behind him. I adjust my sights on him. "He has a rampant mouth but he means no disrespect."

I blink and wait.

"We were at Asperheim."

"With Viktor and Ella? Get to the blasted point." I should watch my mouth with a child present. I already threatened him, and that's bad enough.

The man tries to swell up, too stumpy and fat to be any kind of threat. I'd laugh under normal circumstances. I want to share this sight with Ella. My stomach drops into my legs, and I tense to fight my reaction.

"Yes, and we had previously met Ella before her recent time in Asperheim." He stops, shifting nervously, beady eyes darting around. "George specifically sought her out to see her."

My brows draw together, and I frown. "Why?"

George pops out from behind his father with a defiant expression. "'Cause I knew her from before, and they said she had no memory. And she didn't, she didn't know me. She doesn't know anything but what they tell her."

"Yes." The man clasps his boy's shoulders. "We can tell for certain she is not the same. She has no recollections of her time spent with us a few revolutions ago."

"She asked me things," George mumbles, looking around. "About herself, like she doesn't even know who she is."

I know Ella spent time in Asperheim after I was declared dead, where she received a rune from the monks that freed her from her father's rule. My eyes flicker to the monk and back to the man. "Pedro?"

"Yes, Sir."

"Get to the fucking point."

He blanches, but his kid leans toward me, his face red with rage. "Didn't Ella love you? She was always nice. Even without her memories and all those things Erac does to her, she's still nicer than you. How come you're so mean?"

Marx and Seth grab hold of me as I drop my arms and red flashes before my eyes. I blink, regaining control of myself, brushing them off. The kid is still leaning toward me, glaring. I tip my head back and laugh, crouching down to his level, balanced on the balls of my feet.

I smirk at him. "You've got courage, I'll give you that, kid. Ella was nice. She cared about everyone." I swallow the lump in my throat and drop my voice. "She made me better. All I want is to have her back. I'll do anything it takes to get her back."

He reaches into his pocket and pulls his hand back out, bunched in a fist. I hold a hand out with curiosity. He drops little metal balls into my hand. Bearings roll and clink together in my palm as I scowl down at them.

"What are these?"

"Bearings."

"Yes, I know that," I snap, "but—"

"Your Highness," the father speaks in a cautious voice. "The bearings contain her memories."

I clench my fist around them, desperate to keep them safe. A hand lands on my shoulder, and I twitch, glancing up at Seth's grave features. "So, we have her memories? We can put them back, like, when you got your memories back?"

I turn back to the boy. "How do you know they are her memories?"

"Because I heard that purple-eyed man, Erac, say so. He was talkin' to Viktor about what to do with them."

I narrow my eyes at the kid. "How did you hear this?"

He lifts his chin. "'Cause I was spyin' on them."

Tough kid. "What else did you hear?"

"They were talking about Ella, said some stuff about her being the queen piece on the board, and Erac said they should get rid of the bearings with her memories. Viktor didn't want to. He wanted to keep them in case they were useful. So, I stole them."

My eyes flutter open wider, and I rock, almost losing my balance. "What?" I gasp with humor. "How old are you, kid?"

"I'm not a kid. I'm thirteen."

I chuckle. A thirteen revolution old boy outsmarted Viktor and Erac. I tip my head back and laugh. "Alright—George, was it? Alright, George, so you stole these?" I hold up the bearings clenched tight in my fist.

"Yeah." He looks to the ground and toes the floor. He winces and then stares at me with wide eyes. "I was careful. No one saw me; I made sure. They were just in this chest in Erac's room, but—" He looks up at his father.

"But what?"

"He noticed they were missing. He got mad, like really mad. He went after Ella." The boy's face scrunches up and turns red.

My stomach twists. "Erac hurt her?"

George's mouth twists. "He tried."

The right corner of my mouth hitches up. The woman snapped her fingers, wiping out dozens of my men without effort. She wouldn't let that useless dick hurt her. Pride swells in my chest at the thought of my lover standing her ground.

Pedro clears his throat. "There was an altercation. The whole palace shook." He frowns. "When my son told me of what he had been doing, under the guise of doing chores as a keeper, I grabbed him and brought him to Archimago, hoping to keep him and the bearings safe. He called on Wyoma, and she brought us here."

George inhales, his body pulling upward as he exclaims, "She's a dragon!" The court fills with gasps and whispers, but the boy is oblivious, continuing to shout. "That's so awesome, right? They can change from massive beasts to their old selves again."

"Ahem," Pedro grips his son by the shoulders, cutting his gaze to the red-head who is eyeing George with malice. Her expression is like a serpent about to consume an innocently unaware rodent despite not being hungry. "Yes, my son speaks the truth, but *those are secrets we aren't to share.*" He squeezes his son's shoulders to enforce his terse tone.

I glance up at the man, then back to George. Dragons aren't my concern, even something as mind-reeling as that. I open my hand to show the bearings before sealing them in my grasp again. "How many more were there?"

"I got all of them." A triumphant grin spreads over his face.

I open my hand and do a quick count. Sixteen. Sixteen pieces of my lover, my wife. I stare at them and clench them tight enough to make my fist quake. I lift my eyes to George, seeing him watching me in my moment of torrid emotion.

A kid, that's all he is. A kid who cared about Ella enough to stick his neck out because of who she is, an enigma that is nice to everyone. Was.

I wince but reach out and ruffle his hair. "Thanks, kid."

He shoves my hand away. "I'm not a kid."

I stand, swallowing my emotions, locking them away. I fix my sights on Seth.

Seth shrugs. "So, we return Ella's memories to her, and we get her back."

There is silence around me. I stare down at my closed fist. It's not as simple as he makes it sound. Implanting memories helps, but she's never going to be the same. It'll be a long road, but she, like me, may get back to some resemblance of her former self, but there will always be a shadow of something else.

"Declan, Sir," George says.

I raise my eyebrows. I like this kid.

"Before, when she came to us, she wanted to run away from memories," he tells me, wiping his hands on his pants. "But she's not right without them. You need to give them back to her. I liked the old Ella. She was my friend. Promise me you can give them back, or I'll do it myself."

My chest lights up like my lungs are iron. She thought I was dead, and she wanted to forget. I hang my head, squeezing my eyes shut. *Lover. I'm coming for you. I promise.*

I pick my head up and look at my brother. "We need a plan."

"I want to help," George says. "I don't trust you."

Laughter abounds from everyone watching. I lean forward, narrowing my eyes, my lips twisted to one side. "Why not?"

"You might be mean and scary, but that don't make you smart."

A hand lands on my shoulder and pulls me up. "He's a kid, Dec," my brother whispers over my shoulder.

I scratch at my jaw and the hair growing on it. "I don't know. He seems pretty intelligent." I smirk at George. "You know Asperheim? And a way in, right?"

"Yeah."

I hold my free hand up, palm toward him. "Then you get to help."

George smacks his hand against mine. "Yes!"

CHAPTER 39

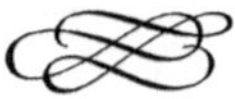

DECLAN

For all Legia's irritating chatter, earsplitting squeals, and her love of fashion, she cleans. I never would have ever guessed she would even touch a cleaning cloth. The way she glares at dirt would be enough to make a grown man tremble.

"Get rid of this, please." She hands a rat, skewered on an arrow to Seth.

He reaches out to accept it, eyes wide. "This thing is massive. Why is it dead?"

"Because I shot it with an arrow."

"But why? Look at this cute little guy. All floppy and—" he yelps. "Warm still. Gia," he groans. "We could have given him a name, kept him around, like a pet."

"A pet?" She gawks at him. "It's a rat."

"As big as my head." He laughs, holding it up for comparison.

Sitting on the lone couch, waiting, I raise an eyebrow at them as they go back and forth. Aron's personal library has new curtains, every spec of dust having been obliterated by Legia's warpath to cleanliness.

There's a squeak, interrupting Legia's response. She snatches her bow off a nearby desk, notching an arrow. She peers into the darkness. I hear tiny claws moving on stone, the shrill squeaks. I listen, tracking for the source, the way Legia is with her sight.

"I know where it is." Seth points.

"Me too," she answers.

I hear the snick of her arrow loosing, the whizz of it cutting through air. I move, grabbing the arrow, twirling it into my grip. I drop it on the ground, peering at the biggest vermin I have ever seen, and I've been in some questionable places.

"Hey," Legia whines. "That was a damn good shot."

I stay on the balls of my feet, moving fast and light, lunging to grab the thing by its tail. It lets out a string of squawks as I lift it in the air. It flails, trying to get loose. It manages to claw at my hand.

"What, are we playing a game to see who can kill the most?" Seth asks.

I shake my head. "I'll take him somewhere else where he doesn't have to die, and he won't bother her." I jerk my chin toward Legia.

There's a gasp. "Cool." I glance over to see George traipsing through the room, eyes pegged on the rat. "Can I keep it?"

I lift the thing up, and it starts making more noise. "Sure, kid. Whatever you want." My gaze scans the room and focuses on Aron. "A little help with a cage?"

He holds a hand out, and a cage appears on the desk closest to me. I flip the lid, drop the thing inside, and lock the clasp in place. I pick it up by the bars and get bitten for my troubles.

I curse, almost dropping the thing, and glare at it. "Little fuck. That wasn't very nice for sparing your life." I offer the cage to George under the distraught gaze of his father. "Hold it by the bottom with two hands. Don't grab the bars until he gets used to this. He doesn't understand, and his teeth are sharp."

George beams, holding the cage on outstretched arms. "This is awesome."

I watch the bite heal on my finger and then turn to Aron. Asena is next to him, and I frown. "What are you doing here?"

She tilts her head with sass, cocking a pose. "This is my court."

I sigh out my nose. "I'm getting sick of those answers. Marx said you weren't aware we were here."

Asena laughs. "I am. Seth reached out."

I turn to my brother with a raised eyebrow but drop it as Marx materializes.

He flashes a grin until he sees his daughter and his face tenses. "Am I late?"

"Right on time," Seth tells him.

Marx turns with a sour expression. "The next time, I'll break every bone in your body."

I cock an eyebrow. "Next time?"

"Good luck." Seth laughs. "You look strong, but you're not strong enough. Shades have dense bones, hard to break, and I'm a lot faster than you."

Marx flashes a grin. "And you have no magic. A mage is not such an easy opponent. I'm sure your brother can tell you."

Legia drops onto the couch. "Can you two please stop trying to prove who has bigger balls and move this along? We need to put this plan together."

I slip my fingers through the bars on the cage and tug on the rat's tail as it moves to bite George. It squeaks and squirms, looking around, but I've pulled back to safety. "Keep your hands away from the bars," I tell him.

He frowns. "But, he's my pet now." George gazes up with a forlorn expression, those dark eyes big and wide in his round face.

"Yes, well," Pedro shuffles, looks horrified. "We can talk about that later."

"What's there to talk about," he whines.

"It's a rat, George," his father says in a stern voice. "It's not a pet."

"But King Declan gave him to me." He scowls into the cage.

"It's a dumb, dirty animal that doesn't want to be in that cage. We will throw him out. We don't even know what they eat."

"They aren't picky," I say. "They'll eat anything, even flesh."

Legia shudders. "So gross."

George perks up, beaming at me with wide eyes. "That's so awesome."

"George." His father's voice sounds full of worn patience.

I stare down at the black beady eyes glistening. The tip of the nose twitches as it sniffs the air in fear. George sticks a finger through the bars and pokes it. The thing squeals, moving away in fear.

I sigh and run a hand down my face. "How about I keep him for you, and you can visit him anytime you want?"

George shrugs. "Fine." Still, he grasps the cage and moves to another desk, and sitting on the edge, he stares down into the cage. "Can I name him?"

"Sure." I drop my hands on my hips. "Aron, how's that cage to hold Ella coming along?" My eyebrows crease together as I stare at the space above his head. He looks too much like Erac for me to look at him straight on.

"Things went smoothly. I am nearly finished." He wraps his arms in front of him, no doubt an old tick from hiding his hands in the sleeves of a tattered jade robe. He smiles, his violet eyes crinkling at the corners. "It should work to prevent her from controlling the elements. Marx, your assistance was invaluable."

I bob my head. "And George, you can tell us how to get into Asperheim, where she is?" I glance at him to see him watching the rat, trying to touch it again. "Something other than the front door?"

"My son and I can tell you where her rooms are located. We can draw you a map of the palace. It's a vast maze of corridors, so we will walk you through it a few times."

"Yeah, and you can go through the aqueducts." George seems a little too excited, still gazing at the rat with hungry eyes.

Seth holds his hand up. "Do we sneak in, in the dead of night, and hope we aren't found out? Or do we create a diversion and hope it catches the attention of the right ones?"

Legia frowns. "Which are the right ones? Anything too big, and it'll be obvious. Or if Ella is helping Viktor, it might draw her away from where she would be."

"That could work to your advantage." Marx shifts his weight.

I lean against a desk. "How would you do it?"

He nods, head bobbing. "Something minor will put Viktor on alert. Anything possibly arranged by an enemy, he'll consider an attack. He will be suspicious of everything, just as he was of my offer to show Ella Dis."

I laugh. "Maybe, but she came anyway. She's not listening to him."

Marx turns to me. "She came to Dis?"

"I had a few minutes."

"Did you build trust? Or act impulsively?"

I cock my jaw and narrow my eyes. "What do you think?"

"That you lack patience. Haven only knows why because I tried to teach it to you."

"You're a right old bastard for whatever you did to my brother," Seth snaps. "Fucking prick, keeping him away, taking his memories."

"Hey," Asena snaps, eyeing him. "That's still my father."

Seth curls his lip. "Dec's a bloody, arrogant, sadistic prick these days, so thanks for that."

"You're welcome," Marx answers with a grin.

"None of that matters," I grind out through clenched teeth.

"We have the bearings, we can get Ella her memories back, but we need to move fast. They know the bearings are missing. That useless dick went after her for it, so we know they know. It's only a matter of time until Erac comes looking."

Aron sighs. "We need to discuss how you plan to manage my brother."

"He's fucking dead." Seth laughs. "That's how we manage him."

"Watch your mouth," I snap. "There's a kid."

"I'm not a kid," George says. "I'm thirteen."

Marx drops his arms. "Let me think on how best to approach this situation. We need to be delicate in how we do this. We will only have one chance." He turns to me. "There is one other opportunity we have, but it will be a last resort."

I smirk. "When you walk through the front door and surrender?"

"Speaking of surrendering." He tosses an envelope on the desk next to me. "I have received an invitation to reconsider my hesitation, a peace offering if you will. Read it if you wish. You might see something I missed. In the meantime, my boy," he fixates on me, drawing a circle in the air, "we solidify whatever this is."

Seth stands at my shoulder. "What's to stop him from stabbing us in the back?"

Marx chuckles. "If I wanted to stab you in the back, there are for more convenient ways, ones that involve limited or no risk to myself."

Asena leans against Marx, nudging him with her shoulder. "Dad," she draws out.

"If you stab me in the back," I growl, "you'd better make sure I'm dead."

"If I wanted you dead, boy, you'd be dead. I kept you alive when you were bleeding out. It was your own mother who slit your throat, yes?"

Seth and I bare our teeth at each other.

"Yes," Marx says with a chuckle, "that's what I thought."

Seth crosses his arms, eyes narrowing. "We sure about letting him know the plan? Honestly, what's stopping him from betraying us to Viktor?"

Marx rubs his hands together with glee. "Why in Haven's name would I ever do that? I want to keep my court and crown, thank you very much, boy. I have no use for Viktor ruling over me." Marx shakes his head. "How have you three managed to get this far without dying?"

I breathe out my nose, pinching the bridge, then drop my hand. The thought of seeing Ella again, the way she glowed over a stupid pin, was choked up about seeing her ridiculous name scrawled in a worthless book, it is all too much. The whisper in my mind is swirling and stretching out, a haze of fury forming over my eyes.

He frowns at me. "You are going to—"

"I want my fucking wife!" I roar.

"Haven," Asena whispers.

"What?" I snarl as she takes a step away from me.

Seth wraps an arm around the front of her shoulders and squeezes. "It's okay. It happens when we're angry. He's not losing control." He directs his attention to me and shrugs. "You're eyes."

I scowl and clench my fists, trying to remember the last time I satisfied my blood lust. A few days ago, when Seth forced me to drink. I exhale through my nose. "No. I'm not losing control of myself, just my temper."

Marx straightens. "I'll be back for your final decision. In the meantime, I have someone who is searching for you. He might be of assistance in our plans, though I doubt it. I'll send him in my stead for now. You never know when a well-placed pawn might be more useful than a queen piece."

Another body forms in the space as Marx vanishes.

Spaulding bends over, glowering at the ground. "Damnatus, I am never going to get used to dissipation."

"Don't train as a mage," I tell him, offering him a hand. "Why are you here?"

He brushes my hand to the side and stands. "I'll keep that in mind. I make my choice this solstice, so three cycles. Selene is dead."

"I'm shocked," I say, with no real surprise. "What else?"

He grimaces. "Pretty sure Ella did it. Although I didn't see it done, I did see the body. It was awful." His voice drops to a whisper, the color draining from his face. His eyes go out of focus, his mind somewhere far from here.

Seth claps him on the shoulder. "Welcome to Ella under Viktor's control."

Spaulding jerks back to life. He clears his throat and rubs a hand over his chest. "I am king now–of Byron, but it's just a title, I answer to Viktor."

"Great," I grunt. "What the fuck are you doing here then?"

Shaking his head, Spaulding sighs. "No, nothing like that. I'm engaged to Skylar, back under my father's rule." He shudders. "None of this is right. I don't want any of this. I came to help you fix this."

I scoff. "Buddy, go back to Byron, keep your head attached. That's the best you can do right now. We'll let you know if there's something you can do."

He nods. "Yeah, right. I haven't even joined a guild yet. I don't have a lot of skills but, please, if there's anything I can do."

I stare back into his wide eyes and grimace. He's still just a kid, like George. With a sigh, I reach out and clasp his shoulder. "It's going to be okay," I lie.

CHAPTER 40

DECLAN

"Are we sure this is going to work?" Seth eyes the cage. "That thing doesn't look like it could hold me or Dec."

Aron tucks his hands in the sleeves of his robe in front of him. "The cage is not designed to hold a shade. There would be different measures taken for either of you. Ella is not capable of the strength you two possess."

I reach out, gripping a bar. "Are there ways of holding one of us?" Eyeing Aron, I jerk my head at my brother.

"Yes, and likely ones Erac has taken. My brother, for all his faults, is no fool."

I stare at the bars and into the cage. "Debatable."

Seth chuckles. "Right? He kidnapped Ella. I mean, what was he thinking? We're going to tear him to pieces for it."

Aron sighs. "Erac and I... I'm not proud of this." He holds a hand up and takes a step back, glancing to the side. "We have done thorough research on shades. Our experiments were not always pleasant, but they were necessary to achieve knowledge."

Seth bares his teeth, taking one step toward Aron. I raise an eyebrow and cross my arms. "You experimented on shades as if we are animals?" The words are a harsh whisper ripped from my throat.

He takes another step under our glare. "I am the only one capable of manipulating the elements in this cell, and while you may be able to reach me before I can command anything, you will not win this fight in here."

Seth steps beside me, arms across his torso and chest puffed up. To me, the sight is comical, but Aron takes another step, and I note the hand held up to ward us off is starting to tremble. "Yes, we did, and any in-depth knowledge you two have learned from Ella's research has been derived from those actions."

I clench my jaw, lips peeling back to expose my sharp front teeth. "Get to the fucking point."

"Erac is versed in shades, extremely intelligent—"

"Still not sure about that one," Seth mutters.

"And is determined enough to have Ella that he betrayed me, his own brother, and we share a lifeforce."

My ears twitch, and some of my rage sinks to the bottom of my legs. "You two are linked, bound to each other. Ella's talked about that."

"Yes," Aron nods, dropping his hand, standing a bit taller. "Erac and I performed a blood ritual, tethering one life to the other—and I'll repeat this again, you won't win a fight against me, not even together, in this room."

Seth snarls, and I glance over in surprise. His face is contorted. "Are you helping him?"

Aron shakes his head, hands tucking into the sleeves of his robes as he hunkers down, shifting his shoulders. "No, and yes. Our souls and bodies are bonded; it is how we stayed alive, sharing two souls, all the power between us. What is done to him is so done to me. For example, if you were to cut my hand, Erac would also be injured."

"I watched him slit your fucking throat."

"The caveat." He sighs, eyes dropping to the floor. "A bond of this nature requires immense trust in the other individual. That individual is your weakest point, not only if they were to be injured, but also because they can harm you without repercussions."

I cock my jaw and stare at him for a beat. "You know that makes no sense, right?"

"Not even a little bit," Seth barks out with an abruptly cut off laugh. "So, if we kill you, Erac dies too?"

I smirk. My brother may be more like me than I have realized. Aron goes pale, leaning back on his heels. My lips spread in a grin as I turn to Seth. "That would be a yes, little brother."

"I know what it meant. Are we going to kill him or not?"

Aron drops his hands to his sides. "I know you two are both very fond of Ella—"

Seth and I both roar with laughter. He leans forward, dropping his arms, and I tip back a bit. The noise echoes around the room as I chuckle, and Seth swipes at his mouth.

I glare at him, my smiling fading. "Not even close."

"Not even a fucking little bit," Seth manages, still chortling.

"Erac is going to die," I say in a quiet voice, but the way Aron twitches tells me he heard. "Now, later, it doesn't matter when, and if I am the one to do it, he will die slowly, painfully." I drag the last words out.

Aron's face hardens. "We are well aware of what you are capable of. We were aware of you, watched you collecting our father's runes from around Caleum, the things you did to get information, to find the runes. I am all too aware of what I face in my brother's betrayal." There is a tone in his voice, a quiet fury I never would have expected. "No one, *no one,* is more enraged than me. He turned his back on me, he has left me to suffer his fate for his own selfish actions, and he did so knowingly."

I watch him and turn to my brother. Our eyes lock, and we

both face Aron again without a word. I scratch at my beard and drop my arms with a sigh. I rest my hands on my hips and cock my jaw.

"Are we or are we not," Seth breathes next to me.

"Not," I say. "Fuck," I curse and glare at the cage. "We're not, not yet. Killing them right this second isn't going to do us any good. It's not going to bring Ella back and, fuck me, but we need his help still."

Getting those words out feels like swallowing melted iron, and I'm panting a bit. I shrug and throw an arm to get rid of Seth's hand on my shoulder. I don't need my brother to pat my back or trying to make me feel better. I need my wife.

Aron looks at me with an expression of pity. "Once we have located and brought her here," he gestures to the cage, "I can reinstall the bearings and break them to release her memories."

"I can do that just as well."

Aron lifts his eyebrows. "Can you, Your Majesty? Breaking a bearing requires a great deal of power. Erac and I were not capable of breaking the bearings in you," he points toward my arm. "We required Ella to do it for us in our weakened state."

"I'm not fucking weak."

"You're capable of manipulation," he says, his volume rising, "that does not make you a mage. Your abilities lie in basic control, shifting elements from one stage to another. There is no real talent in what you can do. Any young mage who has completed the first level of training can do what you do."

Seth is shaking with contained laughter, and I cut my eyes at him, snarling.

"Hey." He chuckles, lifting his hands. "I didn't say it."

Aron sighs. "This is not a conversation that is doing anything to help our situation and one I am disgusted to be having. My temper is getting the best of me." He inclines his head. "I apologize, Declan, you are a skilled fighter—"

"And a shit mage," I cut him off. "I don't give a damn about being a good or bad mage."

"It comes in handy in fights, though, doesn't it?" He smiles. "I've often tried to convince the warrior guild to allow those with the ability to train through the first level of my own guild." The smile fades. "They have never agreed or accepted."

Words from Ella long ago in a life that seems to be long gone float through me. I snicker to myself at the memory. "It's an expensive guild. Sapphires are your primary resources."

Seth gapes at me. "Is that why you were hell-bent that Ella's ring had to be a sapphire and not the custom opal?"

"Yes." I scrub a hand down my face. "The warrior guild, we have a code. We welcome any and all and let you determine your worth through your skill. If you add in those with magic..." I shrug. "It would throw the balance off. There would be damn good warriors who couldn't compete because they can't do what I do."

Aron nods, arms folding together in front of him. "Stupid beliefs of equality in that manner only drag others down. It does not lift others up."

"I'm not going to stand here and debate the guilds. We have work to do."

"Of course." Aron inclines his head. "If we are forced to capture Ella and restrain her, this cell should work."

"Should?" Seth asks. "What do you mean, should?"

I grit my teeth as Aron responds. "She is the most powerful creature any spirit or elemental has ever encountered. The only ones who may have more power are the aspires in the highest dimension and Haven itself. There's no way to know if this magic will hold her."

I jerk my chin at him. "I thought you needed help with a spell?"

"Don't insult me." Aron gives a lopsided grin. "I sent Seth to fetch you to give me time to work in peace."

"That's nice," Seth mutters. "So, what if this doesn't work?"

"We dose her with malwort root, shove her in there, and pray to fucking Haven she can't get out if it comes to this." I curl my lip at the cage and the thought of drugging and locking my wife up in this miserable hovel.

I'm coming, lover. Soon.

CHAPTER 41

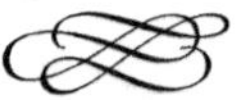

MORELLA

I am shaken awake. With a groan, I blink dry eyes at whoever is there. I expect George, having sent for him again, pleading with any servant that dares come near me, but Erac's face comes into focus. My half-smile disappears into a frown. "Oh."

He smiles, reaching out to brush tendrils of hair that have come loose from the knot done up at the base of my skull in the throes of sleep. "My love, why did you not come to see me today?"

"*Mmphf,*" I cover my mouth as I yawn. "I was tired."

"I can see that." He chuckles. He reaches out, taking my hands in his.

I stare down at them. His hands are bigger than mine, but not large. There are no callouses, his fingernails neat and trimmed. They pale in comparison to *his* hands.

"Morella?"

"Mmm, what?" I wrench my eyes away from our hands to his indigo gaze. His eyes flicker back and forth between mine, and I take in his thin face. The stranger's face had sharp cheekbones and a noble nose, not the same as Erac's flat features. I drop my eyes down and away. "I'm sorry. I'm still tired. What?"

He gives me a tight smile, the expression beginning and dying at his lips. "Yes, I can see that."

Leaning forward, his lips press against mine, flat and clammy. I do my best to not grimace and wait a moment before I turn my face away. He doesn't let me. He grabs my face in his hands and returns to kissing me. I give in, yielding, doing my best to pretend this isn't happening.

When he does release me and sits back, he is beaming at me. "I have missed you."

"Hmm? Yeah." I rub my eyes. "Yeah, you too."

His face draws into concern. "Are you alright?"

"Yeah, I was just…" I stop on a sigh. "I just laid down with —" I stop talking again.

I pull my hands from his and look around for my pin, moving pillows and smoothing the blanket in desperation to find it. Getting to my knees, I scamper over the sheets, searching with my hands until my fingers find the cold metal, and I let out a sigh of relief. I pull it from under a fold of the sheets and cradle it in my hand.

"Darling." Erac's voice is terse. "What is that?"

"Hmm?" I show him, pulling back as he reaches for it. "It's just a pin."

"It's a mage guild pin. Where did you get it?" His eyes seem to darken as he tenses, or maybe that is my imagination.

"I found it, in Dis," I say.

"Viktor took you to Dis when you visited Clemm?" his voice is chock-full of disbelief.

I wince. "No."

He snarls, his face a mask of fury. "No, he didn't. He didn't mention Dis at all, which means you went without him. Alone," he stresses.

"It's not a big deal," I say, rolling my eyes. "It was what, two cycles ago?"

Erac lets out a hiss and smacks his hand over the pin in mine. "It is a big deal. You're lying to me." His fingers wrap around my palm, keeping me from pulling away, and the grip becomes painful.

"I'm not."

"We make these every revolution at the solstice, and whatever we don't use gets destroyed. You didn't just find one."

I frown. "Who are we?"

"Aron and I," he snaps.

"Who's Aron?" My face pinches with confusion.

"He's my—" His face twists as he stops our rapid, fair exchange. "It doesn't matter. You didn't find one. I know you didn't. You lied to me."

"Fine!" I yell, making another attempt to wrench free. His fingers only dig in harder. "I didn't find it. A worker in Dis made it for me."

He lets out a bitter, short burst of laughter. "There are no workers in Dis. It was my home for revolutions, and we didn't keep workers or servants." He releases me, and we wrangle over the pin. The tug of war is short-lived as he backhands me.

Sitting up, I watch him stand, glowering at the pin. He clenches it in his fist, and when he relaxes his hand, it's gone.

"No!" I scream, both my hands delving into my hair at my forehead. "Why? Why did you— Why couldn't I just— Why?"

He leans forward, snarling at me. "Because you lied to me. Because you're still lying to me. Because that stupid thing doesn't matter. Stay where I can watch over you. Stay with Viktor. Stay away from anyone else. It's for your own good, your safety."

I stare at him, the side of my face stinging, my eyes welling up.

"Now, tell me the truth." He shakes a finger at me. "Where did you get it? Who gave it to you?"

I suck in air through my nose, straightening my spine. "A man in Dis. He said he works there."

"What did he look like?"

Narrowing my eyes, I straighten my spine, rolling my shoulders back. "I don't know. Average, like you." I flick my hand at him.

He reaches out, his hand slapping me with an open palm this time. I grit my teeth, and this time I lift my hand to fight back. I send a wave of compressed air elements at him. He has pushed a few paces away, and I try again, this time igniting the air, so it burns.

He ducks behind a shield of air and then stands, glaring at me. I glare right back, ready to attack again.

Something shifts in him, his posture softening. He hangs his head. "Darling."

"Don't darling me," I snarl, getting to my knees and making my way off the bed.

"I get scared," he mumbles. "I get so scared, and it–it doesn't come out right. You're so important to me, and the thought of losing you makes me crazy."

I rub my face. *The stranger wouldn't ever strike me.* The thought hits me like an iron rod to my stomach, as does the realization that the pin is really gone. My chest cracks, the mass in my chest forming fractures.

Tears well in my eyes, and I start throwing pillows at him. "I hate you. Why? Why did you destroy it?"

He ducks the first pillow and catches the second. "Darling, please, I understand you're upset."

The third pillow hits him in the face. He drops the other one on the floor and hangs his head. He sighs, holding out an open palm. A new pin forms, the copper circles gleaming with dull life. He offers it to me, the sapphire in the middle twinkling as he moves closer.

"Ugh," I groan, throwing my hands in the air. "I'm going to the beach, and I don't recommend you follow me."

"My love, please, these are just growing pains," he starts.

"Don't!" I yell. "Just leave me alone."

I close my eyes, clenching my fists and grinding my teeth. Cold tears into my elements as I dissipate. There is no breeze or the sound of crashing waves, though, and I open my eyes to see a fist whizzing toward my face.

I yelp, cowering in a ball.

"What the fuck?" I hear.

CHAPTER 42

MORELLA

The air is full of panting and the smell of sweat. I peek up to see my stranger. He is breathing hard, doubled over, and staring at me with a mixture of emotions. His eyes are dark, full of confusion, but a side of his mouth is drawn back in a half-grin.

He drops down, balancing on the balls of his feet in a crouch. "Fuck." He reaches out toward me, his fingers trembling as they push wisps of hair out of my eyes. "Are you okay?"

I nod, dropping my arms, no longer needing them to protect my head. I am still shaking, though, my nose running and tears leaking from my eyes. Seeing his handsome face, the care and compassion in his voice break me.

As I sob, he mutters and grunts, leaning closer. I cover my face with my hands, dropping to sit on the floor as everything crashes down around me. "I'm sorry," I wail. "I'm sorry. I didn't mean to— I wanted to go to the beach."

"This is a shitty beach."

Surprise draws my face out of my hands. I blink through tears, stuck to my lashes, and glance around. The room is dim, full of broken furniture and debris. I sniffle, swiping at my face. "Where am I?"

He chuckles, sitting cross-legged in front of me. "Dis. An empty room."

Still quaking, I nod, struggling to keep composure. "Oh. I didn't mean to scare you."

He lets out a bark of laughter, then draws a hand down his face. "I didn't mean to almost break your face." His humor dies away. "Really, I'm sorry for almost breaking your face."

I shrug, rubbing my cheek. "It's my fault for scaring you." I do my best to smile. "You didn't, though."

His eyebrows lift. "What exactly do you think you scaring me has to do with me almost punching you?"

Now it's my turn to give him a baffled look. "Isn't that why you tried to punch me?"

He points over my shoulder. "I was swinging at that, and you popped up between it and me."

I glance at the busted cabinet behind us. "Oh." I turn back to him and blink eyes dried by saltwater. "To, you know, be rabid?"

The man gives me a look of shock that turns as his head tilts, and his eyes glaze over. "To what?"

"You know," I say awkwardly, "because you're a shade?"

"What exactly do you think being a shade is?" he asks, on the edge of laughter. His eyes brighten with humor.

"Er…uh, someone told me shades are, um, very animal-like."

"Hmm, is that right?" His eyebrows disappear under the chestnut hair falling before his eyes.

I shrug, hugging my knees against my chest. "Um, don't panic, I won't, but they told me to kill one if I ever saw it, er, him."

He roars with laughter, his head tipped back. One of his hands presses against his stomach as his shoulders shake from the laugh deep within his chest. When he calms, he shoves his fingers into his hair, brushing the strands away, but they plop back, the ends resting against the bridge of his nose.

Still grinning, he shakes his head. "I was in here to work out."

My eyes grow wide. "Oh."

"Yeah," he chuckles and sighs. "Thank you, I needed a laugh."

I smile at him, the fissures in my chest turning to butterflies. "Me too."

His face draws in, and he reaches out. "Did I?"

I flinch, and he stops. I shake my head. "No. Sorry, go ahead, it wasn't you."

His thumb caresses my throbbing cheekbone, our eyes locked together. Reaching up, I wrap my fingers around his wrist, pressing his warm palm to the injury. He grimaces, but his touch remains light as he continues to stroke my face above my eyebrow.

His other fingers find their way into my hair, and my eyes flutter closed. The world should stop, just end and let this moment go on forever. This is all I needed, and I didn't know it.

I tip my head back, staring up at him. "Who are you?" I ask in a low whisper. "I feel like I know you, but I don't have any memories."

At first, his mouth tightens. There's a strain to his eyes, but then he relaxes, nearly smiles. "You know me, lover." The way he says lover sends a warm shudder through my body, drawing desire out of me. He reaches up and tucks a stray hair behind my ear. "You just don't remember."

"Oh."

His hand cups my jaw. It's warm and calloused, strong, and yet his touch is light and gentle. I swallow, nervous but barely breathing with excitement. My toes curl as his face lowers to mine.

His lips press to my forehead, and then he pulls back. My

eyes flutter, half-mast. The action is not one I was expecting, not the fulfillment of desire I wanted. There's a tenderness to the action that makes my lower stomach clench with tension.

I lean forward into him, my hands pressing against his solid chest. The muscles twitch and bunch as he intakes a sharp breath. I lift my gaze to his, lifting my hands. "Should I not have?"

"You can do anything you want," he says, his voice a whisper of breath, pressing his hand against my back to guide my body forward. Everything is so gentle, allowing me to accept what he wants rather than the demanding force Erac uses. I blink, dropping my eyes from his to hide the welling tears as they prick with pain.

"Are you alright?" His voice is full of concern.

"Ha." I force myself to grin up at him, sniffling and blinking away the tears. "Yes, I am fine."

One of his hands reaches up, taking my face in his grasp. The fingers lay against my skin, his thumb running below my lower lip. His eyes drop to my mouth, then lift back to my eyes even as his nostrils flare. "You're not," he whispers. "You flinched when I reached for you. You're crying. Why?"

So many answers to that question course through my mind. *I don't know who I am. Erac is rough. My father is cold. I'm lonely, I feel alone even when I am surrounded, and I don't know why. Something is missing. Things don't make sense to me.*

I part my lips to answer him, but an overwhelming desire takes hold of me, and I reach out, my fingers curling around his neck. I lean in and press my mouth against his. He grasps my hips, pulling me into his lap.

I straddle his torso, one of my hands running up the back of his neck and tangling in his hair, damp with sweat. His hands roam up and over my hips, running down my backside to cup my butt cheeks in both hands. A groan is shared between us, his tongue licking against mine in an open mouth kiss.

I want more, to feel his hands everywhere, knowing they are warm and strong. I know he wouldn't hurt me. I feel it in my core. I can't explain the sense. It's like being able to know when someone is staring at me.

This man is safe and handsome and good at kissing me. I pull back but keep his jaw in my hands. His eyes flicker, opening halfway, dark and hazy with lust. I grin at him as one of his hands presses on the back of my head, guiding my mouth back to his. His lips meet mine, curving to match.

Wrapped in his arms, my mouth and body pressed to his, I let it all go. I lose myself in the taste of his mouth and the secure strength of him. I rip my mouth from his, and he growls but doesn't force anything.

I lean back, eyes widening at the evidence of his arousal pressed between my legs. My gaze drops then lifts back to his. My tongue licks the taste of him from my lips, his eyes flickering like prey at the movement.

Moving slow, I lean in, tilting my head. His eyes stay low, his breath hitching as I move back in to take his lower lip between my teeth. He groans, long and low, his hips rolling up into mine.

The world moves. We both freeze, drawing apart with confusion blooming. I glance around, and then it happens again, the ground shaking.

The cabinet starts to topple over, threatening to crush us. I duck my head, pressing into him, with a mewl of fear, trying to form a shield of protection around us. One of his arms leaves me. He grunts and flexes, and the wardrobe crashes to the floor nearby.

Picking my head up, I meet his eyes. His lips twist with humor. "You're safe. I can handle busted furniture."

I giggle, even as the ground vibrates again. "What is that?" I glance around again. "Is that normal?"

"No idea, and not normal. I don't give a fuck right now, either. Don't go."

Giving him a smile as another tremor rips through the world around us, I hold a hand out. The elements are buzzing, like static electrical shocks. My smile fades. "It's like massive amounts of energy." I turn to meet his gaze. "Is there anyone else here?"

His face tightens. "Yes."

My guts quiver. "I told Erac I got the pin here."

Everything about him tenses. "What did you tell him?"

I clasp his face between my hands, staring into his eyes. "It's okay. He won't hurt you. I told him someone that looked like him gave it to me."

"Oh, yeah, I'm totally safe then," he says with a smirk. "I'm much better looking."

I narrow my eyes, questioning who he is and how he knows me and Erac. "Is there an Aron here?"

"Yes."

"Who is Aron?"

He cocks one brow. "Erac's brother. They don't get along these days."

I groan. "Do they look like each other?"

He leans back, letting go of me to rest his hands. "How do you not know—" He stops and shakes his head. "Never mind. Yes, they're twins."

"Shit. He's here. That's him." Fear pulsates through my chest in droves of sickness and heart palpitations. The ground shudders and the sound of stone screeching rips through the air around us. "I have to—"

"No," he grunts, wrapping his arms around my waist, his nose burying in the crook of my neck. "Don't."

"He'll be furious if he finds me here." I pry his face away from me. "I'm not supposed to be here."

"Fuck that," he snarls. "You're allowed to be wherever you want."

"I'll stay until it's over," I say, the tip of my nose against his. "I'll stay to make sure you're safe, but then I have to go."

He shakes his head. "No. No, you don't have to do anything."

The room shakes again, the broken, busted furniture rattling. Dust rains down from above, and I tip forward into him to hide my face. He kisses the top of my head, strong arms wrapping around me.

The world rattles, threatening to come apart around us, but he doesn't let go. He holds on to me as the explosions continue. Everything fades away like I am in my own little crevice of heaven.

When the world is quiet, and the shaking has stopped, I pull my face from the crook of his neck and blink around. Relief washes through me as my eyes meet his dark gray irises. They flicker back and forth, really seeing me.

His hand lifts, cupping my jaw, and his thumb skims over my lower lip. "You shouldn't be afraid of him. You shouldn't flinch because I move my hand toward you. You shouldn't want to cry all the time." His voice is low and thick, the words whispering through the still air. "That stupid pin shouldn't make you happy. You shouldn't need permission to do anything. You shouldn't—"

I crush my mouth against his. I kiss him, madly, hurriedly like I need this to survive because I do. I need what he offers, the safety and warmth. My eyes scrunch shut tighter, tasting him briefly before I shred myself apart to rebuild in my room.

Standing on my balcony, I touch my swollen lips and stare at nothing. My hand drops away, and I smile. I think I know what love is now. I don't know how I'll convince my father to let me marry my stranger, but I'm going to.

CHAPTER 43

DECLAN

Ella disappears from my lap mid-kiss, and I am left a fucking fool trying to tongue the air. I grunt and fall back on my hands, twisting my face with fury at the place she had been a moment ago.

"Fuck," I groan as I stand and wince. I'm rock hard and throbbing, but she is gone.

The door to the room bursts open and Seth comes skittering inside, eyes wide. "Fucking Damnatus, Erac was here."

"Yeah, I know."

He stops and tilts his head. "You know?"

"Ella was here too. She figured it out." I wave my hand in the air and sigh. "She told him she got that stupid pin here from someone that looked like him, not realizing that was a real possibility. How do you know?"

"Cause I saw him."

Every muscle in my body tenses. "You saw him?" I growl under my breath. "Did he see you?"

"I don't know?"

"You don't—" I stop, clutching at my hair. "How do you not know? Is he still here?"

My brother's eyes stretch wide. "I don't know. What am I? An idiot? I saw him, and I ran as fast as I could."

I narrow my eyes. "What was he doing?"

"Shit," Seth exclaims with a harsh breath of air. "Shit, shit, shit. He was kneeling over Aron. What do we do?"

I give him a skeptical look. I'm not stupid enough to believe I stand a chance against him. He's beaten me twice now. "You're fucking kidding me, right?"

He shakes his head at rapid speed.

"Hide. We hide until we know for sure he's gone."

Using the elements, I shut the door behind Seth, then find the nearest wall to lean against. My shoulders drag down the stone, my skin scraping along the way. I hit the floor with a *whump* and sit there, replaying the last five minutes of my life.

If I'm going to die, I'm at least going to die happy. *She kissed me. My wife grabbed hold of me, kissing me like she was desperate, and only I could save her.*

I am fucking giddy like a boy on his change day. She didn't know me, doesn't have her memories, and she still wants me. I grin at the ceiling and chuckle to myself.

Fuck, lover, you still want me, even after this whole mess. I let out a pleased sigh, and my eyes close to half-mast as I replay it over and over in my head.

"What the hell are you smiling about?" My brother chuckles. I crack one eye open to see him grinning down at me. "What else happened with Ell?"

I sit up, still smiling. "Nothing."

"Then why are you in a good mood?" He lifts his eyebrows to the point they disappear under his curly mop of hair.

"She kissed me."

He turns pink and guffaws. I don't fucking care. My wife kissed me.

"Haven," he chortles, "you're like a lovesick kid."

"Shut up. Don't ruin this for me." I cock my head. "Where were you?"

He grins. "Hanging out with Asena."

The skin on the bridge of my nose crinkles. "Why were you…? Never mind, I don't fucking care. Just shut up and let me have this."

"Yeah, well, just skip over the monumental information I have. Good for you. Now how do we get her back?"

"I don't fucking know. Shut up. Go away. I told you don't ruin this for me," I snarl softly at the ceiling.

"I really hate to burst your bubble, and I mean that. I really hate to because you're not a heartless bastard with her, but kissing her isn't going to fix this." He scratches at his beard. "Plus, I'm not going anywhere. We're hiding, remember?"

"I hate you," I grunt.

Dejection is settling in my gut. He's right. I'm trying to ignore it and focus on the kiss, the way she felt pressed against me and beneath my hands. I can't ignore him or the logic. If I don't bring her home, I'll never get to kiss her again.

I grit my teeth. "Fuck you," I mumble, letting my eyes slip closed. "I really hate you right now."

He sighs, and I open my eyes, staring at him, not hiding the pain in my chest, the sharp stabbing I get every time I inhale that sends ice water through my veins.

He stares back with a broken expression. "I know. I know you miss her, and she's all you're thinking about. I used to feel that way when I saw her with you." I curl a lip back at him, and he laughs me off. "Used to. I don't anymore. I love her, but not like that. Not anymore. Not for a long time now."

He sighs, dropping to the floor next to me. "Aron was on the ground, not moving." He winces.

I shrug. "This whole place was shaking like it was going to fall apart. I'm guessing they were fighting."

"Yeah, but who won?"

I tip my head back against the wall. "Go check." I shove my brother in the shoulder, indicating the door.

He makes a weird "*fft*" sound and shoves me back. "You go check, lover boy. You're the badass. I'm the comic relief."

I smirk, turning to meet his gaze. "I've really been a prick lately."

"Hmm, let's see. Some guy started to come between you and Ell, then we all thought she was dead, and when she came back, Selene screwed the pig by dropping those secrets. You've been trying to fight a war, to stop Viktor, and lost Ell again, lost the crown, and, let's face it, we know they're hurting her. You're kinda entitled to it, but I'll deny ever saying that."

I lift and drop one shoulder. "Yeah. Where's George?"

"Clemm. Where are the bearings?"

"Stashed somewhere a thirteen-revolution-old boy can't steal them."

Seth chuckles. "He's going to be a badass when he grows up."

I snicker. "Yeah. Legia?" There is a long pause, and I cut my eyes to him. "Where's Gia?"

Seth sighs. "I don't know. Asena dissipated me back here, and I went to get blood and damn near walked in on Erac and Aron."

I turn my head to him, one eyebrow lifted. "What were you doing with Asena?"

His face flushes. "We've been spending time together."

My lip curls up with my eyebrow. "Why her?"

"What do you mean, why her? She's beautiful, she's smart, she doesn't take shit from anyone, and she thinks I'm funny."

Tipping my head to the ceiling, I curl my lip. "You know who her father is."

"Well, yeah, but she wasn't involved." He chuckles and hangs his head.

I glare at him. "I don't care. That's not going to be my family. Got it?"

He frowns. "You know what? Fuck you. You were the golden boy growing up, and then you got Ell. I've always had to adjust for your life and clean up your messes."

"My messes?" I laugh. "What the fuck have you had to clean up?"

My brother jerks forward, facing me with a sour face. "Seriously? Helping you with Ell from the very beginning. Putting her back together when you were dead. Being stuck between you two every time you'd fight. Trying to keep you from detonating when we thought she was dead. Helping you fight this war. Manage everything for you when you get all pissy and—"

"Alright," I say, lifting my voice and scowling at him. I raise my hands in defense. "I get it."

"Just let me have this one thing."

I nod, one side of my mouth pulling back. "Yeah, fine. But why her?"

Seth laughs, but there's a lack of humor. "I think I asked myself that a thousand times when you got engaged to Ell. Like, why her? But you know what? I got over it, and so can you."

"Alright, I get it. I really fucking get it. I don't know if you really got over it, but whatever, you and Asena, sure."

He shrugs and settles back. "Maybe. I'll have to get Marx to agree to at least not kill me."

"Save his crown for him, and I'm sure he'll at least tolerate the idea," I say, standing up. "We should see what's going on."

He bobs his head. "Let's go then."

I extend a hand, helping to pull him to his feet. "Where were they?"

"Aron's library."

We stand there, hands clasped, and my heart slams against my breastbone. "I don't know what we'll find."

"Shut up." He grins. "We started this together, and we're going to finish this together, no matter how it ends."

"You'll end up dead in one of my messes. Got it," I say dryly. "Thanks."

He chuckles, letting go of me to throw an arm around my shoulders. "Maybe, but hey, you're consistent."

I shrug him off and walk to the door, steeling myself before I wrench it open. Sticking my head out, I crane to see down the hall, then step out and motion for my brother to follow. I put a finger to my lips, making eye contact.

He gives me a disgruntled look, mouthing at me, "No shit."

We creep down the hall, the only sound the echo of my heart and his in my ears. Every step is harder than the last, but we make our way to the double doors. I stop short, seeing broken chips of wood, one door still hanging by the lower hinge. Something blasted from the inside out.

I take a deep breath and step forward, peering within. Just on the other side of the threshold, Legia is sprawled face down, unmoving.

"Fuck," I step to her, moving orange hair away from her neck so I can check for a pulse. My fingers shake, deftly searching. I try the other hand, my fingers too numb to find the sign of life I'm looking for. I roll her over, and her eyes are open, hazy with a white fog, the brilliance of the blue gone.

Seth crouches next to me on the balls of his feet. "Shit, Gia."

My fingers tremble as I close her eyes, and then I hang my head and clench my fists. Taking a deep breath, I stand, inspecting what is left of the room.

Dust is still falling, the ceiling blown open to the night sky above. Rock and rubble are everywhere, shreds of books and pages littering the room.

I step over a pile of stone and drop to one knee next to Aron. I place my hand on his neck, and his violet eyes pop open.

Jerking back, I flounder and fall on my butt, baring teeth at the air.

Growling, I shift to lean over him. "Aron?"

He tries to smile, blood trailing from all corners of his eyes and mouth. "Erac."

"Yeah, we know."

Seth kneels next to me. "You're alive?"

Aron wheezes, the sound like dead reeds in the wind knocking together. My skin puckers with pimples at the sound. "Not for long." His chest heaves and drops rapidly, eyes flickering. "Erac took—" He coughs.

I bob my head. "Your Vitale rune. He tried to kill you."

"Did." Aron coughs again. "I'm done."

"I thought they couldn't live without that rune," Seth says, eyes on me with twisted lips.

I shrug. "We weren't sure. It doesn't give them—me—life, so I guess pulling it off doesn't kill us. Maybe just keeps us from coming back or healing or whatever it does."

Aron lifts a hand. "I have…just…enough…"

I grab his hand, clenching it tightly in mine. "Just enough what?"

His eyes slip closed, and his breath heaves. The heart in his chest rolls over and takes a second to squelch with life again, barely beating. He exhales, the air whistling out of him, and my elements shred apart.

I rebuild, the world swimming. The ground sways and pitches up to me, and my face meets sand. I groan, rolling over and getting shoved sideways by rolling saltwater.

Soaked, with a mouthful of sand, I stand, trying to figure out where I am. I use my shirt to wipe at my face, the grains scratching my skin. I spit to clear my mouth of the grit, then drop to one knee, catching water of an incoming wave in both hands.

I throw the seawater in my face then shake my head,

blinking to clear my eyes. Getting to my feet, I see my brother stumbling toward me. I fumble forward to meet him.

He laughs, falling to the beach on all fours, then rolling to lay next to me on his back. "That has got to be the worst dissipation in the history of magic."

I snort through my nose, almost laughing. "Maybe the worst dissipation ever, but look." I point a heavy arm at the rocky cliffs.

He picks his head up, and we stare at the spiraling palace. "Asperheim." He chuckles. "That old bastard still dissipated us clear across Caleum on his death bed."

I grunt, getting my legs under me. "Probably with his dying breath. Come on."

CHAPTER 44

DECLAN

The way into Asperheim through the aqueducts leading under the palace was not as easy as George had described. I crawl along the channel, boots slipping, continually falling on the carved stone. I curse and growl as I slip again.

Seth laughs behind me. "This might be easy for a kid, and ugh," he groans, "the smell."

I grunt as I catch myself from falling again. "It was supposed to be the water channel."

"What if we got the wrong entrance?"

I fight onward, the water trembling and pebbles raining down. I wait for the earthquake to pass and glance back at Seth. I peer, trying to make him out in the shadows and darkness. "He said the fifth cavern."

"Sixth," Seth grunts.

"Fifth."

"Pretty sure it was sixth, big brother." He laughs. "We're in the shit tunnels, not the freshwater ones, aren't we?" His chuckle echoes around us in the dark.

"Shut the fuck up. Keep moving." I continue shuffling along

in a crouched position until I reach the end of the tunnel. I crouch, kneeling on the edge work.

I climb into the open room, standing and breathing through my mouth. Seth stands next to me, his shirt pulled up over his nose and mouth. He wiggles his eyebrows. "Sixth."

I search around, ignoring what I was crawling through. "Out," I point to a ladder.

We move, jumping overflowing sewage passageways to reach the ladder. We butt into each other, both in a hurry to be out of this place. I glare at him, grab one side of the ladder, and he shoves me as he latches onto the other side.

"You got it wrong. I'm going first."

I pull my shirt over my face and motion up the ladder. Seth climbs, and I hold the legs. The rickety build of bamboo wobbles under his weight, and I struggle to hold it steady without breathing. My eyes are starting to sting from the stench.

"Hurry up."

He reaches the hatch, extends his arm, and pushes. He shifts, bracing his forearm against the round, wooden door. The ladder lurches as he shoves. I hear the wood rattling and grit my teeth.

"Push harder."

He slams his hand upward into the door, splintering it. I duck my head as particles fall. The ladder waddles, and I glance up, seeing Seth moving up out of sight. I scurry up and through the portal.

Seth gestures at the broken door. "Going to fix that?"

"No, we need to move." I take a step and stop.

Seth asks, "What if they find us? I can't ignore their orders. What am I supposed to do if they say something smart like, kill yourself?"

I give him a look and check our surroundings, taking a deep breath and pulling my shirt down. "At least it smells better up here."

"You're ignoring the question."

"Of course, I am." I breathe with force, glaring. "What do you want me to say? If they have a set of spirit runes, you'll do what they say. If they say kill yourself, then you'll kill yourself."

"Easy for you to say," he mutters in a dark, sour tone. "I'm not ready to die."

"I'll do what I can to keep you alive. Maybe my orders will override theirs," I say, my voice low.

I move to the door, cracking it open. I peer out the slit and watch. I wait, opening the door further, poking my head out.

I turn back to Seth. "Another room, small, three doors."

He chuckles. "Oh, good, we definitely used the wrong cave. Told you it was the sixth."

"We got instructions from a kid. Directions that changed every time he told us."

Seth laughs. "We might be lost in Asperheim, but at least we're *in* Asperheim. He's a kid, don't take your anger out on him."

I open the door and step into the other room. "Hadn't planned on it." My brother lets out a soft whistle. I glare over my shoulder. "Short of mauling him, there's nothing I could do anyway. The little fuck doesn't seem to fear me."

On one wall to my left are two doors. The wall before me has one more. I check the doors next to each other. One leads to a dark passage, the other is a closet. I step to the third door, cracking it open to check where it leads.

I close it, turning to Seth. "We'll use this door."

"Wrong passage," he manages through a grin.

"Will you quit that," I mutter. "Come on."

I open the door, and we slip out. He follows behind me as we snake through passageways. We keep to the walls and shadows. Seth stomps his way along.

I turn around and hold up a hand. "Quiet steps," I hiss under my breath.

He shrugs and crosses his arms. I narrow my eyes and peer around an intersection. My eyes flicker over the area, and I breathe out my nose in relief.

"I think I know this place. This way." I take the left path, passing by the doors of the grand hall. "I remember being here the night I came to get Ella. The map George drew out shows stairs at the far end of this hall. Straight up six floors."

"Now, it's six?"

I press my lips together and take a breath, glaring over my shoulder. *Really?*

We slip up the hall and round and round the spiral staircase. I stop, Seth bumping into the back of me. My feet won't move, and my heart is racing.

Seth pats me on the shoulder as he steps around me. He stops, his fingers digging into my muscles. "Fuck me."

"No, thank you." I shoulder past him.

My skin prickles under the sight of Erac's eyes. He stares me down with hatred. I return the sentiments.

He crosses his arms in ease and shakes his head. "She doesn't want you anymore."

I am not going to let him bait me into a fight. I keep my pulse even with deep breathing. "Why don't we let her decide? Where is she?"

He laughs in a short bark. "She's asleep in my bed where she belongs."

My blood boils in my veins, a hazy red mist clouding my vision. I clench my fists and try to keep my composure. "That's my fucking wife." My voice sounds far away.

"She doesn't know that. She gives herself to me every night."

Seth puts a hand on my shoulder. "Dec."

A dark need to break and maim is pulling at me in the back of my mind, trying to take control of me. "I'm going to rip your fucking head off."

"She doesn't want you anymore. She loves me."

I bare my teeth, muscles in my neck straining. "Why don't we tell her the fucking truth and let her decide?"

He smirks, putting his hands on his hips. "Sorry. She's asleep now."

"I don't care. She'll want to wake up for this."

He chuckles, honestly looking amused. "I'm afraid she's not going to be coherent. She never is after I finish taking her."

My sight goes in and out of focus, my heart jackhammering against my ribs. I pull in a sharp breath. I'm not stupid enough to believe I can win in a fight, even if I am bigger, stronger, faster, and smarter. Elements don't respond to me the way he can manipulate them. "If you fucking touch my wife, I'll—"

His laughter cuts my threat short. "If? I touch my wife-to-be all the time. Little touches. The feel of her soft skin is exquisite."

A growl tumbles from my lips, ripping from my chest with blind hatred. I glare, tensing my shoulders, flexing my arms. "She's my wife."

"How many times do I have to tell you she doesn't know that before it reaches through your pea-sized animal brain." He chuckles, his head tipping back. He grins up at the ceiling, laughs, and drops his head down to smirk at me. "I enjoy the feeling of being inside of her."

I lurch forward and stop as my brother's fingers dig into me.

"The taste of her," Erac continues, "so sweet. She's soft, yielding, the way her body responds, the way she begs my name." His smirk grows.

I lurch a few paces, dragging my brother with me. I'm snarling at the mage, the whisper in my mind excitedly chattering.

Seth laughs, but there's a hollow ring to it, and his words come from far away. "You know she'd never let you near her if she had her memories. It's sick. You're raping her."

"Only the first time. Until she learned."

My vision streaks with gray and red as I snarl and bite at the air.

There's a hollow vibration before me. "She's not your wife anymore. She's mine, to have and to hold and to fuck."

I roar and lunge for the sound of his heart and the foul stench of his skin. I grapple and go flying back from a force I can't hear or smell. I blink, refocusing my eyes to see the bastard holding his hands up and out, contorted as he bends the elements to his will.

The air closes in around me, packed too tight to allow movement. I inhale, using sheer strength and breaking the air around me. I pull my arm back, creating a sharp piece of steel in my hand as I move through a swing.

Erac grunts, jerking back as the blade sinks in his shoulder. He leaves his injured arm hanging, using his good hand to squeeze the air in front of him as if choking me.

I snarl, trying to move forward, but my throat is constricting, and I'm lifted off my feet, all the pressure and weight of my body carried on my neck. I claw at the nothing before me, trying to get enough air for my brain to process information. I need to think, but the building pressure is glazing my sight over, tunneling down to nothing but his sadistic grin. I try to break his control but fail. My arms won't cooperate. They are heavy as lead, hard to move, and growing heavier by the second.

I have never been the weak one in a fight. Losing is as equally mortifying as it is terrifying, and it's the last thought in my mind before my limp arms drop at my sides, and I lose consciousness.

CHAPTER 45

MORELLA

Guards pass by my terrace much to my displeasure. No one would dare attack me, and patrolling my quarters is insulting. I will have to speak with their supervisor and have them reprimanded. I sigh, hanging my head as I lean against the stone railing.

I'm replaying the time with my stranger, trying to find the right words that will convince my father to let me see him. He's nobody, living at Dis, there's no way my father could see him as a threat to me. I ache in my core for this, but I need to find a way to convince my father.

My fingers trace along my lips as I think about my stranger. Around me, shadows are still, the quiet pressing around the edges.

"They caught the Bard brothers," I hear one guard say to another.

"Thank Haven for that. Maybe this forsaken war can cease. I don't care who wins at this point. Just let it be bloody over."

"I have my preferences." The second guard laughs. "Not that I'd let them show."

"What were we going to do," the first grumbles, "say no and have our heads taken off?"

"That'd be a right old blessing if it's that quick."

I tilt my head and peer up at the night sky, trying to recall these brothers. Nothing, as is my usual. I have no memories. Everything is a blank from before, but I know Erac and my father have referred to the men who poisoned me as brothers.

Caught, they say?

My eyes narrow, and I go in search, finding them right where I expect, in the lowest level of the palace. One of the prison cells is open, voices coming from within. A deep male voice is cursing at Erac. I smirk, coming closer.

I lean against the doorway, allowing my eyes to take in the little details of things, calculating the situation. Two men strung from the ceiling in chains, arms over their head, feet dangling. Both men appear to have been here a while, blood evident.

One is larger than the other, with a boyish face contorted with rage. He's yelling, spittle flying from his mouth. The words are irrelevant.

The second man is smaller but by no means a small man. He has a thin face, handsome features pinching with restraint. My lips part as I stare, unblinking, unable to move.

My stranger tries to swing and kick at Erac as he snarls something. The words don't register. As my father punches him in the face, his head snaps to the side, and he spits a mist from his mouth. His eyes lift and meet mine, widening ever so slightly, and I watch his muscles twitch and tense.

Had Erac caught him in Dis? What about the brothers?

My father's white dress shirt is stained with blood, as is the dagger. Erac is speaking to the larger male. I clear my throat, drawing every eye to me.

"Father." I smile at him as he turns, light glistening on his bare scalp, his green eyes finding mine. "What are you doing?"

"Morella. Daughter," he stresses the word, "why are you down here?"

I brush a lock of hair away from my neck and step into the room. "I heard the guards say you caught the brothers." My eyes flicker to my stranger, and he grimaces. I indicate the men. "Who are they?"

"Ell," the larger man grunts. "Haven, you've got to be fucking joking."

Erac swings a metal bar into the man's gut. The skin sizzles, turning red. "Silence."

I eye the gloves he wears, figuring the bar is iron. "I apologize, Sir." I smile. "But who is Ell?"

"Mor–ell–a," my stranger says, annunciating my name. "You go by Ella." He jerks his head toward the man next to him. "He calls you Ell."

"Oh." I press a hand to the bare skin above the low neckline of my gown, fury washing through my chest. "Me?" I force a chortle. "Haven, but no, I am not joking."

"My love," Erac comes to me, wrapping an arm around my waist. He kisses my cheek. My stranger is watching with an intense gaze. "Please, we can deal with these two. Rest," he brushes my hair to the side and kisses my neck. I close my eyes and pretend to enjoy his attentions.

"Mmm, yes, my love," I meet his gaze and smile. "But you didn't answer my question." I step away from him, looking to my father. "Who are they?"

"The Bard brothers."

That information jolts through me like a wave of energy. I raise my eyebrows and blink at my father. "And you saw fit to keep this from me?" I point to myself and narrow my eyes. "Why was I not included in this?"

"Why was that again," my handsome stranger speaks up. He glances at the man next to him. "Seth, did you catch that earlier?"

Seth wiggles his eyebrows back at him. "You know, Dec, I don't remember catching that, just a couple blows to the face."

Dec. My stranger's name is Dec.

Both restrained men fixate their gaze upon me. "I wonder why that is," Dec says, drawing his words out in a soft voice.

My eyes bore into him with the hatred of a thousand lost memories. I don't know who I am because of this man, and he did this to me.

They did this to you. Make them repay in blood.

"Maybe we should ask them?" Seth cranes to see around my father to my betrothed. "Hey, Erac, why didn't you bring Ell in on this?"

My ears prickle at the nickname, some of my sanity returning. George used a shortened version of my name too. Erac stands next to me, an arm around my back to rest his hand on my hip. "The two of you are nothing more than an infestation to be rid of." His face turns to me. "There is no need of you here."

I bristle but turn my face to him. He smiles at me, and I grab his face, pulling it to mine for a kiss. I draw it out, fighting the disgust, and then I eye the Bard brothers, my sight lingering on Dec. The putrid rage he displays makes that whisper growl in the back of my mind.

"My love," Erac's fingers trail down my bare arm. "Please, allow us to handle this. You do not need to trifle with them."

"Why are you trifling with them?" I ask, trying to gaze into his eyes like I love him. "There must be a reason you haven't just killed them."

"Of course, but Morella, this is a simple task. No need to trouble yourself."

I spin out of Erac's arm and shove him toward the door. "I will deal with them. I will get the information." His eyes flicker from me over my shoulder, looking to my father. He is weak, always waiting for permission. I roll my eyes and face my father. "Let me do this. They owe me."

Seth yelps. "What? Ell! Come on, we didn't do anything."

"You broke into our home," Erac says. "And they would have hurt you," he says in a lower voice, eyes on me.

I roll my eyes from him to my father, doubting his words. If Dec had wanted to hurt me, he was given several chances without coming all this way.

My father meets my gaze, contemplating, his eyes searching me. He rubs a hand over his scalp and offers his blade to me. "Get what information you can about their source or the traitor and where the item is now."

I accept his blade, stepping to the Bard brothers. I examine them. Both are in jeans and boots. Dec wears more fitted clothes, nicer boots. I look into their eyes, first Seth's and then Dec's. He is more calculating and intelligent, bound to have more usefulness.

I stand in front of Seth and place a hand on his stomach. "Seth, is it?"

"Hey, Ell." He smirks, exposing blood-smeared teeth. "Damn good to see you."

I give a smile to the man. "Yes, I agree. It is good to see you."

"Knew you couldn't have completely forgotten me."

"Are you going to tell me what I need to know?"

"Come on, Ell, you aren't really going to do this." He gives me another flash of teeth.

I run a hand up my neck to the back of my head and drag fingers through my hair, lifting hair from the nape of my neck for a cool breath of air. I am starting to sweat in this room without airflow, and too much excitement coursing through me.

Something is slithering through my veins, a dark thirst to see him bleed. I test the edge of the dagger for sharpness on my thumb. I glance from the blade to Seth's dark gray eyes, watching me.

His humor fades from his face as I stare. "Oh, fuck, come on,

Ell." He struggles against his bonds. "You wouldn't do this, not the real you, not if you knew—"

I press the blade to the side of his throat, and his annoying words stop. I curl my lips in a closed smile. "There now, that's better." I tap the flat of the blade against his mouth. "Tell me, who is your source?"

He shakes his head at me. "Think, Ell, there's got to be something left in—"

I draw the blade from his neck down his torso to his waist. He hisses and thrashes. I watch with enjoyment and intrigue as the skin knits back together. I glance over my shoulder at my father. "A shade?"

"Yes, they are both cursed with the strain."

"I've never had the pleasure." I turn back to Seth with a newfound glee. "So, when I..." I drag the blade across his abdomen.

He curses, jerking his legs up and kicking at me. I jerk out of reach, but my crown slips from my head, clattering to the floor. I stare down at the thin silver bands intersecting. George picked the simple design; told me I was not elaborate or drawn to fancy things. Rage quickens my pulse.

My eyes fixate on Seth. "Who is your source?"

"Ell," he groans. "You know me, and I know you. This isn't you." There's a desperate pleading to his words. "You'd rather hurt yourself than me. You hated doing this kind of thing."

"Oh, well then." I giggle, stepping to my stranger, meeting his eyes. I draw my blade down his torso, from neck to gut. His face tenses, and he grunts but doesn't thrash the same way his brother did.

Smarter and stronger.

I lift the blade to my lips to lick at the blood. "Then why do I find such pleasure in this?"

I draw the blade against my tongue, holding his gaze.

He smirks. "You've got a sickness in you, like a shade, the thirst for blood."

"Yeah," his brother calls out. I step away from Dec back to Seth, eyeing him as he rambles on. "But you hate hurting others. Doing this makes you sick. You cried on my shoulder a hundred times because Viktor would make you do this."

"Are you going to give me the information I request, or not?" I keep my voice light, ignoring his remarks.

"Not," he snarls, his face contorting. "This isn't you, and I'm damn well not going to—"

I drive the dagger through his chest into his heart. "If you aren't going to give me what I want, then I have no use of you."

His mouth hangs agape. He starts to choke on blood. I stare into his clouding eyes until the light is gone, then wrench the steel from his chest before too long. Turning away from him, I focus on the other brother.

He screws up his face and flails in the chains. I can hear the way his skin sizzles at fresh contact with the iron. He bares his teeth at me, fighting for freedom. I hold the hand with the blade up to my mouth to cover my giggle at the sight of him flopping like a fish from a line.

"Oh dear," I chortle and roll my eyes. "I just killed your brother, didn't I?"

He stops squirming and glares at me. His jaw clamps down. I can see the way the muscles lurch and bunch outward. I watch his eyes for tears, but there is only rage.

Good. He deserves this.

I step to him, cupping his straining jaw. I sigh and drop the dagger to the ground, listening to the clanging of metal against stone ring around in the silence. "Take some time. Think about it." I indicate the corpse of his brother hanging next to him. "Get some sleep, and we'll talk in the morning."

I glance over my shoulder to Erac and Viktor. Neither makes a comment, but both dissipate out of the room. I turn back, breaking the chains holding Seth. His body falls limp and heavy to the floor, although I doubt he'll stay dead for long. Shades heal fast; he might recover. With some effort, I drag the body in front of the remaining brother in his line of sight.

He is staring with a mixture of emotions I cannot decipher. I glare at him. "You shouldn't have lied to me, tried to trick me."

He smirks at me, half chuckling, then shakes his head, eyes on the floor. "Lover, you've lost your fucking mind." His eyes lift to mine with a burning intensity. He jerks his chin at me. "Those fuckers stole it, actually. Let me know when you want the truth."

I pick up the dagger and ram it into his side. "I know the truth. You and your brother poisoned me, and because of that," I twist the blade, "I don't have memories. I don't even know who I am. You ruined me."

Turning my back on him, I take a step, dissipating midmotion to arrive in my rooms. I clench shaking fingers, bile lingering in the back of my throat and my nasal passages. Rage burns through me, white-hot.

I trusted him.

"Let me know when you want the truth."

"Ugh!" I ram my fingers into my hair and grip handfuls in frustration. My eyes scrunch shut, and I scream as loud as I can for as long as I can.

"Your Majesty?"

I blink, looking up at the dozen guards standing in my room with wide eyes. I snarl at them. "Get out!" I point at the door.

"Are you alright?"

"Get out, or I'm turning you to dust."

They scamper, each one clamoring to be the first out of my room. The door snaps shut, and I shuffle to my bed. With a groan, I flop down onto it and stare at the ceiling.

~

Someone enters my room. I know it is Erac without a glance. He is the only one who would dare enter unannounced right now.

He sits next to me on the bed and bends over to kiss my shoulder. "You astound me every day, my love."

I meet his violet gaze, the same eyes I have, although I think mine are of a brighter coloring. I hum at him. "Why is that?"

He brushes my hair away from my neck. "You are incredibly strong, staring down the men who tried to destroy you and even killing one."

"I see." I was hasty in putting the blade in his heart. The euphoria I feel in death overcame the desire for information. I feel hungover, and I massage my temples. I let my emotions get the best of me. He should be disappointed in my lack of control.

"…a sickness in you, like a shade, a thirst for blood…"

"What is wrong? Are you not happy?"

I hum at him again, staring out the window. "Why was I not included in the interrogation?"

"Why was that again? Seth, did you catch that earlier?"

"You know, I don't remember catching that. Just a couple blows to the face."

"I wonder why that is?"

"Maybe we should ask them? Hey, Erac, why didn't you bring Ell in on this?"

Seth was emotional, quick to humor. Dec was smarter. He wanted me to question why I was not part of the interrogation. He got to me. I shake my head and roll my shoulders.

"Never mind." I wave a hand in the air at my betrothed. "Silly question?" I smile up at him from over my shoulder.

He nods his head. "It is, my love, of course, it is."

The smaller Bard is not stupid. He calculated his words for maximum effect, pointedly speaking. I frown. There is no reason for me to believe anything he says. He is with the resistance. They poisoned me, did this to me.

"Mor–ell–a. You go by Ella. He calls you Ell."

George called me Ella, said I go by Ella. I sigh as I feel Erac brushing my hair from my neck and pressing his face in its stead. I roll my eyes, knowing he wants to be arduous.

"Not tonight." I shove him away, annoyed by his interruption of my thoughts. "My head hurts."

He grabs my chin, forcing me to look at him. He is not displeasing to the eye, but Dec—my stranger—is conjured in my mind. That is a gorgeous man, one I still want to kiss again.

Erac scowls. "What has gotten into you, Morella?"

I jerk my face free of his grip. "Nothing. I am tired."

A headache is starting to appear, normal after I give in to that whispering voice begging for blood. I get a high and then come crashing down.

"Darling, love." His hand rests over my clenched hand. "Are you sure everything is alright?"

I snap at him. "Why do you keep asking me that? Nothing is different. Nothing whatsoever."

"I am trying to protect you," he says with a heavy sigh. He kisses my temple and sits back on his heels to stare at me.

"Protect me from what?" I laugh. "There is nothing that can affect me."

"When I first brought you here, when you first woke up again, you were in my room."

"Yes." I draw the word out with irritation.

He nods. "Yes, to keep you safe. I spelled the room with powerful blood magic so that only I may use magic there, like the cells beneath this palace, where only we can use magic."

"I remember," I respond coolly.

"Without magic—and they have that same magic I do—you are helpless." He sits forward, taking my hands in his. "My love, please, understand, this is all to keep you safe. You are impressive, a force to be reckoned with, but only where there is magic." He kisses the knuckles of one hand and then the other. "If they trap you again, they will poison you again, and I will have to go through the trouble of saving you again."

I tilt my head back and stare into his eyes. *Go through the trouble of…? Do I mean so little to you, my husband-to-be?* I purse my lips and nod at him. "I understand."

I watch him leave, then get up and walk out on my terrace for fresh air. I feel so trapped, and that nagging feeling is still present in my gut. I search the sky, lost in the hurricane, tearing me apart inside.

CHAPTER 46

DECLAN

My shoulders hurt. My throat is raw. I swing my legs, using momentum to throw my body upward, grabbing hold of the chain I am suspended from. The iron burns, my skin hissing as I grip the iron, but I pull myself up, relieving the tension on my joints.

I hold on for as long as I can, but my muscles are protesting, tremoring with fatigue. I let go, snarling as I drop, and my shoulders jar as my weight snaps toward the ground. I groan and lean my head back, staring upward.

I try not to think about what she did to Seth. She didn't hesitate or flinch, just watched him die without a single emotion. I remind myself she's partially a shade. She's got a hunger for this kind of thing. Still, I know she loves him. My lover wouldn't have hurt him. She would have cried, paled, blanched, fought against killing him.

She dragged that blade across me, ran her tongue against the blade to taste my blood. Seeing her do it was worse than the feel of my skin slicing open. My throat is dry, and I try to swallow. It doesn't help. I need blood to quench the thirst.

I stare at Seth's body and squeeze my eyes shut. She stabbed him in the heart and didn't even care. *Fuck, lover, what the hell?*

A groan draws my eyes open, and I watch Seth sit up, running a hand over his chest. He blinks up at me and grimaces. "Damn. Dying hurts."

I narrow my eyes. "Usually, death is permanent. Why aren't you dead?"

"Glad to see you too." He winces and rolls one shoulder behind him. "Shit that hurt."

"There are worse ways to die. She made it quick and clean." I peer at him. "Seriously, how the fuck are you alive?"

"Slit the throat, or remove the head, drain out all the blood somehow, or I mean, if you go stabbing, you leave the blade in the heart." He rubs an errant hand over his pectoral again. "Shit, they really messed with her head."

Grunting, I look at the ceiling for a way out. I'm glad he's not dead. I am. But my shoulders are killing me right now, and I can't think about much else. "Congratulations, you know how to kill us properly. Now, will you quit sounding so chipper and get me down?"

Seth inspects the chain. "How?" He eyes me. "Can't you just change the chain to air or something?"

"I can't use magic here. Something's blocking it, keeping me from controlling the elements. Now, fucking figure it out."

He crosses his arms. "I'm not in the mood for your pissy attitude. I just died." He motions to the floor. "And Ell did it. I mean, damn." He rubs a hand over his face.

I attempt to kick him. "Get over it."

"Easy for you to say," he grumbles, coming closer and grabbing me by my legs, taking tension from my shoulders, "she didn't kill you."

"She didn't kill you either, apparently. She just stabbed you." I try to release the pressure on my joints by wrapping my hands around the chains and lifting some of my weight. Every muscle in my torso burns with disgust at the abuse. "Are you going to stand here and hold me, or are you going to get me down?"

"You're cranky. Worse than usual."

"I just watched her hurt you. That's not Ella. I've been hanging here too long in iron chains. Everything hurts. I want my fucking wife back, and I want down from here."

He sighs and hoists me higher. "Don't move too much; your balls are in my face."

I breathe out through my nose in annoyance. "I don't need you to tell me where my balls are. What are you doing?"

"Getting you up high enough for you to crawl up the chain. You're gonna have to pull it out of the ceiling."

My eyes train upward to the mounting bracket. "You're fucking joking."

"I'm not. You're always talking about how strong you are. Time to prove it," he grunts. "I'm going to throw you up to the mount, so grab onto the chain and don't smack me in the face with your dick."

I clench my jaw and glare down at him. "You're on my last fucking nerve."

"Get over it."

He throws me up, and I slam into the ceiling. Stunned, I free-fall back down. He moves out of the way as I drop. The chain stops me with an abrupt snap, my shoulders popping.

I growl and lash out at him. He steers clear of my reach and laughs. "Oh, fuck. Sorry, Dec." He is still laughing. "That was great, though."

"Come here."

He leans back with a smirk. "Depends. Are you going to kick me?"

"Get the fuck over here." I want to rip his arms out of their sockets the same way he just dislocated mine. He moves to grab my legs, and I snarl at him. "Don't fucking do anything, just stand there."

I use my knees and feet to climb up his body and stand on his shoulders. He wraps his hands around my feet, helping me balance, doing something useful this time. I eye the chain and take a deep breath.

Accepting what comes next, I shut my eyes and focus on something more pleasant. I think about Ella and roll my shoulders. The ball and sockets snap into place, my body pulling things back to proper placement, and the ripping burn of healing rolls across my chest and down my arms.

"Need help up there?"

"No," I snap, glancing down at my brother. "You've done enough. Just stand there and let me do this."

He lets go of one of my feet to salute me. The motion rocks his body, and I grip the chain, iron singing my skin. I bare my teeth at him as he snickers. "Got it, Your Highness."

"I'm going to beat you fucking bloody for this." I tighten my grip on the chain. "Now, don't move. I'm going to push off you."

I jump from his shoulders, getting my legs over my head to hang upside down from the chain with my feet on the ceiling. My muscles aren't happy, burning with the exertion, already exhausted. I grit my teeth.

Why the fuck am I not stronger?

I position my feet on either side of the plate and grapple with the links, pulling them taut. Pushing with my legs and pulling, I strain with every ounce of energy left in my aching body.

The links separate, pulling apart. I make a couple of short, brutal jerks, one link opening far enough for me to slip the connecting piece out. I grip the chain above the link in one hand, wrangling the other apart.

I glance beneath me. "Move."

Seth steps back, hands up, and I release my grip, twisting as I fall to land on the ground. My knees crack with jarring pain even as I let my legs bend to absorb the force. I hit the floor and roll, laying there panting.

Fuck this shit, I growl in my mind.

"You alright there, big brother?" he asks, standing over me, chuckling.

I kick at him, grunting when I find solid purchase. His noise of pain lets me know I made my point, and I sit up. Swinging my arms in front of me, chains rattling, I do my best to keep my composure. "No."

Seth stands over me, stretching and rolling his shoulders. "Sure, I know you're not okay deep down, but right now, physically, are you?"

Pinching the bridge of my nose with my eyes closed, I take a deep breath. "Fine. I'm fine. I've already healed." My eyes find the door, waiting for guards to come rushing in. I could stand to hurt something. I need blood.

The door is still and closed. My brother offers me a hand. "What can I do?"

"Nothing." I pry my wrists apart, the iron cuff around my wrists separating. "You did enough."

He sucks his teeth between his lips and chuckles. "I'm sorry," he starts bursting into laughter, "but seeing you hit the ceiling and come back down…"

With my hands now free, I whip him with the chain. He catches it in both hands and uses it to help haul me to my feet. We both drop the chain, and I watch the blistered skin of my palms bubble and heal over.

My brother drops his arm around my shoulders and leans against me. "I mean, look at that, healed in seconds. She knows how—or she should—know how fast shades heal. She should have known that wouldn't kill me." He lifts eyes full of fury and pain to meet mine. "They screwed her up bad. What if… What if we can't fix this?"

I don't know if he's waiting for me to share in his pity party. I'm not giving up. I glare back. "You're acting like her pulling the blade out is the fucked up part of *she stabbed. You. In. The.*

Heart!"

"I'm really trying not to think about that, alright?" He rubs the back of his neck.

I reach behind his back, clasping his opposite shoulder. Glancing up at him with a smirk, I say, "If she did know better, you'd be dead, so let's just be thankful for the small things."

His eyes dance with contained mirth. "Didn't realize you cared so much."

I sneer and glance around the room, but I don't contradict him. I have a heart. Somewhere. I shove him away from me. "Get out of here before they realize you're not dead."

"I mean, come on though, she should know better."

"Oh." The word is a light breath of whisper in the air.

My ears twitch, and I turn to the door again. Ella leans against the doorway, one arm across her stomach, and the other bent up for her to inspect her fingernails. Her eyes meet mine, and she smiles. "I do know better."

Fuck.

I tense and stare at her, then my eyes cut to Seth. "Get out of here."

"Great plan. How?"

Keeping my eyes on Ella, I watch her step into the room. She's still wearing that silky black dress that shows too much skin for me to focus. Her eyes never waver from mine as I hold my hands up.

"We surrender?" I give her my best cheeky grin.

One corner of her mouth pulls back. "You think you're so charming, don't you?"

I can still make her laugh. Bonus points. "Maybe."

"Yeah, Prince Charming, that's Dec," Seth laughs over my shoulder. "He's not a stoic, salty bastard or anything like that."

Still holding my gaze, she lifts just one eyebrow, her features lighting with entertainment. "I want answers, and you are going to give them to me."

For a split second, I think things might go well. I think she'll ask questions and we'll give her answers. We can tell her the truth and walk right out of here.

She throws out her hand, and I fly back, slamming into the wall. Pressure builds against me, pinning me to the wall like a living portrait. The force builds, and I grunt, my bones cracking.

I am a fucking idiot.

Stepping forward, her fist clenches, and all the air is ripped out of my lungs. I can't breathe in, the weight against my chest threatening to splinter my ribcage into a million shards. Suffocating, I catch sight of Seth choking and coughing for air in my peripheral vision.

She snaps her fingers, and I feel the freezing pressure of dissipation. I'm blinking, coming back to myself. My eyes roam around me, my head throbbing, throat raw like I gobbled down gravel. I'm flat on my back, arms stretched over my head. I try to move, twisting and jerking, but every limb is secured in place.

Fuck.

I struggle, feeling iron burning and thick leather straps straining against the bare skin of my arms and torso. I give up, panting, trying to dissipate. My elements stay pieced together. I open my eyes and stare at the barren ceiling above me.

"Fuck."

I hear her laugh then see her face above mine.

"Oh, fuck, lover. What the hell are you going to do to me?"

CHAPTER 47

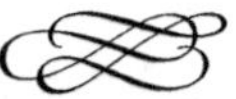

DECLAN

She eyes me, standing there, dressed like a fucking queen in a black dress, watching me struggle. I hate this, letting her see me helpless. I stop trying, the iron burning my skin. The bonds are strong, but I'm surprised the thing I'm attached to hasn't broken.

I squeeze my eyes shut and grit my teeth. My throat is raw. Blood. I need to drink, but maybe if I am consumed with bloodlust, I'll be able to break free. I open my eyes to see her still watching me.

Fuck, she's beautiful. She looks great in black and silver, so small and delicate.

I try to focus on something else. Feelings aren't going to help me. She's going to rip me to pieces, and the last thing I need involved is my heart. I need to remember this isn't my wife right now, but her face is hard to ignore.

I cock a brow, trying to reclaim any of my dignity with a collected calm.

Not that I have any dignity left.

I'm strapped half-naked to this forsaken table with my hands over my head, completely exposed and helpless. The situation isn't ideal, but I have her alone in a room, maybe I can do some good.

She sits next to me, the silky fabric of her dress pressing against my side. My skin reacts with pleasure. Thoughts of holding her against my flesh in the dress and drinking from her stir desire in my lower stomach.

She is staring down at me. "Who are you?"

Too many answers race through my mind. I relax and close my eyes, pretending that question didn't hurt worse than anything else she could possibly do to me. "Declan Dean Byron." I crack one eye at her. "Nice to meet you, Your Highness."

She smirks, pulling a blade from thin air. Small, black leather-wrapped handle with a loop on the end. That blade brings back memories. She drags the blade down my chest. My skin splits, blood seeping out.

I hiss through bared front teeth. "Fuck, that does not feel good."

She chuckles. "Yes, I'm sure."

I breathe, feeling my skin knit back together. It's a feeling of warmth and spiders crawling across my chest.

She hums and runs fingers up her neck and beneath her hair. "I asked who you were, not what your name is. I don't care about a name."

"Who am I?" I sigh, then try to grin, but it's hard. "I'm the son of a duke long dead, brother to the Duke of Kennelton. I was King of Byron." I clench my fists. "Your husband." Those words come out of me with an onslaught of emotions. My voice shows it, too, a weakness she is going to notice.

She scoffs. "Not likely. I have a betrothed." She flutters her fingers in front of me.

"That prick couldn't make you choose him, so he fucking took you, and now he's left my ring, my fucking ring, on your finger." I tug at the straps holding my arms over my head with all the fury that brings. It doesn't help enough. I give up, letting my muscles turn to flab. "Fuck. What are you going to do to me?"

She rakes her fingernails down my chest. My eyes damn near roll into my head at that. The woman can turn me on even in the worst fucking moment possible. *Damn, I miss her.* I grit my teeth and wait.

"The mind is an interesting thing. Give it an idea, and it will pick at it, conjuring up some of the worst things imaginable based upon your own fear."

"So, you're going to let me sit here and think about it?" I pick my head up and smirk. "That's fucking cruel."

"It's the middle of the night. Everyone else is asleep. I have all night, and it's just you and me."

I try to see around the room. "What did you do with Seth?"

She jerks her chin over my head. "He's there."

Doing my best to crane my head back, I stare from the tops of my eyes. My brother is strapped to the wall spread-eagle, head hanging down, chin to chest. I look to her. "Is he alive?"

"Yes."

"You didn't kill him?"

She shrugs. "No, but I made sure he'll stay quiet for now."

I raise my brows with intrigue. "You'll have to share how you managed that." I laugh. "He never shuts up."

She tips her head back and laughs. "His lips are sewn together with iron, that's how. I doubt it will be pleasant when he regains consciousness." She rests the tip of her dagger in the middle of my chest, spinning the blade by the pommel. "I want to know everything."

"Yeah? Well, I want to kiss you." I'm further lost than I realized as the words slip from my tongue. I never should have said that.

There's surprise in her beautiful face. Ever since she came back from Medius, she's been even more gorgeous, glowing with power and stronger than ever, in magic and in herself, but her face hasn't changed. It's an open book to me, her features giving away every tiny thought in her head. She used to annoy me with all those thoughts, but I missed them then, and I miss them even more now. Hours. That's all I had before she was stolen away from me again.

She leans over me, dragging her breasts covered in that incredible fabric against my chest, and I feel ready to burst. I pant as she brushes her lips against mine. I don't know what is worse, that my loving, caring wife is so cold, or that I kind of like it.

"What would my betrothed think? Hmm?"

"He can fuck himself."

Her teeth sink into her lower lip as she giggles. "I have a very long list of questions that I expect answers to."

I breathe out my nose, long and slow. I rest back into the table and sigh. "I'll tell you anything you want to know."

She sits upright, taking the exquisite feeling of her against me away to play with the dagger. I eye it, then focus on her gaze. She meets mine with hard, dark eyes.

Oh, fuck, she's mad. I do my best to pull my arms free, tensing my abs, trying to sit up, to use the strength of my core and arms in conjunction. I strain. I grunt. I give up, panting.

She reaches out, and her fingers land on my stomach. Small fingertips cool against my flesh. The tip of the dagger resumes spinning in my skin, dead center of my chest, her eyes watching. This time she adds pressure, the metal biting into my skin. A stinging sensation starts, followed by the burning of my body healing as quickly as she opens the skin. The feeling is maddening, and I flex my hands, pulling at the bonds around my wrists.

"How did you poison me?" she asks, her voice soft and low.

I shake my head. "I didn't."

She removes her fingers from my skin to drive the blade through my sternum. My eyes cross and roll at the crunch of bone, my chest spasming with pain, my lungs filling with warm blood. I choke, blood filling my mouth. I can't breathe. Every pull for air in my lungs makes the pain pulsates worse, sharp and hot.

She hisses and wrenches the blade back out. "Don't lie to me." In a pain-induced haze, I smirk at her. She glares, pressing the blade to my neck. "You find this humorous?"

In some ways, this situation is funny. I can't breathe enough to share some intelligent quip. I can't even get through the cloud in my mind to think of one. I just know there is one somewhere.

I keep my eyes open, though I can barely see. My chest heals, bone snapping back into place, and the pain lightens. The dagger point presses against the underside of my jaw. "What did you do to me? How did you trap me? What poisoned me and rotted my mind?"

"Viktor and Erac." I breathe the names, barely moving my mouth to avoid injury. I thought after the first time, this wouldn't be so damn hard to get carved up by her, but it is. I close my eyes and picture Marx is carving me up instead. "Erac took you, took your memories."

"I want to know what you did to me that made them take my memories."

I laugh and get the blade embedded in my side. The laugh transitions to a growl as I jerk in response. "You want answers, stop carving me up long enough for me to answer you."

She rips the blade out and sits on the table, leaning over me. Her face is pinched with concentration. "Fine. Tell me what you poisoned me with, why my father and betrothed were forced to wipe my mind clear."

I take a couple of breaths and loosen the tension in my jaw, wiggling it side to side. "I can't answer you. I— Will you fucking not?" I snap, the blade hovering over my stomach, pointy end ready to impale me again. I glare at her. "You can keep putting that blade in me, but I didn't poison you, and no matter how many times you stab me, that truth isn't going to change."

"Maybe." The word is crisp. "Or maybe you're lying to me."

I scoff. "We didn't do a damn thing to you. You weren't forced or coerced by us. We're your friends, family..." I hesitate, fumbling over the word "love" so that it comes out as an unintelligible mumble.

"Stop." The blade sinks into my abdomen, and I flinch, biting back a groan. "Lying." It rotates. "To." It's moved in a half-circle. "Me."

She rips the blade free, and I jolt. I sit up as much as I can, straining. "I'm not. They're the ones lying to you. All I ever did was fight for your freedom!"

My roar rings around the room. She stares at me with those eyes. Almond-shaped, bright violet eyes that I know so well. They haunt me when I close my own.

I lay back, and the healing burn rolls through my gut. Maybe the warmth is my blood. My throat is begging for a drink, a tiny drop of blood. That's another two holes my body is healing. I need blood.

My eyes roll around the room. I don't know why or for what. She grabs my face, her grip forcing me to look at her. I don't want to look at her. She's beautiful. She looks like my wife, but she's not.

My eyes focus on the pulse in her neck, my thoughts scattering at the thought of blood. My eyes close. Blood, the thought of the tangy taste against my tongue, gets me to lick my lips in anticipation.

She stares down at me and then cocks a brow. I shake my head, trying to adjust. "Lover."

The blade is rammed through my leg. I groan.

"Stop calling me that."

Her voice is calm. There's no rage or care to the words at all. Whatever heart I might have shatters. "Yes, Ma'am," I manage and stare at the ceiling, telling myself I am not going to cry. Still, my eyes are burning worse than my throat.

My eyes slip closed against the wetness welling up. I grit my teeth and clench my fists, wishing I had long fingernails to bite into my flesh. The sensation would be a welcomed distraction.

She's my lover. Why can't I call her that? I fought for that right, earned it like any man should. Fucking bastard Erac. I'm going to kill him for this.

I open my eyes and bare my teeth at Haven as the blade wrenches out of my leg. I grunt and glare at her. "Damnatus, that fucking hurts."

"I would assume so." She stands there, eyeing me.

The silence ticks by with each clap of my heart as she stares down her nose at me.

My mind is racing. The bottom of my left foot is itching. A few slashes. A couple of impalements. She's been easy on me so far, but I doubt that will last. She's fond of fire, the easiest element for her to control.

I imagine her slicing, running fire over my flesh as it helplessly tries to heal. She'll find tender flesh, like the soles of my feet, the back of my knee. I twitch.

She hasn't touched you yet. Don't torture yourself for her, I tell myself. My skin crawls with a sickening anxiety. *Fuck, lover, what are you planning?*

The anticipation is gnawing at my gut, making me queasy. It's worse than if she were doing anything. The thought of my wife… I crush my eyes shut to stop the tears. I exhale through my nose. I twitch, like I'm going to pinch it, an old habit I formed to keep my temper in check.

When is the last time I cried? When I declared her dead? No. That was rage and guilt. I could go for a drink. That line of thought ratchets my heart to full speed. *Blood. I want blood. Need it.* The craving for the hot, tangy liquid makes me struggle.

She loves fire. Maybe she will set me on fire. That's not so bad. I mean, fuck, it hurts, but I'll heal. If she burns all my skin off, will the spirit runes come back?

Fear trickles down my spine. *Fuck. I'm going to heal. She's going to inflict pain over and over again. Maybe cut my flesh off, then set me on fire, the muscles. What if she cuts my fingers off? Will they regrow? I've never had to try to grow anything back.*

I lift my head and glance at my dick and balls. *Oh, fuck, what if she cuts those off?*

"Give the mind an idea, and it will pick at it."

I lay my head back and laugh. It rips at my throat like swallowing sand.

I need blood. *Maybe she'll give me blood, make this take longer. That might be worth it. If it's her blood. Taste her one last time.*

I can't believe I told her I wanted to kiss her.

She's not going to kill me, not right away. It's not her style. She's downright cruel. When that voice in her head takes control, it wants blood and pain before death.

"Breaking so soon?" Her laugh wafts over me, my ears twitching. She drops the dagger on my torso, and I jerk when her fingers circle my belly button.

Oh, fuck me, don't do that to me. I like that. I grit my teeth and hiss through my nose. "You're killing me."

"Not yet." Her touch vanishes.

I try again to lift my arms, straining and grunting with exertion before giving up and collapsing into my bonds. "What is this table made of?"

"Steel, leather, iron, and bound with magic. It was designed so not even a shade could escape."

I laugh. "Of course, it was. They knew I'd come for you." I slam my body back into the table with as much force as I can muster. With a sigh, I shake my head and try to get comfortable. "Now what, then?"

She tilts her head at me. "Now, you tell me what I want to know."

I force myself to relax, working blood into my hands and catch my breath. "Fuck, lover—" I squeeze my eyes shut. "If you want to know the truth, I'll tell you. I'll tell you anything you want to know."

Her finger draws down over my cheek. There's something wet there. I blink a burn out of my eyes and stare up into her face. She looks down at me with a longing.

CHAPTER 48

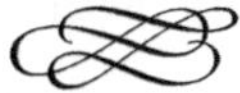

MORELLA

I stare down at him, and he looks ready to break. I want to hurt him for lying to me, the whisper in the back of my mind wants to watch the way he heals again, but part of me is fighting back for the first time, not wanting to give in.

I want to trust him. Everything inside of me had known he was safe. I had believed he was safe, that he wouldn't ever hurt me. My temper sparks to life, and I grip the hilt of my dagger in my sweating hand. "Who am I?" I ask, my voice warbling.

He lifts his eyebrows and smirks. "Morella Rowena Annabelle Byron." I start reaching for the dagger in the middle of his chest, but he goes on, "Before you go all stabby on me, you were Princess of Byron, then Queen, and then... Then everything went to shit."

"I know my name. I want to know who am I? I want to know who I am. Am I nice? Do I like to read?"

A laugh bubbles out of his chest, and he wheezes. "If someone wanted to find you, they'd search the library first. And nice doesn't compare." He grins, his voice ticking up with the smile. "Although you do have a wicked temper."

"Erac says you poisoned me. He made me drink something at first, blue and frothy and—"

"And bitter," he interrupts, skeptically gazing at the blade. He sighs, making a face of disgust. "It's the flower of dreamwort and tastes like hell. And Erac's a fucking dick. I should have realized he's talking about our bond. The poison? He liked to call our bond that."

I lift my scarred forearm before his eyes. "And this? This is your poison too?"

He lifts his head off the table and inspects my arm. His lip curls. "Those are scars from bearings. I have them too." He jerks his chin up, eyes rolling to the tops of the head toward his arms.

"What's a bond?"

He stares with eyes half-closed. "I claimed you as my mate. Shades can claim—or bind—a mate to them. It's like a blood bond but doesn't require a full exchange of blood due to the venom in my bite." He smirks with a humorous hitch of breath in his throat. "It hurts, gives you a nasty headache because of the soul swap."

My face twists to shock. "Soul swap?"

"Yeah," he drawls. "Half your soul goes to me, and half mine goes to you, and we get a mental link."

I narrow my eyes, pressing the tip of my blade against his side. "So, you're the voice in my head? This whole time it was you?"

His eyebrows push together and up, the skin of his forehead wrinkling. "What? What voice? Oh, that voice." He shakes his head. "First of all, the flower of dreamwort interrupts the bond, so I couldn't use the mental link, and second, that voice is all yours, lover."

He winces at the pet name. I ignore it and the warm jitters in my stomach at the way it rolls off his tongue. "I stopped drinking it. Erac said I didn't have to anymore."

"Right after he killed me, I assume," he scoffs. "Yeah, death breaks the bond."

I peer at him, my mouth pinching. "Library?"

He gives me a look of surprise. "Yeah."

I bob my head at him. "There was blood. Erac told me it was a heart bleeding up from beneath the surface."

His face contorts into a mixture of shock and horror. "A what?"

"Never mind." I wave my hand. I toy with the dagger, still wanting to stick him and fighting the urge. His story lines up with the facts that I have. It doesn't change the fact that he deceived me, though.

"You've been giving them hell, haven't you," he snickers, drawing my attention outward. "Asking questions they don't want to answer?"

"The voice in my head," I start, "it's not you or this bond thing?"

He shakes his head. "No, that's the bloodlust."

"Bloodlust?" I repeat in a questioning, timid voice.

He stares up at me, eyes smoldering intensely. "Bloodlust. Like something else talking to you in your head. A voice buried so deep in your subconscious that you can't tell if it's you or not, whispering sick, twisted things. All shades have it. The urge to break and watch things bleed, to taste it."

"I'm not a shade," I say, but it comes out more as a question. I don't know who I am, who am I to say what I am.

He scoffs with disdain. "A long time ago, there was an emperor named Tyle—"

"I know who Tyle is," I snap, bristling. "I still like reading."

He smirks, relaxing into the table. His features soften, a smile toying with his lips. "Yeah, I saw you asleep in the library. That's pretty common for you. So you know about Tyle? What he did to make shades?"

"Yes."

"Then, you'll understand when I tell you that Viktor injected you with his blood."

"What?" I gasp. A turmoil of disgust and shock slide into my gut. "That's—"

"Yes. You want to know who you are? You're the daughter of a dragon and spirit, left in an alleyway in Cato to be found, and found you were, then taken to Viktor, who thought you were just a human baby. He injected you with his blood to transform you into an elemental, but all he did was instill utter obedience in you."

I lean over him, my eyes stretched wide. My gaze drops to my left arm, the rune George mentioned surfacing in my mind.

Dec chuckles and flexes against his bonds. "You hate orange juice and dancing and Viktor. You always want to help everyone. I watched you run into the middle of an angry mob to save a kid right after I told you they didn't like the royal family, and you did it without flinching. You despise being the center of attention, and you love being outside. Your favorite place in the world was your window seat, and your favorite thing has always been magic."

My eyes prickle as he grins up at me, spouting off facts like they are nothing. I want to reach out and collect the words, gather them together, and hold them close. Reaching up, I rub the end of my nose and blink.

I swallow the distress lodged in my throat. "What else?"

"You owe a favor to a servant because it was the only way you could convince him to accept your help. You've got a wicked right hook, and you're ticklish under your toes." He gives me a lopsided grin, and my heart skips a beat. His eyes light up in a soft gray, and I find myself reaching out to touch the gorgeous smile on his lips.

Closing his eyes, he tips his mouth up to me, letting me trace his lower lip. "While you're there," he says, "can you scratch my jaw?"

Pleasant surprise lights up my chest, and I laugh, happy to oblige. My nails delve into the darker, wiry hairs along his square jawbone. He twists his head, exposing the underside, and I work from one side to the other.

"Thanks. Damn beards itch like crazy."

My hand trails down his neck and stops in the middle of his chest. I meet his eyes, open half-mast, and my cheeks burn. Clearing my throat, I look away. "Why don't I have memories?"

"Erac was pissed when you married me. Jealous bastard stole you and used bearings to wipe your memories away."

I frown and turn away to stare at the wall. My world is fracturing. What I thought I knew, everything Erac and my father told me, are lies. There is an undertow drawing me into a spinning oblivion of confusion. My hands shake, and my breathing becomes shallow and rapid.

The world blurs around me, a thousand words repeating in my mind all at once. The din is deafening, and I put my hands over my ears to try and block out what is replaying in my mind. All memories overlay as they crash down over my head like bricks burying me alive.

One memory swivels dead center, George standing in my rooms in his dirty, stained orange robes telling me he found out my fiancé's name is Declan. I gasp, eyes popping open, and I fixate on his handsome face with lips peeled apart in shock.

"Declan," I say.

He smirks at me, and then his features twist with disgust. "I'm not telling you a fucking thing."

I frown, face drawing in with confusion until I glance over my shoulder. Erac stands at Declan's feet, fury scripted in his eyes. I know better than to let him realize what is really happening, so with a sigh, I grab the blade from Declan's chest and ram it into his arm right above his armpit.

CHAPTER 49

DECLAN

"Fuck," I howl as I writhe. I growl from the back of my throat. "I'm not telling you a damn thing. I told you to fuck yourself. And what do you want fuckhead?" I lift my head to glare at Erac.

The blade drags what feels like miles up my arm, and I curse at her again.

She shrugs, face blank. "I wouldn't recommend insulting my betrothed."

Tilting my head back, I meet her eyes to smirk at her with adoration. "I'm going to rip that spineless coward's head off and keep it as a trophy."

She wrenches the blade free. A creeping burn starts as the healing begins. I feel her hand drawing down the searing flesh. My skin tickles and twitches.

My scalp starts to sweat, and I try to fidget, strapped too tight to move. "What the fuck are you doing?"

"Maggots." She shrugs. "I figure they'll keep the wound from closing if they're in there, eating your flesh."

My stomach twists. That's fucked up. Brilliantly fucked up.

She's so damn good. *Why is she so damn good at this? Fuck, why do I like that she's good at this?*

She is grinning down at me, eyes crinkled at the corners with genuine mirth. "I want to know who it was that stole from Erac."

Those things in my split flesh are crawling and writhing around. "Fuck, that's—" I squirm. I struggle, trying to yank my arms free. "Fuck, get them out of there. Fuck, I can feel that, feel them fucking moving." I wish I was pretending. They are digging around in my arm, pricks of pain like tiny bites.

"Try cutting his dick off and filling that hole with maggots, my love."

I whip my head up to glare at Erac. "Piece of shit. It's bigger than yours, isn't it?"

Erac draws a blade of his own from the air, and I tense. *Fuck, he's going to do it. I can't stop him. Shit. Wrong time to bait him.*

"Darling," Ella sighs, holding out a hand to stay him. "I'll get to it later. I thought I made it clear I would be handling this?"

Those things are still crawling around in my flesh. My arm is twitching and shaking. I am starting to feel them everywhere, in my bicep, my armpit, working their way into my chest. "Fuck, please, please get them out of there."

Erac scowls, crossing his arms. "I'm not interfering."

She slams the dagger down into the table next to me, but I still flinch. "Then what are you doing here?" she asks.

My arm is burning and shaking of its own accord. Those things are moving under my flesh, squirming, and feasting. The sensation is maddening, to know I am being eaten alive.

Dropping his hands to his hips, Erac takes a hardened stance. "I told you, I'm protecting you."

Ella laughs with bitter coldness. "Do I look like I need protection?"

His face screws up, and I start trying to pull my arms free

again, thrashing as if I could shake those creepy crawling larvae out of my flesh.

Erac shakes his head. "You have no idea what you need protecting from. I know what they did to you, what they are capable of. You don't."

She wrenches the blade free and points it at him. "I don't need your help or your protection, and I'm not a child who needs to be watched over. I'm dealing with this."

Those things are worming into my shoulder socket, my armpit filling with a crawling sensation. "Oh, fuck, please, they're moving, they're moving, get them out of there," I beg Ella, eyes glued to her.

They square off, both staring, and Viktor materializes out of thin air. I bare my teeth at him. He contemplates me, then his gaze shifts away, taking in the scene.

"I want to have a conversation with Declan," Viktor says. "Both of you will leave this room."

We all snarl at him, and he lifts his eyebrows in surprise. Ella rests the dagger next to me again and huffs. "Why? I'll get you your answers."

Viktor holds a hand up. "This is none of your concern." His eyes shift from her to Erac. "Either of you. This is between him and me, and I want privacy."

"Fine," Erac says, stepping forward to grab Ella by the arm.

I grunt, flexing, and trying to get free. "Don't fucking touch her."

Erac smirks at me. "Just make sure when you're done, this animal is dead. I'll take Ella to bed."

She rips free of him and shoves him in the chest. "I'm not going anywhere with you."

My arm is twitching, and I am whimpering. The creepy crawlers have made it into my chest. "Get these things out of me," I plead in a tormented whisper. "Please make it stop."

She draws her hand from my wrist down to the hollow base

of my arm and socket. The sensation leaves, but my arm still twitches, and I whimper again. She bends over me, her face close. "They're gone."

I shudder and stare at her. "You're pure fucking evil."

Erac's voice snaps around the room. "We're leaving. Now, Morella." She is pulled away from me. I blink, and both are gone from the room.

I breathe out, my head falling to the side, my eyes rolling in their sockets. Viktor's face looms over me, and I do my best to give him a dirty look. "The fuck do you want?"

His mouth twitches down in a quick frown, and he checks his watch. "How long has she been at it? And you're already begging?" He gives me a flashed smirk.

I curl my lip in disgust. "She put maggots in me. You try dealing with feeling things crawling around inside of you."

Viktor slides his hands in his front pockets and contemplates me. "I have an offer for you, son. Can I call you, son? You did marry my daughter, after all."

Rage streaks through me, and I do my damnest to break free, so I can throttle him. I want to beat his flesh against the walls and paint the stone red with his blood. "You fucking fuck! You knew. You've known, and you let him, you gave her to him! I'm going to kill you. I'm going to break every bone in your body. I'll skin you alive, I'll—"

"Mr. Byron," Viktor yells over my roaring.

I snarl and snap at the air, my vision hazing at the edges, a burn rolling through my body that has nothing to do with wounds or healing. This is pure, undiluted rage, the whispering teasing new and creative ways to maim him.

"Really, Declan, this behavior is unbecoming," he mutters.

I roar with laughter. "You fuck."

"Yes, well, moving on then." He rolls to the balls of his feet and stares down at me. "I have a proposition for you."

"Yeah, what's that?" I struggle against the straps.

"My daughter," he says, eyes blazing.

The bait dangles over me, precious and beautiful. I snarl at him. "She's a woman, not a sheep to barter with."

"Be that as it may, she is stubborn, starting to get ideas of her own."

"Imagine that," I mutter, giving up on the idea that I'm getting up without help.

He sighs and runs a hand over his mouth. "Do pay attention please, I loath to repeat myself."

"Well, I'm as captive an audience as it gets. Get to the point of what you want so I can say no."

Viktor checks his watch. "I already got my four hours of sleep, and so I have all day to deal with your..." he hesitates, "charm."

I imagine giving him a rude gesture. "Fine, talk. I'm listening." I face straight up, inspecting the stone ceiling.

"I have a problem."

"I think you've got several, mostly mental ones."

His face doesn't so much as twitch. "You are a delight as always, my boy."

"Yeah, a fucking dream."

"Erac has become cumbersome," he says.

The skin on the bridge of my nose crinkles, my upper lip peeling back to expose my teeth. "That bastard is a fucking useless, spineless—"

"Other than the abuse of language, I agree."

I jerk in my bonds and blink at him, then chuckle. "We have found rock bottom if we agree on something."

"Certainly," he drawls. "Nonetheless, the problem remains. I have come to realize that in her current state, Morella is going to be difficult and, honestly, useless to me. Erac is still under delusions that he can persuade her to enjoy his company, while I am not inclined to agree." One side of his mouth twitches. "She can be rather stubborn."

I smirk. "Yeah, damn woman getting ideas of her own and wanting freedom."

"Erac failed to consider what would happen when he broke the bond. Replacing the half of her soul, we were unable to remove memories from previously, and any efforts to remove her memories again may destroy her mind beyond repair."

I clench my jaw and fists. "You're a proper heartless son of a bitch for what you've done to her."

"I have done what I saw as necessary. I am leaving behind a legacy not of my own, but for my daughter as well."

I cock a brow. "You're fucking nuts."

"The problem is I now am faced with how to proceed. Morella is proving she will likely be uncooperative, and Erac is acting on emotions."

"And you love irrational behavior." I smile. "Get to the point of this conversation."

"I want you to take Erac's place."

My ears are ringing as I gape at him. "The fuck did you just say to me?"

"Your language is hardly acceptable. Watch your tone and tongue with me, or I'll remove it."

I cock my jaw, considering if I want to push the issue while strapped to this forsaken table and helpless. *Helpless, again, still, something like that.* I squeeze my eyes shut and clench my jaw.

Viktor sighs. "You have likely already convinced her to believe the truth."

"Funny how well the truth works." I shake my head in disbelief.

"I will need insurance against Morella retaliating against me and give her proper motivation to perform."

The skin down my spine twitches as realization blooms in my brain. "Me?" My voice is low and tortured. "You're going to use me."

He smiles, lips pressed together, but something akin to

humor is dancing in his eyes. "Yes, my son, you. A blood bond should do the trick, tethering your life to mine so that if she or anyone else tries to kill me, she'll be motivated to reconsider or take preventative measures against my death." He pulls a hand out of his pocket and checks the time. "She'll have what she wants, of course. You." He tilts his head toward me.

"And what do I get?"

He blinks at me. "Besides my daughter?" His brow furrows. "I'll give you Erac. He has run his course of use."

"I want to talk to Ella."

"Not until I have an answer."

"What's the fine print on this contract?" I ask, narrowing my eyes.

He rolls his shoulders back. "You are taking Erac's place. You will put on the proper face and pleasantries when required, showing allegiance and doing what I require of you. If you fail, I will use my daughter for motivational purposes."

I snarl at him but realize he might not realize that blood bond requires trust in who you share a life force with. My ears twitch as I recall Aron claiming that the two lifeforces linked can hurt the other without repercussion.

Sighing, I raise an eyebrow,. "How does this blood bond work?"

"What is done to you is done to me. If I bleed, you will bleed. Erac mentioned it as the reason why we couldn't kill his brother."

I wait for him to mention the weak point, but seconds tick by as I listen to my heartbeat. I wonder if he knows Erac killed his brother anyway. "And I get to rip that fucker's head off? And Ella?"

"Yes."

I consider. "Voices in my head?"

"Thankfully, we will be spared a mental link in the way you

and my daughter have. The bond will only reflect physical conditions."

"How long do I have to decide?"

Viktor checks his watch. "Erac knows nothing of this. You may want to consider quickly. I don't know how long I can persuade him to leave you alive."

"What about getting the information on the stolen goods?" I lift an eyebrow. "That's got to buy me some time, even with you."

"Hardly. It's obvious. That servant boy is to blame, hardly a viable threat at this point. If I kill you and—" he gestures at the back wall where my brother hangs, "—you know, I have forgotten his name."

"Right. I get the point. Can I at least get blood to think clearly?"

He doesn't answer me, frowning down at his feet. I try to crane to see if there's something worthwhile but can't manage to see anything. I give up and wait.

Viktor lifts his eyes to me with an emotion I can only assume is murderous pain. "Did she suffer?"

"Who?" I ask, cocking a brow.

"Your mother."

"Regrettably," I draw the word out, "no."

He bobs his head in an uncharacteristic manner, slow and even movements like the weight of the world draws him down, and he fights to rise. "Thank you. I'll leave you to consider your options."

CHAPTER 50

MORELLA

I rebuild in Erac's room. I hiss at him and slam a closed fist against his chest. "I hate you."

Erac's hand closes around my throat, squeezing. He walks me backward, up against a wall, eyes blazing with fury. He leans in close, mouth near my ear. I struggle to breathe with the grip crushing my windpipe.

He laughs, low, bone-chillingly and dark, leaving every hair on my body standing on end. "I knew leaving you alone with Declan Bard was too dangerous."

His hand clamps down harder, and I struggle to get any air. The pressure in my head is starting to build. "Erac," I beg, clawing at his hand. "Can't breathe."

The death grip releases, and I fall into him, coughing and gasping for air. I put a hand to my throat and gape up at him.

He stares with rage down his nose at me. "You are a very stupid girl."

I wince and rub my neck. "Why is that? Because I won't love you?"

He backhands me, and I fall sideways to the floor. My hand rests against my cheek as I gape up at him. "There is something very wrong with you that you'd chose an animal over me."

I swallow hard and stand, dropping my hands to my sides. "Better an animal than a monster like you."

He sneers. "You're never going to talk to Declan Bard again. He'll be put to death tomorrow morning. I'll make sure it's a classic public execution, drawing it out so that bastard suffers."

He reaches out, dragging me toward the bed. I try to resist, dragging my feet. My fingers try to peel his from my wrist to no avail.

"No!" I yell, struggling harder, thrashing in his grip as he bends down and picks up the chain attached to his bed. "No, let go of me," I beg, fighting as hard as I can.

"You were born to be beautiful and powerful. They shackled you, made you believe you were meant to serve." He takes my legs out from under me, and I hit the floor on my side. Stunned, I lay there as he locks the cuff around my ankle. "They weakened you, softened you, ruined what you should have been."

My chest aches. Drawing air is difficult, like my ribs have turned to iron, burning and restricting me. "You did this to me," I whisper. "You took my memories to make me what you wanted me to be."

"And now I'm going to have to start over, to try again, and this time I am going to kill that fucking animal you love so much. I'm going to make sure he's really dead, make sure the bond is gone." He checks the chain, and I watch, knowing there is nothing I can do, not while here in this room where I have no control over the elements. "That poison is still there. I only had half of your soul to remove memories from. Half your soul to clear and start over with. This time I'm going to make sure I have your whole soul in you when I clear the ledger."

I lurch to my feet. "It wasn't them at all—the brothers—it was all you, everything."

He starts toward the door, and I follow, the chain jerking me to a stop several feet from it. He halts and looks back at me. There's something soft and sad to the expression he wears. "I love you, and you keep choosing that fucking animal over me. He's rotted your brain, made you think you love him, that you should hold back when you were born to be a queen, to use your power."

He sighs, stepping toward me, reaching out. I take a step back. "Don't touch me," I snarl. "You don't get to put your hands on me ever again."

His lip curls back in rage. "Fine. Stay here. I only regret you won't have the bond to feel it when I cut his heart out, and then you'll beg for me to take your memories again."

"You said doing it again would rupture my mind, that I'd be like a doll!" I scream.

He smirks, "A pretty doll that won't fight back."

My jaw drops as fury snakes through my veins. "You're disgusting. You're— You can't be serious."

Laughing, he reaches out and grabs hold of my face. "I'm very serious, Morella. If you won't love me, then I'll have you any way I can." He brings his mouth down on mine, bruising my lips.

I refuse to open my mouth to scream or curse in fear of his tongue invading me. I claw at his hands, prying myself away from him. I spin my back to him, my body heaving and retching.

"Someday very soon," he murmurs, brushing hair away from my neck to drop little wet kisses on the top of my shoulder. "You are going to do and be everything I want."

I squeeze my eyes shut until I am sure he is gone. I take a deep breath, using shaking fingers to feel around the cuff. I've spent too many hours of my life in this chain to think I can break free. I had tried to break the chain, the cuff, the bed it's linked to, everything I could think of. My mind is racing.

I stand up, trying to reach the door to no avail. I've done this a hundred times already, but I can't give up. Somehow, someway, I won't be here when he gets back. I wrack my brain for any new idea and try to see if I can talk to Declan, but there's nothing there. My chest compresses at the thought that he might be dead.

I grit my teeth and glare at the door. This time I'm smarter, and I'll be damned if I can't figure out how to get free.

CHAPTER 51

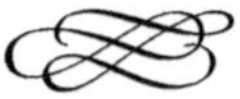

DECLAN

"Dec?"

I pick my head up and stare at her by my feet. My eyes lock on the pulse in her neck, the steady clop of her heart echoing in my ears. I lick my lips with a dry tongue. "What?" I ask in a soft tone. "What's wrong?"

She shakes her head. "I don't have time. I need—I need something. Erac is going to hurt me if I don't give him back the bearings."

I scowl, trying to swallow. I close my eyes, trying to focus on her words instead of the sound of her beating heart pushing blood through her veins. "Useless fucker. You can beat him. You have more power than he does."

"Please," she whispers. "At least tell me who took them so I can prove I was getting information."

I curl my lip at her, then run my tongue along the front row of my teeth. "Let me up." She shakes her head. "The bearings are hidden somewhere only I can get them."

"What if you die?"

I give her a look that says, *are you kidding me*? "Let me up, I can—"

"I don't have time for this!" she yells, her eyes glassy, her lower lip trembling. "Just tell me who took the bearings."

I narrow my eyes at her, eyes dropping toward her neck and flickering back to her eyes. I know every look she has, the little ways her features shift, and what they mean. I've never seen her this way. I don't know that look, but the bloodlust is setting in, and my mind is hazy.

"Ella—"

"Please, just trust me."

I shake my head, panting, the world too hot. "If you tell Erac who it was, he'll kill them, like he killed Aron when you told him about the pin."

Her lips twist with fury. "He's going to hurt me. Don't you care about me? Please, please don't let him hurt me."

I groan and flex against the straps, taking a deep breath. "George," I say. "It was George. He knew something was wrong. He spied on Erac, found the bearings, and brought them to me for me to help you."

"Thank you," she says, her voice deepening.

Confused, I pick my head up and watch her face change. The eyes grow darker, the delicate, angular features turning wider and fuller. Erac smiles at me as the hair shortens, turning dark blond.

"Fuck." I stare at him, my heart ratcheting up about twelve notches. The clunking echoes in my ears between my empty head. For a moment, he stares back, that stupid grin on his face.

"Thank you," Erac says. "If you'll excuse me, I'm going to take care of that insolent boy. Don't go anywhere." He chuckles.

"If you lay a hand on him—if you harm one hair on that boy's head, I'll kill you," I growl. "Do you hear me Erac? Do not touch him. He's a kid!"

Erac picks at nothing on his dress shirt and shrugs. "He stole from me. I can't tolerate that. You understand, don't you? This whole thing," he waves a hand at me, "is because I stole from you, isn't it?"

I snarl. "Don't you fucking hurt him. He's a kid! Take it out on me. Come on, you hate me more than anything else. You'd rather torture me, so do it." I twist around, trying to see the straps on my arms and a way out. Fear is clearing the haze from my mind. I jerk and strain, pulling against the straps until they are digging into my flesh, and I am exhausted.

He smiles, chuckling softly. "I do hate you, but you see, I'm going to kill you and him," he says, his eyes lifting over my head. "And the boy and anyone else who would meddle so when I rip Morella's mind apart, there will be no one left to take her from me."

"You fucker!" I roar. "You flaccid useless cock. You—"

He disappears, and I struggle against the straps, praying to Haven there is give. I try to bend my legs, fighting against the tethers around my ankles and calves. I jerk and pull and thrash and fight, but nothing works.

"Come on!" I yell at the ceiling. "This is for a fucking kid. He's just a kid."

I get no answer, and there is no give to my bonds. I lay there, muscles burning even at the thought of moving. My limbs are aching and heavy, no amount of force breaking free.

I slam my head against the table, eyes burning and nose running. There's no give, no breaking, no hope. "Fuck," I manage, losing my composure.

~

Hours creep by before I hear the rustle of air that follows dissipation. My head whips toward Erac, standing at my feet. He is still, watching me with an odd expression. I can't tell if he hates me or is going to cry.

His eyes drop from mine. "Why does she love you?"

My ears twitch, and I chuckle, refocusing on trying to get loose. A shadow looms over me, and I glance up at him now to the side of me. He is frowning as he reaches out and splays his hand, the skin and tendons flexing and tensing.

My lungs burn, refusing to work. I choke, my abs clenching and fighting against whatever is suffocating me. Turning my head toward him, my body throws the wetness out of me, but not enough. I still can't draw in air.

I keep trying to regurgitate the liquid from my chest, my vision graying and hazing. I manage to throw up enough to draw air into my burning lungs. Wheezing and spluttering, I spew out more and then close my eyes.

Breathing in deep through my nose sends molten iron through my skull. The scent of George lingers in my nasal cavities. My eyes snap open, and I glare up at Erac, eyes trying not to focus on the blood splatter across his face and shirt.

He keeps staring at me with that dejected, rage-filled pained gaze.

"Fuck you." My voice is hoarse. I take another breath through my mouth to avoid smelling George again, like it matters now. "Fuck you. He was a kid, a defenseless kid."

Erac conjures a stool and perches on it beside me, strumming his fingers on the surface next to my ribs. "I don't understand," he whispers. "Why does she love you? You're an animal, a monster that feasts on blood. The control you maintain over the elements is crude, and you are crass, arrogant, dominant. There's nothing noble about you." He sighs, ceasing the irritating noise of fingers tapping, and sits up straight. "I want to know how you did it."

I get as far to the other side of the table as I can manage, maybe a few hairs width difference, but it makes me feel better on the inside. "Did what?"

"How did you make her love you?" The words are a tortured whisper from his lips, his eyes glowering at me in the dim light.

I curl a lip back. "You can't make her do anything."

"You're lying," he says, rolling his shoulders back and then slouching down. "There's no reason she should love you and not me." His eyes meet mine, barely open. "She doesn't even have her memories, and somehow she still doesn't love me. Why? Tell me what you did to make her love you, and I'll kill you quickly."

I laugh. I can't help it. It just comes out, and his face ripples with rage. He draws a short sword from the air, ramming into down through me, skewering me to the table. I groan with pain, trying to breathe as his hand contorts again, filling my lungs with fluid.

My body starts to make attempts to dispel the liquid, and I spit it at him. My muscles scream in protest as they work against the intrusive metal. I can feel the sharp edges cutting deeper.

I struggle, straining my arms, which only clenches my abdominal muscles further, flesh searing as the steel cuts further. I gasp and gurgle, glaring at Erac as he watches me with a contemplative stare. His hand drops, and I work to clear my lungs to breathe.

He sighs. "You couldn't stay away, leave her alone, leave her to be happy with me." He crosses his arms, frowning down at me. "I need to know how you did it. When I wipe her mind clean, I need to recreate your tactics."

I scoff on a chuckle. "You want to know what I did? I fucking cared for her, tried to protect her. It almost cost me my life—it did, and it's going to again, and I'd do it again and again because she's worth it. That woman is worth it."

"I see. Show her I am willing to die for her." His head bobs. "She loved you before that, though. What did you do to make it happen?"

I fucking lose it, choking on laughter, tasting blood on my tongue, the scent of that metallic ambrosia thick in the air. I lick my teeth, wanting, needing a taste of that sweet scent. "I might be a monster or an arrogant bastard, but I'm not a fucking prick, not to her. If I have to tell you how to treat a woman, you don't deserve to have fucking balls."

My eyes dart around at his slight movements, and as he stills, so does my sights, set on the pulse in his neck. I snarl and run my tongue around the front of my top teeth. My torso is throbbing, but the pain is receding. The only thing I care about is blood and how I'm going to sink my teeth into something and get what I need.

Erac slides the protrusion from my gut and holds it aloft. I strain, inching over toward it, snarling and licking at the air. The blood is crimson, glittering over the steel like beautiful water. I want it, need it. I try to reach for it, get close enough to lick it, my tongue feeling the tangy taste as I lick inches away from it.

Erac chuckles. "If she could see you now," he muses. "A fucking animal, rabid like a dog."

The blade inches closer, just out of reach. I push my head back into the table beneath me, breathing through my mouth. I've been here before. I can control this. I grip my hands into fists and glare at him.

"I'm going to skin you alive," I growl, more animal than man.

"You are going to die." There's a sick glee to his words, probably the same euphoria bound to them as when I talked about ripping his head off or his spine from his body. "But I'm not quite done with you yet."

"Rot in the inferno."

"What did you tell her to convince her she loves you? I could see it in her eyes when I left her. She has no memory of you and yet cares for you after a few short hours. I need to know how you managed that."

"I'm not fucking telling you how to make my wife love you. I don't care what you do to me."

"So, it can be done? I can make her love me?"

I pull at my bonds in a futile action for the thousandth time. The wound in my abdomen screams in a vivid reminder of its existence. Even through the haze of bloodlust, the pain is overwhelming. I pant, trying to catch my breath. "You're fucking insane. You've really lost your mind."

"No." He digs his fingers in the wound barely healing in my stomach. I groan, tipping my head back, eyes closing against the radiating intrusion into me. "You're not healing."

He's right. I snap my head up and glare. "I'll fucking die then, and you can fuck yourself. It doesn't matter how many times you wipe her mind; she's never going to love you."

He smirks, pulling away from me. He wipes his fingers on my sweating chest. "I always thought we were so different."

"We are," I say with a laugh.

"We're both willing to do anything for Morella. I'll wipe her mind as many times as I must, to start over again and again until I get it right. I don't care how long it takes. I don't care how much damage it does. Eventually, I'll get it right."

"Do you even hear yourself?" I shake my head, then I bare my teeth at him in a malicious grin. "Do you?"

"Yes," he says flatly.

"If you really want to make her love you, you'd have to be me, you useless sack of blood."

He *tsks* and puts his hands in his pockets. "Why would I ever want to be a rabid animal?" He shakes his head. "No, I want to know what you did, what you said to make her believe you."

I snarl, my voice on the edge of violent growling. "The fucking truth, which you can't use. You've hurt her, lied to her, and even without memories or me, she still didn't love you, did she? She still fucking didn't want you even when she didn't have me." I spit at him, the drool spraying his face. "You can't make her love you, you fucking prick. You're a sorry excuse for a man."

He holds the short sword up, and it morphs into a smaller blade. "Let's see how much of a man you are without the proper equipment."

I struggle against my bonds as a twisted smile crosses his face. There's no give to the straps or what's beneath me, but there's no chance I'll give that part of me up without a fight. I use every ounce of strength I have, managing zero progress.

"Aron and I experimented on shades," he says with an eerie calm. "We tried all manner of mutilations and torture to test their abilities and bloodlust. All those books Morella loves to read so much are based upon our research. It won't grow back." He grins, his whole face distorting.

Fuck, I curse as I continue to thrash. This is going to hurt. I'm already not healing. Bloodlust is going to take over, and I really am going to be a rabid animal. I take a breath through my nose and close my eyes.

I feel the bite of steel against my neck. "I will give you one chance. You can agree to tell her she can save your pathetic life if she agrees to do as I say and love me."

I know I am never going to trade her life for mine. I smirk, the left side of my mouth hitching, and I open my eyes. "I'm not telling her anything for you. Go fuck yourself."

He sighs and shakes his head. "You really are arrogant, aren't you? Let's see if you're any humbler without your balls."

"Not likely, asshole."

CHAPTER 52

MORELLA

I break, curling in on myself on the floor, sobbing until I can't breathe. I heave, getting enough air to continue crying. I lay there as my eyes dry, trying to breathe, my body revolting and hiccuping, breathing in short, desperate gasps. My lids stretching tight over swollen, sticky eyeballs, and I grip my knees to my chest as hard as I can.

My mind is numb and hazy. Picking my head up, my eyes flutter and squint against the dark, then stretch open wide, and I jerk upright. Whipping my head around, I search the room. Everything is in place, and no one else is present. Moonlight bathes the room in shadows and crisp relief.

I am alone, but I am not the same woman who woke up in this room. I know magic this time, how to control the elements and weave spells. I know my name and that I had a life before this, a man who loves me, who was willing to be tortured, maybe killed just to get to me.

Rage slithers in my veins, and I welcome the burning sting my blood carries through my limbs. Erac is going to regret what he did to me and rue the day he ever taught me to control the elements.

I test the limits of the chain around the room. I can reach the window, so I go to it, sectioned and grouted in a fancy design. I look around and find a bookend to throw through the window. I use the other to break pieces of the window off, dropping larger, jagged shards on the floor, thinking they might be useful weapons later.

I reach through the opening, trying to see if I can manipulate the elements outside of the room. I close my eyes and picture a dagger, the weight and cold metal dropping in my palm. I pull back, bringing it inside.

Staring at it, then out the window, I realize that I can control the elements outside of this room. I drop the blade and stick my hand out the window again, concentrating on the library, desperate for a book. If I can't get out, maybe there is a way I can save my mind before it is wiped clear again. A heavy spine materializes in my hand, and tentatively, biting my lower lip with anxiety spurring my heartrate, I pull the tome through the window. I lose my grip, and the text thumps heavily on the floor. I grin, crouching down and flipping through pages.

I curl against the wall, hidden from view of the door by the bed, squinting in the moonlight to read the flourished script. I skip and scan in a hurry to have the bare minimum knowledge as a plan forms in my mind. I set the book aside, crawling to the window.

I gather as much glass in my hand as I can hold, feeling it cut my skin. I stick my hand out the window, releasing the glass. My blood clings to the shards, and I force them together, changing them into an orb. It's near the size of my head, but I keep it suspended in the air as I lift another shard from the ground and use it to cut the side of my hand.

I use a drop of blood on the sphere, concentrating wholeheartedly on the goal I want to accomplish. There is no telling if this will work, being in this room, but I can't give up. Using the sharp end, I stab into my skin, drawing runes on the orb as it hangs in the air outside the window, over and over until the orb is coated in bloody runes. Concentrating, I watch my blood seep into the glass ball and swirl until the glass is clear once more.

I reach through the window, plucking the orb up in my palm and using both hands to compress it down, shrinking the orb to the size of a pea. My eyes dart around my body for a place to seat the bearing that will go undetected. Not my wrists, Erac grabs those. Not my torso as he enjoys looking at me. I eye my feet wondering if Erac has ever paid any attention to them.

I need a part of my body that can extend out the window, something that will go unnoticed. My eyes land on the ornate, gorgeous ring on my third finger. I leave the tiny glass ball to suspend in the air outside the window and then pull the ring off, dropping it to the floor.

I stick both arms through the window and press the orb to the skin of my third finger, on the backside, where the ring will hide it from sight. It sinks into my skin, my flesh burning and sizzling. My eyes cross with pain, and there's a ripping sensation through my mind, a throbbing deep in my core. I manage to stay conscious, and I pull my hands inside, searching for the ring among the pieces of shattered window.

I drop to the floor, panting and getting the ring back on my finger. With any luck, he'll leave it on me when he tries to rip my memories out again. I sit there, gripping the skirt of my dress in sweating fingers, and wait.

My heart berates my breastbone as Erac materializes in front of me. He glances at the window then scowls at me. "What did you do?"

"Threw a tantrum at being locked up against my will by a man intending to kill my husband," I mutter, smoothing the skirt of my dress over my legs.

"Let me show you your precious fucking husband," he snarls.

Cold rips through me, and I blink, standing on my feet in the dark, damp cell. I hear growling and thrashing. I stare, fear slithering through me. There is blood everywhere, splatter on the walls, covering Declan's torso. My eyes lock on the ripped and mangled part of him where his stomach and legs meet.

"Did you cut his legs off?" I gasp, taking a step toward Declan.

Erac reaches out, fingers digging in my hair and gripping hard enough to send pinpricks of pain across my scalp as hair rips free. I cry out, but it only makes him hold tighter. "I cut his dick and balls off, carved him up a bit." He laughs, soft and dark. "This is what you wanted?"

He throws me away from Declan behind us into the wall. I get my hands up, ready to set Declan free and pull Erac to pieces, but he laughs, louder, the noise echoing. "I fixed this cell," he snarls at me. "I am the only one who can control the elements in here."

That doesn't stop me from trying, but nothing happens. I grit my teeth and glare. "You think he's the bad guy?" My eyes are burning as much as the blood running through my veins. I welcome the feeling. "You're the monster," I whisper.

Erac draws a blade from the air. For one terrible second, I think he's going to attack me, but he slices his forearm, holding it aloft. Declan howls and struggles, his efforts seeming to double. The table is shaking and groaning but still holding. He growls and snaps at the air, fighting hard enough that I worry he is going to hurt himself.

"That!" Erac screams, pointing at Declan. "That is a monster."

I track blurry eyes from him to Declan and then back to Erac's eyes. They are ablaze with hatred and rage, and I swallow my fear. I lift my chin and glare at him. "I hate you."

He starts and stops. His face screws up, and then he sets the blade down next to Declan, who is still thrashing. It clatters on the floor, the sound reverberating around us, dislodged by his thrashing.

Erac chuckles, his eyes fixating on Declan. "You won't. You won't even remember this, and next time he will be dead, and you won't have any reason to not love me back."

I force myself to grin. "I might not remember, and he might be dead, but I am never going to love you."

He closes his eyes, reaching up to swipe at his face. I lunge forward, grabbing the blade. He kicks me in my side, but my fingers curl around the hilt. He kicks again, and I slash with the dagger, feeling contact. I scramble, even as he fights with me, trying to get a grip on the blade.

I back up, holding my arm out close to Declan's mouth as I distract Erac with the blade. Teeth sink into my forearm as Erac tries to pry the dagger from my grip. The bite is mild, the forceful clamp of Declan's jaw leaving my arm throbbing under the pressure, but I don't pull back. I let him drink even as I kick Erac in the gut.

My eyes roll and flutter as my head cracks like I've been struck with an ax in the back of my skull. Erac wrenches the blade from me as I falter from the sensation, and I stare through watering eyes at him. He steps back, brandishing the dagger as Declan sucks on my arm.

Erac's smile turns to choler, his eyes locking on what is happening. "You'd feed it? Even now? Seeing what it truly is?"

My bloodlust is screaming through me, spurning me on. I resist pulling away from Declan, biding precious time. Erac stomps forward, and I lock my fingers around his wrist, getting a leg between us. His force pushes me back onto the table.

I'm getting woozy, the world too warm and foggy, like a rain cloud has settled around me. I grunt as Erac drops the blade, trying to dislodge my arm from Declan. Searching blindly for the buckles on the straps, I pull and tug at one and then another as I lay there limp, letting Erac and Declan fight over my arm.

Warmed leather meets my fingers, the iron mixed in, burning my fingertips. I try to ignore it, still pulling at a buckle. Declan's thrashing combined with our weight tips the table. We crash down, my pounding head smacking off the stone floor, and I tuck and roll, my arm now out of Declan's mouth.

I get to my feet and start screaming at Erac. Words twisted with sharp vinegar and rage.

He jerks back, then steps into a full-blown swing. The lower portion of the right side of my face sears. A tangy metallic taste lingers on the top of my tongue.

I glare up through welling tears at him, standing over me as he bellows. "Ungrateful. Disrespectful. Stupid. I should have known better. You wretched and pathetic— Memories aren't the root, it's your soul. I should have broken you like he said. You're too soft, too caring, such a waste."

My brain is too addled to comprehend the words he is shouting. I blink at him, sprawled on my side on the hard, cold marble floor. My hip hurts like I landed hard on the ground.

I twist to my feet, lunging at him, clutching his shoulders, throwing my body into him. He topples back, grabbing at my arms. I get my right hand free, swinging with a closed fist the way I did at the air. The contact of my fist against his face feels so good, so I pull back, swinging again.

A shock wave hits me, throwing me back into the wall. I see double, my head burning, my ears ringing. Erac holds out his hand, fingers splayed. Chains wrap around my wrists and neck, the metal burning, leaving my skin to sizzle at the contact.

He kneels, putting two fingers under my chin to lift my head. "You'll watch him die, both of them. They both came for you, thinking they love you. You're going to watch, and then you'll beg for me to pull the memories out of you."

I spit in his face, and he pulls back, wiping the saliva from his chin. His eyes turn cold and dead in his head. He yanks on one of the chains behind me, tethering me to the wall, making sure it is secure. I stay on my knees, glaring up at him.

"Feeding that animal was stupid. Now it'll just take longer." He swings around on his heel, turning his back on me. I kick him behind the knee. His leg gives, and he topples. He snarls at me, and I stare back with every ounce of fury I have running through me, and he balks, taking a step back. He stands and whirls to glare before getting to his feet. He uses the elements to right the table.

I stare where he was a moment ago, rage burning through me like boiling water poured over hot coals. My head is throbbing, and my throat is thick, like I haven't drunk water in days. I turn, eyes flickering for something, anything. I can't control the elements within the confines of this room.

But I can control them everywhere else.

I close my eyes and focus, picturing Asperheim. I will pull this whole place apart piece by piece. There will be nowhere for him to hide, nowhere for him to run. It's time I proved to him that he is weak. I'm the most powerful being in all of Caleum, and he's going to repay in blood what he stole from me.

CHAPTER 53

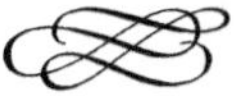

DECLAN

I blink, Erac's grinning face materializing over me. I lick my teeth and lips, the sweet taste of blood still there. The flavor is like tangy honey. Ella's blood.

I snarl at him, thrashing in my bonds. I need more, more blood, more of her. My head tips and falls side to side, eyes searching for the source. Pain rips through my torso, and I snap my focus onto the blade drawing through me.

Rabid, snarling, floating toward conscious thought, the pain begins to drag me back down. I can smell her, the scent of her blood on me.

I growl, baring teeth to snarl at Erac as he starts ramming the blade into my chest between ribs. He doesn't speak, his violet eyes gleaming mean with fury as he tries to bleed me dry.

The whole world trembles and Erac pauses. We both glance around, and his face contorts with rage as he glares into the corner. I crane my head, catching sight of Ella chained in the corner, eyes closed, her features twisted in a beautiful rage. Erac narrows his eyes, and she flies back into the wall. I hear the crack of her head against the stone, my own head racking with brilliant pain at the sound. My heart lurches into my throat, but she lifts her chin and opens her eyes. They glow, brilliant purple, her whole face lighting up with the glow of energy.

Oh fuck.

CHAPTER 54

MORELLA

I fly back, hitting the wall. My head cracks, and it hurts, but it fuels my rage. I open my eyes and bare the hatred burning within me to him.

He is yelling, his mouth moving, but I don't hear him over the screeching of splitting rock. The walls of the room crack before my eyes, deep black ravines ripping through the stone, breaking the spell that prevents me from using magic. I can see the fear in Erac's eyes.

I will the chains gone and stand. I draw air in, compressing it over and over, the world still shuddering around us. He fires a few shorter spells at me, which I absorb and then hurl the frigid bomb at him. It detonates against his shield, and I see him hit a cracked wall.

Someone runs in front of me, lips sewn shut, large hands grabbing my shoulders. Seth shakes me, his eyes stretched wide. I brush him away from me. He flies back, colliding with the wall. I ignore him, stepping toward Erac.

Part of the ceiling falls between us, and I dissipate in front of him, grabbing a shoulder and pulling him up, still snarling.

I focus, wanting him to hurt, wanting him to scream and

bleed. I need to see what he will look like inside out. His flesh ripples, splitting open and rolling back, muscles then bone exchange places until I am staring at his eyes through his skull.

His mouth is open, I can see his lungs working, I think he is screaming, but I cannot hear anything over the sound of the raging hammer strikes of my heart, the deep rumble of the world around us.

I use my free hand to grab his lungs, squeezing until I feel them collapse, and my nails sink into the slick warm organ, the texture of smooth muscle. The scent of blood encourages me, and I drag my nails through a lung.

His eyes roll back in his head, and I let him fall on the ground, a heap of bone and bloody tissue, a fucking mess. I kneel over him and smirk as he stares up through hazy purple eyes, a single lung quivering and pulsating with desperate gasps.

He might already be dead, but might be isn't good enough. I clasp his heart in my hand, squeezing it until those eyes turn foggy, then rip it away from the rest of what is left of him.

I hold it up, grinning. It's still hot to the touch, slick with blood. The muscles twitch once, and I bite into it, muscles sinking into the thick rubber. I chew it and swallow, then take another bite, grinning down at his hazed eyes as the warmth of my saliva and the fluids spill over my lip and down my chin.

He'll never heal. He won't have all the pieces of his body to heal. I crush the remainder of his heart in my hand, watching it harden to rock and crumble to dust, letting it fall like sand between my fingers to the floor.

The room collapses in a loud shriek, and I throw up a shield as rock tumbles down on me.

CHAPTER 55

DECLAN

The whole palace is crumbling as Seth half carries, half drags me through corridors. A passage caves in, and he turns away, bracing against a wall, shielding me from the rubble and dust. I groan and fall to the ground.

"Dec."

I snarl and sniff the air, my nose met with rock dust.

"Dec." He shoves his wrist in front of my face.

The veins throb, my eyes focusing on them. I sink my teeth in his arm and warm blood spurts into my mouth. It tastes horrible. I pull back, spitting it out and gagging, a burn rolling through my throat.

"Dec, come on, you need blood. I need you to focus."

Something collapses overhead, and I look up, the ceiling cracking.

I shove him away. "Not yours." I try to spit out whatever is left in my mouth. "You taste awful."

"I don't give a shit what I taste like, you prissy precocious fuck. I need you to focus and dissipate us the hell out of here!"

I growl and grab his wrist. Black lines are running around my bite, faint smoky lines. I hold it up and then throw it at him. "Look. You're not healing. We're poison to each other."

He winces and pulls back. "Must be the venom."

"No shit," I grunt, trying to stand.

He grabs me against him, getting under my shoulder to hoist me up. Together we start running, me doing a weird galloping limp and getting carried along with him.

"There!" he yells.

"See it," I manage.

Stairs leading up. We take them two at a time and spiral our way up and up. We hit daylight and stop. Wherever the steps lead to is gone. I glance around us. The jump isn't too bad.

"On three?" Seth asks.

I nod, staring down. "It's going to hurt."

"I just watched you—" loud screeching pauses his words as the ground shifts beneath us "—get tortured for hours."

"Don't like heights."

"You sit on the roof all the time, you fucker."

"Don't like falling."

He groans. "On three. One… two…"

"Where's Ella?"

He gives me a wide-eyed gaze. "She's lost it. I tried to—"

I shove him away, turning to go back.

"Dec, she's fucking lost it. This is her." He points around us at the crumbling palace. "I tried to get her, and she blasted me to a wall with a wave of her hand. I got you out of there and ran."

I limp back down one step, and the whole staircase slips down a few feet. My heart hammers and I fall against the half wall remaining.

Seth grabs me, hauling me against him. "There's nothing we can do."

I shove him away, and he grapples with me. I break free, and he clocks me in the face. The world goes off-kilter, and I blink at him.

"There's not a damn thing we can do!" he yells. He grips me by the shoulders and meets my eyes, his black and ringed with red. "There's nothing."

I grit my teeth as the stairs rumble and threaten to come down. I glance over the edge, gritting my teeth. The stone structure cracks away from the support wall.

Fuck.

I jump just as the stone breaks and crumbles beneath me, doing my best to shove outward. The warm air whips past me as I descend. My arms move in circles, flapping as if that is going to do me any damn good. The ground comes rushing up to meet me, and I land on my feet. My legs snap and crumple, and I roll headfirst, broken legs flopping over me to hit the ground on my back.

"Fuck."

Seth hits the ground with a *whump* and a few curses but rolls and pops up onto his feet. He grimaces and extends a hand. I shake my head but take it. He tugs, and I jerk up, my legs still shattered bones and shredded muscles.

I flop, unable to stand. I grit my teeth, latching onto him. He grunts and swings me over his shoulder. "We are never speaking of this."

He laughs and runs. I lift my head and watch the remnants of Asperheim's massive conical shape collapse into a pile of broken rubble.

Seth keeps moving, passing by servants and guards, all scattering from the premises. He scales large slabs of stone, going upward, shifting me on his shoulder, so my ass is in his face. He hoists us up and then pulls me off his shoulder.

"You know all those times you've been a major prick?"

I narrow my eyes, dangling in his grasp. "Yeah?"

"Just think of this as payback."

"What?"

He lets go of me, and I drop straight down. My legs hit solid ground again at velocity from the short drop, and then I topple and hit my back once more. He crouches on the broken wall, and I watch him jump off, landing feet first. I can hear the crunch in his legs, and he stays in the crouched position, laughing.

"Fuck you," I groan, but I'm grinning at him.

He chuckles and shakes his head. "It was either that or cradle you like a babe."

"Yeah, no, this was so much better." I sit up, curling a lip at my destroyed legs. I search around us, the wind blowing sand in my eyes. There are others, all milling about, most covered in white grime and dust. I jerk my head at a couple of guards. "Go fetch. I need blood to heal."

Seth puts two fingers in his mouth and whistles, waving his arm in an arc. "Hey, over here!"

I cock a brow at him. "That's just lazy."

"Why hunt when the food comes to you?"

~

I shove the second guard away from me, wrinkling my nose and wiping my mouth with the back of my hand. I check his pulse, making sure the poor bastard is still alive, and then grimace at my brother. "That tasted like old socks."

Seth shrugs. "I hope you can use your legs. We've got company." He jerks his chin.

I glance over my shoulder to see demons stomping across the dune toward us. I sigh. "Great."

"This isn't over," he says, standing and wiping his hands on his shirt.

I stay on the ground, even drop to my back to stare at the

remains. There's an earth-shattering scream as the whole thing caves in. My heart jackhammers, splintering into two pieces, one lodging in my throat and the other settling in the bottom of my gut.

Fuck. Lover.

I squeeze my eyes shut and draw in a shaking breath, forcing my lungs to keep working despite my shattered heart. "There's no way," I mumble, eyes burning with tears. "No fucking way she'll survive that."

Seth gets a hand under my arm, hauling me up. "Come on. It's Ell. She's stubborn enough to survive."

I am limp in his arms, blurry eyes pegged on what once was a mountainous palace but is now massive slabs of broken stone. A hand locks around my other arm, and I get ripped around and dragged through the sand. I stare at my wake, wide-eyed servants and guards watching me go. I let my head drop forward, shutting my eyes against the emotions threatening to spill out.

My backside is raw by the time I am dropped. I groan and rub a hand over my face, trying to get rid of the sand in my eyes. Rolling over, I pop up on my knees and see Viktor. He is covered in white dust from the broken rock but otherwise unharmed. He is staring hauntingly at the pile of rubble.

I laugh like something is uproariously funny. "There's no way she survived that you useless blood sack."

"She survived, somehow. She always does."

"No thanks to you, you sadistic fuck."

Viktor won't take his eyes off the decimated palace. He hums at me.

"A fucking hum? Like, what the fuck is that for a response?" I've never seen him like this. He looks lost. In some very fucked up way, that man does love Ella. "You are fucked up. Incomprehensibly mind-fucked. You're staring at that heap, thinking she somehow survived, and you're still going to get what you want."

Viktor turns to me for the first time. His eyebrows come together. "What do you know about what I want?" He turns back. "She survived. I have to believe she did, or I will have nothing left."

"No, you'll have nothing left after I wring the life out of you and pull those runes off."

Viktor chuckles, sliding his hands into his pockets. "You still won't give up, will you?"

I snicker. "You let my wife torture me. You took her memories and—"

"Erac did those things, my boy. I merely capitalized on them."

"You know…" Seth's voice is strange. Glancing at him, I see his eyes are puffed up and pinkish. I frown, and he shakes his head. "I always figured you'd push too far and kill her one day."

The apple of his throat bobs. I bare my teeth at him and turn to Viktor. "If she's dead—I'm going to kill you either way—but if she's dead, I'm going to make you beg for it first."

"My daughter is not dead." He jerks his head at me with his eyes on a demon. "If you're doubting her power even for a moment, then I was wrong. You don't deserve her."

I gape, seeing the butt of an ax handle coming toward me. I try to duck too late, feeling it crack against my temple, and everything goes black.

CHAPTER 56

DECLAN

I come to on my side, my head tipped at a sharp angle. Groaning, I roll to my back. Taking a few deep breaths, I sit up and roll my neck. I freeze, opening my eyes and reaching up to feel the thick band of metal encapsulating my throat.

Digging my fingers under the band, I try to pry it free to no avail. I hold a hand in front of my neck as if I were going to choke myself and will the elements to obey my desires, but the collar remains. Rolling my shoulders, I shudder, accepting I'm unable to remove the band.

I sigh through my nose and pinch the bridge. When I drop my hand, I look around me. The room is familiar, albeit painted yellow with obnoxious furniture. My knees bend, and I curl up, grabbing at the back of my neck. I open my eyes and stare down at my crotch. I hiss between bared front teeth and lift the waist of the sweat pants to peek underneath.

Dick. Balls. I groan and drop back in relief.

Staring up, I catch sight of my brother sitting in the window seat. He points to the low table between chairs and couch, not turning away from the window. He's slouched against the wall, knees bent, staring out at the dying light of the soul star. There are deep shadows cast in his forlorn expression.

I look where he points, glass bottles filled with dark red liquid. My throat constricts with need. I lurch, crawling over to lift one of them, popping the metal tang holding the cork in place, pulling the stopper out of the bottle. I chug, not even caring that the blood is room temperature and congealing.

One after another, I down the fluid until my stomach churns, and I exhale a burp with a disgusting aftertaste. "What is this?" I ask Seth, pointing at the collar around my neck. "And we're in Byron?"

He lifts and drops one shoulder. "Ell's rooms. You were right. Selene really wiped everything of her away in here." He grimaces and turns to face me. "And that, I'm supposed to tell you, is to prevent you from doing magic. He said something about learning from mistakes and not using runes because you can tear down a room or something. You know how Viktor is."

I cross my arms, flexing my neck. "Old bastard is a lot of things, but stupid isn't one of them." I breathe out my nose and scratch at the hair on the underside of my jaw. I almost shake my leg like a dog. Might as well since I'm collared like one. "Why aren't you collared?"

He lifts his eyebrows. "I can't control the elements for shit, and I don't have spirit runes. It's real easy to make me do anything he wants." He shudders. "I have a whole new understanding of what Ell went through."

We both stare out the window, out across the gardens, the city of Cato, and to Salt Canyon in the distance. My eyebrows push together, my eyes narrowing as my lips pinch. There are so many memories in this room for me that it hurts to breathe.

I turn and glance at the door. "What's to stop us from leaving?"

"If you leave this room without permission, I'm supposed to kill myself."

I shift back to face him and watch him lift a dagger. I curl my lip and rub my eyes. "Fine. Then what?"

My brother sighs and shifts, twisting, so his legs hit the floor, and he sits with his back to the windowpanes. "Now, we wait."

I drop down on the couch, laying back to stare at the ceiling with an arm behind my head. About three seconds in, I sit up. "This thing was not designed to be used."

"Kind of like Selene, but you still found a way," he says, his lips twisting to one side with humor.

I sigh and shift, so my legs hang over the armrest and flop back. "At least I've gotten laid." I grab my dick, thrilled it grew back despite Erac's assurance it wouldn't.

"So have I."

I bolt upright and stare with one side of my nose wrinkled up, lips pulled to the same side, almost curled up in shock. My fingers latch onto the side of the couch to help my aching abdominal muscles. "What?"

Seth laughs, but the sound lacks any humor. "Yeah, Asena."

"What the fuck," I chuckle.

"It was a disaster too." He runs a hand over his face as he laughs.

I grin. "The first time is never good."

"Marx walked in on it," he says, his face turning pink.

I roar with laughter, clutching my stomach with one hand. I laugh so hard, my eyes water.

"Laugh it up, lover boy," Seth grumbles.

"What the hell did he do?" I manage, still grinning ear to ear.

"Oh, he turned red. I thought for sure he was going to kill me, his daughter naked and straddling me. I think my whole life flashed before my eyes." He rubs the back of his neck. "That's what the threat about breaking every bone in my body was about. Pretty sure I'm on borrowed time."

"He just left?" I ask in skepticism.

"Hell no." Seth tips his head back and laughs. "I threw her off me and ran."

I burst into peals of laughter again, falling back and clutching at my stomach. The muscles are freshly healed and protesting this abuse, but there's nothing I can do about it. I calm down, running a hand down my face, still chuckling. "Wish I could have seen that."

"My bare ass and dick swinging as I ran for my life?"

"He's definitely going to kill you. Did you at least get to finish?"

"Nope," he says, drawing the word out with a dry tone. "Not even a little bit. My dick has shriveled up. Every time I even get halfway excited, all I can see is his face of rage, and it dies. I think I've suffered some permanent kind of trauma from it."

I snicker. "You've got the absolute worst luck with women."

"Tell me about it."

I could, but that would be plain mean. Instead, I let the silence stretch and watch the shadows elongate on the ceiling. Selene put in some stupid crystal chandelier that starts to twinkle from the light of the moon as time stretches on.

The door creaks open, the scent of cooked pork fills the room, and I jerk up, twisting to see who enters the room. Viktor moves in, kicking the door shut behind him. He sets the tray of food on the low table and takes a seat opposite on one of the floral upholstered chairs.

I eye him as he shifts with a face of discomfort. "Who redecorated this room?" he asks.

"Selene," my brother and I say together.

Viktor purses his lips. "She's a fucking idiot."

I smirk and sit up, reaching for the tray. "I'm shocked that one of your children could be so stupid."

Seth plops on the couch next to me. "Haven, this thing really is bad."

"Selene was never my child," Viktor says. "The only use she had was finally getting rid of her mother on my behalf." He gives a wry expression.

"So, what is this?" I ask, jerking my head at Seth.

"This is simple. My daughter will come for you."

I smirk. "She has, so many, many times."

Viktor clears his throat, choking on air. "I would prefer our conversation stay polite."

"I'd prefer to rip your throat out." I shrug. "I thought about your offer. My answer is no. Specifically, fuck no, you disease-ridden cockroach."

Viktor nods. "Not surprising." He gives me a smile. "I know when I am beaten."

I study his forlorn face. The lines and wrinkles in the skin are deeper than ever. Exhaustion weighs the angular features down.

"You know she's dead," Seth says.

No one says anything, and I bow my head, picking at the shredded pork on the plate with my fingers. The scent is no longer appetizing, the tender meat tasteless in my mouth.

Viktor rests his elbows on the sides of the chair and presses his fingers in a steeple. "My daughter does seem to… It does seem that way." His face is openly displaying emotion, the buttons of his dress shirt left undone at the collar. He is disheveled.

"You messed up," I say, my voice raw with surprise. "You didn't plan for this."

Viktor's eyes lift to mine. "My daughter has always found ways to astonish me."

Seth lets out a low whistle.

Viktor gives a rare chuckle. He gets to his feet. "I need some time, boys. I need to figure out my next steps."

I cock a brow. "And us? What are we supposed to do?"

Viktor smiles. "You know, I have no idea, but it's always best to keep as many pieces as possible. There is no telling when a pawn can be of use."

He is in an oddly weird mood for having every plan and contingency destroyed. I give him a rude gesture. "I'm more than a pawn."

"Would you prefer to be a rook or bishop?"

Seth shakes his head, and I laugh despite myself. "Fuck you."

"Stay here. The collar will prevent you from controlling the elements." His eyes shift from me to my brother. "You, however, are coming with me."

I lurch to my feet. "Like hell."

"Mr. Byron," Viktor says, sliding his hands in his front pockets.

I twitch at the name. The whispers start back up, begging to watch his skin split and bleed. I blink, tensing up to fight the urge.

Viktor lifts his brows at me. "You and I both know how this works."

My fists clench at my sides. "I'll stay put. I'll give you my word."

"And I am to trust you?" Viktor inclines his head with humorous cynicism. "You and I have been playing this game for a long time. We are both on familiar ground, and even without the use of magic, you still carry a viable threat to me."

"And," I shove through bared teeth, "we both do exactly what we say we will."

He tilts his head, contemplating. "I'm sorry, my son, I am, but I cannot take even the smallest risk at this time. Seth, follow me."

As Viktor turns away, I meet my brother's eyes. He gives me a flashed smile and claps me on the shoulder. "It's okay, big brother." He winks. "I'll be fine. Just stay here, yeah? So I can be fine?"

I jerk my chin at him. "Yeah, I'll be here."

"Breakfast and dinner will be delivered," Viktor calls out over his shoulder as he exits the room. "You're free to do anything you want within the confines of this room. Should you leave this room without my permission, there will be repercussions for your brother."

I stare at him with zero humor. He closes the door. I don't hear the telltale click of a tumbler, which means he didn't even bother to lock it.

CHAPTER 57

DECLAN

I wake up in the middle of the night, my chest constricted with fear. I rub over my lungs, my skin clammy with sweat. My lower leg is throbbing, and I throw the covers to the side, expecting blood and bone sticking out of the leg to match the intensity of the pain, but there's nothing.

I rub the back of my calf, unable to shake the extreme tightness of panic in my chest. I sit up against the headboard and stare out the window at the moonlight. I bend my knees and elbows, curling into a sort of ball, burying my face in my hands.

The overwhelming panic spikes, and I jerk my head up, blinking at the shadows around Ella's bedroom. Everywhere I look is wrong. There are so many mirrors. I grimace and shove my hand through my hair, feeling it damp with sweat.

Something is wrong. I close my eyes and pinch my nose, digging deep into my mind. A full-blown panic smacks through me, and my eyes snap open. "Ella," I whisper.

I reach out again. *"Ella? Lover? Can you…? Is that you?"*

"What is this?"

"A bond. Blood magic. Did I bite you?"

"I fed you—you were—"

"Yeah, got it. I don't need you to finish that sentence," I snarl at the empty air before me. I rest back, tipping my head against the headboard and closing my eyes. I breathe in through my nose and try to find calm to shove through our link to her. *"Where are you?"*

"I don't know. It's dark. I can't see anything, hear anything."

"You're hurt."

"My leg."

"I can feel it. It's okay. Just breathe. Listen to me and take deep breaths."

The panic ebbs away, the tide pulling back from shore, still present but less.

"Okay," I think, *"good. Just keep calm. Can you control the elements? Make a light, try and tell me where you are."*

"Oh, Haven, I'm buried, I'm buried!" The fear comes rushing back through me like a tidal wave, and I grit my teeth, my own heart jacking to full speed in my chest.

"Ella, calm down."

"It's caved in all around me. My leg it's stuck. It's crushed."

Pain lights up my leg, and I double over, clutching at it in reflex. I grunt, rubbing the place below my knee. *"Stop trying to move it."*

"I'm stuck. I'm stuck! I can't move. I can't dissipate like this. I tried to blast my way out, and it all caved in closer."

I pinch the bridge of my nose and try to fight through her fear. I need to calm her down. I rack my brain for what I do when I'm afraid. I need to distract her, so I feed memories through to her, my favorites that I've played on a loop over and over for the last five cycles.

"I was this close to ripping your throat out," I shove out through clenched teeth. *"I have to go."*

"Feed on me," she begs in a soft whisper.

My knees almost give out. "Ella."

"Feed on me," she repeats in a shaky voice, lifting her eyes to mine with determination like she needs me.

I work my jaw side to side to release the tension, then work my hands open and closed to bring blood back to the extremities. I try to stay calm, but when she stands on her toes and clasps my face, I tense up, freezing and baring my teeth in warning. She blinks at me, and I close my lips, pressing them together hard. Her lips press against mine like she doesn't care that I'm about to lose control. Like she isn't afraid of me.

Getting her naked, running hands over her skin, feeling her respond to my touch and moan in pleasure. Bringing her to orgasm and thrusting into her. Sinking my teeth in her arm when I find my own release, the pleasure and taste of her satisfying my most primal urges.

I get an arm under her, moving her from the middle of the bed up to the pillows. She's limp and light as a feather, easy for me to tuck in and slide behind. I press her to me, one arm over her, keeping her close and safe.

I brush the hair away from her face and stare down at her, head throbbing in time with my heart like every other part of me. She's half-unconscious already from being fucked, and I grin down at her until I catch sight of the bite mark on her arm already bruised.

I slide the ring on her finger as carefully as I can with haste. I'm not taking a chance, not wasting another second, terrified she might change her mind after what I've done. I get the band over her knuckle and stare down at the dim yellow sapphire, thinking I ought to have cleaned it up first.

She smirks at me, lips pulled to one side, a mischievous light to those eyes. "I agree to commit to a bond."

I lose my breath, my stomach dropping away. I can't decide if I want to puke or kiss this woman. I can't believe she's agreeing to this, to me. My hand grips hers tighter as I echo those words, staring at her, waiting for her to recoil with hatred, but she doesn't.

"Consider yourselves married," Sordello says, and there's some whistling and clapping. I don't care. I have what I need, and now I want to be alone with her. I dissipate us to the only place I can think of where no one is ever going to find us.

My heart rate is slower, my limbs too heavy to move. I relax into the mattress and ignore the wet leaking out the corners of my eyes.

"Declan?"

"Memories."

There's a whole lot going on in her head, a barrage of fear, longing, pain, and heartbreak. I smirk. *"You just have to get to me, and it's all yours. I'm yours. And your memories. I have them. You can have them back."*

"I can't."

"Lover, you have more power in your little toes than any other being in Caleum. You can. You just need to stay calm. Clear your mind." I open my eyes, fixating on all the details of the room around me. I see it all and hold it in my mind, my heart beating hard in my chest. *"You can do this."*

The air crackles and the strum in my chest elevates, not my heartbeat but the drain of energy. I sigh, giving in to it, letting her draw from me whatever she needs.

The pull ceases, and I blink my eyes open, pushing myself into a sitting position. She stands at the foot of the bed, the scent of her blood punctuating the air. It stains the side of her face, clotted on her forehead from an open wound. As my eyes meet hers, she whimpers, eyes welling.

"Fuck," I growl, scrambling to her.

She limps one step forward, falling as her injured leg gives way. I grunt, ignoring the pain knowing my leg is fine, and catch her against my chest. I wrap my arms around her, wanting to latch on tight but fighting not to so I don't crush her.

She sobs, and it wrenches my lungs, setting my chest on fire. I bury my nose against her hair, the scent of honey. I bare my teeth and hold her as she comes undone. Her tears are wet against my chest, like acid eating my skin as they fall, and I'm helpless to stop it.

I can't stand doing nothing, so I pry her blubbering face away from me and meet her eyes. She sniffles, her lower lip quaking, and snot leaking from her nose, but she's beautiful. I kiss her forehead, the tip of her nose, and then her mouth.

I press my lips to hers and move away. I keep finding new places to kiss, and she quiets, pulling her face away to wipe her nose with her hand. She draws one shaking breath then blinks at me with clumped lashes and swollen, red eyes.

She is staring at me. She's lost. I can feel her, and I throw myself into our bond. I throw every ounce of my shrewd, shrunken heart through to her. Her eyes well up, and it ties my chest into knots.

I stare back, watching, waiting. She swallows and leans into me, but there are no more tears. All that is left is the chasm of agony yawning within our minds, threatening to swallow us and drag us to the very depths of despair.

"We can figure this out. You and me." There's a ball of emotion strangling my voice, but I don't try to hide it. "You promised me. You don't remember, but you promised me."

She leans into me, breathing unevenly and sniffling. I crush her against me as if I could make this go away with sheer force. I ease up, pulling her into my lap. She mewls with pain, and I run my hands over her legs, up her sides. I want to take her pain away.

"You really love me," she whispers.

"Lover," I say with a grin, "you have no idea."

"I do," she answers in the same soft voice.

She is thinking about Erac, and it makes me want to peel my flesh off and dig this bond out of my skull in a highly physical manner. She trembles with a small laugh. My lips twitch. At least she still finds me funny.

"Haven," she says on a breath and snuggles into me. "Declan?"

She doesn't call me Dec. I try not to react.

"What was that?" She picks her head up. "You just…" She frowns. "I felt something."

I breathe out slowly. "Dec, you always call me Dec."

"Oh."

"It's okay. I called you princess when I lost my memories, and you hated that, so this makes us even." She hums at me, relaxing, her weight settling against me. I kiss the top of her head. Getting my arm under her legs and twisting her body to cradle her in my lap, I press my lips against her temple. "I've got you."

She nods, hiccupping.

"I've got you, and I'm never letting go." My words soothe the angry wounds inside her. I rock her, keeping her close. "I'm going to stand up now."

Her hands reach out, curling around my neck, her nails digging into my skin. It doesn't matter. I have her.

Forcing my numb legs to work, I get them under me and stand, hoisting her with me. I limp to the bed and lay her in the soft safety. I brush the hair from her face and kiss her forehead again, ignoring my urge to lick the blood from her cheek.

"Do you want me in bed with you?" She tenses, fear coiling. I grunt. "I know what that prick did to you, and I'm not going to do that. I'm not going to hurt you either. You need sleep. I'm not going to fucking touch you unless you want me to."

The fear uncoils, dissolving, and she turns her face against my chest. "I believe you."

"Damn well better fucking believe me, princess."

I go to the other side of the bed, rolling into it and shifting next to her. I lay on my side, giving her space so as not to smother her or scare her, but she reaches for my hand, weaving my fingers in hers.

I close my eyes, blinking, and when I open them, the room is full of light. I come to face down, one arm stuck out next to me, smothered in something warm and soft. I lift my head and groggily stare at my wife asleep next to me. That thought sings through me.

For the first time ever, I get to wake up next to my fucking wife.

Something in me crackles, like breaking glass.

Oh fuck.

I ram fingers and thumb into my eyes and rub hard. I blink, stretching them open, and repeat.

She's snoring away still, but my arm is numb. It's aching and tingling, but I don't want to wake her. With the patience of the saint I am not, I drag my arm from beneath her, then inch close enough to put an arm over her.

CHAPTER 58

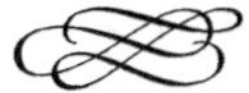

MORELLA

Bright light exists behind my eyes, the air tasting fresh and cool on the back of my tongue as I breathe through my nose. Fingers are running through the strands of my hair, a gentle caress. My eyelids flutter open, and I blink against the harsh glare of my surroundings. Trying to focus my blurry sight, my eyes start to water, and I rub them to be rid of the phosphorous and wetness.

I bolt upright, glaring around. Declan lifts his eyebrows at me, his features soft, his eyes a bit swollen. I frown at him and scrub a hand down my face.

Looking around us at the unfamiliar room, I cross my arms over my chest, curling into bent up knees. "Where are we?"

"Your rooms."

I cut my eyes, thinking these aren't my rooms.

He shakes his head. "Your rooms in Byron, your rooms before you lost all your memories."

I look around at the gilded, fancy furniture. There are about a dozen mirrors hanging on the walls or sitting on the chest of drawers. The walls are a cheery yellow, the wood golden, and the curtains lace with bright floral embroidery.

"This is *my* bedroom?"

"Sort of." He laughs. "Your disdain is understandable. Your sister Selene redecorated."

I get the image of the room with dark mahogany, done up with dark violet and creamy whites. Turning my head to him, I frown. "Is that you?" He nods. "Oh."

"That's what it used to look like, and if you hate this, you're going to really love your sitting room."

I frown and close my eyes, rubbing my temples. "Do that again."

He pictures the room in our minds again, and I concentrate on it, willing the elements to bend to my desires. The energy strums in my chest, a pleasurable pulse of release. When I open my eyes, the room is transformed.

I throw the covers away from me and slide off the bed with my back to him. I take two steps and stop, staring down at my leg. Blood stains my skin, but the flesh is seamless, and the bone is back inside of me. I eye him over my shoulder and point to it. "What happened?"

He props his head on an arm and smirks. "Spirit runes."

I nod. "Right. Where's the bathroom?"

He nods at the double doors leading out of the room. "Across the sitting room on the right."

"Thank you."

I step into the sitting room and stop. The furniture is white with pink, blue, and purple flowers painted on all of it. The curtains are white lace, the walls a bright yellow that hurts my eyes. "What's this room supposed to look like?" I yell over my shoulder.

He finds it funny, and I get a mental image. I fix the room and stomp to the dark wood door on the far wall. I rip it open and step inside. Flipping the light, I study the gold fixtures and massive mirrors. I sigh and shove my fingers through my hair.

"What about this one?" I yell. He's laughing. I can feel it. I squirm and rub my eyes. *"This is weird."*

"You get used to it," he says.

I glance back at him, standing shirtless behind me. He juts his head into the room and laughs. "She really liked mirrors."

I massage each temple with two fingers. "Show me."

A knock on the door makes me twitch, and I turn around. He puts both hands on the doorway and blocks me inside. He shakes his head. "I'll get it. Shower," he jerks his chin to the room behind me. "I'll explain everything."

I narrow my eyes. "If you—"

"Lie to you? Try to trick you? Hide something?" He wiggles his eyebrows at me, guides me further into the bathroom with gentle encouragement, and closes the door. *"How am I supposed to fucking lie to you when you can hear every thought?"*

I turn around and face the room. *"There are so many mirrors."*

A clear image comes into my mind, and for a third time, I fixate on his mental picture to alter the room. I shower and clean up, scrubbing myself clean until my skin is raw. I exit the bathroom in a short black dress with a loose skirt and high neckline.

Declan is sitting in the window seat, staring out the window. The morning light plays well on his features. He notices my eyes on him and turns toward me. I smile with closed lips, spinning the ornate yellow sapphire on my finger.

He stands, still shirtless. I look down, rubbing the back of my neck and shoulder. "Ahem, do you have a shirt?"

"Why? Want me to put one on?"

Startled by his teasing tone, I meet his eyes. My eyes roam over his bare torso cut with rippling muscles. My cheeks warm with embarrassment as I look away.

"What's wrong, lover?" His voice has dropped to a husky whisper. "Too much for you to handle?"

I glance at him, my eyes sliding over his skin, black cloth

pants slung low, cut hips and a trail of dark hair leading beneath. "Haven." I turn my back to him. "Put a shirt on."

He laughs, the sound coming from his chest. He presses against my back, the warmth of his skin soaking into me. "I can smell—"

"Stop," I squeak as his hands grip my hips, pressing me back into his own arousal.

His lips brush against my neck, and he whispers in that deep, growly voice that I feel between my legs. "What I was going to say, or what I am going to do to you?"

I swallow, every part of me tensed. I'm struggling to breathe evenly. I squeeze my eyes shut, and spin around. He lets me move freely but keeps his hands on my waist. I open my eyes to see him staring down with a hunger in his.

"You're an incredibly attractive individual," I manage with a breathless voice. "There's not a woman who would not be attracted to you."

He smirks. "I hope you think I'm attractive. I'm your fucking husband."

I clear my throat. *"Why in Haven's name could I have not woken up with no memories but with this man instead?"*

"Because that prick took you and stole your memories to keep you from me."

My eyes stretch open wide. I hiss and shove him away from me. "Stop doing that."

He laughs and grins at me. "Fuck, lover." He rubs a hand over his mouth, but he's still grinning when his hand drops away. *"Feels damn good to hear you again."*

"Sit." He jerks his head to the couch, grinning at me.

I shuffle forward, plopping down in front of a tray of food. My stomach grumbles and clenches and I dig in without hesitating. The eggs are fluffy, the fruit fresh, and I enjoy every bite.

Declan chuckles as he settles next to me. I take a drink of water and glance at the empty tray. "Did you already eat?"

He shakes his head. "No, that's all there was."

Guilt pangs in my stomach. "I'm sorry."

His hand rests on my knee, and his soft gray eyes meet mine. "Don't. I ate dinner, and I suspect you didn't."

I sigh and hesitate, my hand hovering over his. I can't decide if I want to put mine on his or rip his away. He pulls back, and I lift my eyes to his once more. "Declan— Dec, I..." the words die in my throat. I don't know what to say.

"You don't have to say anything." His eyes never leave mine. *"I'm not going to push you, but you're going to have to accept that old habits die hard. I'll try, though."*

I smile, reaching out to take his hand. He lets me, not fighting or helping, just limp in my grasp to let me do whatever I want. I set his palm on my thigh at the edge of my skirt again, laying my own over it.

"It's okay." I clear my throat. I conjure a comb to work through my hair.

He's watching me. "Why did you cut it?"

I lift my eyes to him. I frown, staring down, trying to remember. "I don't know. I don't remember cutting it, so I must have done it before?" I look up into his scowl.

He shakes his head. "The last time I saw you before this whole mess, you had hair down to your ass."

I grab at the ends around my shoulders. "I didn't do it then. I woke up like this."

"Prick." He sighs, squeezing my thigh.

"I can fix it."

He gives me a weak, one-sided grin. "If you want. I don't mind; it's just different."

I nod, staring at the comb in my hand. "Right. Explain..." I say, trying to put into words what I want to know. I grit my teeth and clench the comb. "What happened?"

He shrugs, leaning back into the couch, head back to the ceiling. "I don't know much. We were drugged, and then I had my throat slit. I was too incapacitated to know what was going on. Marx kept me alive somehow." He picks his head up to meet my gaze. "It was a fucking shit show. I know that much from reports, but I don't know much more. I was bleeding out."

I nod, returning to working through the knots in my hair. "And then?"

"And then..." He takes a deep breath and winces. "I was getting information from Selene, figured out where you were, and then..." He stops.

My chest constricts, and a sickness burns in my stomach. I exhale and form an O with my mouth.

His jaw clamps and he turns his face away from me, his palm a bit damp against my skin. "I felt him rape you."

I stare down at his trembling hand on my leg. "I don't remember it. I guess that's why he removed my memories a second time."

Declan lets loose a bitter sound, halfway between laughter and a groan. "That prick is going to die for what he did."

"He's dead," I say. "Permanently. I ate part of his heart and destroyed the rest so he couldn't heal."

His eyes never waver from mine despite my expectance of disgust. One side of his lips twist up. "Lover, I don't give a fuck if it means he's gone, and you're safe."

"Anyway..." I clear my throat and exhale. "Where are we now?" I ask, shifting to angle myself toward him.

"Your suite in Byron Palace."

"And this?" I reach out and tap the metal band around his neck.

His lips twist to the side with disgust. "That is a gift from Viktor. It works to keep me from controlling the elements."

I frown, wrapping fingers under the band and force it to change to air. Relief washes through me that I suspect belongs to him. "I guess that's better?"

He bobs his head, running a hand at the base of his throat. "Thanks."

I nod. "My father is here?"

"Yes, and he's got Seth somewhere. The rules of the game are I stay here in this room until he decides, and Seth stays safe."

My lips purse. "Seth, your brother? The really tall one with lots of frizzy brown hair, right?"

"That's the one."

I recall putting a blade through his heart. "Sorry about that."

He shrugs. "He's not dead. He'll get over it. He doesn't stay mad about things. It's a perk with him."

"Seth," I say, getting a strange elation in my chest. I cock my head at him. "Is that you?"

He shakes his head. "That is you, probably your soul. When Erac killed me, you got your half from me back. It's going to remember things even if your mind doesn't. I had it when that asshole ripped your memories away, so it still remembers."

I rub the space between my breasts and frown. "It feels…" I hesitate, "like happiness."

He reaches out and tucks wet hair behind one ear. "You two have a thing," he says, twisting the word. "And I don't like it."

I giggle. "I can see that, just by the look on your face."

He hums and cocks a brow. "And you think it's funny? I've nearly ripped his arms off because of it."

I shake my head at him, my mouth curved in a smile. *"This is nice."* I lift my eyes to his and soak under his gaze. *I can't believe I forgot his face, the sound of his voice. How did I forget a man like this?*

"Blood magic," he says curtly. "It's a bitch. So is getting your memories back, by the way. That's a hellish experience all its own."

My smile fades. "I want them back."

He holds his hand up, the other still on my leg. "Easy. I'm not keeping them from you, just giving you a forewarning."

I nod. "Okay."

We settle into the silence, but I feel him inside my mind. His anxiety and trepidation. His concern for me, what they've done to me, if I'm alright, if I'll still want him.

"Yes," I say, whispering to the air. "Yes, to all of it."

I turn, putting a hand on his face. I smirk and scratch the underside of his jaw. His eyes roll back into his head, and his mouth turns up in a lazy grin.

He wraps his fingers around my wrist in a light grip and plants a kiss in the middle of my palm. "I've missed the ever-living fuck out of you."

I hum at him, fury streaking through my chest. I'm pissed that I didn't miss him. I should have. "You said my father is here?"

Lifting a hand, he stares at me with a serious expression. "First, Viktor, not your father, and you only called him by his first name. Your father is a spirit named Sordello."

I swallow, my hands starting to shake. He has all the answers I've longed for, begged for, and he's throwing them out like random words that mean nothing. "Anything else?"

He smirks. "Not right now."

"Good." I stand, rage churning in my stomach. "Where is he?"

"I don't know." Declan stands, taking my trembling hands in his, meeting my welling eyes as the fury overcomes me. He grimaces and nods once. "We'll find him."

I grip his hands tighter and close my eyes, fixating on the image of my father. I don't know where he is. It doesn't matter. I'll find him. Exhaling, I focus on being with Viktor, the cold seeping through me as my elements tear apart.

"He's going to pay for it, all of it, in blood and pain."

CHAPTER 59

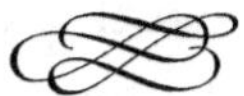

MORELLA

I lace my fingers in Declan's as I rebuild us. My eyes open, and I stare around a massive white marble room. Viktor stands in the middle, the outer edge lined with finely dressed individuals. I tear my eyes from my surroundings to focus on Viktor, and his jaw goes slack as our eyes meet.

"Declan, my boy. I thought I had made it clear you were going to stay put?"

Declan's fingers tighten on mine, and he shrugs. "In my defense, she made me." He points to me.

"Ah, you brought me my daughter. I knew you wouldn't let me down."

My eyes cut to him. He frowns back. *"Really? You're going to think I was helping him?"*

Aloud he clears his throat and flashes a smile. "Oh, I brought your daughter to you, but I think you're going to regret it." He lifts my knuckles to his curved lips, his soft gray eyes dancing.

I tilt my head. *"What are you so happy about?"*

"The last time two times you let loose, you destroyed a palace, and I didn't get to see it either time. Now I want to see it. Give him hell."

I narrow my eyes and pull my hand away from Dec as I step toward Viktor. His smile falters, and I grin. "Hello, Viktor."

He purses his lips, his eyes dropping to his polished dress shoes. "I see."

"Where is Seth?"

He rubs the back of his neck, the left corner of his mouth twitching. "He is somewhere tucked away nicely."

My blood begins to boil, the pressure hissing in my ears. "You won't tell me?" I ask in a whisper full of rage. "Fine."

I throw my arm out and splay my palm, eyes slipping closed as I picture Seth. The air rustles, and the energy strums out of me. Opening my eyes, I glance over to see Seth gaping at me.

"Ell." He laughs and takes a step toward me.

I hold my hand up. "You stand there and shut up," I snap, dropping my hands to my hips, facing down Viktor. "Look me in the eye and tell me the truth. You owe me that much."

Lifting his head, Viktor meets my gaze, his eyes the color of poison. "Morella."

"Ella." I draw the shortened version of my name out. "I go by Ella."

He slips his hands in his front pockets. "Yes, your friends have given you that nickname."

"Thanks, I hadn't learned that on my own. Was there anything else you wanted to tell me?" My heart is hammering, my vision tunneling, and widening in time with the beats.

The left side of his face flinches. "You are my daughter."

"No." I hold a finger up. "No, what I am is pissed off. You stole my memories. You lied to me. Was there anything you didn't lie to me about?"

There are whispers in my ears. I don't know if they are in my head or the world beyond my skin. My hand is shaking before me as I wait for him to answer.

"Please, understand—"

"What did you do to George?" I breathe in fire. "He tried to tell me the truth, and you punished him. He was a kid trying to tell the truth, and you hurt him for it."

He jerks his chin up, so he stares down his nose at me. "That boy was an insolent servant, beneath your status. You deigned to talk with him, and he—"

"He knew the truth!" I scream, leaning toward Viktor. "He was going to tell me the truth, so you kept him quiet. How?"

My father—Viktor—rocks on his heels and slides his hands in his front pockets. He stares at the floor, the thinking frown obscured. "A few lashes to encourage his cooperation and a conversation. Nothing he wouldn't recover from."

I scream, clawing at the air. Viktor recoils like I slapped him, a gash left behind in his cheek. He steps back, eyes wide, as he lifts a hand to the wound.

I lift my hand, he flies upward, and I draw it down. His body slams into the ground with an agonizing splat. I grit my teeth and back off. I want him alive. I want to hear the truth.

"How many lies, Viktor? How many lies did you tell me? I killed for you. I delivered the spirits to Damnatus for you! All those souls trying to save me from you, and you made me kill them for it."

He starts to sit, twisting to get off the floor. "You do not understand," he says through clenched teeth. "Everything that I have done, I did for you."

I laugh with a bitter hollowness. "Me? You ripped my mind apart, kept me away from a man who loves me and left me Erac. Do you know how many times he hurt me?"

"Yes, trusting Erac was a miscalculation."

"Miscalculation?" I repeat in a hysterical laugh. "Everything you did, you did for yourself. You're pathetic, seeking daddy's approval."

"Enough!" he roars, daring to take a step toward me. "That is quite enough, Morella. Now, you have had your tantrum."

My head tips back, and I cackle with all the hatred breaking free of my blood. I fixate my eyes on him, lifting my hands and gathering air between them. I feed the hatred into the air, my hands shaking, and the ground starting to quake.

"Morella, you will not."

I release it, every feeling of rage, fury, heartache, the nights Erac touched me making me sick, the blinding need to know who I am, the air shattering like a bomb of emotion. It detonates into Viktor, and he lets out a blood-curdling scream. He falls to the floor on all fours.

Blood drips from him, his shirt staining red in the blink of an eye. I step forward, watching him cough and spit blood on the floor. I reach down, digging my fingers into his bleeding shoulder, wrenching him to his knees so I can stare down into his eyes.

"A thousand cuts for a thousand lies," I snarl. He gapes with eyes muted in pain, which brings a grin to my face.

I shove him back, and he gives with no resistance. He hits the ground on his back and groans, breathing raggedly. His eyes fall half shut as he watches me. "My daughter."

"I am not your daughter!" I scream, slamming a shock wave of compressed air down into him. "You lied to me. You used me. I almost killed children for you. How much blood do I have on my hands because of you?"

My sight is blurry, my eyes stinging as they blink. Wet is cold against my cheeks as I draw in a shaky breath.

Viktor's chest shudders, and I watch as he struggles to push himself into a sitting position. He stares up at me, blood leaking from every inch of him with an unfocused gaze. "Erac brought you back to me. He stole your memories, gave me another chance."

I hiss at him, reaching down to grab his chin, forcing him to meet my eyes. "Have the decency to look me in the eye. Or are you not man enough to manage that?"

"I wanted you to understand, to take your place with me," he says, his voice thin with agony.

Tears are starting to burn my eyes, not of pain but rage and fury. "I had no memories. All I had were your lies."

"I was trying to help you."

I shove his face out of my hand, snarling. "You were helping *you*. I almost killed the Bard brothers because I believed you. Did you know he was my husband when you poisoned me against him?"

Viktor rips rage-filled eyes to me. "Yes, I knew."

I take a step back, my heart hammering as I gape at him.

He sneers, trying to sit up again, his arms flopping, grunting with pain. "I admit, I have made mistakes, that being one of a larger of them. I helped to steal your memories. I kept you close. I wanted a chance to make you see how much I love you, my daughter."

I draw in a shaky breath, staring at him with my fists clenched and vibrating at my sides. Every muscle in my body is quivering.

"Do you even know what love is?" I ask him, blinking tears out. They roll down my cheeks, my voice trembling in time with my lower lip.

"I do. I know what love is, and believe me when I tell you, I love you."

I glance over my shoulder at Declan, standing with his arms crossed and eyes pegged on me. One side of his mouth pulls back, and he jerks his chin at me.

"Go on. I'll be here when you're done." He smiles. *"Loving the fuck out of you."*

Turning back to Viktor, I push the whispers begging for me to rip him apart away. I want him to hurt. He should pay in blood, but it's not enough. I want more. I glance down at the ring on my finger, the glass bearing beneath it, and smirk.

I pull air elements together, heating them and spinning them together to form glass. His blood lifts off the floor under my command, churning, and I feed it into the small orb. I focus, wanting every wicked memory of pain and the nightmares he's suffered to collect.

I leer at him with a twisted smile. "I'm not going to kill you." I grab at the air, pulling every good, kind, blissful memory from his blood until it churns in the air. "That's every last single decent thought or moment you've had in your life."

His eyes shift from me to the swarm. He grunts, his gaze moving back to me. I kneel next to him, holding the glass bearing up for him to see.

My voice is a hoarse whisper. "And that is every terrible moment in your life. You're going to relive every terror you've ever lived over and over for eternity. Every embarrassment, every heartbreak, every pain you've ever suffered, over and over again." I eye the blood churning with his pleasant memories, throwing my hand toward it, so it dissolves to nothing.

"No," he groans. He reaches, swinging to grab hold of me. His arms twitch, and he winces.

I kneel next to him, meeting his gaze. "I'll let you live. I'll give you a crown. You'll be emperor of your own hell, locked away somewhere I can come to enjoy your screams whenever I want."

"Please, Morella."

I ram the orb into his forehead to plant the nightmares deep in his mind. "It's Ella."

Viktor collapses back, starting to whimper, his eyes rolling in the back of his head. I sneer down at him as he flinches and croons on the floor.

Two hands run up my arms, and I flinch, turning my head to the side. Declan kisses my forehead and then cranes over my shoulder to stare at Viktor. "Seth might want to say hi now, and he deserves this fate," he says, jerking his chin over my shoulder, "but until Viktor dies, the spirits are trapped in Damnatus."

I turn in his hands, lifting my eyes to his. I expect fear or disgust, a revulsion to what I've done, but there is none. I bob my head, leaning into him. The whispers are fading, and my knees buckle as I sob.

He catches me, lowering us to the floor. He holds me as I cling to him. Footsteps approach and someone settles down near us. "Aw, I'm not one to pass up a group hug."

Declan's chest rumbles with laughter, vibrating with his deep voice as two arms squeeze me from behind. "Get the fuck off me, little brother."

"Shh," Seth hushes him. "I need this more than I care about your feelings. Are you crying, Ell? It's okay. I forgive you for stabbing me in the heart."

A laugh trickles out of me, and I smile against Declan's chest, embraced in solid warmth. I squeeze my eyes shut and breathe deep. For the first time in my life—as I remember it anyway—I am whole.

CHAPTER 60

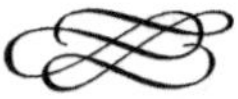

DECLAN

I fish her memories out of the room in Dis as Ella watches. I shove the massive four-poster bed to the side and pull up the stone slab, digging my fingers in the dirt beneath it, relief filling my chest as my fingers lock around the leather pouch.

Pulling it out, I turn my head to her, holding it up for her to see. I stare at her in the black dress. I'm tempted to tilt my head closer to the ground to catch a glimpse under the short skirt. Her eyes narrow at me, but she's fighting back a grin.

She holds an open palm out, and I twist to my feet, trying to hand the bearings over, but the pouch is gone from my grip and in hers before I can blink. I smirk, stepping to her, grabbing her by the hips.

I nuzzle her neck. "You can trust me, you know."

She bats me away, pulling the pouch open to dump the bearings into her hand. She frowns at them, picking one up and holding it against her arm. She's measuring the size, gauging if I'm telling her the truth. I bite my lower lip and laugh at her even as she lifts blazing eyes at me.

I hold my hands in front of me. "You can try to catch me in a lie, but lover, you hear every thought, and I'm not lying."

She sighs, sliding all the bearings back into the pouch. "Fine. What now?"

I twist my lips, glancing around, and then tilt my head, studying her face. "You need somewhere to put them in and break them. Somewhere you'll be comfortable." I grin, thinking of the perfect place.

She nods, stepping into me, her face against my chest. "Show me."

Closing my eyes, I hold tight to the image of the top floor of the Byron library, where we used to meet during our betrothal. The indention in the floor is full of cushions, perfect for lying on to stare through the glass dome above. It all feels like eons ago, the image hazy, but she picks up on my thoughts, wanting to know more.

I shake my head. "We'll get you your memories back, and you'll know everything." She rolls her eyes, and I smile at the gesture. I tuck hair behind her ear and kiss her forehead. "Come on, just dissipate us to the dining hall. You need to eat something. Trust me, you'll want something in you before you do this."

She inhales deep, eyes closing. "I do." Her eyes flitter open. "Trust you."

I clasp her face in my hands and kiss her, slowly, savoring her. She leans into it, into me, and the tension between my ribs lessens. When I crack one eye and pull back, she's grinning, her eyes fluttering open.

I grin, taking her hand, bringing her knuckles to my lips. The cold tingle spreads through me as she tears me apart. I don't mind when she rips me to pieces in this fashion, but I'm hoping it's the only way that I'm ever torn up again.

We sit on our own. A servant approaches, tall and lanky with blond hair and purple eyes. He grins, taking a seat across from us. "Ella, thank Haven, you're back."

She gives him a timid smile, eyes shifting to me.

"Dean," I say, then narrow my eyes at him. "Food, and back the fuck off for a few. You're on a long waiting list to talk to her, but you're all fucking waiting until she gets her memories back and her head on straight."

Dean bobs his head, rubbing the back of his neck. "Makes sense." Still, his gaze fixes on her. "Whatever happened, though, I'm glad you're back. I'll keep defending you. I owe you everything."

"Bourbon, food," I say flatly.

"Please," Ella whispers. Her hand reaches for mine on the table, splaying over it, her fingers nestling between mine. She squeezes, her heart rolling with pleasure at the way I guard her. "Thank you."

I turn, pressing a kiss against her forehead as she leans into me. "You know you don't need me," I whisper, resting my chin on the top of her head. "You've never needed me. Wanted me, maybe, yeah, but you've never needed me."

"I do," she whispers back. "I need this."

One side of my mouth pulls back. "I love the ever-loving fuck out of you, and I'm not going to stop, but we're still in one hell of a fucking mess, lover. Things aren't going to be easy, and come what may, I need you to know you can stand on your own. You've always had more power in your cute little toes than anyone else in their whole body."

She breathes out, moving closer. "Dec."

"Right here. Not going anywhere, not letting anyone near you right now either. You're safe."

She nods against me as Dean serves up a meal. His eyes draw over Ella and me, and he smiles. "You two need anything, just send for me. I'll take care of it, okay?"

I lift my chin and direct him away with my eyes. Ella slides the plate closer. Together we pick at the meat in silence, the broken pieces in us stretching tentatively closer.

The others around the hall give curious glances, the Duke of Deveraux even approaches, but I shake my head at him. He stops short, frowning. I wince, knowing I need to tell him the truth sooner or later, but right now, I'm not ready. Neither is Ella. We need time, and it's been less than a day.

When she shoves the plate away, I stand, draining my whiskey and offering her a hand. "Come on."

"Where are we going?"

I shake my head. "We're walking, give the food in you time to settle so you don't throw it up, but we're going to the library."

She gives me the saddest grin I've ever seen in my life, and I groan, pulling her against me. I spin her, tucking her under my arm, and move us out of the dining hall. I warn everyone away with glares and narrowed eyes when they have the courage to meet my gaze, and I use the elements to open the door for us to exit.

She grips the bearings tight, holding them against her chest. We weave through the corridors, and I glance behind us, the sense of being followed tickling at the hairs on the back of my neck. But when I turn, I don't catch sight of anything out of place. I sigh, directing her down a passage on the left.

We reach the massive carved double doors of the library and stop. Her lips part and she steps before me, eyes glued to the doors.

I chuckle. "I thought you'd want to see those again like it was the first time."

She nods, not looking at me. Her hand reaches out, touching the carved wood. "Yes."

I give her time to stand there and stare, her head tipped back. I step to her, hands gripping her shoulders, massaging the muscles connecting to her neck. She sighs and droops against me.

"Alright." I kiss her temple and use the elements to open the door for her. "In we go, up to the top."

Without commenting, she steps inside, eyes opening wide. She stops inside the door and inhales deep. I know she's savoring the scent of books, and I laugh, scooping her off her feet.

Her eyes pop open and stare up at me. "Dec?"

"Go on, enjoy it. I'll carry you while you do your thing."

She smiles, her head tipping back. "Have you always been so incredible to me?"

I wince. I really want to lie to her right now but shake my head. "Honestly, no. Fuck no. But if you give me a chance, I'll try a lot harder from now on."

She frowns and picks her head up, lifting her eyes to mine as I glance down at her while climbing the stairs, spiraling around. She studies me, and I cock a brow. She puts her head back down and nestles against me.

"You know," she says, "I really doubt that you've been awful to me."

I chuckle. "Lover, you need to get your memories back. Just keep in mind you've already forgiven me for all of it, though, okay? You said yes. You married me."

She chortles, snorting through her nose and nuzzling her head against my shoulder. "Are you going to start demanding that I love you?"

"I'm going to break if you don't, but no, that's entirely up to you if you do or don't. Just promise me..." I stop, shifting her and grunting. "Promise me again that we'll figure it out, and this really is the last time we have to."

"Promise," she whispers.

I drop my eyes to see hers closed again. The heart in me swells. If Haven thinks that it can keep us apart, then it hasn't been paying attention. There is nothing, *nothing,* I wouldn't do to stay by her side. I smile, getting us to the top of the library, and walk through the shelves to the center where the floor opens and is cut out, full of cushions.

I step to the indent in the floor and kneel, lowering her into the cushions. She opens her eyes, staring up at me. I stay there, staring right back, reaching out to brush the hair away from her face, my thumb trailing over her cheekbone.

Fuck, she's beautiful.

Her eyes shift, her lashes lowering to hide those bright purple irises from me, a blush creeping across her face. I smirk, sitting and sliding down to join her.

She turns into me, holding the bag of bearings close against her heart but cuddling into me. I get my arm behind her, and my lips find her temple. Holding her, breathing her in, my eyes close, and my body starts to relax for the first time in revolutions.

Sitting up, I nudge her. "Come on. Get your memories back; I'm not going anywhere."

She flounders, trying to find stability, then kneels next to me. I take the pouch from her, setting it on the side, and dig my fingers into it, offering up a couple of bearings. She takes them, moving to line them up with the scars.

Footsteps draw my eyes, and I watch Seth and Asena stroll up. Seth stops, his features twisting to one side of his face. "Guess this was a popular idea."

Asena giggles, tucked under his arm. She's not too much shorter than he is, and I can see the way he's lit up with her. I shake my head and sigh, turning back to Ella.

"We can go somewhere else," I tell her. *"Whatever you want."*

She shakes her head. *"No, and I think I want Seth around."*

I curl my lip and then turn back to my brother. "She's getting her memories back."

"About damn time." He grins.

They hop down into the den of cushions with us across the way. Asena curls up, lifting Seth's arm to drop it around her as she moves in close. I meet my brother's eyes, and he grins.

I raise my eyebrow at him, and he shrugs his free shoulder. "Let's do this."

I turn back to Ella, offering up two more bearings. "Get those in you, but then, just break one."

She takes them and freezes, her eyes snapping to mine. "You aren't sure what's in them?" she asks in livid rage.

I hold my hands up. "Cut me some slack. I'm relying on information from a kid."

She frowns, lining them up, and they sink into her arm partway with no resistance. "Where is George? I want to see him."

Nausea slips through me, and I grimace in guilt. "He's…" My words falter at the flash of rage that scares even me in her violet eyes. I swallow. "Erac."

Seth picks his head up. "What now? What happened to the kid?"

Her hands shake with the last bearing in her fingertips. I hang my head. "I was strapped to that table, losing my mind to bloodlust, and he…" I wince. "Erac showed up looking like Ella saying I needed to tell her the information or Erac was going to hurt her."

Asena frowns. "Skilled mages can alter appearances. It's convincing."

I snarl. "No, I should have known better. I should have been able to smell—"

Seth laughs. "You weren't even healing by the time I got us out of there. No way were you in the head place to pick up on something like that, and any threat to Ell would have—"

"I should have fucking known," I snap, rubbing hands down my face. "I knew something wasn't right. She had a weird expression."

Ella curls her lip back and then turns back to pushing the bearing in her arm. "Erac lied a lot. I don't blame you if you thought you were protecting me, but I'm not happy. Now what?"

"Break the bearing," I tell her. "Last time, the brothers—Erac and Aron—they told you to treat it like shifting iron, overpowering the elements that make up the bearing."

Her shoulders drop, and she turns her face to me. "What?"

"Don't ask. It's a long story, and it'll be so much easier to just give you back your memories."

She gives me a disgruntled look but turns back, holding a hand up over the bearings.

I reach out, turning her arm away. "Just one. Let's make sure George was right, and then make sure you don't get the blood spray out of them on you. That really is poison—used blood from blood magic—and damn near killed you once."

Ella opens her mouth, eyes sharp as they settle on me. She wants to know, digging in my mind for answers. I try to open up to her, letting her root around, not hiding anything.

I hold up my hand. "Just get your memories back. You'll have all your answers."

Her lips press tight, and she focuses on the bearing. The stream of energy starts, the tug in my chest. I exhale, giving in to it and her. The bearing bursts, a fine mist of blood releases in the air, and a rush of color and noise slams behind my eyes.

We groan together in unison. My eyes close, and I ram the heels of my palms into them, pressing hard to see spots of color dancing in the dark. "Fuck."

The too many memories settle like dust in my brain, filtering down into the crevices, but then it starts up again, the onslaught of information of a thousand hours all crashing through my mind at the same time. I get maybe a minute before the screaming, streaming pictures behind my eyes return as she breaks the other bearings. My eyes slip closed against the torrent of color. I am dizzy, my head tipping and swaying on my neck.

I put my arm around her, hauling her by the hips against me. I kiss her forehead, my head feeling like a spike is splitting it open.

She cuddles into me, and I half roll on her, keeping her shielded from the world. A petite whimper escapes her, her fingers curling around my arms.

She's clinging to me, too many visual cue cards exploding in our minds. I feel like the fucking room is spinning in circles and brace myself.

"Dec."

"Lover?" Her mind is slipping out of consciousness, and I squeeze her tight. *"I'm right here, with you. Fuck, I'm with you on this. I never wanted to go through this hell again, lover, but I'm here."*

My mind is heavy and hazy, but soon enough, it's passing, and I blink, sitting up. She pushes me away, wiping at her face. I reach out, swiping the tear off her cheek that she missed.

Her eyes lift to mine. *"That was awful."*

I nod. "Nothing I ever wanted to live through again, that's for damn sure."

She winces, rubbing the place between her eyes. "But," she smiles at me, "I remember our wedding."

Laughter bursts from Seth. "It wasn't much of a wedding, but sure, you're married."

I cut my eyes to him with a scowl. "Shut up."

She smiles. "I remember committing to a bond, and that you didn't exactly ask me to marry you."

I grin, holding up my hand with her ring on it. "You still did it, willingly too."

She rolls her eyes, fighting against a smile. "I'm not complaining." One of her hands lifts and presses between her breasts. "I can feel how happy I was."

"Yeah, just hold onto that feeling when you get the rest of

your memories back. I'm going to need the help." I reach for the bearings, digging my fingers in, scooping some into my hand.

I turn, opening my fist and offering them to her. My ears tingle and twitch, the little hairs on my body standing up. I whip toward the bearings as movement catches my eye.

Samuel reaches a hand toward the bearings. I growl, arm snaking out to grab the pouch, but my fingers close on dust.

My heart stammers and stalls, gaping at the particles slipping through my fingers. My eyes lift to his as he grins triumphantly. "For Gemma," he says, "for all the lives—"

Samuel disintegrates, joining the remnants of the bearings. My eyes stretch open, and my head turns to Ella in slow motion, the world streaks of color as my eyes refuse to focus.

Ella is livid, a hand held out, limb shaking. I grip the last bearings we have in my other hand as the room starts to crackle and pop. The air zaps with energy building like a brewing storm.

"Ella," I reach for her, taking her face between an open palm and closed fist. She shows me teeth, but I chuckle. "You'll ruin all these books."

The air is supercharged against my skin, but her eyes narrow before she relaxes, and the energy releases. She sticks her arm out, and I put the last five bearings on her arm. As I push the last of them in, I raise my gaze to Seth.

Asena wears a horrified expression, lips parted and eyes wide, unblinking as she stares.

Seth shakes his head but laughs. "Fucking Damnatus, Ell, you're terrifying."

She frowns at the bearings in her arm. It starts to shake, and her fingers curl tight. Pain and fury are rippling in the air between us, echoing in our minds.

I reach out, tucking hair behind her ear. "It's okay. It'll be okay."

Her eyes lift to mine, burning with the promise of pain. I grimace as she snarls at me under her breath.

Seth crawls over, putting a hand on her shoulder. "It's fine. You don't need those stupid balls. Dec's got big enough balls for the two of you, and we can tell you everything. We know everything between the two of us, all your memories."

Ella jerks away from him, eyes glassy. "How do I know you aren't lying to me?"

I smirk, and my brother howls with laughter. I shove him away and meet her gaze. *"Because, lover, I can show you too. Like I did before."*

She drops her chin to her chest and sighs. "Fine, but I want to know everything. All of it."

She tilts her arm away and frowns at it, the remaining bearings rupture, and my eyes cross at the overwhelming memories all playing at once in my mind. I grit my teeth and pull her against me, my head starting to throb in time with our heartbeats.

Leaning back, I tip my head against the side of the hole we sit in and breathe, waiting for it to pass. Everything behind my eyelids grows dark and still, and I pick my head up. Ella's limp against my chest, her eyes closed.

My eyes lift to Seth, and he grimaces at me. "Is she okay?"

Asena's face twists with abhorrence. "Are you kidding me? She just turned that guy to ash, and you two aren't batting an eye at it. What's wrong with you?"

Seth frowns, shifting toward her a bit. They stay cuddled together, so I'm hoping this tiff won't change anything. My brother needs someone, and I'm not fond of Marx, but if it makes him happy, I'll shut my mouth. Besides, he might back off Ella.

"We'll justify a lot of scars because we love the person holding the knife," he says, with no trace of humor to his words.

I lift my eyebrow at her, breathing out through my nose. "When everything you want and need and love is ripped away from you so harshly, all that you are filled with is rage and hatred and revenge. You can't even see it, and it takes something pretty strong to break through and bring you back." My eyes fixate on my brother's, hoping he might understand he's a big reason I've ever found my way back.

He shakes his head. "How much darkness has she been living in? Sure, that wasn't great, but he destroyed pieces of her, her life, her soul, something that makes her who she is. What would you have done if you had that kind of power and someone destroyed part of you?"

Asena nestles closer, resting her cheek on his shoulder, and stares across the way. She doesn't answer, but her eyes pinch with contemplation.

I tilt my head, eyeing my sleeping wife. She's truly beautiful, alluring, and breathtaking the way most deadly things are. I smile, pressing my lips against her forehead and inhaling the scent of honey through my nose.

There's a sigh, and my eyes flicker to Asena as she shifts against my brother, turning her back to his chest. She's frowning, but Seth tips his head against the back of hers, eyes closed.

I turn to her, eyes narrowing. Asena's narrow back, and I smirk. She grins and shifts closer to my brother, her eyes closing, but her lips stay curled up at the ends.

I tip my head back and stare up at Haven. *Fucker, this better be the end of this shit.*

EPILOGUE

ELLA

I stand, arms crossed, looking out over the ocean. A storm is blowing in, my long purple-tinged red hair whipping free in the cool wind as the dark storm clouds brew. I narrow my eyes at the lightning striking the waves in the distance.

Lips press against my temple, and large warm hands run across my forearms as strong arms wrap me in close. I tip my head back, staring up at my husband. His eyes are soft gray, an expression of contentment pulling on his sharp features. Wind tosses his hair into his eyes, and I smile, reaching up to brush them back into place.

He squeezes me, a reassurance, a need to know I am there, but not hard. "Come on, everyone's here."

I nod, turning to face him. "Okay."

"If you're tired, I can make excuses."

I roll my eyes. "Visiting the spirits in Medius wasn't hard; it was fun." I hold a hand out, flexing it, and then let it fall to my side. "I love burning energy like that."

He smirks, silver eyes crinkling at the corners. "Did you feed George?"

I roll my eyes again and groan. "For the thousandth time, we are not naming the rat George, and yes."

"Sure," he chuckles. "I'm pretty certain George would have loved it, though."

There's a pang shared between us. I try to shove it away, turning back to face the sea. Rebuilding Asperheim took almost as much power as dissipating the spirits home. Declan insisted we kill Viktor, but I want him to suffer, locked in the dark beneath this palace. So, instead, I moved the spirits home. Sordello wasn't sure if it would work, but then he claims my magic is capable of many things thought impossible.

The dead were buried with honor and care. I cried for them, for never getting to say thank you for what they did to help me, but George was the worst. Declan has told me about my older brother, Marcus, and I ache that I'll never get to meet him. All I will have of the man who was more a father than Viktor, a friend, and brother who did so much are memories.

The Duke of Deveraux bawled when Declan and Seth told him about his daughter, Legia. I did too and I asked so many questions that they all answered in broken voices. So many good lives were wasted in Viktor's pursuits.

I gave them each their own statue in our gardens, plaques to memorialize them for all eternity for their courageous deeds. George got a rat on his shoulder, an ice cream cone in one hand. It's next to my favorite bench where I curl up to read when I have time. Sometimes I talk to him, whispering nothing important, sometimes reading aloud as if he could learn the stories of the past with me.

I stretch my neck and sigh. "Alright."

"He was a real badass," Dec whispers in my ear.

I nod my head, energy pulling through my chest as I change my clothes from tight black to a flowing dress of charcoal gray, the color of Declan's eyes the first time I met him.

"When you ran into me in Dis, you mean." He sighs. His

hands squeeze my shoulders. "Fuck, that was miserable. All I wanted to do was grab hold and never let go."

I snort through my nose. "Pretty sure I would have killed you for it, given the lies I believed at the time."

"Which is why I refrained," he says. "We'll be back later, George," Declan calls over his shoulder with a mischievous grin.

I shove him in the middle of his chest, stepping into him as I dissipate us down to the great hall. We rebuild, and he finishes his step back, clutching my shoulders to pull me against him and kiss me. I lean into it, standing on my tiptoes.

His lips curl as he chuckles, pulling away. His head lifts, and I glance around at everyone watching. I drop a curtsy, clinging to Declan's fingers with my free hand. "Welcome to Asperheim, and thank you for coming. I'm sure there are quite a lot of questions; I still have a few myself, but let me try to answer some."

I glance at Declan, and he squeezes my hand. I turn back to the hundreds of eyes watching me. "I am Ella, and while I have not met most of you personally, you probably know my father —" I wince, hoping Sordello is not watching from above, "— Viktor Byron."

My eyes travel over the room, my heart racing. I don't know why I ever thought this would be a good idea. Taking a breath, I go on as Dean nods at me from the front of the crowd.

"Viktor was a bastard and a prick and a lot of things. He made me a lot of things, things I don't want to be. The courts are not mine to claim, and I have no interest in finishing what my father started. However," I say, drawing the word out and glancing around, "I understand some of you may still be angry. I know I am."

Declan steps next to me. "Understand that any part that Ella played in this mess was not done of her own volition, and I'm going to strongly discourage any recourse be taken. The King of Byron, Spaulding, has absolved Ella of any wrongdoing given the circumstances and reinstated their family connection."

I nod. "For those of you still unaware, I was manipulated through blood magic. Any attempt at retaliation, either against myself or my husband, will not be tolerated. And let me assure you, you will lose that fight, and retribution will be swift." I stare around the room with narrowed eyes, then relax my face and smile. "The mage council voted and agreed that I take the Gammet brothers' place as high mage. The council will move from Dis to here, and Declan and I will be taking on the duties of keeper as well."

No one says anything, and I glance over at Declan to see if there is anything else that needs to be said.

"Enjoy your evening, and know that if you ever need help, find someone else."

I whack at him with the back of my hand as laughter slithers through the room. "We are here to help, and please enjoy your evening."

Declan pulls me away, twisting his lips. "We aren't helping. Caleum can go fuck itself; we're done."

I narrow my eyes back. "No, and no."

He stops, moving me in front of him, one hand on my waist, the other picking mine up. He steps back, drawing me with him, and I groan. *How the hell did I not notice he was taking me to the dance floor?*

He smirks even as I step on his toes. "I just wanted to make sure some things aren't going to change."

I roll my eyes, but Declan stops as a hand lands on his shoulder. We turn to Seth, grinning ear to ear.

"Hey, Ell, mind if I cut in?"

Declan curls his lip but steps aside. "Five minutes, little brother, then I want my wife back."

He winks at me. "You always want your wife back." Dec punches Seth hard enough that he tips sideways. He rights himself, laughing. "Too soon?"

I wrinkle my nose at him and shake my head. "Don't antagonize him."

"Come on," he pulls me forward and starts moving in time to the music. "You okay?"

I sigh. "Getting there."

Declan stands to the side, shaking hands with two large dryads. Gamal and Lumor, two friends who fought at my side and Declan's. Declan gave them co-captain of the guard positions here at Aserpheim to reward their bravery and loyalty. He says he wouldn't trust anyone else with our lives. I hope to get to know them well, to learn what they can tell me from the time before.

Seth sweeps me away from them in a circle. "Let me know if you need me to take care of my brother. He can be a real jerk."

I smile. "Honestly, everything is a dream compared to what it's been, and while the bar was set pretty low, Dec has been wonderful."

Glancing over his shoulder, Seth tightens his hold on me and turns. "Come on, I want to talk to you for a minute and not here."

He pulls me away from the crowd as Declan growls in my mind. We stop at the edge of the expansive stone balcony overlooking the beach, waves crashing, and the air sweet with the promise of rain.

Seth lets go of my hand and pulls a small box out. My eyes grow wide as he opens it. "What do you think? Think Sena will like it?"

I take the box, tilting it and inspecting it. The opal shimmers with pinks and oranges. "Yes." I nod. "I think she'll love it."

He grins, stashing the box in his pocket. "Marx gave his resigned approval earlier, something about me helping him keep his crown, but if he ever catches me under his daughter again, he'll still break every bone in my body. But it was a yes, so I'm taking it."

"That's great."

He stares out across the sea, his eyes shifting a bit darker.

I put my hand on his arm, tilting my head at him. "But?"

He shakes his head. "No buts. But…" He smiles. "I love you, Ell, always have, always will. And I still expect my spirit runes." He stares at me pointedly.

I smile. "I talked to my dad about it this morning. The spirits are willing to give you a set since you fought with them and helped get them home."

He nods. "Good, because you two would be hopeless without me."

Declan appears next to us, frowning. His eyes narrow at Seth, toying with the idea of ripping his arm off and beating him with it. I laugh, head tipping back.

"Hey, big brother." Seth chuckles. "Which body part are you thinking about pulling off?"

"Back the fuck off, or one of these days, I'm going to do it. Go find your own woman."

Seth grabs the ring out of his pocket and tosses it in the air. "Already did, and she's incredible."

Declan snatches it, popping the lid. He grunts and snaps the lid closed, tossing it back. "Then, I'm taking mine back now."

"Come on." I smile. "Both of you, let's get back to the party."

They start back inside, but I turn at a clap of thunder, staring out on the horizon. Rain starts to drizzle down from overhead, and I tip my head back, catching the drops against my face, letting them wash it all away. I am not going to ever get all my memories back, but at least I know the truth now. I know who I am. All the anger and pain is fading, being washed away by the love from the Bard brothers.

The water trickles down my skin, cleaning away all the poison in my soul. Two pairs of hands from two different men grab hold of me, pulling on me to get me out of the storm. I laugh, letting them tug me inside.

Neither hand grips hard enough to hurt or leave bruises, allowing me to accept it, and I do.

THE END

Thank you for reading Declan and Ella's story!

THANK YOU

Thank you for reading Poison!

Please leave a review!

Write a customer review

You, my dear reader, control the success of my humble story. By leaving a review you help others discover a story they can enjoy.

I love hearing from my readers!

Send me an email at cjwallingsford@outlook.com or find me on Facebook or Instagram to chat.

ACKNOWLEDGMENTS

This trilogy has been an obsession that my husband, Eric has endured for years. I've spent days of my life cursing the voices in my head, scowling at a computer screen, and ripping my hair out over an open notebook as I played a game of chess no one else could see. I have been absorbed in plotting, trying to mash those puzzle pieces together to avoid any mistakes. I do loathe inaccurate character behavior and plot holes.

Eric has listened to me rant and rave, has offered advice, and been there through the whole ordeal in full support of me playing with my imaginary friends. He's been a major help, like telling me when my ideas are stupid.

Thank you to Brittany Santagato, who read every word twice before anyone else and provided invaluable feedback. She was the sole beta reader, gave Seth the love he deserves, and encouraged me to share this story with the world.

Thank you to KillingItWrite for the editing and feedback that helped to create this story.

Thank you to Storywrappers for the beautiful cover.

I love music, listening to it constantly while writing. There are so many artists who have helped to shape my words through their lyrics. There are far too many for me to list them all, so I will stick to the top five: Slipknot, Taylor Swift, I Prevail, Crown the Empire, and STARSET.

A head nod to Dan Hermeyer, who has slandered so many sentences of this book, twisting them to sound incredibly dirty.

ABOUT THE AUTHOR

C J Wallingsford is a lover of writing and traveling. When not exploring new places and tracing down history, she lives in St Louis with her husband and two dogs, Jovina and Rat. This is CJ's third book, and the completion of The Spirit Runes Trilogy.

www.ingramcontent.com/pod-product-compliance
Lightning Source LLC
LaVergne TN
LVHW020039110826
845155LV00029B/557